D1098811

VICTORIA SCHWAB

New Beginnings

Second Chances

Last Wishes

SCHOLASTIC

Published in the UK by Scholastic Children's Books, 2020
Euston House, 24 Eversholt Street, London, NW1 1DB, UK
A division of Scholastic Limited.

London – New York – Toronto – Sydney – Auckland
Mexico City – New Delhi – Hong Kong

SCHOLASTIC and associated logos are trademarks and/or
registered trademarks of Scholastic Inc.

Everyday Angel: New Beginnings
First published in the US by Scholastic Inc, 2014
Text © Victoria Schwab, 2014

Everyday Angel: Second Chances
First published in the US by Scholastic Inc, 2014
Text © Victoria Schwab, 2014

Everyday Angel: Last Wishes
First published in the US by Scholastic Inc, 2015
Text © Victoria Schwab, 2015

The right of Victoria Schwab to be identified as the author of this work has been
asserted by her under the Copyright, Designs and Patents Act 1988.

ISBN 978 0702 30156 8

A CIP catalogue record for this book is available from the British Library.

All rights reserved.
This book is sold subject to the condition that it shall not,
by way of trade or otherwise, be lent, hired out or otherwise circulated in
any form of binding or cover other than that in which it is published. No
part of this publication may be reproduced, stored in a retrieval system,
or transmitted in any form or by any means (electronic, mechanical,
photocopying, recording or otherwise) without prior
written permission of Scholastic Limited.

Printed by CPI Group (UK) Ltd, Croydon, CR0 4YY
Papers used by Scholastic Children's Books are made
from wood grown in sustainable forests.

1 3 5 7 9 10 8 6 4 2

This is a work of fiction. Names, characters, places, incidents
and dialogues are products of the author's imagination or are used
fictitiously. Any resemblance to actual people, living or dead,
events or locales is entirely coincidental.

www.scholastic.co.uk

New Beginnings

To Carla, for always knowing how to lift my spirits.

South Dublin Libraries
www.southdublinlibraries.ie

chapter 1

GABBY

"Ready . . ." said Gabby, stretching. "Set . . ."

She got halfway through the word *go!* before her brother, Marco, took off.

"Cheater!" she shouted, sprinting after him.

The woods behind their house grew up instead of out; trees densely piled onto hills like the one Gabby and Marco Torres were racing up now. Marco was older by three years, but Gabby was quick on her feet and knew the shortcuts. Marco always took the paths, but Gabby climbed the un-paths, the places where roots and rocks made stairs up the side of the forest.

"Come on, Gabs!" His voice rang out through the trees. "Keep up!"

Her lungs burned as she ran, twigs snapping under her shoes. She had never beaten him to the top. Even when he didn't cheat. But maybe today . . . She caught a glimpse of his bright blue T-shirt cutting between trees, and she sped up. She was so focused on catching him that she didn't see the fallen branch until it snagged her sneaker and sent her stumbling to her hands and knees on the damp ground. She sprung back up, but by then, she'd lost him.

His laughter rang out, and she sprinted on until she burst through the tree line, breathless, and grinning. "Marco!" she called. "I won!"

But Marco wasn't there. She stood at the top of the hill, catching her breath, waiting for her brother to get there and give her some line about *letting* her win. She waited, and waited, and waited.

"Marco?" she called nervously, looking around the field.

The hill was suddenly too still and too dark. The laughter that had followed her through the woods before reached her again, but it was twisted and wrong. It was her brother's voice, but he wasn't laughing anymore, not at all.

He was coughing.

Gasping.

Choking.

And that's when Gabby woke up.

She wasn't standing on a hilltop but slouched in a stiff hospital chair next to a bed. In the bed, Marco was doubled over, coughing. A nurse rubbed his back with one hand and adjusted his IV with the other.

"Hey there . . . Gabby," Marco said between coughs. "Sorry . . . didn't mean . . . to wake you."

"It's okay," Gabby mumbled, rubbing her forehead. "Bad dream. Are you all right?" she asked as Marco settled back against his pillow, his face flushed.

"Right as rain," he said, still struggling for air. "Don't tell anyone, though," he whispered loudly. "I don't want them to kick me out." The nurse toying with the machine laughed a little, and Gabby managed a thin smile. Marco was always joking.

But the coughing fit had clearly winded him. He looked tired. These days, he always looked tired. Gabby knew it was because of *the bad*.

When the doctors explained Marco's condition to Gabby, they didn't call the sickness by its proper name. They referred to it only as *the bad*, as if she didn't know how to search the Internet and find out what *the bad* really was. Now she knew the proper term — *osteosarcoma* — but still found herself thinking of it as *the bad*. Not because she wanted to dumb it down, or make it seem smaller, but because it was easier for her to picture the thing attacking her brother's body not as a many-syllabled word but as a monster.

Monsters could be fought. And Marco was fighting.

He looked at her and frowned his big-brother frown and said, "You were supposed to go home last night."

Gabby glanced down at her crumpled clothes and thought about how wrong it felt to call the new apartment *home*. *Home* was a place in the country with wooded hills and laughter and a healthy big brother. A place Gabby seemed to get back to only in her dreams. And as bad as the hospital was, the apartment was worse. It was a ghostly shell, empty and dark — their mom spent every free minute in the hospital with Marco.

"I like it better here," Gabby said, picking up the cheerful tone he'd dropped. "And the food's good. Way better than Mom's."

Marco chuckled carefully. "That may be true . . ." he said, letting out a sigh, "but you can't keep sleeping here. Not with school starting tomorrow."

Not just school, thought Gabby. *A* new *school.*

Grand Heights Middle School.

The thought of starting seventh grade there filled her with a mixture of fear and hope. When Marco had first gotten sick last year, everything had changed. Not just for him but for Gabby, too. Suddenly she couldn't go anywhere without being smothered by everybody's concern. Teachers, classmates, friends — their pity became like a low wall around her life. People wanted to look over and say hi, but the wall stopped them from getting too close. That was the weird thing about sickness. Even when it wasn't contagious, people kept their distance.

Even Alice and Beth, who were Gabby's closest friends, started acting strange around her. They got weird and quiet and went out of their way to be polite, and she hated it.

When Marco got transferred to a new hospital in a new city over the summer, Gabby had almost been relieved to leave.

Grand Heights Middle School would be filled with strangers, but it would also be a fresh start. Maybe she didn't have to be that girl with the sick brother.

Maybe she could just be Gabrielle Torres.

Marco cleared his throat. He was looking at her expectantly, and Gabby realized she'd gone quiet. She did that sometimes.

"¿Dónde estás?" he asked. *Where are you?* But what he meant was, *Where is your head? Where have you gone? Come back.*

"Sorry, I'm here," she said, blinking. And then she remembered. "Oh, hey, I got you something."

Gabby fetched a plastic shopping bag filled with school supplies from under her chair. She had picked them out herself. Her mom hadn't been able to take her shopping, but the mall, like the apartment, like the school, like *everything else*, was in walking distance from the hospital. Gabby dug through the bag until she found the blue-and-white-striped notebook and pen. "For your homeschooling," she said.

"Hospital-schooling," corrected Marco. He was fifteen, and should have been starting tenth grade at Grand Heights High. Instead, he'd be here with a tutor.

Gabby dropped a fresh pack of colored paper on the pale hospital bed. "And this is for the rest of the time," she said.

Marco's eyes lit up. He was an *expert* paper-airplane maker, and they spent the next half hour folding the paper into planes to throw from his third-floor window and into the parking lot below. Gabby had just succeeded in landing her third purple plane on a white minivan roof — Marco cheering her on — when the door opened behind them.

"Gabrielle Torres," said a quiet voice with mock scorn. "Are you letting your brother have too much fun?"

She turned to see Marco's new friend, Henry, coming into the room in his wheelchair. Henry reminded her of paper. Not the rich, colorful kind that she and Marco had been making into airplanes, but a worn and faded white. He was pale to start with — she'd seen photos from when he was a kid — and paler from being sick, his hair a watery blond, and his eyes a gentle, washed-out blue.

Gabby shook her head, and Henry tsked.

"Didn't he tell you," Henry went on, wheeling himself up to the bed, "what'll happen if he has too much fun here?"

"They'll kick him out?" ventured Gabby.

"Exactly!" said Henry, knocking his knees against the metal bed rail. "You don't want him to get kicked out, do you? Who would entertain *me*?"

"*You* could have too much fun," offered Gabby. "Then they'd kick you out, too."

Henry's smile turned sad at the edges. "Nah, they like me too much to let me go." His eyes fell to the plastic bag on the bed. "What have we here?"

"School supplies," said Marco. "Gabby starts tomorrow."

"Wow," said Henry with a soft, soundless laugh. "School, already? Time really does fly when you're having fun."

"Do you miss it?" asked Gabby. Henry was the same age as Marco, but she knew he'd been sick a lot longer, and a lot worse, and wondered how long it had been since he'd hefted a backpack onto his shoulder, or heard a shrill class bell.

"Nah," he said with a shrug. "Best part of being here is I don't have to go to school."

7

Gabby didn't believe him. She could see it tucked away in Henry's eyes, how much he missed being a normal teenage boy, even if normal meant school and homework and chores. She could see it starting in Marco's eyes, too, even though their mom was still dragging him through the motions so he wouldn't fall too far behind. Henry looked as if he might never catch back up. The thought shot like a pang through Gabby's chest, but she didn't have a chance to dwell on Henry's condition, because Marco started coughing again.

Gabby winced as two nurses appeared out of the hospital cracks, one doing her best to get Marco settled, while the other wheeled Henry away. The bag of school supplies tumbled off the bed, and Gabby was on her hands and knees, trying to gather up the pens and notebooks, when her mom rushed in.

"What is it?" asked Mrs. Torres, only adding to the commotion. "What's wrong? Marco? Are you all right? How long has this been going on?"

"He'll be fine," urged a nurse, but her calm somehow made Gabby's mom more flustered, and Mrs. Torres gathered up the colored papers on the bed in a single sweep and dumped them into a chair. She muttered to Gabby in Spanish about making a mess as she rubbed circles on Marco's back to help him breathe.

Gabby backed out of the room and into the hall. She slumped against the wall beside the door, every muscle in her body tense, as if she'd been the one coughing. She looked down and realized she was still holding some of the school supplies: a pretty journal with music notes and a handful of pens. Through the door, she could hear the scene quieting, but Marco's cough echoed in her head and she couldn't bring herself to go back in — she'd probably just be in the way. So she stayed put in the corridor.

Most of the halls on this floor were painted yellow or green, but this one was blue. Gabby liked the color because it made her feel like a little piece of outside had wandered in. She'd spent a lot of time in hospitals, and so often their pale walls and fluorescent lights reminded her that she was definitely *not* outside. Now, if she stared at the wall and let her eyes unfocus, she could *almost* believe she was staring at the sky on a nice day, warm and sunny and blue.

chapter 2

ARIA

Outside the hospital, it was a cloudy day.

No blue sky. No sunlight. No shade. So it was strange when a shadow formed in the middle of the parking lot.

It started as a blot and spread across the pavement. Even if there *had* been a sun out, casting shadows, there was no source nearby — no car, no lamppost, and certainly no person — to cast this particular one.

The impossible shadow grew until it was roughly the size and shape of a twelve-year-old girl with long, wavy hair. And once it was done growing, the shadow *changed*. It went from dark to blinding white, as if a hundred lights had been turned on somewhere deep inside of it. And out of the light came a girl.

In one slow, fluid motion, like coming up through water, the girl rose out of the mark on the ground. And when she was standing on top of the girl-shaped puddle of white, the blinding light inside went off like a switch.

The girl looked down at her shadow approvingly.

"Nice work," she said to it.

The shadow seemed pleased, fidgeting happily beneath her feet. The girl looked around, marveling at the fact she was *here* — even if *here* was a hospital parking lot on a cloudy afternoon — and a thrill ran through her at the thought of being somewhere.

Being *someone*.

There was only one problem.

The girl in the parking lot didn't know who she was.

That is to say, she knew *what* she was, but this was her first day as a *who*. And now that she was a *who*, she couldn't help but wonder what type of *who* she was. She brought her hands up in front of her face, as if they would tell her, and in a way they did. A blue bracelet circled her wrist, bare except for a pendant with a name carved on it in small, delicate script.

Aria.

She tested the word on her tongue a few times and liked it.

"My name is Aria," she told her shadow. It gave the slightest nod.

And then she looked down at herself for the first time. She was delighted to find she was wearing a green shirt and a white skirt with pockets and a pair of bright blue leggings that ran right into her sneakers. The laces on the shoes were white, until Aria — she really did like the name — decided she'd rather have purple ones. As soon as she thought it, color began to seep down the shoestrings, turning them violet.

Aria smiled and caught up a chunk of her hair, holding it in front of her eyes so she could see the color. Even in the gray day, flecks of coppery red glittered in the brown strands.

Delightful, thought Aria. She let the strands slip from her fingers as her eyes (a greeny blue, even though she didn't know that yet) drifted up to the white building that loomed in front of her. It was very large, and she bit her lip and wondered how she would find whoever she was looking for in a place that big.

Well, thought Aria decisively, *one thing at a time.*

First, the shadow.

She couldn't just run off and leave it there in the lot (well, she *could*, but that would be strange). So she located its head behind her, and its feet in front of her, and then she took two small steps forward so that her shoes nested cleanly into the shoes of the shadow instead of standing on its stomach. Aria then rolled from her heels to her toes and back a few times until she was sure the shadow had stuck, moving when she moved, stopping when she stopped, and behaving in all ways like a perfectly normal shadow.

Once she was satisfied that it wouldn't come loose, Aria smoothed her skirt, tucked a strand of hair behind her ear, and made her way to the hospital.

A dozen steps led to a set of glass doors, and a man and a woman were sitting halfway up the stairs, huddled side by side despite the warm day. The woman seemed upset — *very* upset — and Aria wanted to help. But she couldn't. She *shouldn't*.

Because there was no blue smoke.

Aria knew she wasn't supposed to get involved unless she saw the blue smoke. It was the reason she was here. The smoke would show her the person who needed her help. The fact the shadow had brought her to the hospital meant someone inside would be marked by it. The people on the steps weren't. As sad as they seemed, they must not need the kind of help that Aria — or someone like her — could provide.

Aria reached the revolving glass doors, and stopped. Not just because the door itself was strange and vaguely concerning. But because there, in the glass, she saw something for the first time. Herself.

It was one thing, looking at the pieces — hands, shoes, skirt, hair — but it was such another, bigger, better thing to see herself as a whole. Well, *almost* whole. Her eyes hovered on the empty space above her shoulders, the place where her wings should be . . . *would* be, once she'd earned them.

Just then the revolving doors jerked into motion, and Aria jumped back as a man came through the turning portal. He left the glass spinning, Aria's reflection coming and going and coming again. She darted forward, jumped back out on the other side, and found herself inside the hospital.

The lobby was filled with people, some in white coats, moving briskly, and some in regular clothes, slumped in chairs. Others still were pacing or waiting or talking to one another or to no one. Aria scanned the crowd, but she didn't see any smoke.

"Good afternoon," said a woman behind the desk. "How can I help you?"

Aria approached the desk. "I'm just trying to find someone."

"Who are you looking for?" asked the woman.

"Oh, I don't know," said Aria brightly. "I haven't found them yet." The woman frowned, but before she could say anything, Aria smiled and added, "Don't worry. I'll know them when I see them."

And with that she set off down the hall on the left.

If the woman had been looking closely, she might have noticed that each of the fluorescent lights overhead grew a little brighter as Aria passed beneath them. Or that the scuffs on the linoleum faded under her shoes, leaving the floor clean and new. But she didn't notice. No one did. They were small changes, the kind you sensed but couldn't put your finger on. Aria made the world a little nicer just by being in it.

She explored two floors in search of the smoke — scanning halls, peering through windows and around doors — until she stumbled upon a common room. Several children clustered around a TV, a few others sat around a table with a puzzle, but it was the boy by the window who caught her eye.

He was pale and blond and wreathed in smoke.

The dark plumes hung around him like a cloud as he stared out the window. But as Aria drew closer, she frowned. His smoke was the wrong color. Aria was meant to find *blue* smoke. But the cloud circling the boy's shoulders was a dark, bruised purple. Almost black.

He was definitely marked, but not for Aria.

"Henry," said a voice, and the boy by the window looked up as a nurse carried a cup of water over to his wheelchair.

Aria wondered why Henry was here, and why he was shrouded in such a grim cloud. She looked around, searching for someone like her, maybe someone with a charm bracelet to match that particular shade of purple-black smoke. But no one stood out. In fact, Aria was the only person in the common room who didn't look like she belonged there.

Until another girl came in. She was about Aria's size, with warm, tan skin and rich, dark hair. But what caught Aria's attention wasn't the girl's skin or her hair or the notebook she was clutching to her chest. It was the blue smoke swirling around her shoulders.

Smoke the exact same color as Aria's bracelet.

The girl wove absently through the tables and chairs, lost in her own thoughts, and flopped down onto a couch in the corner. Aria hesitated. She'd been so focused on finding the smoke, she didn't know what to do now. So she stood there, watching, hoping the girl would give some clue as to what was wrong.

The girl didn't seem *sick*, not like the other kids in the common room. But that didn't surprise Aria. After all, the smoke had nothing to do with sickness. It marked a person only if Aria could help them, and she couldn't help sickness. She wasn't a healer. (She didn't even know if those existed.) Aria was just . . . Aria. And whatever was wrong with the blue-smoke girl, Aria was pretty sure she wouldn't figure it out by standing there. Plus she was beginning to feel awkward about staring. So she took a deep breath, walked up to the girl on the couch, and said hello.

chapter 3

GABBY

Gabby had been squinting up at the ceiling, trying to decide if the lights in the room had gotten brighter, when someone said, "Hello!"

She looked over to find a girl perched on the opposite edge of the couch. The girl had coppery hair and bright blue leggings and a cheerful smile. The thing about hospitals was that few people smiled like that. They grimaced with worry, or pursed their lips with pity, and on occasion they beamed with relief, but they rarely seemed *cheerful*.

"Hi," said Gabby cautiously.

"What's your name?" asked the girl. She looked like she was Gabby's age. There were a few other twelve-year-olds here, but all of them were sick. In fact, Gabby hadn't seen a girl her age who *wasn't* sick all summer.

"Gabrielle Torres," she said, then added, "Most people call me Gabby. You?"

The girl's smile brightened, as if the question thrilled her.

"My name's Aria." She held up her hand and Gabby could see the name etched into a metal pendant on the girl's charm bracelet. "See?"

Gabby nodded. It was a pretty name, one she hadn't really heard before.

A beat of silence fell between them. Gabby realized Aria was staring at her. Gabby stared back.

"So . . ." said Aria. She tapped her fingers on her knee, her gaze wandering over the room like she was searching for something — anything — to say. When her eyes found the far green wall, her lips curved up.

"What's your favorite color?" she asked.

Gabby's eyebrows rose. People asked a lot of questions in hospitals — *How are you feeling? Can you rate your pain? Do you need anything?* But *What's your favorite color?* wasn't one of them. She shrugged.

"I'm not sure," Gabby said. She knew Marco's favorite — green — and she knew what hers *used* to be — purple — but it had been so long since she thought about something silly like that. With so many big questions out there, how could she care about something stupid like colors? The black music notes on her notebook stared up at her from their white background, not helping.

"Don't worry," said Aria. "I'm not sure, either."

"Really?"

Aria nodded. "Really. Or at least, I can't decide. I see one color and I think that might be it, my favorite, but then I see another and I change my mind. It's so hard to pick only one. Like my laces," she said, gesturing to the shoestrings, which were now hot pink. "I've changed them twice so far today."

Gabby almost smiled. Aria was weird.

"There is one color I don't like," admitted Aria. "The color they've painted the hospital steps. That sad gray. It's almost like a noncolor. It's . . ."

"Sickly," offered Gabby.

"Exactly," said Aria, shaking her head.

Something moved at the edge of Gabby's sight, and she turned to see the nurse wheeling Henry away. Gabby waved and Henry waved back.

Aria watched him go, too, with a strange look on her face.

"That's Henry," said Gabby. "Do you know him?"

After a pause, Aria shook her head. "Not really. Why is he here?"

Gabby smiled sadly. "If you ask him, he'll say it's because the doctors like him too much to let him go." Her smile fell. Wouldn't it be nice, to live in a world where that was true? "He's really sick," she added. "I don't know if he's going to get better."

"The smoke," Aria said to herself. "It's really dark."

Gabby frowned. "What are you talking about?"

Aria's attention snapped back to her. "Nothing. I just . . . I hope he gets better."

"Me too," said Gabby.

She squinted at Aria. What was she doing in the hospital? Unlike Gabby, she didn't wear the battle scars of those bound to the sick. No bags under her eyes from spending nights here. No cringing at the sound of a distant cough. Nothing tired or worn or tense about her. In fact, she radiated health.

"Do you have family being treated here?" asked Gabby.

Aria shook her head.

"Then why are you here?" asked Gabby, hoping she didn't sound rude.

Aria looked down at her pink laces. "I'm just here to help."

"Oh," said Gabby, "so you're like a volunteer?"

Aria hesitated, scrunched up her brow, and then nodded decidedly. "Yes, like that."

"I didn't know they let people our age work at the hospital," said Gabby.

Aria hesitated again. "Well," she said, "you have to start sometime. What about you?"

"What about me?" asked Gabby.

"Do you have family here?"

Now it was Gabby's turn to hesitate. She'd said more in the last few minutes than she had in days. It felt nice to talk to someone, and she hated the idea of the girl's smile turning tight with pity. But it wasn't like Gabby could hide Marco's sickness, not when she was *in* his hospital.

"My brother's here," Gabby finally replied. "He's sick."

Gabby braced herself for the *I'm sorry*, but Aria simply nodded and asked, "Is it bad, like Henry?"

Gabby looked down at her notebook. "It's different."

Marco's *bad* had started last year on a soccer field. At first they'd thought the pain in his leg and hip was just another growth spurt — he was tall for fourteen — but it kept getting worse. And then one day when he and Gabby were racing up the wooded hill behind their house, he'd had to stop, he couldn't make it to the top. And they took him to the doctor and found out that it wasn't normal, wasn't natural. The tests confirmed it. A series of tumors — such an ugly word, like a kind of beast — were attacking the bones in Marco's left leg. From his knee all the way up through his hip.

And they were growing.

Fast.

In a matter of weeks, the Torres family's life had been overtaken by *the bad*. Marco began an aggressive treatment plan to stop the tumors from spreading. The doctors explained that they had to shrink the tumors first. So that when they operated on Marco, it would be easier to remove them all.

Nothing about the treatment had been easy. But Marco had done it. He'd fought his way this far. And now it was time to operate, or it *should* be, but . . .

"Gabby?" pressed Aria.

"We're waiting," she said, willing herself to say the words out loud. "We moved here over the summer so my brother, Marco, could have an operation, but a couple weeks ago he got sick. Not a big kind of sick. A small kind, a bad cold, but still. They keep putting his surgery on hold. And now we're waiting."

The truth was, every time Marco coughed, every time his temperature went up or he slept too long, the panic in Gabby's chest got worse. What if they *couldn't* clear him for surgery? What if *the bad* came back before they could operate? What if —

"It's okay," said Aria softly, as if she could hear Gabby's worried thoughts. And Aria's tone did make Gabby relax, just a little bit.

"I'm starting school tomorrow," Gabby went on, "and I'm worried about Marco, but there's this part of me that can't wait to get away from here. When I'm here all I can think about — all *anyone* can think about — is my brother's sickness. But when I go to school at least I can pretend for a little while that things are okay. Normal. That I'm not just the sister of a kid with cancer."

The moment she spoke those words, Gabby felt horrible. She wasn't ashamed of Marco or his illness. But if she could have anything in the world, it would be for him to get healthy. It wasn't Marco's fault he was sick. *This is why I should keep my mouth shut*, Gabby told herself. Half of the time her thoughts didn't seem important. The other half of the time she hated herself for even thinking them.

Gabby started to take back what she'd said, when Aria said, "That makes sense."

"It does?" asked Gabby.

Aria nodded. "Sure. Your brother's sick. You're not."

Gabby found herself nodding. "I know it's wrong," she said, "but I'm just tired of . . . I don't know. . . ." She fumbled for the words. "In a hospital, the only people who matter are the ones in the beds. But when someone you care about is sick, you get sick, too, in a different way. . . ."

Just then she heard a text come in on her phone. She dug it out of her pocket.

"What was that?" asked Aria as the phone made another chirping sound.

"My mom," said Gabby, getting to her feet. "I have to go." She couldn't believe she'd told the girl so much, but it felt good. "Thanks," she added.

"For what?" asked Aria.

"For listening."

Aria smiled. "That's what I'm here for."

At that, Gabby's heart sank a little. Sitting there, talking to Aria, she'd felt special, important. She'd totally forgotten that Aria was a volunteer at the hospital. It was probably just her job to make people feel better.

"I'll see you around," said Gabby, quickly turning to go.

Aria shoved her hands in the pockets of her skirt, and smiled. "You will."

chapter 4

ARIA

Aria watched Gabby walk away, the blue smoke swirling around her shoulders. She waited a moment, then hopped up from the couch and followed. Gabby had vanished around a corner, but thin tendrils of smoke trailed behind her, and soon enough Aria caught sight of her near the end of a pale blue hall. She was standing outside a door, staring in.

Aria hesitated. She wanted to go over to Gabby, but she thought it would seem strange, her showing up so soon after they'd said good-bye. Better if she could stay with Gabby for a little while without the girl knowing. If only she could watch *unseen*.

Was that possible? Aria wondered, looking down at her hands. Some things she knew with absolute clarity — what she was, what she was meant to do, what she *couldn't* do, what she *mustn't* do. But what she *could* do and what she *should* do, those things were muddy, blurred.

Only one way to find out, thought Aria.

Staring down at her hands, she willed herself to disappear. At first nothing happened. And then, between one blink and the next, she was gone. She'd expected something slow and spreading, the way color did through her laces, but she didn't bleed out of sight. She just vanished.

She could still feel the linoleum beneath her shoes, but there were no shoes to *see.* Aria shivered a little. She didn't like it. What if she couldn't undo it? She wanted to undo it!

And just like that, she was there again, green top and blue leggings and pink laces in the hall.

Aria sighed with relief.

What an unpleasant thing, being invisible. It made her *feel* less real. But it was necessary. And now that Aria knew she could undo the illusion, she took a deep breath, made herself invisible again, and joined Gabby in front of the door.

Gabby was peering in through a glass insert, and as Aria looked over her shoulder, she could see what Gabby saw in the room. A boy in a bed.

It had to be Gabby's brother, Marco. He was propped up against several pillows, sleeping. He wasn't what Aria had pictured, not frail like that other boy, Henry. No, Marco was broad-shouldered, with dark brown hair and golden skin.

Gabby was about to turn the knob when a woman called to her from down the hall.

"Gabrielle," said the woman, her voice tense. She had a crease between her eyebrows and circles under her eyes, and she looked like an older, sadder version of Gabby. Aria guessed that she was her mother.

"Where have you been?" she asked.

Gabby's hand fell away from the door. "I was wandering."

"Well, you've had *me* wandering all over this place looking for you."

"I'm sorry," said Gabby automatically. "I was just trying to stay out of the way." She turned back toward the door. "How's Marco?"

"Sleeping, again," answered her mom, softening. "I'm going to stay with him awhile longer."

"I can stay, too."

Mrs. Torres shook her head. "I want you to go home."

"It isn't home," muttered Gabby under her breath.

Her mom tutted. "Don't talk back. Just go." Gabby's shoulders slumped. "And if I'm not there by nine thirty," added her mom, "I want you *in bed.*"

"But you'll be there in the morning, right?" asked Gabby. "To wish me luck?"

Mrs. Torres's brow crinkled in confusion, and then her eyes widened. "Yes, yes, of course," she said. "Big day, *mija*. You have everything you need? All your supplies?"

Gabby nodded. "I think so."

"Seventh grade," said her mom, voice tight. "When did you grow up?"

It was a small question, said more to herself than her daughter. Aria saw the pain in Gabby's face, but the girl only shrugged and said, "I need to grab my things." She slipped silently into Marco's room.

Aria stayed in the hall with Gabby's mom. Aria could see the question flickering like a light behind the woman's eyes — *When did you grow up?* And for a moment it was like Gabby's mom had looked at her daughter and actually *seen* her. Aria willed Gabby's mom to hold on to that glimmer, but a second later Mrs. Torres's pocket gave a shrill double-beep. By the time she dug out the phone, the glimmer was fading. By the time she answered, the glimmer was gone.

She started talking rapidly in Spanish and was halfway down the hall with her cell pressed to her ear by the time Gabby reappeared, shopping bag in hand.

Aria watched Gabby watch her mother. Gabby's mouth was pressed into a small, sad line. Aria realized that that moment when Mrs. Torres saw her daughter was just that. A *moment*. And Aria could tell from the disappointed look on Gabby's face that it was a rare moment.

Even though Gabby was trying to hold it together in the hall, Aria could tell that she was upset. Hurt. And suddenly, Aria understood something.

Gabby wanted to be noticed.

She wanted to be *seen*.

And Aria was the one who was going to help her. She didn't know exactly how, but she would find a way. It was why she was here. It was her job. Her purpose.

Gabby started off down the hall, and Aria followed. Down the elevator and through the lobby and past the revolving doors — Aria nearly collided with the glass because she couldn't *see* herself in it — and down those horrible gray steps.

Aria paused to cast a last glance back at the hospital. The sun was sinking, the low light glinting against the building, making it look sharp, unwelcoming. When she turned back, Gabby had gotten a ways ahead, and Aria had to run to catch up.

As she reached her side, she noticed something.

Gabby had started to hum.

It was nothing more than a small, wandering melody, but it was lovely. Aria didn't know if all people sounded as nice when they sang, and she was about to try when she remembered her current invisible state. So she kept her mouth shut and listened, the sound filling her with warmth. The melody had an effect on Gabby, too. As she hummed, her shoulders began to loosen, the strain going out of her face.

And then Gabby came to a stop in front of an apartment building and looked up. The humming trailed off, the easy song replaced by heavy silence. Gabby took a deep breath, climbed the steps to the front door, and went inside. Aria moved to follow, but by the time she got to the door, it had fallen shut again. When she tried the handle, it didn't move. Aria frowned. It hadn't been locked. Gabby had gone right in (she could hear her fading footsteps), but when Aria tried it again, it wouldn't budge. She *willed* the door to open, the way she'd willed herself invisible, the way she'd willed her shoelaces to change colors.

But it didn't work.

Weird, she thought. It should be so simple, opening something that's closed, certainly easier than disappearing.

31

But Aria couldn't do it. Was she not strong enough yet? Or was it somehow breaking a rule?

Aria gazed up at the building, which was eight stories tall and five windows wide, and wondered which apartment belonged to Gabby. She thought about going for a walk, or making her way back to the hospital. But now that she'd found the blue smoke, found Gabby, it was like a thread connected them, a thread with only so much length, and Aria felt an uncomfortable tightness in her chest at the thought of testing its reach.

Overhead, a light turned on. Four floors up and one window over. When Aria squinted, she could almost see a curl of blue smoke up there. Gabby's apartment.

Aria looked around. All she needed was a way *up*. The simple answer would be to fly, but Aria didn't know if she could do that without wings. She closed her eyes and tried to picture herself airborne, but when she opened her eyes, she was still standing on the ground. Fine then. If she couldn't fly, she would climb.

The moment she thought it, a ladder appeared, simple and wooden and running all the way from the grass to the apartment roof eight floors up.

Strange powers, thought Aria as she brought her hand to a lower rung and began to climb. Up four stories she went —

she wasn't afraid of heights — until she reached Gabby's window.

Gabby was nowhere to be seen, but Aria could hear humming and the opening and closing of drawers in the kitchen.

She took one hand off the ladder and tried to open the window. It wouldn't budge. Aria made a small, indignant sound. A ladder! A ladder, out of nothing, and she still couldn't manage to open something closed! It *had* to be a rule.

Aria mentally added *cannot trespass* to the short list of things she knew she couldn't do, right under *cannot heal the sick* and *cannot fly (I think)*. And then she sighed, wrapped her arms around the ladder, and tried to decide what she *could* do. She couldn't — well, she *shouldn't* — just stand there outside the window all night. It was uncomfortable, and probably a little creepy, even if she was invisible.

She either needed to climb down, or climb up.

The setting sun was streaking colors across the sky, and Aria wanted to be closer to it, so she chose up. The ladder ended just at the lip of the roof, and Aria swung her leg over. Then she stood on top of the apartment building, feeling as if she were on top of the world.

She finally allowed herself to become visible again. She looked down at her hands and let out a relieved sigh, surprised at how much effort it had taken to be *in*visible. Every moment she couldn't see herself she felt the need to *remind* herself she was still there, still real. She spent a few moments making sure every bit of her was back, from legs and arms to laces — still pink — and her bracelet.

In the fading light, she examined the blue circling her wrist and noticed something she hadn't before. There were small loops woven through the material, rings where charms could be added. Three of them. Her heart jumped. Was that how many people she needed to help? Was that how she would earn her wings?

Aria's spirits lifted at the thought. Three people. True, she hadn't even succeeded in helping *one* person yet, but she would. She would help Gabby get rid of her smoke, and she'd be a full step closer to a pair of wings.

She turned her attention back to the sky. It was mesmerizing, the way it changed. She watched the oranges slide into pinks and then deeper purples, shifting and then fading into darkness. The sky made her think of Gabby. Gabby, who was fading, too, becoming invisible even though she didn't want to be.

Marco's sickness was loud and bright and big enough to make everything else feel small. It wasn't his fault. It wasn't anyone's fault. But it was time for Gabby to find her light. Find her voice.

Aria smiled. She couldn't wait for tomorrow.

Because tomorrow, Gabby would go to school.

And Aria would be with her.

chapter 5

GABBY

"Hello?" Gabby called out, even though she knew the apartment was empty. Her *abuela* — her mother's mother — always said that when you came home, you had to let any ghosts know you were there. Gabby's grandmother always stomped her feet on the mat and clapped her weathered hands and made a racket every time she entered an empty room.

Gabby didn't believe in ghosts, and even if she did, she thought a *hello* was probably enough. Still, as she made her way through the apartment, she went back to humming. She sang to herself as she kicked off her shoes and dropped the bag of school supplies on the table.

Ghosts can't just come in, her *abuela* had added. *Not unless you let them.*

Are ghosts the only things? Gabby had asked.

Her *abuela* had tutted. *No,* mija. *Ghosts and monsters and angels and all those magic things, they all need your permission to come in.*

Why?

Why? Why? Because it's a rule. They have different rules than we do. Rules about right and wrong, and what is theirs and what is ours.

Her *abuela* was a strange, superstitious woman.

Don't ask why, just know it, her *abuela* had said. *And keep the door closed.*

Gabby wished her *abuela* had come with them — she still lived in their old town. She called all the time, but it wasn't the same. Gabby's mom said she was too old to travel, but Gabby knew the truth: she had a fear of hospitals — *too many go in, too few go out* — and would rather light candles for Marco from home.

Gabby found a frozen lasagna in the freezer and popped it in the microwave. She rapped her fingers on the counter, humming under the sound of the food cooking as her gaze wandered over the empty apartment. Her mom's room sat dark, practically unused, and down the hall Gabby's room was almost as lifeless. No dent in the wall from where Marco had thrown the ball and she'd failed to catch it. No scratch on the floor from where she'd tried to roller-skate indoors.

No notches on the doorframe from where they'd measured her height. Every time she flipped on the lights, she still found herself looking for those notches, as if one of the marks might have come with them from their old house. But none of them had.

Marco had a room, too, but he'd only slept in his bed one night between moving here and getting checked in at the hospital. Still, his was the only room that looked the least bit warm and welcoming, as if that would will him to get better faster, to come home. Not that this place felt like a home.

The microwave dinged. Because she couldn't eat and hum at the same time, Gabby turned on the TV, and a game show filled the apartment with hollow, high-pitched sound while she picked at the cheese on her lasagna.

"Marco?" Gabby called out, breathless from running.

He'd been right ahead of her. He'd been winning. And now he was gone.

She called his name again, hearing only the echo *Marco, Marco, Marco*, through the trees. Nothing else, not even his playful answer, *Polo, Polo, Polo*.

Gabby kept climbing up the hill, but when she got to the clearing at the top, it was empty. And quiet.

Fear began to claw at Gabby.

"Marco!" she cried out, but this time there wasn't even an echo. The world ate up the words and left only silence, thick and smothering, interrupted at last not by her brother's voice, but by a harsh, metallic alarm.

Gabby woke up, her throat and eyes burning as the alarm on her bedside table blared.

"Mom?" she called out, her voice shaky from the nightmare. No answer. She climbed out of bed and padded through the apartment, but there was no sign of her mother. She felt a wave of sadness, followed by panic.

Maybe there was a good reason her mom had stayed over at the hospital. Maybe something was wrong with Marco. Gabby went back to her room and grabbed her phone from her dresser. She hated that calling had become the easiest way to get her mom's attention.

It only rang twice before a voice said, "Hello?"

"Hey, Mom, it's me. I just wanted to make sure everything's okay."

"Yes, of course, why wouldn't . . ." She could hear her mom fumbling with the phone and pictured her looking at her watch. "Oh, *mija*, I'm so sorry. It got late and I was tired and I just closed my eyes for a moment. I was going to wake up early and come home in time."

"It's okay," said Gabby. "I just got worried."

"Do you want me to come home?" asked her mom.

Yes, thought Gabby. "No," she said. "It's fine."

She wanted her mom to insist, to say she was leaving, was already in the lot, was on her way. Instead, her mom said, "Okay."

Gabby's heart sank. Her mom was tuned to the slightest changes in Marco's mood, but Gabby felt like she had to shout if she wanted to be noticed. And she couldn't bring herself to do it. Couldn't find the voice.

"Have a great first day," added her mom.

"I'll try." A few tears escaped down Gabby's face before she could wipe them away. She hung up and shook her head, chiding herself.

This was seventh grade, not elementary school. She wasn't a little kid anymore. She didn't need her mom to see her off to class. This was her chance, her fresh start, and she couldn't let a silly little thing like the lack of a kiss on the cheek ruin it.

She focused on getting ready. Gabby stood at the mouth of her closet, surveying her wardrobe. Everything looked too bright, or too dull, or too big, or too tight. She hadn't gone shopping since before the move, had spent the summer in jeans and T-shirts (and hoodies, because the hospital was always cold). Now she was terrified that there would be some major trend at Grand Heights Middle that she didn't know about. Back home, Alice had always known the latest styles, while Beth chose not to care about clothes. Gabby fell somewhere in the middle. Now, she wondered: *Do the twelve-year-old girls here wear skirts? Headbands? Leggings?*

She thought of Aria's blue leggings from yesterday and dug around in a drawer until she found a pair of green ones so bright they must have been part of a Halloween costume. Reluctantly she tried them on under a frilly skirt. She chanced a look in the mirror and grimaced.

She looked ridiculous. Scrambling out of the outfit before anyone else could *ever* see, Gabby stared down at the clothes littering her bedroom floor. Again she wished her mom could be there to advise, and again she smothered the feeling. Seventh graders, she told herself, did not need parents to offer fashion input.

She finally settled on a version of her summer uniform: a pair of dark jeans, a red T-shirt with a scooped neck, and ballet flats. Not the most exciting outfit — she wasn't as fashion-forward as Alice, as carefree as Beth, or as bold as Aria — but it would do.

Gabby grabbed her backpack, walked out of her room, and took some money from an envelope tacked to the fridge labeled FOOD. She stomped her feet once by the front door to let any ghosts know she was leaving and marched downstairs. There was an orange cat on the front stoop, and she was just leaning down to pet it when she saw the school bus rounding the corner. She ran and reached the stop just as the bus did. Gabby took one last, deep breath, and climbed on board.

It was the first day, and the bus was only half full, but everyone on it seemed to know one another already. The kids huddled in groups, chatting about their summers. Gabby slid into a seat alone and looked out the window at her apartment building as the bus pulled away. She saw the orange cat stretching on the steps, but as her gaze drifted up the seven — no, eight — floors, she could have sworn she saw someone standing on the roof. A girl. She squinted, but a second later, when the bus rounded the corner, the figure was gone.

chapter 6

ARIA

Aria sat up abruptly.

She'd been lying on the rooftop, sprawled out on a few blankets. She'd summoned them, along with a pillow, the night before, the same way she had the ladder (it seemed summoning useful objects was firmly on the list of things she *could* do).

She hadn't fallen asleep exactly, but her mind had wandered off, and by the time she pulled it back the sun was shining and the air was cool and a small gray bird was pecking at her shadow. She shooed the bird away and got to her feet. It took a moment for her thoughts to collect, and when they did, they shaped into a single word.

Gabby.

And then another.

School.

Aria burst into motion, the pillow and blankets turning to fog and then to nothing around her feet as she hurried to the edge of the roof. She got there just in time to see Gabby stepping onto the school bus. Oh no.

With a last glance around the roof, Aria swung her leg over the edge of the ladder. But she'd made it down only a few rungs when someone cried out, and she froze.

A man on the sidewalk below was shouting up at her and waving his hands. At this height, she couldn't hear what he was saying, but one thing was clear. A twelve-year-old girl clinging to a ladder eight stories up was *not* normal.

The bus had turned the corner, taking Gabby with it, and the man was shouting frantically, and the front door of the building opened as a handful of other tenants came out to see what was going on, and in that moment Aria knew one thing: she needed to disappear.

It happened instantly, just as it had the day before, but then she'd been standing firmly on the ground and this time she'd been clinging to the ladder, and the sight of her fingers vanishing from the rungs made her lose her balance.

And in a moment of panic, Aria let go.

And she began to fall.

The man on the sidewalk stopped shouting, not because the other tenants were trying to calm him, but because he couldn't see Aria plummeting down. He couldn't see her at all.

But Aria was still there, and she was still falling very, very quickly toward the ground below.

Three seconds before she hit the ground, she realized very concretely that no, she could not fly.

Two seconds before she hit the ground, her shadow appeared beneath her, waiting.

And the second before she hit the ground, her shadow filled with brilliant, blinding light. And when Aria hit the ground, and the shadow, she fell straight through into the white.

The shadow took shape on the sidewalk across the street from the school.

If the hundreds of sixth, seventh, and eighth graders had been looking back at their parents' cars and the school buses instead of straight ahead at the front doors, they might have seen it. As it was, nobody saw the shadow that sprung up out of nothing. Nobody saw it take the shape of a twelve-year-old girl, and nobody saw it glow with light, and nobody saw the coppery-haired girl stumble up and out of it and onto the sidewalk.

Nobody, except a sixth-grade boy. He was standing on the sidewalk and had watched the whole thing with wide eyes. He watched the girl brush herself off, sigh with relief, and say, "Good shadow."

The shadow seemed pleased with itself, its light flickering a little before going out.

Well, thought Aria as the edges of the shadow reattached themselves to her heels. *That settles that.*

"Settles what?" asked the boy, and Aria looked up, realizing that she was visible again, *and* had spoken out loud.

"Can't fly," she said.

The boy's eyes widened a little more. "What are you?"

Aria sighed. Not *who*, which would have been easy to answer, but *what*. No one had asked Aria that, and she chewed her lip, and opened her mouth, and was about to answer when a bell rang in the distance. She cracked a grin.

"Late for class," she said, then waved good-bye and jogged toward the school.

On her way, she noticed that one of her laces — still pink — had come undone. She knelt to retie it, and while she was there, she decided to make them yellow instead. As her fingers redid the knot and then the bow, color slid out from her touch and along the shoestrings. She retied the laces on the other shoe, to make them even, and by the time she finished, both shoes were sporting laces the color of lemons. Aria smiled, and straightened, and looked up at the school.

GRAND HEIGHTS MIDDLE SCHOOL, read the marquee over the doors. This must be Gabby's school. Aria followed the wave of students inside, scanning the hall for signs of the other girl. She didn't see her. To be fair, it was a very large school, and there were a lot of kids. The hospital had been large, too, but Gabby stood out there, and here she'd blend right in.

Except, of course, for her blue smoke.

Not that Aria would be able to see it, with so many people — some of them tall! — in her way.

"There you are!"

Aria spun, but the girl who'd shouted those words wasn't talking to her.

"Move it, loser."

Aria frowned and turned, but the boy who'd said it was nudging someone else.

"I've missed you."

"Clear a path!"

"No food in the hall."

"Ugh."

Laughter. Slamming lockers. Scuffing shoes. A group of boys jostled for a soccer ball. A huddle of girls flipped

47

through the pages of a magazine. The whole school hummed with a kind of terrifying energy, and Aria hoped that wherever Gabby was, she was okay. Grand Heights Middle School wasn't just large, it was *loud*. A quiet person could drown in this much noise.

But Aria wouldn't let her.

Another bell rang, high and sharp over the sounds of the students, and the hall began to empty. Aria shifted her weight from foot to foot. Everyone was going to class, and she knew she couldn't just keep wandering around, looking for Gabby. Somebody — a teacher — would catch her and ask questions, as long as she was visible.

Still shaken from her last vanishing act and the fall, Aria took a deep breath and braced herself for the strange, vaguely uncomfortable feeling of disappearing.

But nothing happened.

Aria stared down at her hand and the blue charm bracelet around her wrist, both still visible. She thought again that she should probably be invisible. Again, she wasn't.

Aria didn't know if she was drained from the morning's mishap, or if the magic didn't come because she didn't *need* it, or if deep down, she didn't *want* to be invisible. Whatever the reason, it looked like Aria was going to be playing the role of student, and that meant she'd need to blend in. She looked around at the other kids in the hall. There didn't seem to be a uniform, or any standard outfit — most of them wore jeans and T-shirts — so she could keep her blue leggings and her white pocket skirt, but she needed a backpack.

A moment later she felt the strap in her hand and Aria was pleased to discover how bright the backpack was, a kind of iridescent fabric that changed colors in the light.

She caught her reflection in a glass case and marveled. She looked like a student!

The hall was almost empty, and Aria was about to pick a class at random when she saw something vanishing into a room ahead. Blue smoke.

Aria smiled and ran to catch up.

chapter 7

GABBY

"Hey, how was break?"

"Dang, you got tall."

"I love your hair."

"Still scrawny, Parker!"

"Where did you go this summer?"

"Where did the summer *go?*"

All around Gabby, kids were talking, but none of them were talking about her. Or Marco. None of them looked at her with worry. Because none of them looked at her at all.

Gabby quickly realized that the best thing about Grand Heights Middle School was also the scariest. No one knew who she was. As she made her way down the hall she told herself that's what she'd wanted. The chance to be somebody new. But she hadn't thought about the fact that until she became that somebody, she was *nobody*.

Marco could walk into a room and say hello, could start new relationships with one word. Gabby couldn't even will her feet forward. She *imagined* walking up to a group of girls at a locker and saying hi. But she couldn't.

The conversations happening all around her were like closed loops. She couldn't seem to find a way in. Everyone had these strings running between them, connecting their lives. And Gabby knew that all conversations involved questions. Such as:

What did you do this summer?

How would she even answer?

I just moved here.

Oh, really? they might say. *Where did you come from? Why did you move?*

And what would she say to that?

Lying would feel like a betrayal to Marco, but telling the truth would ruin everything. They'd stop seeing Gabby and start seeing some sick kid's sister instead. Maybe they'd retreat. Or maybe they'd look at her the way Alice and Beth had started to. Maybe they would hang out with her out of pity.

Gabby couldn't stand the thought of *that*, and she was saved from the anguish by the morning bell, which rang out overhead. The chattering students broke apart and hurried

51

into classrooms. Gabby hoisted her bag onto her shoulder and followed them.

Her first class was English. The room was filling fast, and most of the groups from the hall had simply reformed around the desks. Gabby sighed, slid into an empty chair, and put her head down a moment on the desk.

"Is this seat taken?" asked a familiar voice, and Gabby looked up to find Aria standing at the desk beside her, one sneaker resting on the chair, her laces sunshine yellow. Happiness rolled through Gabby. She didn't realize how badly she wanted to see someone she knew . . . or at least, someone who wasn't a total stranger.

"I didn't know you went to Grand Heights," Gabby said.

"Me either," said Aria cheerfully. "It's my first day. I mean, I guess it's everyone's first day, but it's my *first* first."

Gabby frowned. "You didn't go here last year?"

"Nope," said Aria. "I just moved to Grand Heights." She brightened. "Like you! We should stick together," she added.

Gabby smiled a little, caught up in the relief of not being alone. The teacher rapped on the board.

"Hello, class! My name is Mr. Robert." Gabby already knew this because his name was written in three different places in the classroom — on the door, on the board, on the desk — as if the teacher was afraid the students would forget.

"I know what you're all thinking," he continued. "No, I'm not one of those hip teachers who goes by his first name." Gabby doubted anyone was thinking that. "My first name is Bertrand," said Mr. Robert. "But don't call me that. . . ."

Mr. Robert passed a stack of papers down each of the rows as he talked, and the girl in front of Gabby — who was tall and blond, with a high-wattage smile — turned and handed her a page. The girl bobbed her head back and forth as Mr. Robert rambled on, mouthing along, and Gabby nearly giggled.

"Charlotte," warned Mr. Robert, and the blond girl winked at Gabby and then spun forward. "Now, on to roll call."

He went down the list, and Gabby tried to remember the names and the faces that went with them, but she quickly lost track. Was the boy with the short black hair Evan or Ethan? Was the girl with the red glasses and the ponytail Mandy or Morgan? Gabby stole a glance at Aria and was surprised to find her staring intently at the paper in Mr. Robert's hand with a small frown. He made it all the way down the list before he called her name.

"Here!" said Aria brightly.

"Aria, I'm afraid I only have your first name," said Mr. Robert, taking up a pen. "What's your last name?"

Aria's brow furrowed. "Oh, no," she said. "I'm pretty sure it's always been Aria."

The students around her began to laugh. Gabby smiled. Mr. Robert sighed.

"I mean your *last name*. As in, the one that comes *after* your first name."

Aria frowned, and began to fidget with the charm bracelet around her wrist. "Oh," she said, looking down at it. "Um . . . blue!"

"Blue?" said Mr. Robert, raising a brow. "Like the color?"

Aria nodded. "Exactly. Aria Blue."

Mr. Robert shrugged, wrote in the last name, and set the sheet aside.

"All right, class. Let's get started." He leaned back against his desk. "You might think this is just an English class, but it's not. It's an *expression* class. We're going to be learning to use our words to tell our own stories. To that end, I want you each to dedicate a notebook to this class. You'll be given journal assignments over the course of the year. Some days you'll take the journal home, and some days you'll leave it with me, so don't think this is going to be one of those projects you can skip out on. I'll be checking in. And I hope you'll all embrace it, because we're going to start today."

The class groaned. Gabby groaned with them.

"Everyone take out a notebook."

Gabby took out the journal covered with music notes.

"Now," instructed Mr. Robert. "Turn to the first page —"
A hand shot up. "You cannot possibly have questions yet,
Jordan." The hand came back down. "Your first writing assignment is as simple as it gets. An introduction. I want you to
introduce yourself to me. To the reader. I know that a blank
page can seem daunting . . ." he added, "but I think you'll find
that once you make the first mark, the rest will follow."

He turned and rounded his desk and wrote on the board.

Introduction.

Fun facts.

How I spent my summer.

All around the room, pencils and pens began to scratch
and glide across the paper, but Gabby's pen hovered over the
blank page. She couldn't think of a way to introduce herself,
not without introducing Marco, and she couldn't tell Mr.
Robert about her brother. When her old teachers back home
found out, life became *Oh, Gabby dear, if you need more
time . . .* and *Oh, Gabby, I know it's been hard . . .* and *Oh,
Gabby, if you can't focus . . .*

She knew they didn't mean to make her feel different, but they did, and if Mr. Robert found out, it would happen all over again.

To her surprise, Gabby wasn't the only one struggling. She stole a look at Aria's journal and saw that it was blank, too, except for *My name is Aria Blue and I*

Gabby wondered how someone like Aria could have trouble finding words. She seemed so . . . *interesting*. The kind of girl who'd have tons of things she'd want to write about. But staring at the girl's blank page, Gabby realized something: she knew absolutely nothing about Aria Blue.

When the bell rang, Gabby's notebook was still blank. The blond girl in front of her — Charlotte — had filled half a dozen pages, and the other students Gabby could see from her seat had all written at least a few pages.

"Your homework," announced Mr. Robert, "is to finish introducing yourself and to introduce your family. Be specific. Be observant. Life is a story, so tell it."

Gabby and Aria got to their feet with the rest of the room and went to leave with the rest of the room, but Mr. Robert stopped them.

"Miss Blue, Miss Torres," he said. "Unless you've developed a new way of writing that doesn't involve moving your pen, I'm guessing you did not participate in today's exercise." He held out his hand. "Your journals, please."

Gabby's heart pounded as she reluctantly offered her teacher the notebook. He flipped it open and clicked his tongue at the blank pages. Her gaze went to the linoleum floor.

"I didn't know how to start," she mumbled.

"Yes, well, starting is the hard part. Do *you* have an excuse for not working, Miss Blue?"

Aria shrugged. "I haven't lived enough to write about it."

Mr. Robert gave her a sad smile. "How very existential," he said. Gabby didn't know what that meant, but then again she didn't really understand half of what he said. "But I'm willing to bet you've got something to say." He handed the journals back. "I'll be collecting these tomorrow at the end of class, so I suggest you find *something* to write about."

Gabby's heart started to sink, but Aria flashed her a smile.

"Don't worry," she said. "We will."

chapter 8

ARIA

Aria carried her lunch tray to the register in the cafeteria. When the lady told her how much she owed, Aria hesitated. She'd never needed money, but money was a *thing* and she was pretty good at making things out of nothing. So she dug her hand into the pocket of her skirt, and willed the money to be there, and a second later produced a fistful of cash and coins. She handed it over to the lunch lady without counting, and the lunch lady marveled at the fact it was *exactly* the right amount of money — not a penny more, not a penny less.

"Smart pockets," explained Aria with a smile.

The noise in the cafeteria was deafening. Aria saw that Gabby had already gotten her food and was standing at the edge of the sea of tables. She was clutching her tray and looking terrified. The blue smoke swirled nervously around her shoulders.

Aria had to admit, the cafeteria *was* daunting. But Gabby didn't have to face it alone.

She bumped Gabby's elbow.

"Let's find a seat."

They snagged a small table in a corner of the room.

"Everything on your plate is red," observed Gabby.

Aria looked down at her plate. It was true. She'd grabbed an apple and some kind of pasta with sauce and a bowl of Jell-O (even though it scared her). She'd never eaten before. She knew she didn't strictly *need* to eat, but it looked enjoyable. Besides, she was a student now. Other students ate. But her tray was looking less and less appetizing.

"I thought it would be fun," she explained, "to pick by color." She poked the Jell-O with a fork. "Everything was so bright and pretty piece by piece, but all together it's kind of a mess." Aria thought about the way she felt seeing herself for the first time, the whole so much better than the parts. "I guess food doesn't really work like people."

Gabby looked at Aria like she'd said a strange thing but then smiled.

"So, Aria Blue," she said. "That's a really cool name."

Aria beamed. "Thanks!" She was pretty proud of it. She hadn't realized when she'd imagined her name on the roster that she'd need *two*. At first she'd been at a total loss, but then she'd seen the bracelet and thought *blue*. It was the color of the smoke that circled those marked for her. It was part of her identity, just like a name. "I really like yours, too," she told Gabby.

Gabby shrugged. "It's a family name. Gabrielle. It's my grandmother's name. And my aunt's. And, like, four other relatives. When that many people have something, it starts to feel a little less special."

"There may be other Gabrielles," said Aria, "but there's only one Gabby."

"Actually, I'm pretty sure there are other Gabbys, too," said Gabby.

Aria ran a hand through her hair and accidentally snagged her charm bracelet. "What I mean," she said, tugging it free, "is that there's only one *you*. Only one *me*. And we get to be whoever we want, and no one can be us like we can. Isn't that exciting?"

Gabby gave a half-smile. "You're really different."

"One of a kind," said Aria with a wink. "Sooo" — she poked at the Jell-O again — "is Grand Heights Middle School everything you wanted it to be?"

Gabby shrugged lightly, but Aria watched the smoke coil and twist around her.

"My mom wanted to homeschool me," said Gabby. "She thought it would be easier, and maybe it would have been, but I begged her not to." Gabby picked at her food. "It wouldn't be homeschooling. It would be *hospital*-schooling, and I thought, if I was trapped in that place all day, every day, I'd just . . . disappear. But I'm here, surrounded by all these new kids, and I *still* feel kind of invisible."

"I see you," said Aria. "But I know what you mean."

"You do?"

Aria gave a somber nod. "I've been invisible. It's awful." Gabby looked surprised. "I mean, not . . . literally . . . of course," amended Aria hastily.

"But you're so . . . bright," said Gabby.

Aria looked down at herself. "I guess so."

"I didn't mean it in a bad way," said Gabby. "Just that you stand out. . . . I wish I did."

Aria shrugged. "I wear these colors because they make me happy, not because they make me stand out. I don't really think wearing loud clothes is the only way to be loud. I mean, sure," she added, "if you go around wearing neon-pink pajamas, people are going to look at you, but that doesn't mean you're going to be *seen*." Aria took a cautious bite of her apple. "I think there's a difference."

"Maybe," said Gabby. "I don't really *want* to be loud. I just don't want to be invisible." Gabby's eyes escaped to her tray.

Aria looked around. "Well, the cafeteria is full of people. Why don't we make friends with some of them?"

Gabby gave her a withering look. "It's not that easy."

"Why not?"

Gabby chewed her lip. "Because it's not. Not for me."

"It'll be fine, come on!" Aria sprung up from the table, but Gabby grabbed her arm.

"Please don't," said Gabby, shaking her head. "Please don't make a scene."

Aria didn't understand, but Gabby seemed genuinely worried, so she sat back down. What Gabby needed was a little confidence. A chance to stand out in her own way.

Aria watched as Gabby hurriedly finished eating and then pulled a printed flier out of her bag.

"What's that?" asked Aria, trying to read upside down.

"It's a club list. Didn't you get one with your class schedule?"

Aria shook her head. "They must have left mine out," she said, which wasn't strictly a lie. "What's it for?"

"Grand Heights Middle has a bunch of after-school clubs," said Gabby, "and you can pick one, and I was thinking that maybe . . ." She looked down at the list and shrugged. "I don't know . . . maybe it's lame but —"

"This is perfect!" said Aria brightly.

"It is?" asked Gabby, surprised.

Aria nodded, and plucked the list out of Gabby's hands. There were more than a dozen choices. Cheerleading. Painting. Pottery. Track. Dance. *Perfect*, she echoed to herself. Gabby could find her own way to stand out!

"Which one are you going to pick?" Aria asked, handing the sheet back.

Gabby shook her head. "I don't know. We have all week to try them out before we have to decide. Do you think you'll do one, too?"

Aria could hear the hope in her question.

"Yeah, sure!" said Aria. "Sounds like fun."

"Which one do you think you'll choose?"

Aria hesitated. She didn't want to sway Gabby. "Tell you what," she said. "I'm not picky. Whatever you choose, I'll go with you. For moral support."

Gabby's eyes widened. "You would do that?"

Aria beamed. The fluorescent cafeteria lights brightened a fraction overhead. "Yep. So what do you think?"

Gabby looked down at the sheet. "I used to run track. . . ."

"Do you like it?"

"I did," said Gabby. "I'm not sure anymore."

"Well," said Aria as the lunch bell rang, "only one way to find out."

chapter 9

GABBY

"I don't think this is such a good idea," said Gabby after school. A sick feeling was forming in her stomach.

"Nonsense," said Aria, guiding her down toward the track. "It's a gorgeous day," she added.

It was, but a strange tightness was working its way into Gabby's chest. It had started back in the cafeteria and followed her through the afternoon classes and past the last bell, worsening as she changed into gym clothes and made her way out the doors to the rubber ring that ran around the soccer field.

She tried to swallow her nerves as she and Aria reached the dozen or so students gathered at the edge of the track, standing around a coach with a clipboard.

"All right, guys!" boomed the coach, even though everyone was well within earshot. "Huddle up!"

A couple of thin, long-legged girls — *they look like deer*, thought Gabby, *born to lope* — chuckled. A boy sniffed his armpit. The coach passed the clipboard around and everyone signed their name and then started to stretch and warm up. Aria mimicked them, but it was obvious she had no idea what she was doing.

"Are you sure you're up for this?" asked Gabby. "Have you ever run before?"

Aria looked down at her laces, which were now teal — Gabby could have sworn they'd been yellow this morning — and then back up. "I'm a fan of new experiences."

"Now," said the coach, "a few things you should know . . ." He started rambling on about track rules — no pushing, no tripping, et cetera — and Gabby's gaze drifted past the track to another group of students huddled in the middle of the field. Eighth graders, by the looks of them, passing a soccer ball back and forth. The tightness in her chest got worse.

"Hey, you okay?" asked Aria, and Gabby dragged her attention back and nodded absently, automatically, even though she didn't feel very okay.

"Yeah, why?"

Aria chewed her lip. "Well, it's just, he blew his whistle,

and everyone else started running and we're still standing here."

Gabby whipped her head around to see that Aria was right. All the other students were jogging around the track, at least a quarter of a lap ahead.

"Anytime now . . ." shouted the coach. Gabby drew a deep breath and took off.

Gabby hadn't run in more than a year, but she was still good at it. And for a moment, as the rubber track fell away under her shoes, everything was fine. She remembered the thrill of pumping legs and pounding heart. She'd forgotten how good it felt.

And then she thought of being in the woods behind their old house, racing Marco up the hill, the moment when she passed him and looked back and knew that something was wrong. The thrill dissolved into panic, and Gabby staggered to a halt halfway around the track, unable to breathe.

"What's wrong?" asked Aria, catching up and coming to a stop beside her.

Gabby squeezed her eyes shut. *This* was wrong. This was all wrong without Marco. Running was something she did because of him. Something they were supposed to do together.

"I can't do this," gasped Gabby.

"Sure you can," said Aria.

"No, I mean, I can't do *this*. I can't do track. I don't want to."

Before Aria could say anything else, Gabby turned and hurried away. She cut across the field to the bleachers and sank down onto a low metal bench, her head in her hands.

A few seconds later, she felt Aria sit down beside her on the bleachers and then a hand come to rest on her shoulder. Gabby usually hated those small physical gestures — nurses and doctors used them all the time — but she didn't mind it from Aria. It was strangely calming.

"I started running because of Marco," Gabby whispered without looking up. "He wanted to get in shape for soccer, and I wanted to spend time with him. He's the one who taught me how to sprint. It's hard enough that I'm going to school and he's not. I can't do track without him. I can't take it away from him."

"You're not taking anything away, Gabby," said Aria gently.

"I'm sorry," said Gabby, shaking her head, "but this is his. It doesn't feel right without him. I need something else. Something that isn't so . . . full of memories."

She closed her eyes and took a few long, slow breaths, in through her nose and out through her mouth, the way the doctor had told Marco to breathe if he felt a wave of panic coming on.

"She okay?" Gabby heard a girl ask from the track.

"She will be," said Aria. When Gabby opened her eyes she saw the girl — one of the graceful runners — jogging away. Then Gabby looked over at Aria, who was holding the sheet with the electives on it and looking over the other options.

"We'll pick something else for tomorrow," Aria said cheerfully. "Something brand-new."

chapter 10

ARIA

"What about cheerleading?"

"No way."

"Debate?"

"Are you kidding?"

They were making their way to the hospital. Gabby kicked a pebble down the sidewalk while Aria crossed out after-school options with a blue pen.

"Foreign language?" she offered.

"Two languages is enough for me," said Gabby. "Do you speak any others?"

Aria shrugged. "I don't think so."

"My *abuela* only speaks Spanish," explained Gabby, "so Marco and I grew up speaking both that and English. My dad knew how to speak Spanish, but he didn't like my grandmother much, so he went out of his way to speak English when she was around."

Aria hesitated. Gabby hadn't mentioned him before. "Where's your dad now?" she asked carefully.

"Gone," said Gabby, kicking the pebble hard enough to send it skittering into the street. The blue smoke swirled and curled around her shoulders. "He left way before Marco got sick." She found another pebble and began to knock it along down the road. "Can I ask you something?"

"Sure," said Aria.

"Why didn't you write anything in your journal?"

Aria shrugged. "I didn't have anything to write about."

"What about your family?" asked Gabby.

Aria's steps slowed. "What about them?"

Gabby shrugged. "Couldn't you write about them? What are they like? What do they do? Do you have any brothers or sisters?"

Aria's heart twisted. She wasn't sad, not exactly — she knew she didn't need a family, knew that wasn't part of her purpose — but the questions left a strange emptiness in her chest. "It's complicated," she said at last. It wasn't a lie.

"I'm sorry," said Gabby. "I didn't mean to be nosy. I shouldn't have —"

"It's no problem," said Aria with a smile. "It's just . . . ooooooooh!"

She caught sight of a shop window and veered off the sidewalk and up to the glass. Inside was a shelf filled with brightly frosted cupcakes.

"So many colors," whispered Aria, peering in through the glass.

Gabby laughed. "It's tinted frosting," she explained. "Food coloring —"

But Aria had already gone in. The whole shop smelled sweet like sugar, and when she breathed in, she could taste it on her tongue. She spent several minutes wavering between a chocolate cupcake with pink icing and a vanilla cupcake with blue icing and a swirl cupcake with purple icing and ended up asking for half a dozen, two of each, so she and Gabby could both try all three.

They sat on a bench outside with the open box. Aria couldn't believe the cupcakes tasted even better than they smelled! She tried to pick her favorite and couldn't.

"Can I take one of these to Marco?" asked Gabby before biting into the swirl cupcake with purple icing.

"Of course," said Aria, who was now cutting two cupcakes apart and putting them back together in new combinations.

Gabby carefully nestled a vanilla cupcake with blue frosting into the container to keep it safe.

"Does Marco like cupcakes?" asked Aria.

"He likes anything that's not hospital food," said Gabby. "And I think it might cheer him up."

"You're a really, really good sister, Gabby," said Aria, taking a big bite of cupcake. Gabby blushed.

Cupcakes devoured, the girls continued on toward the hospital. As it came into view up ahead, Aria yawned.

"What was that?" she asked, surprised.

"Sugar crash," said Gabby, suppressing a yawn herself. "It happens when you eat a lot of sugar and get really hyper and then you get really tired. Maybe you shouldn't have tried *all* the cupcakes."

Aria yawned again. "Tired?"

"Yeah. Tired. You know. The feeling you get when you need to sleep."

Aria stared at Gabby. "But I don't . . ." She trailed off with a frown, then said, "I don't normally get tired."

"Well, you don't normally eat a pound of sugar, do you?"

"No," she admitted, yawning a third time as they crossed the parking lot.

"Do you have to volunteer today?" asked Gabby. Aria shook her head. "Then why did you come with me?"

Aria shrugged. "I just thought I'd keep you company."

Gabby started to smile. And then they reached the gray hospital steps, and her smile faded. Gabby's shoes came to a stop, her fingers tightening on the cupcake box as she stared up at the revolving doors. Aria watched the blue smoke, which had calmed a little, swirl into motion again, engulfing her. But before Aria could ask Gabby a question, the other girl took a deep breath.

"Let's go," she said, and started up the steps.

chapter 11

GABBY

Gabby cradled the cupcake box as she and Aria wove through the halls toward Marco's room. She knew he would be in a bad mood from missing school, so the cupcake seemed like the least she could do.

A tiny bit of blue sky, she thought, holding the box close.

When they got to his room, Gabby peered in through the window and let out a small sigh of relief when she saw that he was alone. It was easier that way. Marco liked to pretend things were normal almost as much as she did, and sometimes, if they were careful, they could get through a whole conversation without mentioning his condition or the hospital. They could carve those pieces out and focus on the other parts, ignoring the holes. When Gabby's mom was there, the holes were all she saw.

"Hey, Gabs," said Marco, looking up from his school-work as she and Aria came in. He gestured to the textbooks scattered on the bed. "I hope your first day was way more fun than mine."

"I survived," said Gabby, looking around. "No Henry?"

"He came by earlier," said Marco. And then his eyes went past her, to Aria. "You have a shadow."

"Marco, this is Aria," said Gabby. "Aria, Marco." She felt herself smile when she introduced them and realized she was proud to have gone to a new school and returned with a new . . . friend? Yes. Aria could definitely be considered a friend. "We go to Grand Heights together, and Aria also volunteers here," Gabby added.

"Aren't you kind of young?" Marco asked Aria.

"Do you have to be a certain age to help people?" asked Aria, sounding genuinely curious.

The edge of Marco's mouth went up. "No, I suppose not."

"We brought you a treat," said Gabby. "Better eat it before Mom shows up."

Gabby handed him the cupcake, and Marco nearly wept as he pulled it out of the box and dug in. He took only a couple of bites of the cupcake before he had to stop — these days his stomach couldn't keep up with his eyes — but he cradled it in his lap as if it really were a piece of blue sky, of freedom.

And then Gabby's mom came in.

The first words out of her mouth were, "Marco, what on earth are you eating?"

She swiped the cupcake out of his hands and deposited it on the side table, then produced a napkin and began wiping the frosting from his fingers.

Marco rolled his eyes. "If anything kills me," he said, pulling away, "it won't be a cupcake."

"Marco!" Gabby's mom scolded, appalled. He slumped back against his pillow as tears brimmed in Mrs. Torres's eyes.

Gabby sighed and said, "It was my fault."

Her mom turned and blinked, seeming to notice her for the first time.

"Gabrielle," she scorned, "you should know better."

"I know," said Gabby. "It's just, we stopped on the way back from *school*," she added, giving her mom a weighted look, "and I thought it would be a nice treat."

Mrs. Torres softened, then reached out and smoothed Gabby's hair. "Well, that was very sweet of you. And yes, school!" She perched on the nearest chair and took Gabby's hand. "How was it? Were your classes all right? Did you have what you needed?"

77

Gabby felt a hand at her shoulder as Aria whispered, "I'll be right back," and then both the hand and the voice slipped away. Gabby nodded absently, not wanting to lose her mom's attention.

"Go on. I want to hear all about it."

Her mom *said* that, and Gabby wanted to think she meant it, but she'd barely opened her mouth when a knock came at the door and a nurse came in, saying something about paperwork. Mrs. Torres's hand slid from Gabby's as she straightened and nodded and said *of course*, and followed the woman out.

Gabby stood there a moment, staring at the door, a tangle of emotions wrapping around her like smoke, thick and suffocating. And then a voice reached her through the cloud.

"Hey, Gabs," said Marco gently. "Forget her. Tell me. And remember I'm trying to live through you over here, so make it good."

Gabby hesitated, then nodded, and slid into the chair beside his bed.

"Now," said Marco, lifting the cupcake from the table and taking another, much smaller bite, "start at the beginning."

Gabby told Marco almost everything: from how left out she felt on the school bus to the journal assignment in

English to how she and Aria sat together at lunch. She didn't tell him about trying to run track and the fact that she couldn't bring herself to do it without him. It would only make him upset.

"Where did your friend run off to?" asked Marco when Gabby was finished.

She looked around the room, as if Aria might simply be hiding in a corner. "I don't know," she said, trying to hide her disappointment. "She probably went home."

"Speaking of, you should go, too," said Marco. Gabby frowned at the thought of the empty apartment but didn't complain, only dragged herself to her feet.

"Hey, Gabs," Marco added. "Thanks for the cupcake. It tasted like —"

"A piece of sky?" asked Gabby hopefully.

Marco smiled. He knew what she meant. "I'm not sure sky has that much sugar or artificial coloring, but yeah. It tasted like normal, and that's exactly what I needed today."

Gabby smiled back. "That's what I'm here for."

"I hope you don't feel like that," he said. "Some days I don't feel like I'm more than this — this sickness — but you are, okay? Don't be this place. Don't be . . ." He trailed off and then picked back up. "Just be you."

Gabby wondered who that was but didn't say that, only nodded.

"Night, Marco."

"Night, Gabs."

The orange cat was back on the apartment steps, catching moths. Gabby knelt and scratched behind its ears, wishing she could coax it to follow her up into the empty apartment, for company. Marco wasn't allergic, but when he got sick, Mom decided all four-legged creatures were germy carriers of evil.

Gabby went upstairs. She stomped on the floor and said hello to the ghosts and hummed while she made herself dinner. Then she turned on the radio and sank down onto her bed to do homework. It was a nice evening, and she left the window open, relishing the fresh air — not fresh like the woods behind their old house, but miles better than the hospital — while she worked.

Most of the assignments were easy enough, but when she got to English, she found herself staring down at the still-blank journal.

I'll be collecting these tomorrow at the end of class, Mr. Robert had said. *So I suggest you find something to write about.*

Gabby tapped her pencil against the page.

My name is Gabrielle Torres, she wrote.

I am twelve years old, and I don't know who I am. I know who I was when I was eleven, before my brother got sick, but somewhere between then and now I've lost it. Myself, I mean. I don't know how to find it again. I thought a self was something you always had, something that grew up with you. Something you couldn't lose. I thought you only got one self, but if that's the case, then what happens if you lose it? Do you try to find it, or replace it? I want to go back to being the person I was before, but it doesn't work that way. Before-Gabby doesn't exist anymore. And now? Now I don't know who I am.

That's what she *wanted* to write.

That's what she *should* have written.

But she couldn't do it.

Instead, she wrote a lie. It started as a small one — *My family just moved here so my mom could start a new job* — and then got it bigger — *My brother, Marco, is in tenth grade over at Grand Heights High* — and bigger — *He's going to try out for soccer soon* — spiraling away before Gabby could stop it. She wrote a paragraph, and then a page, and then two, all of it what she wanted to be true. A life where Marco had never gotten sick. A life where everyone was happy and healthy and Gabby didn't feel invisible.

And Gabby knew she should stop, knew this was wrong, but she liked the girl on the page more than she liked the one writing on it, and she wanted it to be real, even if it only felt real for a few moments.

So she kept writing.

chapter 12

ARIA

One minute Aria was sitting on the couch in the common room, and the next a hand was shaking her awake. For a dazed second, she had no idea where she was, and then she blinked and remembered. She'd been wandering through the hospital, trying to shake off the "sugar crash" and give Gabby some space.

She wanted to be there for her, of course, but she couldn't *always* be there. And it wouldn't do Gabby any good if she learned how to be herself only when Aria was with her.

Aria had made her way to the common room, hoping to see Henry and find out more about his purple-black smoke. Only he hadn't been there, and she couldn't stop yawning, so she'd decided to sit down and then . . . had she fallen *asleep*?

"Young lady," said the nurse, whose hand was still on her shoulder. "Visiting hours are over. It's time to go home."

Home? Aria nodded absently and looked around the common room, still groggy. Beyond the window, the sun was going down.

"Do you have family here?" pressed the nurse. "Is someone coming to pick you up?"

Gabby. Where was she?

"I live close by," said Aria, getting up.

She regretted the cupcakes as she trudged back through the hospital to Marco's room. When she got there, she saw Marco sitting up in bed, writing in a journal, but no Gabby. She double-regretted the cupcakes as she made her way downstairs and out the revolving doors onto the ugly gray steps of the hospital. And then she realized that she couldn't remember the way to Gabby's house.

The sinking sun and the glow of the hospital cast her shadow like a door on the concrete. Aria tapped her shoe, and the shadow fidgeted.

"I need to find Gabby," she told the shadow. "Take me home," she said, and then frowned and corrected herself. "I mean, take me to *Gabby's* home."

The shadow obligingly filled with light, and Aria said thank you and stepped through. An instant later she found herself stepping out of the glowing pool and onto the sidewalk in front of Gabby's building. The light went off inside the shadow, and Aria took a small step forward, nestling her shoes in the right place just as Gabby herself came through the front doors, a bag of trash in hand.

"Aria?" she asked, surprised. "Where did you come from?"

"The hospital," said Aria, grateful Gabby hadn't walked out a second sooner.

Gabby dropped the bag she was holding in the garbage bin. "What are you doing here?"

"I live nearby," said Aria. "And I thought I'd come and say hi. So . . . hi."

"Hi," said Gabby. A moment of silence fell between them. Aria waited. Gabby fidgeted. Finally she said, "You want to come upstairs?"

Aria smiled. "I'd love to."

She hopped up the steps but hesitated at the entrance. What if she still couldn't go in? But then Gabby held the door open for her and said, "You coming?" and Aria's shoe crossed the threshold without any resistance. She smiled and followed Gabby inside.

"Here we are," said Gabby when they reached her apartment.

Aria looked around. She'd never been in a home before, but she'd imagined it would feel . . . homier.

Gabby kicked off her shoes by the door, and Aria did the

same. She started to follow Gabby toward her room when she noticed a photo in the hall and stopped. It was the only decor in the hallway, and it had obviously been taken before Marco got sick. Gabby and Marco and their mom were all sitting around a table in a big backyard, wooded hills behind them. The photo wasn't faded, but there was something about it that made them seem far away. Gabby's mom was in the middle, her arms around her children, and they were all smiling.

"It's weird, right?" said Gabby, coming up beside her. "How different we look." She reached out and touched her fingertips to the glass. "We were a team until . . ." Her words fell away, and so did her fingers. "My room's this way."

Aria thought Gabby's room was nice — she didn't have any others to compare it to — but nothing about it really screamed *Gabby*. Then again, nothing about Gabby screamed *Gabby* yet. That was the problem. Aria thought about turning one of the walls a color — they were all a soft white — but she didn't know which color to make it, and besides, that might be hard to explain, so she held off.

Gabby flopped down on her bed. "Make yourself comfortable."

Aria wandered around the room, taking in the details. Gabby's closet door was open, and Aria could see dozens of outfits inside. Shirts and pants and skirts and shoes. Aria looked down at her own ensemble. It had never occurred to her to change. Aria made a mental note to do so at some point. She turned back toward the room. There was a radio on the table by Gabby's bed, and Aria crossed to it, mesmerized, and began pressing buttons, searching through stations.

"So you came just to say hi?" asked Gabby.

"I didn't want you to think I'd bailed on you," said Aria. "I fell asleep at the hospital."

Songs poured and crashed and seeped and sprang out of the radio as Aria clicked through.

"Can I ask you something?" said Gabby, getting suddenly quieter. "Why are you hanging out with me?"

Aria looked up from the radio, surprised. Gabby's smoke was swirling around her again, and Aria could practically hear the doubt spilling out of Gabby's head before she spoke.

"Is it because of my brother?" Gabby asked quickly.

Aria shook her head. "No. It doesn't have anything to do with Marco."

"Is it because you feel sorry for me?"

"I don't."

"Then why?" pressed Gabby.

Aria chewed her lip. "Because I want to help."

"So you *do* feel sorry for me."

"*No,*" said Aria. "But I can tell you're going through a hard time, and I'm hanging out with you because I *want* to. Because I think you're really cool, even if you can't see it."

Gabby blushed, her eyes going to her bedspread. She mumbled something that sounded like, "No, I'm not."

"You are, too. The thing is," said Aria, searching for the words, "I have this . . . this superpower."

The corner of Gabby's mouth twitched. "No, you don't."

"I do!" said Aria cheerfully. "When I look at someone, I can see the way they are *and* the way they're going to be." It wasn't a lie, thought Aria. Not really. After all, she could see Gabby's smoke, and she knew she'd be better, happier, brighter, once the smoke was gone.

"And when you look at me?" asked Gabby.

"I see someone who's going to be *amazing.*"

Gabby smiled, and the smoke around her wavered ever so slightly. "You really think so?"

"Yeah," said Aria. "I do."

Aria landed on a pop station, filling the room with cheerful music. She fell into a cushy chair in the corner and pulled out her homework. It seemed silly to do it, but as long as Aria was helping Gabby, she figured she *was* a student. For a second she wondered what would happen when it was over and time for her to go, but she pushed the thought away.

Gabby started humming along to the song on the radio. Aria didn't know the words, but she tried to sing along. She wasn't much good at it, but it didn't stop her from trying, and the two ended up giggling more than once when Aria managed to both be totally off-key and replace all the words with nonsense ones at the same time.

A couple hours later, Aria was in the middle of a particularly horrible sing-a-long when Gabby's phone rang. Gabby's smoke coiled around her, tensing, as she answered.

"Mom? Is everything okay?" The voice on the other end said something, and Gabby's shoulders relaxed visibly and then slumped. She mumbled something in Spanish and hung up.

"Everything all right?" asked Aria.

Gabby nodded. "She's going to stay awhile longer. Told me to go to bed." She yawned and looked at the clock. Aria could tell that it was time for her to leave.

"I better get going," she said.

"Do you need to call someone to come get you?"

"No," said Aria. "I don't live that far away."

Gabby looked out the window at the dark. "Do you want me to walk you home?"

Aria shook her head. "No," she said with a smile. "I'll let myself out."

"Hey," said Gabby when Aria had reached the bedroom door. "Thanks."

"For what?" asked Aria.

"For sticking with me."

Aria beamed. "I'll see you at school tomorrow," she said before slipping into the hall. She got to the front door and saw her shoes sitting in the foyer. Then she hesitated. Did she *have* to go? Would Gabby's mom come home? Would Gabby be all alone? It didn't seem right to leave Gabby by herself, not if she didn't have to, and even if Gabby couldn't see her, maybe she would feel less alone if Aria were there.

Aria made her decision. She slid into her shoes and considered her teal laces for a moment before willing them, along with the rest of her, to disappear.

"You pick," said Gabby at lunch the next day.

Aria was looking over the club list again. That morning, she'd managed to duck out of the apartment while Gabby was in the shower and met her on the front steps of the apartment building so they could ride the bus together. She'd even summoned up some new clothes and was now sporting a pair of jeans and a striped T-shirt.

The girls were at their table in the cafeteria, and Aria was determined to find Gabby the right after-school activity.

"I'm not picking," said Aria, "it has to be *your* choice."

"Why?" pressed Gabby. "It's your club time, too. You have just as much right to pick."

"You're only saying that," said Aria, poking the food on her tray (it was all orange), "because you don't want to choose."

Gabby sighed. "How am I supposed to?" she asked. "If the whole idea is to try something new, then I have to choose something I don't know if I'll like. It would be easier to just pick at random."

Aria brightened. "Okay! We'll do that."

"Wait, no," said Gabby, "I don't actually —"

Aria held up her hand. "This is a good idea," she said. She grabbed a pencil from her backpack, and she quickly counted the number of remaining options: eleven. She then numbered the activities out of order.

"Pick a number," Aria told Gabby, "one to eleven."

"But there are things on there that —"

"It's only Tuesday," said Aria, "and you said we have all week. If we don't like the club today, we'll pick a new one tomorrow. It'll be fun."

Gabby took a deep breath. "Okay. Seven."

Aria turned the paper around to show her what she'd chosen. *Dance.*

"Dance?" asked Gabby nervously. "But I don't know how."

"Perfect!" said Aria. "Neither do I!"

Dance did not go well.

Aria really liked it, but Gabby hated the mirrors in the studio. Every time she began to relax, even a little, she'd catch sight of her reflection and get self-conscious all over again.

The next day, they tried yearbook (option eight), which was a total bust because Aria wasn't very good with computers, having never seen one, and Gabby didn't know anything about the school or its students.

Thursday afternoon, they found themselves in painting (option two), and things weren't going much better. Aria was getting nervous because Gabby still hadn't found something that was *hers*, and they were running out of options, and out of time.

Aria sat at her easel and swirled the pigments on her palette. She liked the *idea* of painting but was frustrated by the fact that mixing two, three — even four — awesome colors didn't always result in a *more awesome* color. In fact, most of the time it just resulted in brown. She frowned down at the mess on her tray while one easel over Gabby seemed to be struggling with her own paints.

"Find form," the teacher told Aria when she saw the abstract swirls on the paper.

"Let go," the teacher told Gabby when she saw the rigid shapes on hers. Gabby's smoke rippled with frustration.

This *definitely* wasn't the right club, and Aria was almost relieved when Gabby turned toward her too fast and accidentally painted a streak of red across the yellow sundress Aria was wearing.

"I'm so sorry!" said Gabby, scrambling for paper towels, but Aria only smiled and waved her way.

"It's fine, don't worry," she said. "It'll come out."

Before Gabby could say anything else, Aria ducked out of the studio and ran her hand over the stain, the color vanishing with her touch, leaving the dress beneath spotless. Aria sighed and leaned back against the wall. If only fixing Gabby's problems were that easy.

One day left, she thought, pulling the list of options from her dress pocket. There had to be something here.

And then, just as she was about to head back into the art room, Aria heard the singing. It was soft and far away, and she followed it through the halls until she found a door covered in music notes, just like Gabby's journal. Aria pressed her ear to the door, listened, and smiled. A bunch of different voices were singing together inside the room. It was beautiful. She'd liked the music pouring out of Gabby's radio, but this was better.

Gabby could do this, thought Aria, pulling back.

Gabby would be *so good* at this.

Aria had heard Gabby humming when she walked and when she did homework and when she showered. She sounded great, but she did it only when she thought she was alone. And that was Gabby's problem, wasn't it?

But this. This could be her solution.

Aria hurried back to class, bouncing with excitement because she finally knew how to help Gabby find her voice.

chapter 13

GABBY

The next day at lunch, Gabby picked number six.

"Let's see. . . ." said Aria, squinting at the list. "That's choir!"

Gabby frowned. "I thought choir was number three."

Aria waved her hand. "No, it was totally number six."

"I don't know about this," said Gabby when they reached the music room. When she first saw the music notes covering the door, her spirits began to rise. But her excitement quickly gave way to nerves as she heard the students laughing and chatting on the other side of the door.

"Come on, Gabby," said Aria, rocking from heel to toe. "It'll be fun. And besides, you have a great voice. You're always humming."

"That's *humming*, Aria. This is *singing*. In front of people. There's a big difference."

The difference was that humming made her feel calm. The thought of singing in front of people made her feel sick.

"It's singing *with* people," said Aria. "And really singing is just humming with more words."

Gabby hesitated. But it was Friday, which meant it was the last day to test out activities, and she was running out of chances. She took the smallest possible step toward the door and stopped. "Are you sure about this?" she asked. "Don't take this the wrong way, but singing isn't exactly *your* greatest strength."

"Lucky for you, I don't mind looking silly," said Aria.

Gabby's shoulders loosened as she laughed, and before she could come up with another protest, Aria put her hands on her back and pushed her into the room.

It was larger than Gabby expected, one wall holding instruments and the other made up into a small mock stage. A dozen kids sat on foldout chairs in a messy circle.

A pair of twin girls was trying to land candy in each other's mouths. Gabby recognized them from math class, and knew their names were Emmie and Ellie but couldn't remember who was who.

A boy she didn't know was lying on the floor with his head on his backpack, wearing massive headphones. Another boy was rapping to a group of three girls huddled in a circle, all clearly pretending to ignore him. Gabby remembered seeing the trio in the hall the first day, elbows linked even then in a way that very clearly said *This group is closed.*

The trio turned as a group, sizing up Gabby and Aria as they came in. Gabby could feel herself starting to shrink when someone laughed loudly. Gabby looked over to see the tall blond girl from English class. Charlotte. They'd said only a handful of words to each other all week, but she'd always seemed friendly. Today she was chatting with a boy nearly a foot shorter than Gabby, and he was passing a soccer ball from hand to hand as they talked.

When Charlotte caught sight of Gabby, she waved but didn't interrupt the boy, who was gesturing enthusiastically, clearly telling a story.

Just then the door swung open again and a woman came in on a wave of sound. Her bracelets chimed and her earrings tinkled and her skirts *shhhhshhh*ed and her voice when she spoke had a musical rhythm.

"Afternoon, my dears," she said. "I'm Ms. Riley. Gather 'round." The room filled with the sound of scraping chairs as the kids made a tighter, cleaner circle, and Gabby and Aria joined the group.

"We have a few new songbirds today, I see," said Ms. Riley, nodding at Gabby, Aria, and the boy who'd been lying on the floor and was now sitting in a chair, headphones hanging around his neck. "Whatever brings you here, welcome. I hope I'm not a last resort." Ms. Riley clapped her hands. "Now, let's loosen up those voices and those nerves and play a singing game."

Gabby fidgeted nervously in her seat, but Aria gave her an encouraging smile. Ms. Riley passed out a few pages of songs and explained the rules. The whole group would sing the first stanza and the chorus, and then they'd go around the circle, each singing a line, then everyone would do the chorus, and so on.

"A vocal hot potato!" Ms. Riley explained excitedly, and Gabby realized she liked this teacher. "Charlotte," Ms. Riley said. "We'll start with you."

"You want me on piano?" asked the short boy with the soccer ball.

"Not right now, Sam," said Ms. Riley. "Voices only at the moment. Ready? Let's go."

Charlotte cleared her throat, and began to sing. Her voice was beautiful and clear as a bell, and Gabby started to think she'd made a horrible mistake, letting Aria drag her here. Her chest tightened at the thought of singing after Charlotte. But then the song passed to Sam. Sam was nowhere near as good, but he fumbled cheerfully through the line. He reminded Gabby of Aria, the way he didn't get embarrassed or shy. The boy with the headphones came next, and he was good — *very* good — and then it was Aria's turn and she was just as delightfully bad as Gabby remembered. Gabby bit back a giggle as Aria missed the notes.

And then it was *her* turn.

For a fraction of a second, Gabby froze. The song hung in the air, the sound dying off. Panic tightened around her chest.

But then she shook it free. What was she afraid of? Messing up? Sam had. Sounding off-key? Aria had. It wasn't such a big deal.

Gabby drew in a breath and began to sing. She was a beat or two late, but she picked up the line and didn't drop it. A rush of relief flooded her face as she got the last note out and passed the song along.

Charlotte winked at her across the circle. Gabby smiled, and when the group picked up the chorus, she was there, singing as loudly as the rest, and when the song came back to her, she didn't fumble it at all.

By the end of the third song, Gabby had forgotten her fears and was actually starting to *enjoy* herself. She didn't have to think, didn't have to find words. She could just focus on the music and the lyrics. They swept her up, carried her along, and the current was enough that when she was sing-ing, she nearly forgot about . . . everything. And then the song trailed away, and Gabby found herself back in reality.

"Very good, very good," chimed Ms. Riley as everyone gathered up their bags. "Gabrielle, Aria, Brendan," she said, offering them each a piece of paper. "You'll need to get this signed if you're going to stay." Her eyes found Gabby's. "And I really hope you do."

It was a permission slip. Gabby had collected them from track, dance, yearbook, painting, and now choir.

"Just bring the slip back signed on Monday," said Ms. Riley, "and you're in the club."

Gabby folded the paper and tucked it into her bag and was halfway to the door with Aria when someone called her name. She turned to find Charlotte and the boy with the soccer ball, Sam.

"How long have you been singing?" Charlotte asked Gabby.

Gabby shrugged. "I've never really done it before."

"Seriously?" said Sam.

"You're really good!" said Charlotte.

Gabby blushed.

"You're going to join the club, right?" pressed Charlotte.

Gabby shrugged. She hated herself for shrugging, but she didn't know what else to do. It was one thing, sitting in a circle, but it was another getting up onstage and singing in front of people.

"You should," said Sam. "It'll be fun."

"Yeah," added Charlotte. "And you're a natural. You'll fit in perfectly."

By the time Gabby caught up with Aria in the hall, she could feel herself beaming.

"Well?" asked Aria, bouncing on her toes, clearly pleased with herself.

"Much better than painting," said Gabby.

Aria nodded. "And way less messy."

chapter 14

ARIA

Aria's heart thudded happily. She'd done it. She'd found something for Gabby.

When Gabby had started singing in the circle, her smoke began to shift, to change. Aria had watched it ripple and — for a little while — thin. The smoke had come back, of course, by the time they reached the hospital. But it was a sign, a step — even a small one.

"What are you smiling about?" asked Gabby as they ambled down the sidewalk.

"Nothing," said Aria. "Just thinking."

They walked in an easy silence up the hospital steps. They'd fallen into a routine, heading there together each day after school. Later on, Aria would follow Gabby home — now that she'd been invited in, she could come and go — and make sure she was okay alone. Gabby's mom came home most nights, but Gabby was usually asleep, and even when she wasn't, Mrs. Torres's being there didn't make the house much warmer. Gabby and her mom just sat at the table, eating dinner while the TV rambled in the background.

At the hospital, Aria and Gabby found Marco flipping through channels on a TV mounted to his wall.

"Thank god you're here," he muttered when he saw them. "Mom's at her worst. I sent her on some errand for an obscure caffeine-free healthy soda just to get a few moments of peace."

Gabby frowned. "Why is she hovering? Did something happen?"

He shook his head and tossed the remote onto the bed. "I had *one* small coughing fit. It wasn't even that bad, but I got dizzy and she freaked out."

"Are you okay now?"

"Of course I'm okay." He rubbed his eyes. "I was okay *then*, too. But I'm losing it, Gabs. They better clear me for surgery soon 'cause I can't keep doing this. I can't stay in here. I can't . . ."

His breathing started to tighten, and Marco closed his eyes and rested his head on his knees. Gabby hurried forward and began rubbing circles on his back and whispering in Spanish. Aria hesitated by the door, watching Gabby's smoke engulf them both. Aria didn't know what to do. She wished that she could make Marco better, but her powers didn't work that way.

Gabby picked up the remote. "Let's find something good," she said, flipping through channels. It didn't seem to help. "Do you want me to go get Henry?" she finally asked.

Marco nodded silently.

"I'll go find him," offered Aria.

Gabby gave her a look that was equal parts surprise and relief. "You sure?"

Aria nodded. "He's in 308," said Gabby, adding a small, "Thank you."

Aria wove through the halls to the other side of the floor, stopping outside room 308. When she peered in through the glass insert, she saw the boy sitting in bed, pale as the sheets, his purple-black smoke still hanging cloudlike around his shoulders. Why hadn't anyone like Aria come to help him yet?

A book sat open in his lap, but he was staring past it into space. And then, as if he could sense Aria there, he turned his head and saw her. He gave a small wave.

Aria pushed open the door and stepped inside.

"Hi, Henry," she said.

"Do I know you?" he asked.

She shook her head. "I'm Aria," she said.

"You're Gabby's friend," said Henry. Aria's heart fluttered at the word. *Friend*. She liked the idea of being a *friend* almost as much as she liked being an *Aria*. "Marco told me about you," he explained.

"What did he say?" asked Aria.

"That you were strange," said Henry. A shadow of a smile touched his mouth. "And that you were cool." He tried to hold on to the smile, but underneath it he looked so *sad*. Aria's eyes kept going back to the dark smoke that hung around him like a fog.

"Are you okay?" she asked.

Henry's watery blue eyes took her in. "That's a silly thing to ask someone in a hospital."

Aria felt herself blush. "I'm sorry. I didn't mean big okay," she said, spreading her arms. "I just meant little okay." She brought her hands together, leaving only a few inches between them.

"Just tired," he said, adding, "My parents were here. I'm always tired after they visit." The second part he'd said so softly Aria had barely heard.

"Why's that?" she asked.

Henry opened his mouth like he wanted to say something but thought better of it. "I don't know," he said, picking up his book and pretending to read. She could tell he was pretending because his eyes never moved from the middle of the page. When Aria didn't leave, Henry looked up from his pretend-reading and said, "So what brings you to my rather gloomy quarters?"

Aria chewed her lip. "I came to see if you want to watch TV with Gabby and Marco."

Henry started to shake his head. But Aria knew that Gabby's brother needed him and she could tell that Henry needed to get out of this room, so she said, "Marco's not doing great. I think he'd really like it if you came."

At that, Henry's face changed again. He didn't ask what was wrong, only straightened and nodded.

"Well, then," he said, mustering a smile. "I'll be his knight in shining armor." He pointed to the wheelchair. "Grab my steed."

A nurse stopped them in the hall, and after a few minutes of bickering with Henry over his outing, insisted on accompanying them to Marco's room. Henry sighed and let the nurse push him the rest of the way. Marco looked up when they came in, his eyes hanging on Henry's for a moment.

Henry didn't say *"What's wrong?"* or *"Where does it hurt?"* or *"Are you okay?"* All he said was, "You good, Torres?"

Marco nodded. "Yeah."

"Good," said Henry. And that was that. And looking at them, at the defiance in Henry's eyes when he asked the question and the set of Marco's jaw when he answered, Aria understood why they didn't ask each other silly questions. Everyone else treated them like patients. They treated each other like people. Like friends.

Friends listened when you needed to talk and they didn't make you talk when you didn't want to and they knew how to help you without making you feel like you needed help.

You're Gabby's friend, Henry had said.

Aria smiled. Gabby was sitting next to Marco's bed, and Marco was already chatting with Henry and acting like himself again. Gabby met Aria's eyes and mouthed *thank you*.

"Only thirty minutes," insisted the nurse, still gripping Henry's chair. He waved her tiredly away.

Then he wheeled himself over to Marco's bed and kicked his legs up onto the sheets.

"No time to waste, Torres," he said. "What are we watching?"

chapter 15

GABBY

Marco made the soccer team this week, Gabby wrote in her journal on Sunday. *No one's surprised,* she added. *He's always been the best.*

She paused and reread the lines. Then she added a few about Henry.

In journal-world, Henry lived in the same building as Marco and Gabby, and that's how they first met over the summer.

Henry never seems very happy, wrote Gabby, *but he's good at making other people happy, especially Marco.*

And then, without thinking, Gabby wrote: *I really hope he gets better.*

Gabby froze. The line sat there in the middle of the page, a glaring piece of truth in a book filling up with lies, and suddenly Gabby felt horrible. Horrible for messing up the lie, and horrible for wanting to make the truth go away in the first place.

Gabby began to scribble out the line, and pressed down so hard she tore the paper. She let out an exasperated noise.

"Whatcha doing?" asked Marco. He was sitting in a chair by the window, soaking up sunlight. Their mom had thrown a fit when he wanted to get out of bed, as if a few feet would mean the difference between sick and well, but Marco had won. He always won, when he wanted to.

"Journaling," said Gabby. "For school."

"Can I see?" asked Marco. Gabby shook her head. Marco sat forward. "Come on, Gabs."

She clutched the journal to her chest. *"No."*

She knew what she was doing was wrong — the lies had started small and taken on a life of their own — and if Marco saw what she'd written, the lies she'd told about him, he'd be angry. Or worse, he'd be hurt. She expected Marco to make a grab for the journal — there was a time he would have snatched it right out of her hands — but he simply shrugged and sank back into his chair.

"I have a journal," he said quietly.

Gabby's eyes widened. "Really?"

He gestured to the blue-and-white-striped book Gabby had given him the day before school started. "I started writing in it right after you gave it to me."

"What do you write about?" asked Gabby.

Marco shrugged. "All kinds of things. I write about life before getting sick. Mostly I write about being stuck in the hospital and the strange and random things I notice here. And of course I write about Henry and Mom and you."

"You write about me?"

"Sure. You want to see?"

Gabby found herself nodding. Marco's mouth twitched up tiredly. "A page for a page," he said.

Gabby's heart sank as she shook her head. "I can't."

Marco shrugged. "Fine," he said, tipping his head back and closing his eyes. Stretched out in the puddle of sun, he looked so . . . normal. Sometimes *normal* felt so far away, but looking at him now, she wanted to believe it could happen.

Gabby got to her feet.

"If you ever change your mind," he added as she reached the door. "Let me know."

"Sure," said Gabby softly as she slipped into the hall and went in search of Aria.

Gabby could hear her friend's laughter — it carried, even when she wasn't loud — from halfway down the hall. She was in Henry's room. Gabby heard Henry make a small, laughlike noise, too.

Gabby stopped and peered through the glass and saw Aria sitting there, cross-legged in Henry's wheelchair. She was about to open the door, when she heard Henry ask, "What are *your* parents like?"

And Aria simply said, "I don't have any."

Gabby's stomach twisted. She'd assumed . . . well, she didn't know what she'd assumed. Aria had said it was complicated, and Gabby had let it go. Maybe she'd known, deep down, been able to sense that hole, and stepped around it. But now that she knew, she could feel the pity rising in her chest. The same pity she couldn't stand from other people.

If Henry felt sorry for Aria, it never showed in his voice. "We're all missing pieces," he said. And then his voice lowered, and he added, "Can I tell you something?"

Gabby hesitated. She knew she shouldn't keep eavesdropping, but she couldn't bring herself to leave, or to interrupt him, not once Aria said, "Of course."

Gabby chewed her lip, and pressed her ear against the door.

"Sometimes," he said, "I feel like I spend all day bracing myself for when my parents come."

"You don't want them to?" asked Aria.

"I love them," said Henry. "I really, really love them. But I sometimes think that if they didn't come, if I didn't have to see the pain and the hope in their eyes every single day then I could just . . ." He sighed.

"Just what?" asked Aria.

"I've been sick since I was eleven," he said. "And at first, they thought I could get better, it looked like I might, but eventually . . . it was just a matter of time. The *gift of time*, that's what they call it, when you're not going to get better. They give you a prediction — maybe a few weeks, maybe a few months, maybe even a year — and they call it a gift. I was fourteen when the doctors gave me their prediction.

"Eight months," he said, clearly worn out from talking but determined to keep going. "That's what they said. And I held on, every day, every week, every month, for my parents. And when those eight months were up, I just . . . kept holding on. For them. Still not getting better. Still not getting worse. And every day my family would come and I'd still be here and it would be this miracle. And for a while, it was worth it, for the hope it brought them. But . . ."

Henry's voice tightened and he trailed off. Gabby and Aria both waited for him to go on, but he didn't. Gabby's heart ached. She hadn't known how long Henry had been sick, or that he would never get better. Did Marco know?

"Hey, what's your favorite color?" asked Aria, breaking the silence.

Henry seemed relieved to change the subject. "It used to be yellow," he said, "before they moved me to this hall." Gabby looked around and saw the walls were indeed a faded lemon color. "But now I can't get away from yellow. So it's red."

Aria smiled. "Close your eyes."

"What?"

"Trust me."

What was Aria up to? wondered Gabby. She peered in through the glass as Henry closed his eyes, and Aria tilted her head, as if thinking, and a moment later, something happened: the blanket on Henry's bed *changed color.* Gabby gaped. That wasn't possible. Aria hadn't moved, hadn't *done* anything, but instead of a dull cream fabric, the blanket was now a vibrant crimson red. Gabby hadn't blinked, hadn't looked away for a second, so how had Aria done it?

Gabby remembered that when Marco was eight or nine, he announced he was going to be a magician. He wasn't very good, but Gabby was very gullible, falling for every one of his tricks. But she was older now, and she knew there was no such thing as magic. Coins were hidden up sleeves and in pockets, and fast fingers could make things disappear. But Aria didn't have long sleeves on, and even if she did, she couldn't hide a *blanket* in them!

Gabby started to think she'd imagined the new color, but when Henry opened his eyes and looked down, he let out a small, delighted sound. He obviously saw it, too.

"How on earth did you do that?" he asked, running his hand over the fabric as if the color might rub off. *It wasn't like a magic* trick, thought Gabby. *It* was —

"Magic," said Aria.

"No such thing," said Henry, still touching the blanket in disbelief.

Aria shrugged her shoulders playfully. "Hey," she said. "Why don't you come hang out with us? Me and Gabby and Marco? It'll make you feel better."

At that, the tiredness slid back into Henry's face. "You go on," he said. "I'll try to swing by later."

Gabby came to her senses and backed away from the door just in time to avoid colliding with Aria as she came out.

"Oh, hey," said Aria brightly.

Gabby's mind was still spinning as she said, "Oh, hi! You want to um . . . go . . . get some food . . . or . . .

something . . . ?" Gabby wanted to bang her head against a wall. She sounded like an idiot. This was *Aria*. Aria was strange and apparently capable of ridiculously believable magic tricks, but she was still Aria.

"Sure," said Aria.

It was only after they'd raided the third vending machine — Aria was fascinated by the way they worked — that Gabby remembered the part of the conversation about Aria's parents. Is that why she liked to come over to Gabby's place all the time? Aria was so cheerful, so loud, that Gabby hadn't thought about the fact she might be hiding from something, too.

"I know this is random, and we have school tomorrow," Gabby said, "but do you want to spend the night?"

Aria's eyes lit up. "I'd love that."

They loaded their vending machine bounty into Aria's backpack, and set out.

"Hey," said Aria when they were halfway to Gabby's apartment. "Do you believe in magic?"

Gabby's heart raced. Had Aria seen her spying? Or was she simply asking one of her strange questions?

"I don't know," said Gabby after a long pause. "I'd have to see it to believe it."

But even then, she wondered, would she?

chapter 16

ARIA

One moment Aria was lying in a nest of blankets on Gabby's floor (thinking about how nice it was to be visible and comfy instead of invisible and afraid of being heard) and the next she was being trampled by a very flustered Gabby as she leaped out of bed with a panicked cry and nearly landed on top of her.

"What's wrong?" asked Aria as Gabby mumbled a quick apology and kept going, gathering up clothes before dashing out into the hall.

"The permission slip," called Gabby, turning on the shower in the bathroom. "I forgot to get it signed!" The door slammed and almost immediately reopened. "How fast can you get ready?" she called.

"Two minutes," said Aria, even though she really needed only two seconds, but that would have been hard to explain.

"Great," said Gabby. The door shut. And then reopened. "You can borrow some of my clothes!" It shut again and stayed closed.

Aria got to her feet and went to peruse Gabby's closet, thinking about how easy it would be if they just used her shadow to get to the hospital. It would just take a moment, and the truth was, Aria was getting tired of hiding her secret from Gabby. There was nothing *stopping* Aria from telling her, no force like the one that had kept her out of the apartment. It was just the fear that sharing her secret would make things worse when they were finally starting to get better.

"Are you almost ready?" called Gabby.

"Yeah, coming," said Aria, tugging a blue shirt off its hanger.

They half walked, half jogged to the hospital, Gabby slowing only when she finally reached the lobby.

"See?" said Aria, breathless. "Plenty of time to spare."

"Wait here," said Gabby. "I'll be right back."

Aria nodded and perched on the edge of a chair while Gabby disappeared down the hall. Aria pulled her own permission slip from her bag, and stared at the blank space where a parent was supposed to sign. She wondered absently what it would be like, to have a family, to have a name to fill in the box.

"What's *your* name?" she asked a woman sitting in a chair next to her. The woman looked surprised, but answered, "Delilah."

"That's very pretty," said Aria. She was halfway through filling in the blank — *Delilah Blue* — when a strange tug formed in her chest. It was the kind of inexplicable pull that normally drew her to Gabby, but this one was tugging her in another direction. She got up and followed the pull left beyond the desk and up two flights, frowning as she realized where she was going.

Henry's room.

She was halfway to his door when it opened, and a couple stepped out into the hall. They looked like Henry, minus the sickly pale. *Parents*, thought Aria, as they turned and walked away. They did it so slowly, as if wearing weights. Aria waited until they were gone before she peered through the glass and saw Henry in bed, the red blanket spread across his lap (she'd wanted to give him something he could put away so he wouldn't fall out of love with the color). He seemed so *sad*. His expression was raw, unguarded, and since Aria could tell that the sadness was something he wore only when he was alone, and since it seemed wrong to see it without his permission, she knocked.

"Aria," he whispered as she stepped in.

"Hey, Henry."

"I'm really glad you're here," said Henry. Something was different about him. The dark purple smoke that usually hung like a cloud around him had come unstuck and now swirled in the air above him. "I said good-bye to my parents today. They don't know it, but I did."

"What do you mean?" she asked.

"I'm tired. . . ." He closed his eyes. "So are they."

Aria thought about something Gabby had said to her, about the fact that Marco may be the one in bed, but they were all ill. Sickness did that, infected everyone. But that no one could get better until the one in bed did.

"Your parents won't get better," said Aria. "Not until you do."

There was a long, long pause. "I know," said Henry. He closed his eyes.

Aria got to her feet and was nearly to the door when she heard him whisper.

"Thanks, Aria," he said. "For listening."

"You're welcome, Henry," she whispered back before slipping out.

And then, halfway down the hall, Aria passed a teenage boy.

She almost didn't notice him, but the jingle of his bracelet snagged her attention. He was tall and slim, with black hair and eyes the prettiest green she'd ever seen, and he was wearing a charm bracelet. It was a bruised purple, almost black, but unlike Aria's bracelet, his wasn't bare. On it hung a handful of dark pendants in the shape of feathers.

The boy smiled a faint, sad smile as he passed by her. Aria thought she'd be relieved to see him, but a sinking feeling filled her chest as she watched him make his way toward Henry's room and go inside.

chapter 17

GABBY

Gabby found her mom in the hall talking to a nurse.

"What are you doing here, *mija*?" asked Mrs. Torres. "Shouldn't you be on your way to school?"

"I need you to sign a permission slip, so I can join a club." Gabby unfolded the paper and smoothed it out a little before handing it over.

"What club?"

"Choir," she said.

"That's wonderful," said her mom. "I'm always saying you have a lovely voice."

Gabby hadn't heard her mom say anything like that in years. In fact, on the rare occasion Mrs. Torres heard her daughter humming, she usually shushed her. But Gabby simply nodded and took the sheet back. She was about to leave when she hesitated and said, "I really like this school."

"I'm glad," said her mom, her attention already sliding away.

"I hope we can stay," added Gabby. "I mean, not that I hope Marco has to stay *here* that long, of course, but I hope that after . . . when he's better . . ."

"One step at a time," said her mom. "We shouldn't look over the hill until we reach the top. Marco needs to focus all his energy on getting better."

"I'm not talking about Marco, I'm talking about *me*." Gabby cringed as soon as she said it.

"*Gabrielle Torres* —" scolded her mom.

"I'm sorry," she said. "I didn't mean it like that. I know we're here for Marco. But what's so wrong with having something to look forward to?" Gabby didn't know if she was talking about Marco right now or herself. She decided she should be talking about Marco, so she added, "The high school's right next to the middle school, and it has an awesome soccer team, and —"

Mrs. Torres's phone rang, cutting her off. She held up a hand. "We'll talk about this later, *mija*."

Gabby sighed and nodded, even though she knew they wouldn't.

She headed back to the lobby, but Aria wasn't there.

Gabby was about to go looking for her when the girl suddenly appeared.

But for the first time since they'd met, Aria didn't seem very happy. In fact, she looked a little shaken up.

"You okay?" asked Gabby. Aria blinked a few times and forced something that was almost a smile but wasn't.

"Yeah, sorry," she said. "Did your mom sign the paper?"

Gabby waved the permission slip. "We're good to go," she said. And then she wondered who had signed Aria's paper. If her parents weren't around, then who did she live with? Now didn't seem like the right time to ask.

Even though they chatted on the way to school, Gabby was good enough at reading people to see that something was definitely on Aria's mind. All morning she seemed off, and when she wasn't herself by lunchtime, Gabby finally spoke up.

"What's going on?" she asked. "Is something wrong?"

Aria shook her head. "No," she said. "I'm sorry . . . it's nothing . . . I just . . ." She shook her head again, as if trying to shake away a thought and brightened forcibly. "Cookies. We need cookies. I'll go get us some."

And before Gabby could say anything, Aria vanished back into the lunch line. Gabby stood there with her tray and turned to survey the lunchroom. It had seemed so scary on the first day, when everyone was a stranger and every table a foreign territory, but now it didn't look so frightening. She recognized half the faces, and —

"Hey!" called Charlotte from a table across the cafeteria. "Over here!"

Gabby glanced around, worried she must be signaling to someone else, but Charlotte called out again, this time saying, "Hey, Gabby!"

The short boy with the soccer ball — Sam — was sitting beside her, and they waved Gabby over.

She made her way up to their table, tray in hand, and Sam kicked his backpack off the chair beside him so Gabby could sit.

"Hey there," he said. "I'm Sam."

"I know," said Gabby. "I'm Gabby Torres."

"Listen to you," said Sam with a whistle. "Giving your full name. Just like a star."

Gabby blushed. She'd gotten used to saying her last name because at the hospitals — and everywhere else, before now — she existed in relation to Marco. He was a patient. She was a family member. The last name was how they placed her.

"He's just teasing you," said Charlotte. "And besides, it's a compliment! Got to have a good stage name." She twirled her ponytail. "My last name's Bellarmine, but if I make it big I'm going by Bell. Charlotte Bell."

"Charlie Bell," said Sam, "and it's only a matter of when, not if."

Gabby's chest tightened. *If*s and *when*s ruled Marco's life.

"You're a quiet one, Gabby Torres," said Sam.

Gabby shook her head. "Sorry," she said. "Sometimes I forget I'm not speaking."

"Internal monologue," said Charlotte. "That's what it's called."

"Really?" asked Gabby. "Well, my . . ." She almost said brother, but stopped. She didn't know why she stopped, hated herself for stopping, but she couldn't do it, couldn't will herself to drop Marco into this like a weight. "My mom is always reminding me to speak up."

Two lies. It was her brother who said those kinds of things, not her mom. Because her mom would never notice.

"I bet my mom wishes I had that problem," rambled Charlotte. "She says my voice may be a gift, but the fact I use it so much isn't."

"You're a really good singer," said Gabby.

Sam ruffled Charlotte's hair. "Understatement, Gabby Torres. Charlie here is *amazing*."

Charlotte blushed and shrugged. "I like singing, but I really want to be an actress."

"She'd be president of the theater club," said Sam, "but they won't let a person in her position . . ."

"What position?" asked Gabby.

"Seventh grade," Charlotte groaned. "It's not my fault I'm an old soul trapped in a seventh grader's body."

Sam laughed. Gabby smiled. And then a crash echoed across the cafeteria, and all three turned to see Aria standing there, a wall of cookies and chips overturned at her feet.

chapter 18

ARIA

Aria had been hiding behind the snack shelf.

She'd seen Charlotte and Sam the moment she and Gabby had reached the cafeteria. More important, she'd seen Charlotte and Sam see *Gabby*, and she'd spent the last several minutes pretending to examine the school's dessert selection while secretly watching the trio. And watching Gabby's *smoke*. As Gabby sat down and chatted and smiled, her smoke began to twist. And then it began to thin. A lot.

Aria had been so excited to see it that she'd leaned forward into the shelf, and before she knew it, the whole thing had come crashing down. She stood there a moment, stunned by the hundreds of eyes that looked her way. So this was what the opposite of invisible felt like.

After a second, the kids turned back to their lunch, and

Aria shook off the surprise and stepped gingerly over the mess as she approached Gabby's table.

Aria said hi, and Sam and Charlotte said hi back, and Sam mentioned that everything on Aria's plate was purple — it was — and then a strange thing happened. Aria had been worried that Charlotte and Sam might gravitate toward her instead of Gabby, but she was wrong. In fact, they hardly seemed to notice her. Their attention kind of . . . slid off, drawn back to Gabby. It didn't hurt Aria's feelings. On the contrary, it made things better. Easier. After all, Aria couldn't stay. Sam and Charlotte could.

Aria reached for her drink, and her bracelet knocked against a bowl on her tray. She frowned, thinking about the boy in the hall, and the feather charms hanging from his wrist. Is that how wings were earned? One feather at a time? Would that boy get a new feather for helping Henry? What kind of help had Henry needed?

"I have to ask," said Gabby, and Aria dragged her attention back to the table. "What's with the soccer ball?"

"Here we go," said Charlotte, rolling her eyes.

Sam let it fall forward onto the table and rested his elbow on top. "I read somewhere that athletes, the really great ones, keep their ball with them wherever they go. They bond with it and —"

"That is so utterly ridiculous," cut in Charlotte.

"I don't know," said Gabby. "My brother tried it for a week once." Her mouth snapped shut as soon as she said it.

"You have a brother?" asked Charlotte.

"Yeah," she said slowly. "He's in high school."

"What position does he play?"

Gabby picked at her food. "He was a defender."

"Was?" asked Charlotte, clearly worried.

"He's taking a season off," Gabby said quickly. "He got injured." Aria frowned at the lie, even though she understood why Gabby did it. She didn't want Charlotte and Sam to look at her differently because of Marco, but still . . .

"What position do you play?" Aria asked Sam.

"Sam is, in fact, a horrible goalie."

"Charlotte!"

"Dude, no offense, but you're, like, four feet tall."

"I'm waiting for my growth spurt."

Gabby smiled despite herself. Charlotte snorted. Aria chuckled. Sam ignored them all.

"I want to be as good as possible. Hey, Gabby, maybe your brother could give me some pointers."

"Yeah," Gabby said quietly. "Maybe."

"Sports are boring," offered Charlotte. "Back to music. I can't wait to hear you audition, Gabby."

Gabby nearly spit out her drink. "Do what?"

"Audition," said Charlotte. "You know, so Ms. Riley can assign solos. You didn't think we just sat around harmonizing in a circle all the time, did you?"

"I . . . I wasn't sure. . . ."

"Don't worry," said Sam, resting his chin on his soccer ball. "You'll do great."

Aria watched as Gabby's smoke twisted and curled with doubts. Other people believed in her, and that had made a dent, but she needed to believe in herself. And Aria knew that wasn't something she or Charlotte or Sam or anyone could do for her.

"I just don't know if I'm ready to sing alone," said Gabby. "I'm not that good."

Sam squinted. "Are you doing that thing people do when they know they're good and just want to be told?"

"Sam," said Charlotte soberly, "I think she's being serious. Are you being serious? Because you're good. Like, really good. You sure you've never really sung before?"

Gabby shook her head.

"You don't need voice lessons. You need *voice* lessons."

"I . . . I don't know the difference," said Gabby.

Charlotte took a long, dramatic breath. "I mean

confidence. You know how to sing. But you can't sing your best until you know what your voice is."

"Until you're a *who*!" chimed in Aria. All three looked at her. "Until you know who you are," she clarified.

"Yeah, exactly," said Charlotte, nodding firmly. The bell rang overhead. "So the question, Gabby Torres, is: Who are you?"

chapter 19

GABBY

Ms. Riley smiled when Gabby came in.

"So glad you decided to stay," she said, collecting the permission slips.

Gabby managed a small, nervous smile. She hoped she would be, too.

Choir started the way it had on Friday, with the warm-ups in the circle, but after only a couple of songs, Ms. Riley announced it was time to audition for solos. Gabby's stomach began to twist, and she forced herself to take a few steadying breaths.

Each student, Ms. Riley explained, would get up on the small stage that ran down one side of the room and perform for the rest of the group. They could pick any song they wanted, but there would be no musical accompaniment. Just voices.

"A word," she said, "before we get started. Singing isn't just about notes or lyrics. It's about the things between the words, the pieces of song that don't go on paper. When you sing, you shouldn't be reciting. You should be infusing. It's about expression — Mr. Robert is fond of that phrase, isn't he? Only here, you don't have to find the words. I can give you those. But you have to find the heart."

Charlotte rolled her eyes playfully.

She was up first. And Gabby thought she was fabulous. Her voice was lovely and clear, like bells. *Blue* came after *Bellarmine*, and Aria took the stage next. Gabby knew she was only here for her and she felt kind of bad about getting her into this . . . and then she remembered that she *hadn't*. The whole thing had been Aria's idea.

Aria cleared her throat and started to sing. Gabby smiled when she recognized the song. They must have heard it a dozen times on the radio. And Aria wasn't that bad. She even found the right key once or twice, and when it was over she mimicked Charlotte's bow, and the class gave a dappled applause as she stepped off the miniature stage.

"What do you think?" Aria asked Gabby as she took her seat. "Am I destined to be a star?"

"Definitely," said Gabby. And she meant it. Aria probably didn't have a future as a singer, but she was bright, and she made everything around her brighter. It was weird, thought Gabby, that no one else seemed to notice.

They continued down the roster, until Ms. Riley reached the letter *T,* and Gabby knew what that meant. It was her turn.

"Miss Torres, you're up."

She felt a little ill as she got to her feet and approached the makeshift stage. She knew what she wanted to sing, but as she got up on the platform and turned to face the room, her mouth went dry. The students stared at her, waiting. Ms. Riley stared at her, waiting. The only one who didn't stare at her, waiting, was Aria, because Aria was suddenly nowhere to be seen. Gabby frowned. Had she chosen now of all times to go to the bathroom? Just then, Charlotte whistled, and Sam clapped, the sounds dragging Gabby's attention back. She focused on Charlotte and Sam and started singing.

The first few notes tumbled out, timid and too soft, and Gabby faltered to a stop. In that moment she wanted nothing more than to stop and get off the stage, to hide. Everyone was *listening* and that was terrifying, so Gabby did the only thing she could think of.

She closed her eyes.

And it was funny, but she could almost feel a hand on her shoulder, and the weight of it was calming. She took a deep breath and started again, and whether it was the closed eyes or the imaginary hand, this time, the song came easily.

It was an old song, the kind her *abuela* used to hum, the kind her mom had even hummed back before she'd stopped humming and started stressing, the kind Gabby usually hummed to herself when she was alone, the melody gentle, comforting.

Gabby had to drag the lyrics out of the back of her mind because it had been so long since she'd actually sung them. The melody lived in her head all the time, but the words were tucked away.

But they came to her now, and she sang, and with her eyes closed she forgot that she was singing them to anyone but herself. And then the song ended, and she heard clapping, and blinked to find the whole room applauding. Charlotte and Sam — and Aria, back in her seat like she'd never left — the loudest.

"Brill," said Charlotte, patting her arm as Gabby took her seat, trembling a little.

"Told ya," said Sam.

"You were *great*," added Aria.

Relief and happiness swirled inside Gabby. It felt . . . amazing. To be seen this way. Knowing that none of the attention had to do with Marco's sickness. It didn't have to do with Marco at all.

It belonged to her.

It made her feel, as Aria had said, like a *who*.

The happiness followed Gabby all the way to the hospital. She didn't even mind that Aria was still being quiet, because for once, Gabby felt loud. She couldn't wait to tell Marco about the singing. She knew he'd be proud of her. But when she was nearly at his room, she drew up short.

Something was wrong.

She could hear someone shouting. No, she could hear *Marco* shouting.

But Marco *never* shouted. He hardly ever even raised his voice.

She hurried toward the noise. Aria said something but Gabby ignored her. She reached the door just in time to hear a water glass shatter against it from the other side.

A nurse was hurrying down the hall with a capped syringe in hand, and Gabby grabbed her sleeve. "What's going on?"

"Oh, his friend," said the nurse. "I'm afraid he . . ." She didn't finish, and Gabby didn't need her to.

Her stomach twisted. *Henry.* How had it happened? When had it happened?

Beyond the door, Gabby heard her mom trying desperately to calm Marco down, a stream of soothing Spanish pouring from her lips. But Marco pitched the nearest thing — a book — at the wall and beat his fists against the bed and screamed about how it wasn't fair. None of it was fair. And when Mrs. Torres reached for him, he pushed her away, then buried his face in his pillow as he sobbed.

Gabby wanted to go in, to go to him, wanted to wrap her arms around him and tell him it would be okay. But maybe it wouldn't be. Maybe none of this would be okay. It *wasn't* fair. Life wasn't fair. Death wasn't fair, and nothing Gabby could say right now would make it any easier to bear. Marco was upset, and he *deserved* to be upset. No one in this hospital was ever upset enough. They all treated death like a sad routine instead of a tragedy.

Gabby felt Aria wrap her arms around her shoulders, and she stood there numb, watching her brother rail in his room until the nurses gave him something and he went quiet — quiet, but not calm — and she couldn't bear to see that.

So she pulled away from Aria's grip and escaped to a bench at the end of the hall, sank onto it, and sobbed.

chapter 20

ARIA

Aria had been dreading it all day.

She knew it was coming. Maybe not *all* of her knew it, but part of her knew. Part of her knew as soon as she saw the teenage boy in the hall that morning. As soon as she saw the color of his smoke.

Knowing didn't make it any easier.

Aria hovered, caught between the quieting sadness in Marco's room and the growing sadness at the end of the hall, leaving Gabby alone for a few minutes until her crying subsided.

"I'm sorry," Aria finally whispered as she slid onto the bench beside her.

"What if he was alone?" Gabby's voice trembled a little as she wiped her eyes on her sleeve. "When he died?"

"He wasn't," said Aria, too quietly for Gabby to hear.

"It's not fair," whispered Gabby, balling her hands into fists. "None of this is fair."

Aria looked up at the ceiling and wished it were the sky. "At least he's —"

"Don't," snapped Gabby. "Don't say at least he's at peace now. I hate it when people say that like it makes death better."

"I don't think anything makes death better," said Aria. "But it was time for —"

"It's never just *time*," said Gabby. "And how can you say that?" She shook her head. "I thought you cared about him. . . ."

"I did," said Aria. "I *do*. But Henry was . . . I think he wanted to let go."

Gabby gave her a long hard look. "You knew."

Aria's eyes widened. "What?"

"All day you've been weird. You knew this was going to happen. Or that it *had* happened."

Aria could feel it. This cusp. The chance to tell Gabby the truth.

"You were with him before school, weren't you?" pressed Gabby. "That's where you ran off to. Did something happen? How did you know?"

Aria sighed. She was so tired of keeping secrets. Would it make Gabby feel better, to know Henry hadn't been alone?

To know it was time for him to let go? To know why Aria was here?

"I saw him come this morning," she said quietly.

"Saw who?"

Aria chewed her lip. "The boy in the hall. I'd been waiting for him. He was a different kind of . . ." She trailed off.

"Of what?"

Aria didn't actually like this word. It seemed too large, too heavy, but it was the only way she knew to explain. "Angel."

She'd braced herself for any number of reactions to the too-big word, everything from disbelief to mockery to awe. But Gabby only stared at her, eyes red.

"A what?" she whispered.

"An angel," said Aria again. "Like me. I wasn't sent to help Henry, though," she added. "I only noticed him because of the smoke. He was surrounded by this dark purple cloud. It's a marking, a flag for someone . . . someone like me but not me, and for some reason no one else had come, so I tried to keep an eye on him until they did. And now I think they didn't come because he just wasn't ready for *their* help, wasn't ready to let go. Like I said, he needed a different kind of . . ." Aria trailed off.

Gabby was staring at her, horrified. "If you didn't come for Henry, then why are you here? Is it Marco? Did you come because . . . oh god, is he going to —"

"I didn't come for Marco, either," said Aria. "I came for you."

Gabby's eyes widened. "Am *I* going to die?"

Aria sighed. "I told you, I'm not *that kind* of angel. I'm a . . . a guardian. I'm here to help you."

"I don't need your help," said Gabby. "Marco does."

Aria shook her head. "I can't help *him*," she said. "Not that way. I'm not a healer."

"So you came here just to do *what*?" snapped Gabby, the smoke coiling around her. "Offer moral support?"

"I can't fix people, Gabby."

"But you just said you're an angel."

"I know, but . . ."

"You said you're an *angel*," repeated Gabby, her voice clawing up, traveling down the hall. "Angels do miracles. Angels fix people. *Angels make things better.* If you're an angel, then make this better. Make Marco better. And if you can't, then *just go away.*"

Aria pulled back, struck by the words. Her eyes began to burn, and before the tears could spill over, she disappeared.

chapter 21

GABBY

Gabby stared at the place Aria had been, feeling flushed and breathless.

Good, she thought bitterly as she got to her feet. *Run away.* Gabby didn't know what Aria was — or how she'd disappeared — but she wasn't an angel. She couldn't be. Gabby didn't know if she even believed in angels, but if she did, and they were real, they would be able to help her brother. Aria couldn't.

A tired sadness came over Gabby.

Her mom was pacing up and down the hall on the phone, and she didn't look up, let alone notice Gabby, as she slipped inside Marco's room.

He was lying on the bed facing the wall with his back to the room, clutching his pillow. She could tell he wasn't asleep by the way his chest rose and fell, his rib cage expanding and contracting too much through his shirt.

Gabby kicked off her shoes and climbed onto the bed beside him. Marco didn't say anything, didn't even look over his shoulder, but he scooted forward a few inches on the narrow bed to make room for her. She brought her hand to rest on her brother's shoulder, and she felt him take a small, shuddering breath.

"I'm sorry," she whispered, even though she hated the way people tossed around that phrase in hospitals. But she really, really was.

Marco had known Henry for only a few short weeks, but the two had hit it off so quickly. When she'd asked them about it, Henry had shrugged in his usual, easy way.

"When you're sick," he'd said, "and you don't know how much time you have, it's easy to make friends. You don't sit around and weigh the pros and cons, or wonder if you have enough in common. It's a waste of time, so you just say, 'Hey, I'm stuck here, you're stuck here, let's hang out.'"

And it *had* been easy. Even though everyone could see Henry was sick, and Gabby could see he was sad, he'd brought a kind of light with him, wherever he went.

And now he was gone. And Marco was lost. And Aria had run away.

Strangely, Gabby's mind went to her journal. Why couldn't life be like she'd written it? Marco should be out playing soccer and Henry should be in the stands cheering for him, and instead they were here and he was gone and Aria . . . Gabby didn't even know where to start with Aria.

When Marco rolled over to face her sometime later, his eyes were feverish.

"*¿Dónde estás?*" he whispered. *Where are you?*

"I don't know," she whispered back.

"I heard you shouting," he said. "Who were you fighting with?"

"Aria."

"Why?"

Gabby realized she couldn't answer, in part because it would sound ridiculous — *my new best friend turned out to be an angel who can't save you* — and in part because that wasn't a fair reason to be mad at Aria. But she was mad anyway because she wanted to be mad at someone.

"It's complicated," she said at last.

"Well, go fix it," said Marco.

"I can't," said Gabby. "I told her to go away, and she did."

"Look, whatever you're fighting about," said Marco. "It's

not worth it. Please, Gabs. I lost a friend today. Don't go throwing one away."

Gabby's heart ached. She knew he was right. "I don't know where she went," said Gabby lamely.

"So go find her," said Marco.

Gabby took a deep breath and nodded. She hugged her brother — he felt really warm — and then she got up and went to find Aria.

chapter 22

ARIA

Aria sank onto the hospital steps.

It wasn't her fault that she couldn't fix people. She *wanted* to fix them, and she would have used her power to do it if she could but . . . but she couldn't.

She was there to *help*, not fix.

Aria considered her bare charm bracelet, running her thumb over the three small, empty loops. She didn't seem to be doing a very good job of helping. She drew her knees to her chest and looked down at the dull gray hospital steps. She was tired of their sad gray paint, and thought that maybe, if the steps were a happier color, she'd feel happier, too. As soon as she thought it, color spread across the steps beneath her, overtaking the gray until each of the dozen stairs leading from the lot to the front doors was a different, vibrant hue. Stripes of blue and red and green and yellow. She felt her spirits rising a little at the bursts of color, until she remembered Gabby's words.

Angels do miracles.

Angels fix people.

Angels make things better.

What good was her magic if all she could do was change the color of some concrete? How was that making *anything* better? It wasn't a miracle. It was just a stupid magic trick.

She was about to change the steps back, when she heard a noise.

"Oooooooh," said an old, old woman being helped up the steps by a young man. "Ooooh, Eric, look!"

"That's nice, Nan."

The man tried to guide her up the steps, but she had come to a grinding halt. "They've painted the stairs!"

"I can see that, Nan."

"They've done it. Look at that. They've always been gray, and I'm always telling those doctors you can't paint a place like this gray. No good for anyone. I told them every time I came. Every time! And look!"

She beamed at Aria.

"Isn't it lovely?" the old woman asked her. "I told them, and look!"

Aria smiled a little and nodded. "They must have heard you," she said.

The old woman's head bobbed cheerfully as she continued up the steps, clutching the young man's arm and saying, "They heard me; they heard me."

Aria watched them go inside and decided to leave the steps the way they were. She closed her eyes and took a long, deep breath, and tried to remember the smile on the woman's face. And then she felt someone sit down on the step beside her.

It was Gabby.

Aria braced herself for another fight, but Gabby didn't scream, didn't snap, didn't say anything. She just sat there, looking pale. The blue smoke swirled around her, twisting and curling with questions.

"How long have you been an angel?" she asked.

"Nine days," said Aria.

Gabby made a small sound of surprise. "And before that?"

Aria frowned. "What do you mean?"

"I mean," said Gabby, casting a glance around, "were you dead?"

Ari crinkled her nose. "No. Of course not."

"Then how do you look like that?"

Aria looked down at herself. "Like what?"

"Like . . . well, like that," said Gabby, gesturing toward her. "Like someone who's been alive as long as I have."

Aria examined her hands, and shrugged. "This is what I've always looked like."

"For nine days."

"Should I look like someone else?" asked Aria.

"Can you?" asked Gabby.

Aria frowned. It had never occurred to her. She was happy with how she looked, since it was the only way she'd ever looked, but Gabby seemed curious, and that made Aria curious, too. She could change her clothes, but could she change herself?

Aria closed her eyes and tried to picture a new combination of features, different skin and different eyes and different hair.

"Well?" she asked, opening her eyes. "How do I look?"

Gabby shrugged. "You look the same."

And even though Aria acted like she was disappointed, she was secretly relieved that it hadn't worked. Silence fell again between them, heavy as a weight.

"If you're an angel," asked Gabby at last, "then where are your wings?"

Aria stiffened. "I don't have them *yet*," she said, a little defensively.

149

"So you can't fly."

Aria shook her head vigorously. "No," she said. "And trust me, I tried. It didn't go well."

Gabby's mouth twitched. "But you can disappear."

Aria nodded. "And I have a shadow."

"*Everybody* has a shadow," said Gabby.

"Yeah," replied Aria smiling a little, "but I'm pretty sure most shadows don't work like mine. Watch," she said, getting to her feet and turning so the sun struck her back and cast her shadow out in front of her. She looked down at the dark patch on the ground, pointed a finger, and said, sternly, "Stay."

Gabby looked at Aria the way any rational person would look at someone giving orders to their shadow. But the look slid from her face when Aria took a step back.

And her shadow didn't.

It stayed stock-still on the ground, as if caught in a game of freeze. Gabby's mouth fell open. And it stayed open when Aria snapped her fingers, and the shadow turned on like a light. Gabby's eyes widened in amazement.

That was the look Aria had hoped for when she told Gabby her secret.

"I don't need wings to get around," said Aria. "I have this."

"But what *is* it?" asked Gabby.

Aria considered the shape on the ground. "I guess it's a door."

"Where does it lead?"

Aria shrugged. "Depends on where I need to go."

Gabby bit her lip and looked at Aria's shadow and then at her own. Even though Aria couldn't read her mind, she could tell what she was thinking, as if the thoughts were words instead of smoke, swirling around her. She wanted to get away, to escape.

"Want to go somewhere?" asked Aria.

"Where would it take us?" asked Gabby.

Aria shrugged and held out her hand. "Let's find out."

chapter 33

GABBY

Aria made Gabby go first.

"Why?" asked Gabby nervously.

"Because," said Aria, "you want to know where it will take *you*. If I go first, it might get confused and take us somewhere else."

Aria squeezed Gabby's hand and guided her toward the light-filled shadow. Gabby tensed.

"Are you sure this will work?" Gabby asked.

"No," answered Aria. She started to say something else, but her voice was swallowed up as they stepped into the light.

It felt like falling but slower, like sinking in a pool. For a moment there was nothing. And then, quick as a blink, there was something. Or rather, *somewhere.*

Gabby looked around. She didn't know what she'd expected. Half of her thought that since it was a *magical*

152

shadow, she'd end up somewhere magical. The other half thought the door might take them to another version of her life. One where Marco wasn't sick. The kind of life she pretended was real when she was in school. And some small part of her thought that the shadow would take them to the woods behind her old house, the ones that haunted her dreams.

But it didn't. Aria's shadow took them to school. To the choir room.

"Why here?" asked Gabby.

Aria shrugged. "Maybe it's trying to tell you something. Maybe this place" — she looked around — "can help you." She ran her hand along the edge of the piano. "It's already starting to."

"What do you mean?" asked Gabby.

Aria perched on the piano bench. "Remember how I said Henry had been marked for someone, and you'd been marked for me? Well, that marking, it takes the shape of smoke. And when you feel like you don't matter, like you don't exist, like you're not a person, the smoke gets worse, because that's what your smoke is made of, those problems."

Gabby's eyes went to the floor, guilt rippling through her. "I shouldn't complain," she said. "They aren't real problems. Not compared to Marco's."

"I don't think it's a matter of *real*," said Aria, swinging her legs back and forth. "I think Marco's being sick, is a *loud* problem. So loud it makes every other problem seem quiet. And because they're quiet, you think they're less important. And maybe sometimes they are. But you have to ask yourself, if you didn't have his problems to compare yours to, would they really seem so quiet? Because I have to tell you, the fact that I'm here means your problems aren't quiet, or unimportant, or that they aren't *real*. They're very real. And the fact that I'm here means I can help."

"How?" asked Gabby, shaking her head. It was such a big question inside a small word. "No offense, Aria, but making things bright colors isn't going to help me."

"I think colors are *my* voice," said Aria. "Singing is yours." She tapped a few piano keys. "I wish you could see what happens when you sing," she said. "All that smoke, it gets thinner. Maybe that's why my shadow brought us here. Because this place, and the way it makes you feel, is a good direction. A future. One that belongs to *you*."

Gabby looked down at the floor. "But what about Marco?" she asked, that same old tightness working its way into her chest. "What about *his* future? Does he have one?"

Aria sighed. "I don't know what's going to happen to your brother," she said. "I wish I did, and I know it feels like everything depends on him. But that kind of thinking, it's the reason you forgot how to be you. This is your chance," she said, gesturing to the empty choir room. "And you're going to have to take it, Gabby. No matter what happens to Marco."

Gabby closed her eyes. She didn't want to picture her life *without* Marco. Could she picture her life *outside* of him?

She took a deep breath and opened her eyes and looked around the room. She pictured choir in session, Charlotte and Sam cracking jokes, the way the music lifted her up, the way the singing made her feel like *somebody*.

But at the hospital, she still felt like a ghost.

"They feel like two separate worlds," she blurted. "Here and the hospital."

"That's because they are," said Aria. "You've found your voice here. But you still don't have one there."

"What good is a voice when no one will listen?" whispered Gabby.

"If your mom were ready to listen," asked Aria, walking back toward her shadow, "would you be ready to talk?"

Gabby hesitated. She hadn't thought about it that way. She nodded. "Yes."

Aria smiled and held out her hand. "Then I'll see what I can do."

"Really?" asked Gabby, as she took Aria's hand.

"Hey," said Aria as the shadow beneath them turned on like a light, "I'm your guardian angel after all."

"Miss Torres," said Mr. Robert the next morning after class, "a word please."

Gabby tensed. She was nearly to the door when he said it. She looked back and saw that he was holding her journal. "This is good work," he said.

"Thanks," she said, turning again toward the door where Aria was waiting.

"There's only one problem," he said. Gabby's steps slowed and stopped. She felt dread wash over her. "My son goes to Grand Heights High," continued Mr. Robert. "He's one of the captains on the soccer team." Her heart sank as she turned back toward the teacher. "I asked him if he knew your brother. You can imagine my surprise when I found out Marco wasn't on the team. So I looked into it: he's not even enrolled at the school."

Gabby looked at the checkered linoleum floor.

"Why don't you tell me the truth?" said Mr. Robert.

She dragged her gaze up. Something in her crumpled. She was so tired of lying.

156

"My brother *would* be in tenth grade at Grand Heights High," she said. "And he *would* be the best player on the soccer team, but he's in the hospital. He's been sick for more than a year. We moved here so he could have surgery, but he got a cold and so it's on hold and we're all just stuck waiting and hoping he doesn't get worse, and I spend every moment thinking about it so I really don't want to talk about it, and I really don't want to write about it."

Gabby was breathless by the time she finished. She expected Mr. Robert to say he was sorry, to slip into that too-familiar mode of pity, of false kindness. But instead his brow crinkled.

"I'm going to make you a deal," he said. "You can write about anything you want in here, but it has to be true." He offered the journal back to her. "No more lies. Do you understand? Find a way to tell the truth."

Gabby took the journal and nodded.

"And I know it's none of my business," he added, "but I hope your brother gets better soon. Grand Heights High could use a few more great players."

Gabby almost smiled. "Please," she said, "don't tell anyone."

Mr. Robert shook his head. "It's not my story to tell," he said. "It's yours."

Maybe it *was* Gabby's story to tell, but she couldn't find the words to tell it.

She sat in Marco's hospital room that afternoon, staring at a blank page.

It wasn't that Gabby didn't know what to say. Dozens of thoughts spiraled through her mind, about Marco and Henry and Aria and school and the hospital. But she was afraid that if she started, she wouldn't be able to stop, just like in the classroom when she'd spilled out her thoughts to the teacher.

Gabby wondered if the thoughts were filling her blue smoke, too. Aria said that's what the smoke was made of, things you felt and didn't say. But Aria was off wandering the hospital halls — she could never sit still — and Gabby couldn't ask her, and it wouldn't help her anyway because the page was still just as blank.

In a moment of frustration, Gabby lobbed her pen across the room.

"What did the pen ever do to you?" asked Marco. He was sitting in bed, head bent over his own journal. His face was flushed, and his temperature was up. Stress, a nurse had said, from losing Henry, but Mom was in a panic. She was meeting with the doctors right now.

"I don't know what to write," said Gabby.

"You've filled half the book," said Marco.

With lies, thought Gabby. "That was different," she said. "What are you writing about?"

Marco looked down at his page. "I'm not ready to write about *now*," he said. Gabby knew what he meant. He wasn't ready to write about Henry. "So I'm writing about when we were kids. Going to the beach. Growing up in that big house with the woods behind. It's easier. . . ." he said. "Maybe you should try that."

Gabby looked down at her blank page. She didn't want to write about now, either, but maybe she could write about before, too.

When we were younger, she started, *my brother and I used to race up the hill behind our house. . . .*

The line spilled out across the page, and Gabby let out a small sigh of relief (Mr. Robert was right, starting was the hardest part). Slowly, haltingly, she went on to describe the house and the yard and the woods. The way she and Marco raced, and the way Marco always won.

But when she got to the day he finally lost, the day they knew something was really wrong, Gabby stopped.

She didn't want to talk about that, but it felt good to write, so she jumped down a line, and started another story.

This one was about a camping trip they'd gone on last year, where her mom had gotten into a war with a squirrel. And when Gabby got to the point where Marco's sickness crept back into the story (they had to cut the trip short so he could go in for more treatment), she switched again. She did this, bouncing from story to story, cutting out the bits she didn't want to write (without filling in lies), making a patchwork of memories.

And with each story, she got a little closer to talking about *now*. It hovered at the edges. She even managed to write a little about how she was feeling, even if she wasn't ready to talk about why.

"Hey, Marco," she said when she'd filled five pages, "look how many —" But Marco had fallen asleep, the pen still in his hand, the journal open in his lap. Gabby slid silently to her feet and crossed to him.

Everything in her wanted to read the words on his page. But she didn't.

She reached out and closed his journal, careful not to wake him.

chapter 24

ARIA

Aria had examined the contents of every vending machine in the hospital and was on her way back to Marco's room with a selection of snacks when she rounded the corner and nearly ran into Mrs. Torres.

Gabby's mom didn't even seem to notice her.

"*No sé, no sé*," she was saying into her phone. *I don't know, I don't know.* Aria marveled at the fact she understood the words. She put that solidly in the *pro* column of being an angel. The voice on the other line must have asked about Gabby because Mrs. Torres added, "Gabby's fine. She's always fine. She can take of herself."

Aria wanted to shake Mrs. Torres and tell her Gabby shouldn't have to take care of herself. But that wasn't the way to get rid of Gabby's smoke. Aria had to be clever.

If your mom were ready to listen, would you be ready to talk?

Yes, Gabby had said.

Aria just had to get Mrs. Torres to *listen.*

When Aria got to Marco's room, she peered in through the glass. He was asleep in his bed and Gabby was folded up in a chair, scribbling away in her journal.

That was it! Aria realized, pressing her face to the glass. She smiled. She had an idea.

That night, Aria lay awake on Gabby's floor, waiting for Mrs. Torres to come home.

Soon enough Aria heard the sound of the door open and then close. She heard the soft thuds of shoes being taken off and set by the door, then the scrape of a chair being slid across the floor, a body sinking into it.

Aria got to her feet and made sure she was invisible before wandering out into the apartment.

Mrs. Torres was sitting at the kitchen table.

She stared at the dark beyond the open window, her brown eyes so similar to Gabby's.

The simple fact was that even though Gabby was finding her voice, her mom still wasn't listening.

Aria couldn't make her listen. But maybe she could make her *read.*

Gabby's journal sat on the table a few inches from her mother's hand. Aria had made sure it was there before they went to bed.

Now she reached out an invisible hand, and flipped the journal open. Mrs. Torres looked down at the book and then to the open window, clearly wondering if there was a draft. Aria turned through a few more pages until she came across Gabby's newest entry. Aria had convinced Gabby to write it earlier that night. She told her she had to be honest, had to trust Aria, and Gabby had done both. Now Gabby's mom looked down at the page, at first absently, and then intently as she read the line at the top.

Some days I feel invisible.

Gabby's mom reached out and pulled the journal toward her.

I don't want to be the center of attention, continued the entry. *I just want to be seen.*

Aria held her breath. And then Mrs. Torres turned back to the first page of the notebook, and started from the beginning.

chapter 25

GABBY

The next morning, Gabby talked to a student in each of her classes. Once to ask for a pen, once to hand back a pen someone had dropped, and once just because she thought of something funny. It was getting easier, the talking.

Sam and Charlotte were waiting for her at lunch, and Gabby realized how happy she was to see them. She pictured the smoke Aria had talked about, imagined it thinning, and she could almost feel it, like a weight lifting.

Like a slice of blue sky through clouds.

But the best part of the day came in choir.

"Gather round," said Ms. Riley brightly. She held a crisp piece of paper, as if it were a prize. And then Gabby realized that it was. It was the choir concert roster.

"With the songs and the solos," whispered Sam beside her.

"I hope you get a solo," added Charlotte.

Gabby told herself she wouldn't, told herself it didn't matter, but then Ms. Riley read her name — *her name!* — and she felt herself breaking into a grin.

Excitement flooded through her, followed quickly by terror. The thought of singing in front of people made her queasy. She started to tell Ms. Riley to pick someone else, when Charlotte stopped her with a smile.

"You'll be great!" she said.

"Better than great," said Sam.

And then Aria wrapped her arms around her shoulders and squeezed. "You can do this," she said.

And for the first time, despite her fears, Gabby tried to believe her.

Afterward, Charlotte insisted they all go out for ice cream to celebrate.

"I don't know if I can," said Gabby automatically. She needed to be at the hospital with Marco . . . didn't she?

"Why not?" asked Charlotte.

"We won't be long," offered Sam.

"Just one scoop," added Charlotte. "You deserve it."

"You do," chimed in Aria. It was weird, but Gabby couldn't shake the feeling Aria had gotten quieter lately.

Gabby smiled sheepishly, then nodded. "Okay, but just one."

One scoop turned into two, which turned into three and a stomachache, but it was worth it, and as they sat on the benches outside the ice-cream shop, Gabby's mouth hurt from grinning. Sam and Charlotte were so easy to be around, so comfortable with each other.

"We've been next-door neighbors since we were really little," said Charlotte. "Would you believe there was a time when Sam was taller than me?"

Gabby laughed. "No way."

"I don't appreciate your skepticism," said Sam.

"Aw, it's okay, Sammie," said Charlotte. "Maybe you'll be tall again one day. Or at least average height."

The girls giggled. Sam scowled.

"How about you two?" asked Charlotte. "How do you and Aria know each other?"

Aria started to answer. "We met at the hos —"

"Apartment building," cut in Gabby, shooting Aria a look. "We moved in around the same time."

Aria's brow scrunched up, but she didn't contradict her. Gabby knew Aria didn't want her keeping secrets, and Gabby herself didn't want to keep them. It was just that she didn't want to talk about the hospital, not when things were going so well.

"That's awesome," said Charlotte. "To have a friend right there. Like a housewarming present."

Aria smiled. "Like fate," she said.

"Yeah," said Gabby, as she pulled the phone out of her pocket to check the time. Her stomach lurched when she saw the number of missed calls. She must have accidentally turned off the sound or something.

"Oh no," she said aloud, frantically accessing the three voice mails.

"What is it?" Charlotte asked.

"What's wrong?" Sam asked.

"Gabby?" Aria said softly.

Gabby pushed up from the bench as the voice mails played. They were all from her mom, and they were a blur of *Marco took a turn* and *tests came back* and *there's a problem* and *come to the hospital as soon as you can* and *where are you* and *where are you* and *where are you*.

Gabby tried to force air into her lungs, tried to breathe in that special calming way, but she didn't feel calm, only sick and dizzy as she grabbed Aria's arm and pulled her up from the bench with a rushed, "We have to get to the hospital *now*."

"Wait, *hospital*?" asked Sam.

"Gabby, what's going on?" asked Charlotte.

"I'm sorry," Gabby mumbled, "I have to go. We have to go. I'm sorry."

She pulled Aria around the corner and took her by the shoulders and said, "Please, Aria. Take me there." And Aria didn't waste time asking questions. She stepped out of her shadow and she and Gabby hurried down into the light.

It was *the bad*.

Gabby's mom clutched Marco's hand as the doctor explained. Marco's fever had gotten worse, and by that morning he had a bad cough, too, so to be safe they'd run a panel and done some X-rays to make sure it wasn't pneumonia. It wasn't. It was *the bad*. There was a long word for what it had done — metastasized — which basically meant that the bad had snuck up into Marco's chest.

Gabby closed her eyes and pictured little pieces of it like crumbs, breaking off from Marco's leg and his hip and traveling through his blood to his lungs. She felt Aria's hand on her shoulder, even though the girl wasn't there. Or she was, she'd explained before she vanished, but Gabby wouldn't be able to see her.

"The good news," said the doctor, "is that we caught it very, very early. Your odds are still good. I can't lie and tell you they're as good as they were, but they're good. We'll operate as soon as possible and —"

"But you said it wasn't safe," cut in Gabby's mom. "You said we shouldn't operate while Marco was still sick. You said there was a higher risk of infection."

"There is," said the doctor, "but I'm afraid it's no longer safe to *not* operate. Every day we lose takes odds out of our favor."

"What now?" asked Marco, sitting forward. Gabby looked at him, the stubborn set of his jaw. She knew how much he wanted to get better, but she also knew how scared he was of the procedure. Before, there had been a chance he could lose his leg. Now, he could lose his life. And that was before the operation was even over.

"It's an extensive operation," said the doctor, "even more so now than before. We'll go in and excavate the affected bones in the left leg, as planned. At the same time, we'll need to go in through the chest and clear away the metasta-sized tumors. Even if everything goes well" — at the use of the word *if*, Gabby found Marco's eyes. He found hers. They held on to each other that way — "it's going to be a harder recovery."

Gabby's mom started to cry.

"I *still believe*," said the doctor, "that if the surgery is successful, the hardest part will be over. You won't be out of the woods, Marco, but you'll be on your way." And then, at last, the doctor turned toward Gabby. "Do *you* have any questions?"

Gabby's mind was nothing but questions: *Is Marco going to die? Is he going to be okay? What are his chances? What is going to happen? What can I do? What can any of us do? Why is this happening? Haven't we been through enough?* But the only one she actually asked was, "When is the surgery?"

The doctor tapped a pen against his clipboard. "Tomorrow morning."

"That soon?" asked Gabby's mom.

"Sounds good," cut in Marco. Mrs. Torres started to protest, but he cut her off. "The surgery was going to happen one way or another," he said. "It sucks that this is the reason it has to happen *now*, but I'm sick of waiting, and I'm sick of being sick, and the sooner I can get through this, *which I will*, the sooner I can get better, and get my life back." He finished, breathless and flushed, but his eyes were bright. "Okay?"

The doctor nodded. "All right, then. Let's help you get your life back."

Gabby focused on Aria's hand squeezing her shoulder and the strength in Marco's voice, and she tried to believe that everything would be all right.

chapter 26

ARIA

Gabby was sitting on the hospital steps with her head in her hands when Aria materialized beside her.

"Aria, please," said Gabby without looking up, "there has to be something you can do."

Aria's chest tightened at the plea. Not this again. If there was anything she could do for Marco, she would have done it already. "I told you, Gabby, I'm not a healer."

Gabby drew a shaky breath and looked up. And then her eyes widened.

"You said you saw smoke," she said, grabbing Aria by the shoulders. "Around Henry, before he died. Aria, you have to promise me you'll tell me if you see that kind of smoke around Marco. If you don't see it, then it means he'll be okay, right?"

Aria wished it were that simple, but she didn't think it was. After all, the hospital was filled with people, some of them who would be okay, and some who wouldn't, but those who wouldn't weren't all wreathed in a prophetic smoke. She worried that the smoke only marked Henry because he needed help letting go. What if Marco didn't?

"Gabby, I don't think —"

"Just promise me," begged Gabby. "If you see it, you'll tell me."

Aria sighed and nodded. "If I see it, I'll let you know."

Gabby made her shake on it. As Aria gripped Gabby's hand, she knew with a sinking heart that she would keep her word.

"Gabby?" called a voice, and the two pulled apart to see Sam and Charlotte trotting up the steps toward them.

"What are you doing here?" asked Gabby.

"You ran away talking about hospitals," said Charlotte, breathless. "We were worried."

"How did you know I was here?"

"We didn't. But there are only two hospitals in this area, and we already checked the other one."

Aria got to her feet. She took a step back and stood behind Gabby, watching as Sam and Charlotte sat down on either side of her.

"What's going on?" asked Sam.

And Aria watched proudly as Gabby took a deep breath and told them the truth. About the move. About Marco. Their eyes widened as they listened, but neither of them said anything. And when Gabby was finished, tears brimming and voice tight, Charlotte simply wrapped her arm around the girl's shoulders.

All day Gabby's smoke had been getting thinner. When she'd turned the journal in to Mr. Robert, it thinned. When she'd gotten the solo in choir, it thinned. When she'd laughed with Charlotte and Sam, it thinned. And despite all the hope and fear that came with the news about Marco, as Charlotte and Sam sat there comforting her, there was almost no blue left in the air. *This is right*, thought Aria, even as a strange sadness spread through her. *This is the way it's supposed to be.*

"Why would you hide something like that?" asked Charlotte at last.

"I just . . . I wanted a fresh start. I didn't want you to find out and feel like you had to be my friend out of . . . pity . . . or something."

"We wouldn't," said Sam simply.

"You don't know that," said Gabby, shaking her head.

"We would be *worried*," said Charlotte, "I mean, we *are* worried, but that's part of being someone's friend. We care about you."

Another wisp of smoke dissolved.

"What can we do?" asked Sam. "To help you."

Gabby chewed her lip. "Do you want to come say hi to Marco?"

"Is that a good idea?" asked Charlotte.

Gabby nodded. "I want you to meet him. I think he'll want to meet you."

"Then let's go," said Sam, bouncing his soccer ball. "And just so you know," he added as they made their way inside, Aria trailing behind, "we'd be your friends no matter what your family's like. My dad does Civil War reenactments, and Charlotte's parents decorate their house for every single holiday, even the silly ones. Plus her little sister is a monster in a tutu. But we're still cool."

"Way cool," said Charlotte.

"Super cool," said Gabby as she led them inside.

Aria followed in their wake, watching as more and more of the blue smoke disappeared.

chapter 27

GABBY

Gabby stood alone in the hallway.

Charlotte and Sam had just left, and Aria had gone in search of cookies, and Gabby was now staring through the glass insert of her brother's room. Marco had loved meeting her friends. He and Sam had talked for ages about soccer. Marco gave Sam a few pointers and said that being short could be a good thing out on the field. Charlotte, who was always so sure of herself, had been tongue-tied, not because of Marco's illness but because "he's really, really cute," she'd told Gabby in the hall. Gabby had screwed up her nose. "Ew."

Now they were gone, and Marco was resting and Gabby was standing outside his door, reading through her journal. She had started to go back through and write in the blanks between sections, filling in the things she'd been too scared to talk about before. It seemed important now, to put them down on paper. In case. As she read through what she'd written, she was amazed at how honest she'd become.

She didn't hear her mom come up beside her. When she noticed her, Gabby stepped out of the way instinctively to let her get to Marco.

But her mom didn't go in. She just stood there, next to Gabby, staring at her.

"*Mija*," she said. "I think . . . we should . . . I mean . . . we need to talk."

"About what?" asked Gabby, suddenly nervous. "Marco's surgery?"

Her mom's brow furrowed. "No . . . no, this isn't about Marco. This is about you."

"I didn't do anything."

"I didn't say you did," snapped her mom, and then, softening her voice, added, "I just want to know how you're doing. I want you to talk to me."

Gabby stared at her mom, as if the offer were a puzzle she needed to decipher. Part of her wanted to say no, to walk away. She'd waited for so long for her mom to ask, really ask, long enough that she'd stopped waiting. She'd given up. But wasn't that the problem? Wasn't that why Aria was here?

"I'm scared for Marco," Gabby said at last.

"I know," said her mom. "We both are. But right now I want to talk about *you*."

Gabby chewed her lip. "I like my school," she said at last. "I'm making friends and I don't want to leave, even if — *when* — Marco gets better. And I miss you," Gabby added, eyes burning. "I miss talking to you and I —"

She was cut off by the sound of her mom's phone.

Her heart sank as her mom pulled it out of her pocket. But her mom didn't answer it. Instead, she switched the ringer off.

"Go on," she said. "I'm here. And I'm listening."

chapter 28

ARIA

Aria climbed the stairs, rounded the corner with her stack of cookies, and stopped.

There, at the other end of the hall, Gabby and her mom were sitting on a bench by the window, and they were *talking*. And as she watched, the very last of Gabby's smoke disappeared.

A strange sensation filled Aria's chest. She was proud and sad at the same time. This meant it was time to go. But she couldn't go yet, wouldn't go yet, not until after Marco's surgery. She'd promised to stay with Gabby, to let her know if she saw any smoke around her brother.

And Aria would keep her promise.

Later that night, in the hospital, everyone was asleep except for Marco and Aria.

Aria peered in through the glass insert and saw Mrs. Torres curled up on a cot in the corner and Gabby curled up on the chair, her notebook pressed to her chest. Marco was sitting up in a small pool of light, writing in his journal. And because people seemed to see Aria when she wanted to be seen, his gaze drifted to the door where she was standing, and he nodded for her to come in.

She padded silently into the room and sat in an empty chair beside his bed.

"Hi," he whispered.

"Can't sleep?" whispered Aria back.

Marco shook his head. "It's okay, though," he said softly. He hesitated, chewing the inside of his cheek. "I would rather be awake . . . while I can . . ." He looked at her for a long moment and said nothing. And then he added, "I'm glad Gabby has you, Aria."

Aria smiled, even though that same feeling tugged at her. The one that said Gabby didn't need her help anymore. That it was time to go.

"I hope I've been a good friend," she said, fiddling with the laces on her shoes (she'd made them red, for Henry). "This is all very new to me."

"Hospitals?"

"Everything."

"What do you mean?" asked Marco.

"I mean . . . I'm new to this . . . to being a person."

Marco squinted, confused, and Aria hesitated. It hadn't gone very well, the last time she told someone. But Gabby had been angry and scared when Aria told her, and Marco wasn't either of those things right now. "Want to know a secret?" she asked.

Aria leaned in and whispered what she was into his ear. Sharing a secret felt like a bit of magic, in that both magic and secrets change the people you share them with.

When Aria pulled back to see Marco's reaction, his eyebrows had gone up in surprise.

"You're joking," he said.

"I haven't really figured out how to joke yet," admitted Aria, and at that Marco laughed, then clasped a hand over his mouth to keep from waking anyone.

"Do you believe me?" she asked.

"Does it matter?" he asked, lowering his hand. She thought about that and was still thinking about it when Marco added, "I want to believe you. I like to think that Gabby has someone watching over her."

Aria tilted her head. "How do you know I'm not watching over *you*?"

Marco smiled a little. "Because I don't need you to." He

gestured to the room. "Everyone's already watching over me, looking out for me, trying to save me. Maybe they can; maybe they can't. But everyone's doing their best, and I'm doing my best, and I don't need you. . . ." The words could have sounded mean, but the way he said them wasn't mean at all. It was gentle. "I don't. But Gabby does. Besides, if you were here to save me, I bet you would have done it already."

Aria examined Marco.

"What is it?" he asked.

"I think in some ways," she said, "you're the healthiest one here."

"Tell the doctors that," he said with a grim smile.

"The fact that I haven't saved you," said Aria, "the fact that I can't . . . it doesn't mean you're going to . . ." Aria fumbled for the words. "It just means that's not what I'm here for. . . . I don't save lives," she said at last, wishing for the hundredth time she could. "I just do my best to make them better."

"Well, thanks," said Marco. "For making Gabby's better."

Aria smiled. The reading light beside the bed brightened. Marco yawned then, and Aria got to her feet.

"Good night, Marco," she whispered. "And good luck."

chapter 29

GABBY

Marco went into surgery at 9:15 a.m.

Gabby knew because she'd memorized the time, and had then written it on her hand in case she forgot.

At 8:30 a.m., she and her mom had gotten to say their — not their *good-byes*, she couldn't think of it that way — *good-bye-for-now*s and *good luck*s. Marco had said he'd see them both after, and then he told Gabby she better not peek at his journal.

And then they'd rolled him away. Gabby had asked, as they were wheeling his bed into the hall, when the actual surgery would start, and one of the nurses had said 9:15 a.m.

It was now 3:38 p.m.

That meant Marco had been in surgery for six hours and twenty-three minutes.

Gabby watched the clock in the waiting room click to 3:39 p.m.

Six hours and twenty-four minutes.

Every time a door opened or closed she tensed, expecting a doctor to come out and tell them — she stopped herself. She didn't want to start thinking again about all the different things the doctor might tell them. She'd spent two hours — between 10:20 and 12:20 — doing that, and it had only made her panic worse. Her mom had let her skip school to be here, and she was beginning to wish she hadn't, because there was nothing to distract her. Nothing else to focus on. Not that she would have been able to focus on anything but this.

3:40 p.m.

She didn't realize she was humming until her mom reached over and took her hand. She didn't shush her, though, only squeezed her fingers.

The night before, Gabby had told Marco and her mom about getting the solo.

"Sing it for us," Marco had said.

"I don't know the song yet."

"Then sing me something," he'd said. "Anything."

Gabby ended up singing the song she'd auditioned with. Marco and her mom applauded, and Marco told her that next time he'd be in the audience and she'd be onstage. She told him to promise, and he said he'd do his best.

Marco, she thought, *you better do your best.*

3:45 p.m.

She felt a hand on her shoulder. Aria's. The post-op waiting room was family only, but Aria had promised she'd be there and Gabby knew she was, even though she couldn't see her. Seeing wasn't all there was to believing.

And then, finally, at 3:53 p.m, the doctor came in.

Gabby and her mom scrambled to their feet, still holding hands.

They waited for the news.

"The cancer was extensive," said the doctor, "And the operation was invasive. . . ." Gabby held her breath. "But Marco is quite a fighter."

Gabby's mom let out a cry of relief.

"He's got a long road to recovery, but if he does as well as he did today, he should make it through just fine."

Gabby's vision blurred from tears as her mom folded her into a hug. And then, over her mom's shoulder, Gabby noticed the waiting-room door open and then close, as if pushed by a breeze, or a small, invisible hand.

chapter 30

ARIA

Aria's shadow wouldn't stop fidgeting.

Even though she couldn't see it — couldn't see any part of herself — she could feel it moving restlessly around her feet. *Not yet*, she'd told it as the waiting-room clock ticked away the minutes. *Just a little longer*, she thought. And then the news had come, and Aria's heart had been filled with joy for Gabby and Marco and their mother, and she'd looked down at the place her shadow would be and thought, *Okay. Okay.*

She was halfway to the lobby, and visible again, when Gabby caught up to her and, without warning, threw her arms around her shoulders, nearly toppling her midstride. Aria had never been hugged like that before. A hug filled with happiness and hope.

"You were there," said Gabby.

Aria nodded. "I had to watch for smoke, remember?"

Gabby smiled, but then Aria started walking again, and the smile slid away.

"Where are you going?" Gabby asked.

Aria's heart sank as she made her way to the revolving doors. "I have to go, Gabby."

"But things are still so far from okay."

"I know," said Aria. "But they're on their way. You're on your way."

"To what?"

"To becoming a *who*," said Aria with a smile. "And that doesn't mean life is always going to be good or easy. It just means you're going to be a part of it."

Aria started toward the revolving doors again.

Gabby grabbed her arm. "Why do you have to go?" she asked. "You could stay in school. You could stay with me. We would find a way to —"

Aria shook her head sadly. Part of her really did wish she could stay. "No, Gabby. This is your life. I was just visiting."

She stepped through the revolving doors and out into the sun, the once-gray steps trailing vibrantly away from her.

"I can't do this without you," said Gabby beside her.

"Of course you can."

"Don't you want to know what happens next?"

Aria did, very much. She wanted to see Marco wake up, wanted to watch him recover, wanted to watch Gabby use her voice. But she knew in her chest she had to go. It was a pull stronger than gravity. She'd been here too long.

"You want to know what happens next?" said Aria. "You go to Marco's room, so you're there when he wakes up. He gets stronger every day and you get louder and he's there in the front row at your first choir concert. And you're there in the front row for his first soccer game, and you make sure that no matter what happens — no matter what happens — you don't lose your voice again. You don't forget who you are, because you, Gabby Torres, are amazing."

Tears shone in Gabby's eyes. "But will you come to the choir concert?" she asked. "Will you come back for that?"

Aria couldn't promise. She didn't know where she'd be. She wasn't entirely sure *who* she'd be, though she hoped she'd still be her. "I'll try," she said.

Gabby wrapped her arms around Aria one last time and then pulled away and went inside. Aria watched her go. There was nothing but air and hope wrapped around Gabby's shoulders.

Aria felt a cool kiss on her wrist. She looked down to see that a small blue feather charm had appeared on her bracelet. It made a sweet jingling sound when she moved her hand.

She smiled and wiped away a tear. And then she looked down at her shadow, and her heart thudded in her chest, because there, just above the shadow's shoulders and so faint they were barely visible, were the first hint of wings.

"I'm ready to go," said Aria. She snapped her fingers, and the girl-shaped shadow became a girl-shaped pool of light. And then she took a deep breath and vanished from sight.

chapter 31

GABBY

Gabby forced herself not to look back.

She'd just come through the doors, a lump in her throat, when she heard two very familiar voices.

"No, his name is *Marco Torres*," Charlotte was saying at the front desk.

"I'm sorry," said the man behind it, "only family —"

"We just want to know if he's okay," said Sam.

"We just want to know what room he *would be in*," said Charlotte, "if he were out of surgery."

"Blink once for each floor," said Sam.

And then Charlotte turned and saw Gabby and said ohnevermind and then flung herself at her.

"You guys came," gasped Gabby.

"Duh," said Sam.

"Stupid school wouldn't let us out early," said Charlotte,

still smothering her. "And the stupid bus was late so we just hoofed it and —"

"Let her breathe," said Sam, and Charlotte pulled away.

"Sorry. How are you? I mean, how is he? I mean, how did it go?"

Gabby nodded gratefully. "He made it through the surgery."

Charlotte cheered loud enough that half the lobby turned in their direction.

"Sorry," she whispered, giving Gabby another squeeze.

"We were about to go room to room," said Sam. "What were you doing outside?"

Gabby looked back for the first time, past the revolving doors. There was no one there.

"I was just talking to Aria," she said.

"Who?" asked Charlotte.

Gabby's stomach twisted. "You know, *Aria*. Reddish hair. Colored shoelaces. Can't sing."

Charlotte shrugged. "Never heard of her."

Sam tipped his head. "Does she go to our school?"

Gabby's heart sank. How could they not remember her? Was that how Aria's magic worked?

"She's a friend," said Gabby. "I was just saying good-bye."

• • •

The auditorium was very, very full.

Grand Heights Middle School's first choir concert turned out to be a really big deal. Gabby stood backstage, trying not to freak out about the size of the audience. Charlotte squeezed her hand, and Sam said she could hold his soccer ball, if she thought that would help. And Charlotte said of course it wouldn't, and the two began to bicker playfully in a way that almost distracted Gabby from the stage and the lights and the waiting crowd.

Almost.

Marco couldn't come, not yet. It had been only a couple of weeks since his surgery, and even though he was getting stronger every day, it had been a hard road. But Gabby had put on a warm-up concert for him in the hospital the night before, and he promised to be at the next show. The doctors said he'd be strong enough to go home next week. *Home.* Maybe the house would finally start to feel like a home with him there.

Her mom was here, though, right in the front row.

"I think it's time, Gabby," said Charlotte gently.

"You ready?" asked Sam.

"No," said Gabby.

"Good!" said Charlotte. "True stars never are."

That made Gabby smile. Charlotte was always good at cheering her up. Like Aria had been. Sadness flickered through Gabby at the thought. Nobody seemed to remember Aria, not Charlotte or Sam or Mr. Robert or Ms. Riley, but Gabby did. Gabby would never forget.

She adjusted her outfit — a purple skirt with a white polo shirt and a glittery blue bow, the school colors — and took a breath. Then she stepped onto the stage with the rest of the choir.

The audience quieted, waiting. There were so many people. Gabby found her mother's face, glowing with pride. Gabby grinned and resisted the urge to wave.

Then Ms. Riley appeared. The choir teacher stood in front of the students, with her back to the audience, raising her hands to get their attention.

Gabby was secretly grateful to have something other than the crowd to focus on. Sam went over to the piano, set the soccer ball on the seat beside him, and began to play.

The moment the music started, Gabby's chest loosened. The choir sang three group numbers, and then it was her turn. The audience fell silent as she stepped up to the microphone and waited for Sam's cue. She could barely hear the first keys of the piano over her thudding pulse, but there it was, the beginning of the song. Gabby imagined Aria's hand resting on her shoulder as she closed her eyes and started to sing.

chapter 32

ARIA

If anyone had been standing outside the auditorium, they would have seen the shadow. It spread across the floor until it was roughly the size and shape of a twelve-year-old girl, and then it filled with light, and Aria rose out of it.

"Good shadow," she whispered.

She slipped into the auditorium under the roar of applause as the choir finished a group number. She lingered at the back of the crowd, invisible, and watched as a girl with long dark hair stepped forward, away from the group, and toward the microphone.

Gabby Torres smiled, closed her eyes, and began to sing.

As Aria listened, she could hear everything Gabby had been through, everything she felt, in those notes. Being invisible. Being lost. Being scared. New schools. Fresh starts. New friends. Aria. Henry. Marco.

And judging by the audience, who sat in rapt attention, they could hear it, too.

Aria held her breath the entire performance. When Gabby finished, and the room erupted into applause, Aria cheered with them, as loudly as she could. Gabby wouldn't be able to see her, but maybe she would hear her.

The applause faded away and Gabby rejoined the group, and the next number started. Aria knew it was time to go. But she wanted to do something, to show Gabby she'd been here, watching, listening.

So before she left, she turned Gabby's laces purple.

And then she turned away, the music following her as she crept out again, unnoticed. The shape at her feet filled with light, waiting, and Aria stepped through.

Second Chances

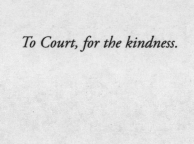

To Court, for the kindness.

chapter 1

CAROLINE

The lunchroom at Westgate School for Girls was like a solar system.

Except instead of being full of planets and moons, it was full of uniformed girls and tables and noise. The school went from sixth grade to eighth grade, and each grade had their own separate lunchtime. Right now, it was the seventh grade's turn, and all sixty-three girls were orbiting the twelve cafeteria tables.

Caroline Mason stood clutching her tray and watching the other girls head toward their tables, drawn by the gravitational pull of friends and laughter and routine. She felt like she was drifting in space.

Everyone had a table. Caroline *used* to have a table.

She reached absently for the pendant that used to hang around her neck — a small half circle — before she remembered it wasn't there. She'd shoved it into the bottom drawer of the jewelry box on her bathroom counter.

Caroline knew she couldn't just stand there, so she took a deep breath and made her way to Table 12. Nobody sat at Table 12. Correction: nobody except for Caroline. She tried to keep her eyes on her tray, tried not to let anyone see how alone she felt as she walked.

But halfway there, her eyes floated up, drawn automatically to Table 7. To Lily Pierce.

If Westgate *were* a solar system, then Lily Pierce would be its sun.

With her perfect black curls and her perfect smile that seemed to make the whole lunch room lean toward her. And away from Caroline. Because everybody listened to Lily Pierce. Everybody did what she said. Whether or not they wanted to be her friend, they definitely *didn't* want to be her enemy. And Lily Pierce had told the entire seventh grade to stay away from Caroline Mason.

Lily and Caroline were at war. Only, Caroline didn't want to fight. She just wanted to go back to the way things were before. Back to before they were enemies.

Back to when they were best friends.

· · ·

"Pick a hand," said Lily.

It was two years ago — summertime, and they were ten. They sat cross-legged on Caroline's trampoline. Lily had moved to their town of Beachwood, California, the year before — into the house right next door — but it felt like they'd been friends forever. Like they'd always be friends. They were starting sixth grade at Westgate together in the fall. They hadn't met Erica yet. Right now, it was just the two of them.

Caroline squinted at Lily's outstretched hands, skeptical. Lily liked to play tricks on people.

"Come on," Lily urged, nodding at her closed fists. "Pick one."

Caroline chewed her lip, and chose left. Lily smiled and turned up her hand. In her palm was a necklace with a silver half circle pendant on the end. Lily then turned over her other hand to reveal a matching necklace with a matching half circle.

"See, they fit together like this," said Lily, linking the pieces so they became a whole circle, like a moon. She looked proud of herself. "We have to wear them," she said. "And we can't ever take them off."

"Not ever?"

Lily shook her head, curls bobbing. "We can't take them off as long as we're friends, which will be forever, so no, not ever. If we take them off, the spell will break."

Caroline crinkled her nose. "What spell?"

"This one." Lily held out the necklace, palm up. "Put your hand over it." And Caroline did. "I solemnly swear," started Lily, giving Caroline a look that told her to repeat the words.

"I solemnly swear," Caroline echoed.

"That as long as I wear this."

"That as long as I wear this."

"I am half of a whole."

"I am half of a whole."

Lily beamed. She handed Caroline her silver pendant. "You look out for me," she said, "and I'll look out for you. And we'll stick together no matter what."

Caroline smiled, and slipped the necklace over her head. "No matter what."

Lily laughed, and the sound traveled through the lunch-room, jarring Caroline out of the memory.

Lily was sitting with Erica Kline and Whitney Abel. Every time Lily laughed, Erica echoed. She smiled when Lily smiled, pouted when Lily pouted, and tossed her straight brown hair when Lily tossed her black curls. She was like a clone, but meaner.

When Lily put her arms around Whitney and Erica's shoulders, it drove a spike through Caroline's stomach. In a way, all of this was Whitney's fault. And she didn't even know it. On the first day of school, Whitney had been nothing. Nobody. A girl with two dull brown braids who barely spoke. Now she was sitting at Table 7, Lily's newest pet.

Whitney said something, and Lily threw back her head and laughed again (a moment later, Erica laughed, too). Then they both leaned in. They were hunched forward over their table, working on something Caroline couldn't see.

Caroline tried to focus on her food, but she wasn't very hungry. She could feel the eyes of Table 7 flicking her way. She didn't want them to see how miserable she was, so she pretended to read through a notebook while the clock on the wall ticked off the minutes until she could go to class. Finally, when the first of the seventh graders started to leave, she pushed to her feet and went to return her tray to the carts by the door.

And that's when it happened.

As Caroline walked by Table 7, Lily pushed back her chair, blocking Caroline's path and forcing her to stop so fast she nearly spilled her tray. She caught it in time, and backed up, straight into Erica.

Or rather, Erica's *tray*.

Erica snickered, and Caroline felt something thick and wet run down the back of her uniform. Caroline turned to see Erica holding her tray not in front of her like a normal person, but up on its side so the whole flat surface was turned toward Caroline. It was covered in a horrible ugly swirl of ketchup and mustard and mayonnaise.

And now, so was Caroline.

The room went quiet as sixty-two pairs of eyes turned toward Caroline and her ruined uniform. Lily smiled. Erica mimicked her. Whitney watched, wide-eyed and silent.

"Ewwwww," said Erica, dropping her tray back on the table. "I got ketchup on my hands."

Lily held out a napkin. "Here you go."

"Thanks," said Erica, wiping her fingers and looking into Caroline's eyes. "Nobody wants to smell like a dirty lunch tray all day."

A glob of ketchup dripped onto Caroline's leg. Her eyes began to burn.

Don't cry, she thought desperately. *Don't cry. Don't cry.*

Lily watched her intently, waiting to see what she would do. Caroline wanted to sob. She wanted to scream. She wanted to punch Erica in the face. Instead she turned, dropped her tray off on the cart, and stormed through the doors, wishing she never had to come back.

chapter 2

ARIA

The shadow took shape on the steps of the school, between two manicured hedges. At first the shadow was just a blot on the stairs, but soon it spread, growing until it resembled the outline of a twelve-year-old girl.

A twelve-year-old *guardian angel*, to be exact.

A breeze blew past, rustling the bushes on either side. The shadow's outfit fluttered, too, and an instant later the whole shape filled with light, and a form rose up out of it. A girl stood there, wavy red hair falling down her back, her shoes resting on top of the pool of light.

Aria blinked and looked around. She had no idea where she was, but she knew *who* she was — still herself — and for that she was thankful.

"Good shadow," she said, and the light under her feet went out.

She nested her heels in the shadow's shoes, and realized as she looked down that she wasn't wearing the clothes she'd had on before. No blue leggings. No green sweater. No pink laces.

Instead, she was wearing a school uniform. White polo, plaid skirt, white knee socks, and black Oxford shoes. The polo had a crest over the pocket with a *W* embroidered on it.

Aria looked up at the stone mantel above the school's massive doors. It read:

WESTGATE PREPARATORY

. . . and in smaller print beneath it:

SCHOOL FOR GIRLS.

Aria's blue charm bracelet still dangled from her wrist, a single silver feather hanging from the first loop. That charm represented Gabby, the first girl Aria had helped. Two rings still hung empty, and as Aria gazed up at the front doors, she felt a little thrill of excitement. Someone here, at this school, was waiting for her, even though she didn't know it. Whoever it was, she would be marked for Aria, wreathed in smoke the same color as Aria's bracelet. And all Aria had to do was find her, and help her, and once she did, she'd be one step closer to earning her wings. When she squinted down at her shadow, she could almost see them. Just the beginnings, of course — a curve here, a feather there — but everyone had to start somewhere.

And today, Aria was starting here. At Westgate.

As Aria climbed the stairs, she considered her shoelaces. They were black, like the Oxfords they were threaded through. Aria chewed her lip. A little color couldn't hurt. As soon as she thought it, the laces turned a pretty purple. She smiled and pushed open the doors, and went in search of a girl with blue smoke.

"Excuse me? Young lady?"

The voice came out of an official-looking office on Aria's right.

Aria turned. "Me?"

"Yes, you," said a woman at a desk. A little nameplate on the desk said she was Ms. Grover, Head of Student Services. "What do you think you're doing?"

Aria looked around. The woman's tone made it clear she was doing something *wrong*, but she had no idea what.

"You can't just come waltzing in late," explained Ms. Grover. "That's an infraction."

"What's an infraction?" asked Aria.

"Being late."

"No, I mean, what *is* an infraction?"

Ms. Grover straightened her glasses and cleared her throat. "An infraction means a broken rule." She pointed to a poster on the wall. It was covered in sentences that began with *NO*. *NO* chewing gum. *NO* cell phones. *NO* tardiness . . . "Three infractions equals a detention."

Aria didn't know what a detention meant, either, but decided not to ask. "Sorry," she said. "I didn't know."

Ms. Grover squinted. "What grade are you in?"

"Seventh," said Aria, because she'd been in seventh grade back at Gabby's school. This school seemed very different, but hopefully the numbers stayed the same.

"What's your name?"

"Aria," said Aria.

The woman's gaze narrowed even more. "You don't go here."

Aria frowned. "Yes I do."

"Young lady, there are one hundred and ninety-three girls at Westgate Prep, and I know them all. I don't know you, so you don't go here."

"I'm new," explained Aria, glancing at the laptop on the desk. "You can check," she added. She'd been able to imagine herself onto a class roster at Gabby's school. Surely she could imagine herself into a computer. At least, she *hoped* she could.

Ms. Grover began typing away on the keyboard. "Last name?"

"Blue," said Aria, proud of herself for knowing now that a last name was a second name, not a name you had before the one you have now.

The woman's fingers tapped furiously on the keyboard, and then stopped. "Huh," she said. "There you are."

Aria smiled. The lights in the office brightened slightly. Ms. Grover did not seem to notice.

"You're still late," she said, pushing a stack of pamphlets and papers across the desk toward Aria. "Surely you've already received all of this in the mail, and had time to read through our policies. Normally, we'd have a student ambassador ready to welcome you, but I'm afraid I didn't know you were coming."

"Last minute," said Aria. "I didn't know, either."

"Yes, well, here's your schedule," said Ms. Grover, tapping the paper on top of the stack. "The seventh-grade girls are still at lunch, but it's almost over. Let me see if I can rustle up someone to show you where to go —"

"That's okay," said Aria brightly. "I bet I can find my way."

Ms. Grover hesitated. "Are you sure?"

Aria nodded. She had a student to find, and she wanted to get going. A faint tug in her chest told her the girl was nearby.

"Very well," said Ms. Grover, already turning away. Aria hoisted the papers into her arms and was nearly to the door when the woman said, "And, Miss Blue?"

"Yes, ma'am?"

The woman offered a small, begrudging smile. "Welcome to Westgate."

Aria could barely see over the stack of handouts as she stepped into the hall. The walls of Westgate, she noticed, were cream-colored but pleasant, and sunlight streamed in through the large windows. A potted plant turned ever so slightly greener as Aria walked past.

What a pretty place, thought Aria, readjusting the papers in her arms. She was about to summon a backpack when a voice behind her said, "Hey, you."

Aria turned around to find a student towering over her. The girl was dressed in the same uniform Aria had on, but she wore a silver badge on her shirt pocket that read MONITOR. She was an eighth grader, Aria could tell, not by her height so much as the way she stood, as if she were very important.

"Your shoelaces are purple," said the girl, as if Aria hadn't noticed.

"I know," said Aria. "I almost went with blue but then I —"

"That's a dress code infraction," the girl cut in, crossing her arms. "I'm going to have to write you up."

Aria frowned. "But I already have an infraction for being late."

"Well, now you have two," said the girl. Aria chewed her lip. She had only been at Westgate for ten minutes, and she was one infraction away from a detention, whatever *that* was, and no closer to finding a girl with blue smoke. She wasn't off to a great start.

The monitor wrote down Aria's name on a purple — how ironic — slip of paper. Aria sighed as the monitor set the paper on top of the already-towering stack in Aria's arms, and then frolicked off, probably to find someone else to punish. As soon as the monitor was gone, Aria willed her purple laces back to black, and started off again down the hall.

She was so focused on not dropping the stack of papers in her arms that she didn't see the girl coming toward her, head down. They collided, and the pamphlets and brochures came down in a shower around them.

"Sorry," muttered the girl as she tried to gather up a few of the papers.

"It's all right," started Aria. "I'm —" But the girl was already on her feet again and hurrying away down the hall. Aria stared after her, eyes wide.

The girl's head was bowed, blond hair falling into her face, and the back of her uniform was covered in what looked like ketchup (Aria had discovered what ketchup was only a few days ago). But it wasn't the ketchup that caught her eye, or even the fact that the girl looked like she'd been crying.

It was the blue smoke.

Tendrils of bright blue coiled around the girl's shoulders as she vanished around the corner.

Then Aria realized she wasn't alone in the hall. A girl with straight brown hair had been standing there, watching everything with a small, cruel smile.

"You're new," she said, surveying Aria. It wasn't a question.

Aria nodded. "First day."

"I'm Erica," the girl said, her smile spreading.

"Hi. I'm Aria," Aria answered as nicely as possible, even though something about Erica made her nervous. Maybe it was the way she hadn't helped pick up the papers, only watched. Maybe it was the way she seemed happy about the other girl being upset. "Who was that girl?" Aria asked.

"That," answered Erica, "is Caroline Mason. And my advice," she added, as the bell rang overhead, "is to stay as far away from *her* as possible."

Aria didn't ask why. She didn't have a chance, since Erica was already walking away. But she knew one thing for sure: She had no intention of staying away from Caroline Mason.

Because Caroline Mason was *exactly* who she was looking for.

chapter 3

CAROLINE

"*It's going to be the best year ever.*"

That's what Lily had told Caroline as they rode to Westgate on the first day of seventh grade. That was only three weeks ago, but it felt like years.

Now, Caroline stood in the doorway of the counselor's office, breathless and upset.

She'd kept her tear-filled eyes on the floor all the way to Ms. Opeline's office. Bumping into that redheaded girl in the hallway had made Caroline feel even worse.

"Miss Mason," said Ms. Opeline, looking up from her work. "How can I help you?"

Overhead, the first bell rang.

"I need to borrow a uniform," said Caroline, her face hot.

Ms. Opeline's eyebrows went up. "What's wrong with the one you're wearing?"

Caroline turned around so the counselor could see the disgusting swirl of condiments that ran from the collar of her once-white polo to the hem of her plaid skirt.

"What happened?" asked Ms. Opeline, sounding genuinely concerned.

"It was an accident," answered Caroline. As if Lily and Erica and Whitney hadn't painted the mess on the tray. As if Lily hadn't tricked her into stopping. As if Erica hadn't held the tray up vertically so it would do the most damage.

"Mhmm," said Ms. Opeline, as she went to a closet in the corner of the room and pulled out a fresh uniform. But when Caroline went to take it, Ms. Opeline didn't let go.

"Caroline," she said, "this is the fourth uniform since school started. And it's only September."

"I know," said Caroline slowly. "I'm sorry," she added.

"Don't be sorry," said Ms. Opeline. "Just tell me what's going on."

Caroline's throat tightened. *Lily Pierce is ruining my life*, she wanted to say. But telling Ms. Opeline wouldn't fix it. It would only make things worse, because Ms. Opeline would tell Caroline's parents, and Caroline's parents would tell Lily's parents, and that would only make Lily hate her more, and that was the last thing Caroline wanted, so she said, "Nothing. Everything is fine."

Ms. Opeline sighed. "Okay," she said, letting go of the uniform. Caroline reached the door before Ms. Opeline added, "But if you change your mind, I'm here."

In the bathroom across the hall, Caroline put on the clean uniform. She stuffed the stained clothes into a plastic bag and shoved the plastic bag into her backpack.

"Did you hear what happened to Caroline?" said someone in the hall.

Caroline froze, listening.

"Whatever," said another girl. "She probably deserved it. . . ."

It was like being punched in the stomach. Caroline's throat tightened. She stood there, listening as their chatter died away. She couldn't tell who the girls were, but it didn't matter. Everyone probably felt the way they did. The bell rang, and the thought of going to class, of sitting in a room with those girls — or girls like them — made Caroline wish she were in outer space.

She met her own reflection over the sink. Her blue eyes were red, and her blond hair was flecked with tiny dots of ketchup and mustard. It wasn't supposed to be like this.

"You look out for me, and I'll look out for you. And we'll stick together no matter what."

A few tears began to stream down her face, but she wiped

them away. The second bell rang, and she took several deep breaths, and finished cleaning herself up.

Caroline was only a few minutes late to science.

Science was her favorite subject, or at least it used to be. She didn't have to deal with Lily or Whitney there, but Erica more than made up for their absence.

Erica scrunched up her nose as Caroline walked past.

"Mr. Pincell," she said, raising her hand. "Something smells."

The science teacher sighed. "I don't smell anything, Miss Kline."

"I do," she persisted, looking pointedly at Caroline. "Like someone's been bathing in kitchen trash."

A few other girls giggled. Caroline grimaced and took her seat.

"Focus," said Mr. Pincell. "Today we're going to work in pairs."

Caroline groaned inwardly. There were an odd number of girls in the class, which meant she'd get to sit there, watching everyone else find a partner, until she was the only one left, and Mr. Pincell would ask the class which pair wanted to work with Caroline, and nobody would answer, and —

217

"Can I be your partner?"

Caroline looked up to see a girl standing over her desk. It was the redhead Caroline had crashed into earlier. It took Caroline a second to process the question because it took her a second to realize someone was speaking to her. Her heart fluttered a little. It was amazing how good it felt, being spoken to.

Westgate Prep was a small school. Certainly small enough that Caroline had memorized the sixty-two students in her grade, and this girl wasn't one of them. She must be new. Which meant the only reason she was talking to Caroline was because no one had told her not to.

Yet.

"I'm Aria," said the girl. "I just started here."

"Caroline."

Aria settled in across the table from her. "So," she said. "Partners?"

Caroline hesitated, then nodded. "Okay."

"Uh," said Aria, scooting her chair closer. "What do partners *do*?"

"Well, right now we're studying crystals," explained Caroline, handing Aria a lump of quartz. "We have to answer the questions on the work sheet."

Aria held the crystal up to the light. "It's beautiful," she said quietly. She then squeezed one eye shut, held the crystal up to her other eye, and considered the class through it.

Aria stopped when she came to Erica's desk and simply stared at her through the crystal. Then she lowered it, and turned toward Caroline.

"That girl keeps making a face at me."

Erica was scowling at Aria so hard it looked like she was trying to burn a hole into her with her eyes. "Erica Kline," said Caroline. "That's pretty much the only face she makes. But also . . ." Caroline looked down at her notebook. "She probably doesn't want you hanging out with me."

Aria looked like she was about to ask why, and Caroline *really* didn't want to try to explain. Except Aria *didn't* ask why. She said, "Oh, I know. She already told me to stay away from you."

Caroline felt her own face drain of color. "Then why did you ask to be my partner?"

Aria smiled and picked up the crystal, gazing through it at the ceiling light. "Because I wanted to."

Caroline stared at her, dumbfounded.

"Ladies," said Mr. Pincell. "Less chat, more work."

Caroline gave him a dazed nod. She and Aria worked in silence for the rest of the class, but Caroline could feel Aria's gaze on her the whole time, and when the bell rang, Aria followed her out.

"Look," said Caroline. "Thanks for being my partner today. But Erica was right. You should probably stay away from me."

Aria tipped her head. "Why's that?"

Caroline sighed. "Because Erica is one of Lily Pierce's minions, and Lily hates me. She told everyone to leave me alone, so if she sees you hanging out with me, it'll make her mad, and trust me, you don't want to make her mad."

"Is that what *you* did?" asked Aria.

Caroline swallowed hard. "Look, I'm trying to do you a favor," she said. Aria's kindness would only make things worse. For *both* of them. "You just got here. You don't know how things work."

"You could tell me."

"I am. I'm telling you that I'm toxic. So unless you want to be Westgate's newest outcast, you should steer clear of me."

"I don't want to."

"Well, I want you to," said Caroline, even though having someone to sit with, to talk to, had made class bearable for the first time in weeks. "So leave me alone." And before Aria could say anything else, Caroline turned and left.

South Dublin Libraries
www.southdublinlibraries.ie

chapter 4

ARIA

Aria watched Caroline walk away from her for the second time that day. She didn't understand what was going on. Who was Lily Pierce? And what had Caroline done to make her mad? Was the whole school really ignoring Caroline just because one girl told them to?

Her thoughts swirled like Caroline's smoke. She looked down at her black laces. She wished they were still purple. She was *sure* she'd be able to think better if they were purple.

She tapped her shoe a few times. And then she got an idea.

Aria ducked into the bathroom. When she entered a stall, she saw a message scribbled on the wall:

Caroline Mason is a waste of space.

Something fluttered in Aria's chest, a sensation she'd never felt before, and it took her a moment to realize what it was: *anger*. She brought her fingertips to the message, and it erased itself.

And then, Aria erased *herself*.

Aria didn't *like* being invisible. It certainly came in handy, but it always left her feeling . . . less than real. Still, if she was going to help Caroline, she needed to understand exactly what was going on, and it seemed like the best way to do that was to watch what Caroline's life was like without Aria in it.

Aria stepped out of the stall, and looked in the mirror, startling a little at the fact that she couldn't see herself in it. And then she went in search of Caroline.

She caught sight of the blue smoke just as Caroline was reaching her last class, art. Aria slipped through the door behind her.

Caroline took her seat, and Aria stood beside her, hoping that even if she couldn't see her there, Caroline might feel a little less alone. Erica sat on the other side of the room next to a girl Aria hadn't seen before. Her backpack said her name was Whitney.

"Good afternoon, class," said the art teacher. He looked exactly like Aria imagined an art teacher would look — cheerful and paint-speckled. His name, she saw on the board, was Mr. Ferris. "It's such a lovely day," he said. "I was thinking . . ."

"That you'll cancel class?" offered a girl.

That started a chorus of "Yeah!" and "Pleeeaasseee," but Mr. Ferris only laughed and held up his hand, and the room quieted again.

"Alas," he said, picking up a notepad. "School policy says no. But I did think we could go outside and draw."

A murmur of approval ran through the room as he began to take roll. "All right," he said when he was done. "The only one we're missing is Lily."

"I'm here, sir."

Caroline stiffened in her seat, and Aria turned to see Lily Pierce standing in the doorway.

"Sorry I'm late," she said, waving a note.

Aria's mouth hung open. Lily had black curls, and pale skin, and a dazzling smile. But it wasn't any of those things that made Aria gape. No, it was something no one else seemed to notice. Something no one else *could* see.

Lily Pierce was surrounded by bright blue smoke.

The art class spread out across the lawn, drawing pads propped on their knees as they sketched with colored pencils. Lily and Erica and Whitney sat in a circle in the center of the lawn, but Caroline sat alone under a tree. She had her

223

head bowed over her paper, and was sketching a fallen leaf, detailing every crack and vein with an orange pencil.

Aria, still invisible, sat beside Caroline, but she couldn't keep her eyes off of Lily. And Lily's smoke. Smoke the same color as Caroline's, a sky blue that matched Aria's bracelet.

It didn't make sense.

Aria had already found the girl marked for her help.

How could there be two?

As she watched Lily smile and laugh and whisper in Erica's ear, a knot formed in Aria's stomach.

The blue smoke marked people who needed her help, but Aria had always assumed that meant people who *deserved* her help. From what she'd heard, Lily Pierce was not a very nice person.

How was Aria supposed to help a girl who was being bullied *and* the girl who was bullying her?

There had to be more to it.

Mr. Ferris paused over Caroline to consider her drawing. "You like science, don't you, Miss Mason?"

Caroline looked up. "Yes, sir. How did you know?"

He gave her a gentle smile, and nodded at her sketch. "You're trying to replicate the leaf, to re-create it on the page, line for line, shadow for shadow. But art is less science," he said, "and more, well, *art.*"

"I'm sorry, sir."

"Don't be sorry, Caroline. Just let go. Hold your pencil looser. Don't be afraid to draw a line in the wrong place. And for goodness' sake don't try and erase it if you do. Just make a new line."

Caroline nodded, and Aria found herself nodding, too. She liked this Mr. Ferris, she thought, as a bright red leaf fell out of the tree and floated into her lap. She smiled and held it up to the sunlight. Fall was so full of color. Aria was beginning to think that it was her favorite season. Or at least, her favorite season right now. She hadn't experienced winter or spring yet, so she couldn't be totally sure, but it was definitely her favorite-for-today.

Aria looked up and realized that Caroline was staring at her, eyes wide.

No, not at *her*. At the bright red leaf in her hand. Aria had forgotten that she was invisible, that the leaf must seem like it was hovering in the air, held aloft by magic. Aria quickly let go of the leaf. Caroline watched it float to the ground, then picked it up, and set it on her notepad.

Laughter burst out across the lawn, and Aria turned to see Lily clasping a hand over Erica's mouth. Aria got to her feet and crossed the grass toward them.

When she saw what they were laughing at, she frowned.

Erica had finished drawing her tree and had added a stick-figure version of Caroline, sitting alone beneath it. Three different sets of handwriting had written the words *Loser*, *Freak*, and *Weirdo* in the space around the sketch. Whitney chewed her pencil. Erica smiled smugly. But Lily didn't. Her laughter had trailed off.

Aria studied Lily. Something was wrong. It was in her eyes, in the beats of silence between her laughs. Like she wasn't *really* happy.

Aria sighed and crouched, inches from Lily's face. A ribbon of blue smoke curled between them.

What is it made of? Aria wondered, squinting at the fog. She could understand why Caroline's smoke swirled around her, and could guess the lonely thoughts and feelings it was filled with. But what could Lily need?

The bell rang, and Aria straightened.

"What a loser," said Erica, packing up her supplies. Aria knew she meant Caroline.

"Yeah," echoed Whitney, a bit halfheartedly.

And then Erica added, "I can't believe you two used to be best friends."

Aria froze. *Best friends?* She looked to Lily — and her swirling smoke — as the girl rolled her eyes and said, "I know."

But how? How could someone go from being a best friend to being a bully?

Lily and her friends brushed the grass from their skirts and strolled away. Aria turned back in search of Caroline, but she was already gone.

chapter 5

CAROLINE

"Just you today?" asked Caroline's mom after school.

"Just me," mumbled Caroline, climbing into the car.

They went through this every day. At first, Caroline made a dozen different excuses for why there was no more carpool — well, there was, it just didn't involve *her* — but she'd run out of good lies and the energy to tell them convincingly.

"How was school?" asked her mom.

Caroline looked out the window, the lunchroom incident burned into her mind. "It was fine," she lied.

Her mom squinted at her. "Are you wearing a different uniform?"

She looked down at the borrowed clothes. "I spilled food on mine."

"Goodness, Caroline, you've gotten so clumsy. That's the third one this month."

Fourth, thought Caroline. The first time, Lily and Erica had stuffed her clothes in the trash can during gym. The second time, they'd put them in the toilet (Caroline had stood, in the flooded stall, watching the blue-and-green plaid swirl in the toilet water). After that, Caroline made sure to put a lock on her gym locker. For a little while it worked, but that just made them more creative. The third uniform had ended up splattered with mud. And now this.

At least she'd survived art. The last class of the day. And the worst. That's where everything had started.

When they got home, Caroline's mom called upstairs to Megan, Caroline's sister. When there was no answer, she asked Caroline to go check on her.

Megan was stretched across her bed, and she was on the phone. She was always on the phone.

"Mom's looking for you," said Caroline.

Megan waved a hand. "I'll be down soon."

Caroline hesitated. Megan was sixteen and gorgeous and without a doubt the most popular girl at her high school. Caroline couldn't imagine Megan *ever* being bullied.

When Megan saw that she wasn't leaving, she lowered the phone and said, "What do you want?" With her tone, she might as well have said *go away*.

Caroline hesitated. "I . . ."

I need your advice, she wanted to say. *School is a nightmare and I don't know what to do and I'm afraid that if I tell someone like Mom or the counselor or the headmistress it will just make everything worse and I —*

"Well?" pressed Megan, impatiently.

Caroline swallowed. "I wanted to borrow your hairbrush," she said, chickening out.

Megan rolled her eyes, tossed the brush to her, and kicked the door shut with her foot.

Caroline trudged down the hall into the bathroom. She dropped the brush on the counter and dug her ruined uniform out of her backpack, dumping it in the bathroom sink. There was a jewelry box on the counter, and somewhere in the bottom drawer was the half-circle necklace.

We'll stick together no matter what.

She couldn't bring herself to throw the necklace away, but she forced herself to not open the box and take it out.

Instead, she tried to scrub away the stains on her uniform, but they didn't come out, only spread, turning the polo and skirt a sickly orange brown.

Caroline heard a car door slam, and a familiar voice, and her chest tightened. It wasn't bad enough that she had to see Lily every day at school. She was also her next-door neighbor.

Through the bathroom window she could see Lily's black hair as she got out of her mom's car. Lily's smile faltered, and then faded altogether — Caroline knew that Lily hated her strict after-school routine, because that was the kind of thing best friends were supposed to know about each other. She watched Lily hesitate on the porch, as though she didn't want to go inside.

For a second, Caroline didn't hate her. She just felt sorry for her. And then she remembered the ruined clothes sitting in the sink, and she snapped the water off. She left the uniform soaking while she went to her room, and lay down on her bed.

Maybe it was just a bad dream. She wished she could wake up.

Or run away. Some days she thought about running away. Starting a new life.

But Caroline Mason didn't want a new life.

She just wanted her old life back.

· · ·

"What about Beth?" Lily pointed across the lunchroom with her fork. It was the first week of seventh grade.

"No," said Erica. "Her sister's in eighth grade here. What about Jessabel?"

Lily shook her head. Caroline knew Lily had a crush on Jessabel's big brother.

"Maybe Caroline should pick," offered Erica.

Caroline frowned. "Why?" she asked. "Why do we need to pick anyone?"

"It's a new year, Car," explained Lily. "We have to send a message. Tell the girls at Westgate that they don't mess with Table Seven."

"But they haven't messed with Table Seven," countered Caroline. "Not yet."

Lily sighed dramatically. "You don't get it."

"No," said Caroline, "I don't."

It wasn't the first time Lily had singled someone out. She used to only go after girls if they did something to make her mad (back in the sixth grade, Lily had been horrible to a girl just because she'd hurt Caroline's feelings). But this time seemed random, and Caroline didn't like it.

"It's preemptive," explained Lily. "We send a message. By the time we're done with whoever we pick, no one will want to take her place. No one will want to get on our bad side. Which

means everyone will want to get on our good side. Do you understand now?"

Caroline didn't. But she didn't want to be on Lily's bad side,
either, and Lily and Erica were both giving her a you're-with-
us-or-against-us *look*, so she nodded, and tried to ignore the pit
in her stomach.

"I know!" said Erica. "What about Whitney Abel?"

"Never heard of her," said Lily.

"She's new," said Erica, pointing across the lunchroom.

A brown-haired girl was sitting at the edge of Table 11, but
not talking to the other girls there. She stared down at her food.

"Her clothes don't look new," observed Lily.

"They're not even hers. They're used."

Lily scrunched up her nose. "Gross."

"It's not her fault," Caroline spoke up. "She's here on
scholarship."

"How do you know?" challenged Lily.

Caroline shrugged. Her mom was on the school board, and
when she found out about Whitney's background — her dad
was a single parent and had been laid off after Whitney was
accepted to Westgate — she told Caroline to be nice.

"New schools are hard," her mom had said. "And Whitney's
had a hard enough time already. Look out for her."

"I think we should leave her alone," Caroline told Lily.

"Overruled," said Lily, daring Caroline to challenge her again.

And Caroline didn't.

The house phone rang, jarring Caroline out of the memory. She imagined picking it up, and hearing Lily's voice saying, "Whatever. This is stupid. Come sit with us tomorrow."

Caroline went downstairs to see who it was. She could hear her mom on the phone in the kitchen, and knew it was just her dad calling from work.

"I noticed that Lily's home," Mrs. Mason said to Caroline when she hung up.

"I know," said Caroline.

"Is everything okay between you two?"

"We're fine."

"She never comes over anymore," pressed her mom. "Are you having a fight?"

A war, thought Caroline. An unfair, uneven, unwinnable war. She knew she should tell her mom what really happened to her uniform. And the ones before. She knew she should tell her — tell *someone* — about the silent treatment, and the other daily torments, and the way it all made her feel horrible and invisible and small. But she couldn't.

Because if she did, it would all be true, and there would be no going back, no making things right. It would be over.

"Caroline?" urged her mom.

"No," she lied, forcing a thin smile. "Everything's fine."

Her mom gave her a long, searching look. "Why don't you go outside? Get some fresh air."

Caroline couldn't say no, not without telling her mom *why* she was avoiding anything that might put her in contact with Lily. So she grabbed a book and trudged out onto the front porch.

chapter 6

ARIA

Aria had waited until the lawn was empty and the students were gone. Then, when the coast was clear, she flickered back into form, letting out a sigh of relief at being visible again.

She did a quick check to make sure she was all there, but when she got to her charm bracelet, she stopped. Something was different. Something had *changed*. The second ring, the one where her new feather would go once Aria helped Caroline, was now *two* rings, linked together. Two rings and two girls. So it wasn't a mistake. They both needed her help.

She looked down at her shadow. "What do I do?" she asked. "Who do I help first?"

Aria was prone to talking to her shadow because it was always there, and because now and again it answered in its own way.

After all, Aria's shadow wasn't an ordinary shadow, not by any stretch. It took her wherever she needed to go. Wherever she was *supposed* to be. Even if she didn't know where that was, the shadow would.

She tapped her shoe on the ground, and the shadow gave a nervous wiggle, and then turned on like a light. Aria stepped through, and found herself no longer at Westgate, but on the sidewalk of a big, pretty street, in front of two houses. One was green and one was white, and each had a mailbox with a stenciled name. One said MASON and the other said PIERCE.

Caroline Mason and Lily Pierce.

They lived next door to each other. And Aria was standing halfway between them.

She frowned down at her shadow. "Some help you are," she said.

There was a tug in her chest, as if a rope ran between her and the girls, but the girls were in opposite directions, and both were pulling Aria. She needed to make a decision. And judging by her shadow, she'd have to make it on her own.

Okay. Whatever had happened between Lily and Caroline, she reasoned, their problems were obviously intertwined. To help one, she'd have to help the other. But she'd found Caroline first, so she would start with her. After that, she'd figure out what to do about Lily.

Aria smiled.

It felt good to have a plan.

Just then, the front door on the green house banged open. Caroline walked out onto her front porch and slumped into a swing seat with a book.

Aria started toward her. Caroline didn't seem to notice her coming. She was staring up at the sky, like her body was there but her mind was somewhere else.

There were two porch swings, and Aria sank silently into the one across from Caroline. She rocked it back and forth with her toes, hoping to get Caroline's attention. When that failed, she finally said, "Hey."

Caroline jumped and nearly fell out of her swing. "Aria?" she asked, straightening. "What are you doing here?"

Trying to help, thought Aria. But what she said was, "I was walking by and saw you out here, and thought I'd come say hi. And I know you said you didn't want anyone to see me hanging out with you but *A*, we're not at school and *B*, I don't really care what people think."

Caroline glanced next door. "You shouldn't be here."

Aria let the swing come to a stop. "Because of Lily?" she asked.

"Because of Lily," admitted Caroline. "If she sees you, she'll think we're *friends*."

Aria frowned. She'd always thought *friends* was the best thing you could be, but Caroline said it like it was a bad word. "I don't mind."

Caroline shook her head. "If you hang out with me, Lily will make your life miserable."

"I doubt that," said Aria with simple certainty. She'd never been miserable before. "And besides, not everyone's afraid of Lily Pierce."

"Name one girl who isn't."

"Me," said Aria brightly.

Caroline rolled her eyes. "Well, you're new," she said. "You don't know better."

Aria shrugged. "Maybe." She paused, and then, carefully, said, "You two used to be friends, didn't you?"

Caroline cringed. She drew her knees up onto the seat, and wrapped her arms around them. "I don't want to talk about it," she said.

"Okay," said Aria. But she didn't leave. She could tell that Caroline *did want* to talk about it — could see it swirling in her smoke — but she'd figured out that sometimes people just needed a little time.

And sure enough, after a few moments, Caroline broke the silence.

"Before you showed up," she said, "I was thinking about how much I miss summer."

Aria smiled. "I like summer," she said. "Until I got to fall, it was my favorite season."

Caroline looked at her like she was weird. Aria was getting used to that.

"Summer has the best constellations," explained Caroline. "At night I'd lie out on my trampoline and look up at the stars. And during the day, Lily and I would sit by her pool or out here on the swings and drink lemonade and read magazines." She wiped her eyes. "It wasn't supposed to be like this. This year was supposed to be perfect."

Aria shook her head. "Nothing's perfect."

Caroline let out a small, stifled laugh.

"Why is Lily being mean to you?" Aria asked.

"To get back at me, I guess," Caroline said after a moment.

"For what?"

Just then a car pulled up next door and honked. Over Caroline's shoulder Aria saw Lily bob out the front door and down the steps of her house. She'd traded the uniform for jeans and a T-shirt. Erica and Whitney climbed out of the backseat of the car to meet her.

"Let's get out of here," said Lily. She threw a glance at Caroline and added, "Something totally smells."

"Yeah," chimed in Erica. "Someone should take out their *trash.*"

Whitney didn't say anything, only stepped aside so Lily could climb in.

Caroline sat motionless. She was gripping the seat so hard her fingers looked white. Aria crossed to her, and sat beside her on the bench, and put her hand on the girl's shoulder.

"Hey," she said softly. "What happened between you two?"

Caroline swallowed hard. "You really want to know?"

Aria nodded. "I really do."

"Okay," said Caroline, looking up. "I'll tell you. It happened in art. . . ."

chapter 7

CAROLINE

*I*t happened in art.

All class, Caroline had a stomachache.

Lily and Erica kept exchanging glances. Caroline knew their plan. And she hated it. It didn't seem right and it didn't seem fair, and her mom's words kept playing in her head.

Whitney's had a hard enough time already. Look out for her.

"We're doing her a favor," Lily had said during lunch.

"Yeah," Erica had chimed in. "After this, she'll have to get herself some new clothes."

Everyone was at their desks, painting different times of day, some dawn and others noon and others dusk. Lily had been painting a cloudy night, so the water in her plastic cup was bluish black. Erica had been painting a sunrise, but she'd used too much paint on purpose to make her water thick and gross, the colors swirling into brown.

Caroline had used as little paint as possible, and hardly rinsed her brush, so her water was still practically clear.

When it was time to clean up, Lily gathered up her cup and Erica's — she passed over Caroline's when she saw how clean it was — and made her way toward Whitney, who was still finishing her sky. She wasn't even looking.

Look out for her.

At the last minute, Caroline stood up, and hurried toward Lily. She only wanted to stop her. It had taken her all class to work up the courage to do it — to think of what she wanted to say, about how this was stupid and wrong and they were better than it — and she reached Lily just in time, and grabbed her shoulder.

But Lily's forward momentum made her stumble backward, away from Whitney and into Caroline. There was a splashing sound, followed by a shriek from Lily, and then the cups tumbled to the linoleum. Everyone turned to look, including Whitney.

When Lily spun on Caroline, the front of her uniform was covered in dirty water.

"What did you do that for?" growled Lily.

"I'm sorry," said Caroline, eyes wide. "I was just trying to —"

"Girls, what's going on?" asked Mr. Ferris.

"It was an accident," said Caroline.

"Yeah, sure." Lily wrung out her skirt, brownish water dripping to the floor.

Erica appeared at Lily's shoulder with paper towels. When Caroline tried to help wipe Lily's shirt, Lily shook her off. "It's fine. Get off me."

"You'd better go to Ms. Opeline and borrow a fresh uniform," said the teacher.

Lily scowled at Caroline, then turned on her heel, and stormed out.

"It was an accident," Caroline called after her, but Lily was already gone.

"So that's why Lily turned against you?" Aria asked. Caroline nodded. "Why did she want to spill paint on Whitney?" pressed Aria.

Caroline explained about Lily's plan, to pick a girl and make an example out of her.

"That's horrible," said Aria.

Caroline stared up. "I know. But it worked. Everyone wants to fit in. They want to belong. Be a part of something.

I just wish," she said under her breath. "I wish I could go back."

"What would you do if you could?" challenged Aria. "*Not* stand up for Whitney? You did the *right thing*."

Caroline felt ill. She'd told herself that over and over but it hadn't helped. If it had been the right thing, then why was she being punished for it?

"I thought it would be okay," she said. "I thought *we* would be okay. But everything changed. Lily didn't come over after school that day, and she didn't ride with me the next morning. And when I got to lunch, Whitney was sitting at Table Seven. In my spot. When I went to sit down, all three of them got up and just . . . walked away. Like I wasn't even there." Caroline felt her throat tighten. It was the first time she'd talked about what had happened with *anyone*. She didn't know why she was telling Aria so much. But it felt good to talk. It felt good to have someone to talk *to*, and it was like once she started, she couldn't stop.

"Does Whitney know what you did?" asked Aria.

Caroline shrugged. "I don't think so. And she probably wouldn't listen if I told her. She's exactly where she wants to be. Where *everyone* wants to be. At the popular table."

"Caroline!" called her mom from inside.

She sighed, and stood up. "I've got to go."

Aria hopped off the swing. "Okay. See you at school."

Caroline hesitated. She didn't want to put Aria in Lily's path. Aria claimed she didn't care, but that was only because she didn't know. But it felt so nice to have someone on her side. It made her feel less like a speck of space dust and more like a planet.

Aria was halfway down the stairs when she turned back and said, "Hey."

"Yeah?"

"Thank you."

"For what?" asked Caroline.

"For telling me what happened."

Caroline shrugged. "It doesn't change anything."

Aria smiled, the kind of smile that seemed to brighten the front yard. "It might."

chapter 8

ARIA

Aria got to the other side of the street before she realized that she had nowhere to go.

Gabby had lived in an apartment building with a nice flat roof for Aria to sleep on. But Caroline's roof had points that didn't look very inviting. The house itself looked like it had extra rooms, but Caroline would have to invite Aria in for her to use them. And since she just left, Aria felt kind of weird about going back.

"Where should I go now?" she asked the shadow at her feet. The shadow fidgeted, trying to decide if Aria wanted it to take her somewhere, but she shook her head and said, "Never mind."

She walked up to to a large tree, and sat down at its base to think. Even though the leaves were changing, the weather was warm enough to sleep outside. But Aria didn't want to get caught, and she didn't want to spend the night invisible, not if she had another option. She leaned her head back and took a deep breath.

Then she saw something up in the tree.

It looked like a house.

Aria raised a brow. She had never seen a house in a tree before, but there it was. At first she wondered if *she* had summoned it — it looked like it was held aloft by magic — but then she saw the branches supporting the floor, and the way the old planks were warped by age, and decided it had already been there. (It still seemed magical, though.)

A magical house for a magical girl, thought Aria with a smile.

There was a rope ladder hanging down, and Aria climbed up. The tree house had no door, only an opening in the floor, and a window between two makeshift walls. The wooden boards groaned under her feet, but the structure held steady.

"Hello?" she called out, even though the house was in fact only one room and she could see that it was empty. Still, it seemed polite to ask.

There was a beanbag in one corner, a shelf nailed to one of the rickety walls, and a couple of candy wrappers on the floor, but otherwise the space was bare. The air whistled through the planks of wood. Aria thought the place was perfect.

Her favorite thing about the tree house was the fact that it didn't have a roof. The branches — full of leaves changing color — made a patchy covering, and past them, she could see the sky.

"This will do," Aria said to her shadow.

She summoned up some pillows and sat down, then emptied the contents of the backpack she'd finally conjured onto the floor. She studied the handouts the front office had given her. Handouts on Westgate's history, its reputation, on what to do, and what not to do, and how to dress (though it didn't say anything about purple shoelaces), and how to be a model student. Handouts on clubs, and sports, and a flier for an upcoming dance with Eastgate, which was apparently the boys' school down the road.

Every pamphlet and brochure featured a smiling group of students walking to class or gathered in the halls. But one of the pictures made Aria stop.

Lily Pierce had her arm slung around Caroline Mason's shoulder, their heads together. They were both grinning. The girls didn't just look happy. They looked *inseparable*.

Aria drew her finger lightly over the photograph, and blue lines appeared, like wisps of smoke, wrapping around the two girls. A small purple thumbtack took shape in Aria's palm, and she pinned the pamphlet to the tree house wall.

Her gaze drifted outside to Caroline's house. The girl in the photo hardly resembled the one across the street.

But that was okay.

Aria was here to help.

"Hurry up, Jess, before somebody sees."

"Stop watching me and keep an eye out."

The girls were in the gym, huddled in front of one of the lockers before the bell rang. They'd gotten there early. And so had Aria. She stood invisible, watching as one of them — Jessabel — squeezed packets of ketchup onto a girl's gym clothes. *Caroline's* gym clothes.

"Did Lily tell you to do this?" asked the other girl.

"No," said Jessabel, tearing open another packet. "It's called *initiative*. You have to take it."

Aria frowned. She had spent the morning invisible, wandering the school, listening to the girls in the halls and the classrooms. Getting to know them, and the things they had to say, about life, about school, about Lily, about Caroline. From what she could tell, the students fell into three camps where Caroline Mason was concerned: those who thought she deserved what was happening to her, those who didn't but weren't willing to get involved, and those who might actually talk to Caroline if she ever talked to *them*. Which she apparently hadn't.

Aria had been in the hall when she overhead Jessabel's plan.

"Almost done," said Jessabel now.

"Hurry up," nagged the other girl. "Class is about to start."

Aria watched, conflicted about what to do.

She thought about becoming visible and stopping the girls, or staying invisible and scaring them away. But neither of those things would make them stop tormenting Caroline. So Aria stood and watched and chewed her lip and waited. And when the girls were done, and they dumped the empty packets in the trash and hurried away, Aria flickered back into sight and approached Caroline's locker.

The built-in lock on the door was broken. Aria pressed her hand to the metal, and by the time her fingers fell back to her side, the door was fixed. And so were the clothes inside. She felt rather satisfied with herself, and went to find her own locker, passing Caroline on the way (Caroline kept her head down, and didn't seem to notice her, even though she was definitely visible again).

The locker room started filling up. Aria watched Caroline as she reached her locker and ran her hand over the repaired lock. She watched her turn the little dials and open the door, watched her shoulders slump with relief when she found the clothes inside untouched.

Aria smiled.

And then someone screamed.

It was more of a screech, actually. Coming from Jessabel's locker. Aria crossed her arms. It had seemed like the only fair thing to do. At least until a second later, when Jessabel tore around the corner, clutching her ketchup-splattered gym clothes. She came barreling toward Caroline.

"What did you *do*?" growled Jessabel.

Caroline's eyes widened. "I didn't —"

"What did you do?" Jessabel shoved the ruined gym clothes against Caroline. Aria frowned. It wasn't supposed to happen like this.

"Hey," she said, coming forward. "It wasn't Caroline's fault."

Jessabel spun on Aria. "Was it you?" She charged toward her. "How? How did you —"

"Jessabel," came a voice, and everyone looked up to see Lily standing there in her gym clothes, Erica and Whitney behind her. "What on earth do you think you're doing?" Lily asked, scrunching up her nose.

Jessabel's mouth opened and closed like a fish as she clutched the splattered gym clothes. "I was just . . . trying to . . ."

"To what?" asked Lily with a smirk. "Look ridiculous?" Erica giggled at Lily's shoulder.

Jessabel turned bright red.

Aria stared at Lily, shocked. Was she *standing up* for Caroline?

"Go get cleaned up, before anyone sees you looking like that."

Jessabel huffed and stormed away.

"I think you upset her," said Whitney softly.

"Serves her right," said Lily, running a hand through her hair. "That's what happens when you mix with *trash*." She looked right at Caroline when she said it.

So much for Good Lily, thought Aria. Blue smoke or not, she needed a talking-to. Aria clenched her hands and took a step toward her, but Caroline caught her shoulder.

Don't, she mouthed.

Lily's eyes slid from Caroline to Aria, and hovered there for a long moment. And then Lily turned and left, her minions bobbing in her wake. Caroline's hand fell from Aria's shoulder as she looked down at her polo. It was splattered with ketchup from Jessabel's attack. Her jaw clenched. The blue smoke coiled around her.

"Hey," said Aria gently. "I have an extra shirt. Do you want it?"

After a moment, Caroline nodded reluctantly. "Thanks," she said, looking around. "But don't let anyone see. It will just make it worse."

"Our secret," said Aria, managing a smile, and producing a clean polo from behind her back. And for an instant, Caroline smiled, too. And then the coach whistled, and the smile was gone. The girls got changed and went to join the class.

Westgate's gym was nothing like the last school Aria went to. Here there were tennis courts, and a field, and a massive track, and a fancy swimming pool with three diving boards at different heights.

The rest of the seventh graders were all on the track, some already jogging. Lily and Erica and Whitney stood stretching, and Jessabel sat on the bleachers wearing a spare pair of gym clothes that were obviously three sizes too large. She glared daggers at Aria and Caroline as they made their way to the track.

Caroline said nothing to Aria as they started running,

and Aria stayed a stride or two behind the other girl. But at least Aria knew that Caroline knew she wasn't alone.

For a while, as they jogged, the blue smoke that circled Caroline's shoulders thinned.

Just a little.

But it was a start.

chapter 9

CAROLINE

The noise of the lunchroom washed over Caroline as she clutched her tray. Here she was again. The worst part of her day.

Once again, she felt lost in space. She found herself scanning the room for Aria, but she didn't see her. Girls shouldered past to get to their seats, one knocking into Caroline hard enough that she nearly dropped her lunch tray. She started to make her way toward Table 12, but she couldn't do it, not after yesterday, not with *something smells* and *trash* still echoing in her head.

So Caroline took a deep breath, turned, and left the cafeteria.

Compared to the noisy lunchroom, the hallway was quiet, and through the doors, the courtyard outside was silent, but not in a heavy, lonely way. It was peaceful. She could imagine she was somewhere else. Caroline carried her tray to the steps, and sat down.

She'd just started eating when someone above her cleared his throat, and she looked up to see Mr. Cahill, the assistant headmaster, staring down at her.

"Miss Mason," he said, gesturing to the tray. "What is this?"

"My lunch?" ventured Caroline.

"I can see that," said Mr. Cahill. "What I can't see is why it — and you — are out here instead of in the cafeteria with the rest of your class."

Because I lost my friends, Caroline wanted to say, *and my table, and no one will look at me, let alone talk to me, and yesterday I got hit with a tray of ketchup.*

But she didn't say that. All she said was, "Because it's a nice day."

"That may be," said Mr. Cahill. "But all seventh graders are expected to eat lunch *together*. In the cafeteria. It's been scientifically proven that eating lunch together creates a sense of community. Don't you want a sense of community, Miss Mason?"

Caroline stared up into Mr. Cahill's face. She felt like she was trapped in some kind of sick joke. "Yes, sir, but I can't . . ." She almost said she couldn't go back in there.

"Can't what, Miss Mason?"

Caroline looked down at her tray.

"Did something happen?" he pressed. "Is something wrong?"

Caroline hesitated, then sighed. "No, sir."

"Then unless you want to be issued an infraction, I'm going to have to ask you to go back inside," said Mr. Cahill. "It may not seem like it, but social interaction is an integral part of —"

Just then the doors burst open, and Mr. Cahill and Caroline both turned to see Aria bouncing through, carrying her tray.

"Sorry I'm late!" she said, plopping down beside Caroline.

Caroline felt a rush of relief. "See?" she said to Mr. Cahill. "I'm not eating alone. There's plenty of social interaction happening here."

Mr. Cahill examined both of them. "All right," he said. "But why are you out here and not in the cafeteria?"

"I just started here," Aria said brightly. "Caroline is my student ambassador. The front office told her to show me around, and tell me how things work so I can get caught up as quickly as possible. Caroline thought it would be easiest for us to meet during lunch so we could talk. No time to waste. This is a hard school, and every moment you're not ahead, you're falling behind."

It sounded like a line from one of Westgate's brochures.

"Besides, it's awfully loud in the lunch room," continued Aria. "And a bit overwhelming. So Caroline agreed to meet me out here where it was calmer."

Mr. Cahill turned to Caroline. "Is that true, Miss Mason?"

Caroline nodded. "Yes, sir."

Mr. Cahill gave a small huff. "All right, but today only, ladies. Tomorrow it's back to the lunch room, understand?"

"Sure thing," said Aria.

As soon as he was gone, Aria slumped back against a stone pillar. "He's pretty stern."

"You didn't have to cover for me," said Caroline, picking at her food.

Aria shrugged. "I don't mind. You *could* be my student ambassador. They never gave me one yesterday. And the lunch room *is* really noisy."

Caroline nodded, and went back to poking her food. When she snuck a glance at Aria's tray, she saw that it was covered in fruit. Apple, banana, orange, grapes, even a kiwi.

"I'm trying to decide which one is my favorite," said Aria, as if that explained everything. "I think it's important to know. And I thought it would be easier if I just focused on one food group at a time."

Caroline laughed. Not a loud laugh, and not a very strong one, but the sound of it still surprised her. And for a second, everything felt a little lighter. "I guess it does make sense," she said. "In a weird kind of way."

Aria beamed, and picked up her apple. "So," she said, biting into it, "what *are* you doing out here?"

Caroline's spirits sank again. "I needed some fresh air."

Aria tilted her head back. "It *is* hard to sit inside when the weather's this nice." She looked back at Caroline. "So it had nothing to do with Lily?"

Caroline frowned. "I didn't want to sit alone."

"There's more than one table in the cafeteria. Why not sit at one of the others?"

Caroline shook her head. "Even if I sat with someone else," she explained, "I'd still be sitting alone." Aria didn't understand what it was like. To be hated. To be ignored. Up until this year, Caroline hadn't known how it felt, either. But now she did, and with that knowledge came a certainty that the other girls at Westgate would never be her friends.

"Well," said Aria, looking up past the buildings. "This is better than a lunch table. Even if it's just for today."

Caroline followed her gaze. The sky was streaked with clouds. Back when she and Lily were BFFs, they'd pick out shapes and make up stories about them. Caroline saw pirate ships and mountains and wolves, but Lily always said she saw castles. Sometimes the castles had princesses trapped inside, high up in towers and guarded by dragons.

But these clouds weren't the kind for finding shapes. They were long and thin.

"Those are my favorite," Caroline said, pointing at them. "People usually like cumulus clouds, those big, puffy ones, but these are stratus. They look like someone drew them with a piece of chalk, but they make the best sunsets."

"Sorry," added Caroline when Aria didn't answer. "I know that's nerdy."

"Don't be sorry," said Aria. "It's awesome. You're really smart," she added. She didn't say it like it was a bad thing. "Why would I tease you for that?"

Caroline sighed. "I don't know."

"Hey, Lily?"
"Yeah, Car?"

"Want to know something cool?"

It was a summer night, a week before the start of seventh grade, and they were stretched out on the trampoline in Caroline's backyard.

Lily propped her head on her elbow. "Sure."

Caroline gazed up at the stars. "Light takes a really long time to travel through space, so when we look at the night sky, we're actually looking at a past version of it."

The universe was so amazing, and vast, and full of cool facts and secrets, and the thought of all the things she knew and didn't know and wanted to know made Caroline smile.

But Lily only snorted, and slumped back down. "You sound like such a nerd," she said. Caroline deflated. "Promise me you're not going to go around sounding off random fact bites when school starts."

Caroline sighed. "I promise."

"Hey now, don't pout," said Lily. "I'm only looking out for you."

The first bell rang, a warning that lunch would be over in five minutes.

Caroline blinked, dragging herself out of the memory. Aria had collected several brightly colored leaves and was twirling them between her fingers. *She's a little strange*, Caroline thought. But she liked how Aria didn't seem to hide her strangeness. Caroline envied that.

She got to her feet with her tray, but the thought of returning to the cafeteria made her feel sick.

"Here," said Aria, holding out her hand. "I'll take it back for you."

"Are you sure?" asked Caroline.

"It's no big deal," she said. "I'll see you in science."

"Hey," Caroline called after her.

"Yeah?"

Caroline hesitated. She didn't want to incur Lily's wrath. But she was tired of having no orbit. "If we pair up again," she said, "do you want to be my partner?"

To her relief, Aria broke into a grin. "Sure!"

She ducked inside, and Caroline stood there, feeling something like hope for the first time in ages.

chapter 10

ARIA

Aria made her way back to the cafeteria without spilling anything, which was quite a feat considering there were still a lot of loose grapes (they were her least favorite) as well as a half-eaten apple rolling around on her plate. She was returning the trays to their proper shelves when a voice behind her said, "There you are."

Aria turned to find Lily, Erica, and Whitney standing side by side, forming a wall of plaid skirts and white polos. Lily was actually a half step in front of the other two girls. Not far enough to seem apart, just far enough to show she was the one in charge. Her blue smoke swirled around her even as she smiled.

"It's Ari, isn't it?"

"Aria," she corrected. "Aria Blue."

"You're new here, aren't you?" Lily asked with a sweet smile.

Aria nodded. "I started yesterday."

"Ah," said Lily, tilting her head. "Well, that explains it."

"Explains what?" asked Aria.

Lily ignored the question. "See, Erica?" she said to the girl on her right. "I told you there was a perfectly good reason. I bet nobody told her."

"Told me what?" asked Aria.

Lily turned her attention back to her. "You've been hanging out with Caroline Mason." It wasn't a question.

Aria stood up straighter. "Yeah. I have."

"You're not supposed to do that," cut in Erica.

Lily held up her hand and gave an exasperated sigh.

"You're new at Westgate, so maybe you didn't get the memo, but Caroline Mason does not exist."

"Of course she does," said Aria.

Lily's smile disappeared. "No. She doesn't. You don't talk to her. You don't hang out with her. You definitely don't become her friend. Caroline Mason is *off-limits*."

"Why?" challenged Aria.

"Because I said so," said Lily. And then she smiled again. "Starting at a new school is hard, Ari. You want to make friends. You want to fit in. I get it. But you want to make the *right* friends. You don't need to waste your time on Caroline."

"I —"

"Why don't you come sit with us at lunch tomorrow?" offered Lily sweetly. "Table Seven. We'll help you settle in." She closed the last of the gap between them. "You get to choose the kind of life you have here at Westgate. I can make it awesome, or I can make it awful. But it's your choice, so make the right one."

The bell rang overhead, and Lily flashed her brightest, whitest smile. "Erica, you and Ari have science now, right? Why don't you walk to class together?"

Aria felt dazed from her encounter with Lily. Looking at Lily Pierce was like looking at two images of somebody at the same time, overlapping so that both of them were blurry. There was Lily, who smiled and bossed and acted superior. And there was Lily's smoke, which was full of sadness and frustration and worry, things she kept beneath the surface, behind that smile.

Aria tried to make sense of it as she followed Erica to

class. Erica wasn't surrounded by any smoke. She seemed to wear her meanness on her sleeve.

Erica didn't say a word to Aria the whole way, and then, just before they reached the door, she looped her arm through Aria's, and flashed her a sharp grin. As they went inside, Erica suddenly laughed, as if Aria had said something funny, even though she hadn't said anything at all.

"Girls," warned Mr. Pincell. "You're late."

"Sorry," said Erica cheerfully, letting go of Aria's arm. "I was just showing Aria around."

Aria glanced at Caroline, who looked confused. Aria wished she could explain, but she knew she had to take her seat. She hoped they'd have to pair up, but it turned out not to be a partner day.

As class started, Erica passed Aria a note.

What's your fave color?

Aria wasn't sure why the girl was asking — Erica didn't strike her as the type to care. *Blue*, she wrote. Then she added *red* below it, before finally writing *purple* underneath, because she couldn't decide. She slid the note back to Erica, and went back to listening to Mr. Pincell. But only a few minutes later, another piece of folded paper found its way onto her desk.

When did you move here?

Aria wrote down *yesterday* and sent the paper back.

The third time the paper came to Aria, it didn't have a question on it. Instead it said, *Caroline Mason isn't worth your time.*

Aria frowned, and looked over at Caroline's desk. She was surprised to see Caroline staring at her, or rather, at the paper in her hand. The blue smoke swirled around Caroline's shoulders and Aria realized what it must look like, what Erica was *making* it look like. Showing up late to class, the hooked arms, the passed notes . . . it looked like they were friends.

Aria didn't send Erica's note back. Instead, she crumpled it up and shoved it in the back of her notebook, and started writing one to Caroline.

It's not what it looks like.

Caroline didn't write back, so Aria sent another.

It's <u>REALLY</u> not what it looks like.

Still nothing. Caroline kept her eyes on the board. Aria sighed, and tried one last time. But instead of writing a note, she drew a picture. Of a monster with rows of teeth and squinty eyes and lots of hair. The monster was dressed in a plaid skirt.

Under it she wrote *Erica Kline.*

She was about to pass it to Caroline when she stopped herself. What would happen if Mr. Pincell caught her and took the drawing? What would happen if Erica saw it? Aria had only been trying to make Caroline smile. It hadn't even occurred to her that she was making fun of someone else at the same time. Putting one person down to lift someone else up. That was something bullies did.

Aria wasn't a bully.

She crumpled the paper and shoved it into her backpack.

A few moments later, Caroline finally passed her a note. *I wish it was a partner day.*

Aria wrote back, *Me too.*

chapter 11

CAROLINE

"So," said Mrs. Mason at dinner that night. "How was school?"

It had become Caroline's most dreaded question. But for the first time in a long time, the true answer wasn't *horrible*. It was still bad. Still full of stress and worry and nausea. But not horrible. Thanks to Aria.

"It was okay," she said. "There's a new girl. I'm sort of . . . showing her around." Even though Aria didn't seem to need much showing around, now that Caroline thought about it.

Her mom brightened. "That's really nice of you. Starting at a new school —"

"— is hard, I know." It was the same lecture her mom had given her about Whitney Abel. "It's not a big deal."

"It is," said her mom. "And I'm proud of you, Car." She turned to Caroline's dad. "Isn't that great, honey?" Mr.

270

Mason, who'd been reading a book at the table, mumbled something that sounded like *yes*. Across from him, Megan was texting. Her mom sighed, and turned back to Caroline. "Well, *I* think it's great."

Caroline asked to be excused, then got up and put her plate in the sink. She headed for the back door.

"Where are you off to?" asked her mom.

"Just out back," she said.

"Car —"

"Let her go," Caroline's dad finally joined in. "A little stargazing never hurt anyone."

"I'm just worried about her. . . ." she heard her mom say before the door swung shut.

Out in the yard, Caroline climbed up onto the trampoline. It wasn't full dark yet, so there were no stars, but she stared up at the clouds. They *had* made a really good sunset, just like she knew they would.

Her mind wandered, as it always did, back to summer, when everything was perfect. When she didn't dread waking up. When the hardest question was what to wear to the mall, and the worst thing she had to deal with was the occasional jab from Erica, who only had an attitude because she was jealous that Lily liked Caroline best.

Lily had an amazing heated pool with a slide and a sloped

271

shallow end like a beach where they could sit, and during the summer they would gather there, with cool, clear water washing up over their legs while they talked.

If Caroline tried hard enough, she could almost hear the sounds of summer, the splash of a pool party, the echoes of laughter. . . .

And then she opened her eyes and realized the sounds weren't part of her memory at all. They were coming from next door. Chatter and soda cans and the voices of Erica and Whitney, and then Lily's voice, calling a meeting to order. Lily loved holding meetings.

A wave of nausea rolled over Caroline as she wondered if the meeting was about *her*.

It was still warm out, but Caroline shivered. She could hear Erica's sharp laugh, and it made her think about her walking into science, arm in arm with Aria. Why was Aria hanging out with her? Yes, Aria had tried to explain in her note, but Caroline still wasn't sure. And she wanted to know, because she really liked Aria. The new girl was starting to feel almost like a friend, but . . .

And then a horrible thought crept into Caroline's head: What if it was too good to be true?

She closed her eyes, and took a deep breath, and pushed

the idea away. And then she heard a voice, much closer than the ones next door, say, "Can I come up?"

Caroline blinked to find Aria resting her elbows on the rim of the trampoline.

"Aria?" she asked, sitting up. "What are you doing here?"

"Your mom let me in," she said, pointing to the house. "So, can I join you?"

Caroline nodded, and Aria hopped up onto the platform and nearly fell over. As she fought to keep her balance, Caroline chuckled. "Haven't you ever been on one of these before?"

Aria shook her head and sank down beside her, sitting cross-legged. The force bounced Caroline up and down a little. "It's like Jell-O," said Aria, poking the elastic floor.

"It's a trampoline," said Caroline. "Here, do what I do."

Caroline stretched out, her head in the center of the trampoline, her feet to the edges. Aria did the same thing, going the other way, and they lay there in the almost-dark as stars began to show up overhead.

There was something about the stars — and about Aria — that made Caroline feel safe.

"Three years," she said absently. "That's how long Lily and I have been best friends. Lily wasn't always so . . . the way she is now." Caroline couldn't believe she was making excuses for her.

"When did she change?" asked Aria.

Caroline squinted, making the starlight blur. "When we started sixth grade at Westgate. Maybe it's because of her mom, but Lily decided that she wanted to be queen bee. She said she *had* to be. And she said she wanted me to be with her. No matter what happened — no matter how she was around other people, or *to* other people — she was always on my side. And I was always on hers." Caroline thought of all the things she'd done for Lily. "It got worse when she met Erica. Lily treated her like a pet project. Erica and I never got along great, but the three of us were fine. Everything was fine. Until now."

Aria drew up her knees. She was still wearing her school uniform, but Caroline noticed that her shoelaces were bright pink. "So," said Aria, "what are we going to do?"

"About what?" asked Caroline.

"About you. About this."

"It's not your problem."

"But I'm here to . . ." Aria trailed off. "I want to help," she said.

"How?" asked Caroline.

"We can stand up to her."

Caroline slumped back against the trampoline. "No," she said. "We can't."

"Yes we can," pressed Aria. "And I bet if we do, others will, too."

Aria obviously knew nothing about Westgate. Silence fell over them, and Caroline realized how much she hated being surrounded by it every day. And how nice it was to have Aria there with her, making the quiet feel warm instead of cold. And since the other girl clearly wasn't going to stay out of things — even if Caroline asked her — she broke the silence and said, "Hey, Aria?"

"Yeah, Caroline?"

"Do you want to ride to school together?"

And even though she wasn't looking at her, Caroline could *feel* Aria smile.

"Yeah," Aria said, tucking her hands behind her head. "I'd love that."

chāptēr 12

ARIA

Aria paced back and forth on Caroline's front path the next morning, waiting for her to come out. Caroline had offered to pick her up, but Aria had insisted on meeting her instead, since she didn't really know how to explain that she lived in a tree.

It was a pretty Wednesday, all blue sky and cool breeze, and Aria had a good feeling about the day. Now that Caroline was finally opening up, she could help her move forward. Stand up to Lily and her old group. Make a new start.

Aria glanced beyond the picket fence to the house next door.

She still didn't know what to do about *Lily*.

As if on cue, the front door swung open, and Lily Pierce strode out, her black curls pulled back by a green headband. Aria squinted at the girl's blue smoke, as if by looking hard enough, she could see what Lily needed. How she was supposed to help.

Lily saw Aria standing there, and smiled.

It was a contagious kind of smile, and Aria found herself smiling back. There had to be more to her than met the eye. More than meanness and control. After all, Lily and Caroline had been friends for years.

Lily wasn't always so . . . the way she is now. That's what Caroline had said. The new Lily was the problem. Maybe there was some of the old Lily left in there somewhere. Aria just needed to find it.

Lily walked over, and rested her elbows on the fence.

"Hi, Ari," she said cheerfully. "Whatcha doing here?"

"Waiting for my ride," Aria replied.

Lily gave her a pitying sigh. "Why don't you ride to school with us? Erica and Whitney should be here any second."

"That's okay," said Aria. "I'm going with Caroline."

Lily frowned. "I thought we talked about this," she said coolly.

Aria looked into Lily's eyes. "You used to be best friends, didn't you? What happened?" she asked, even though she already knew. She wanted to hear Lily's side.

Lily tossed her hair. "I outgrew her," she said. "The truth

is, I only stayed friends with her so long because I felt sorry for her."

But her blue smoke tightened around her shoulders when she said it.

"You know, Lily," said Aria simply. "I don't believe you. I think you still care. I think you miss her."

For an instant, Lily's smile faltered. And then it was back, tighter than before. She leaned closer. "Look, I'm trying to help you. Ride to school with us. Sit with us. You'll be one of the most popular girls at Westgate. I'm giving you a chance to be someone."

"I'm already someone," said Aria softly, but Lily either didn't hear, or didn't listen.

"A lot of girls would kill to be friends with me," she said, pursing her lips. "You should accept my offer."

Aria leaned in. "Or what?" she asked, truly curious.

Lily's smile fell. "Or stay with Caroline, and be a total loser." She pulled away. "It's simple. You can be somebody. Or you can be nobody. It's your choice."

Aria's brow crinkled. "Are those my only two options?"

Just then, someone honked a horn. Lily pulled back from the fence and waved to the car, where Erica and Whitney were waiting inside.

"Well?" Lily asked Aria. "Are you coming or not?"

Aria looked from Erica and Whitney in the car to Lily at the fence, and then up at Caroline's house. She shook her head. "Thanks for the offer," she said, "but I'll stay."

Lily rolled her eyes. "Fine," she muttered, turning to go.

"Hey, Lily," said Aria.

"What?" she snapped.

"It doesn't have to be like this," said Aria. "You don't have to be like this."

Lily sneered. "You don't know anything. You're just like Caroline. A *nobody*."

She marched off toward the car, and Aria sighed. "What am I going to do about her?" she asked her shadow, but her shadow didn't seem to have a clue.

A second later, Caroline came storming out of her own house.

"Oh, hey!" said Aria, trying to recover. "You ready to go?"

But Caroline didn't even say good morning, just got into the car and shut her door. Caroline's mom appeared a second later.

"Someone's in a mood," said her mother in a singsong way.

"Is everything okay?" asked Aria.

"I'm not sure," said Caroline's mom as they walked toward the car. "She's been so up and down lately, I can't keep track." Aria had met Mrs. Mason last night, when she'd come by to see Caroline. Caroline's mom seemed very nice, but Aria could tell she didn't know about her daughter's predicament.

Now Aria climbed in beside Caroline. She'd never been in a car before. There were lots of buttons, but she resisted the urge to push them. Instead, she leaned in toward Caroline.

"What's wrong?" she whispered. Caroline didn't answer. Her smoke swirled furiously around her. Aria's spirits fell. She had really thought this was going to be a *good* day.

"Seat belts," instructed Caroline's mom, tapping the strap across her lap. Aria found the pieces, and fit them together. "So, *Aria*," she added once they were on the road, "that's a pretty name."

"Thank you," said Aria, glancing over at Caroline. Caroline didn't look back.

"And you just moved in down the road?"

"Yes, ma'am."

"Which house?"

Aria couldn't exactly say the *tree* house, so she said the blue one, because the tree house was indeed painted blue.

"The blue one?" said Caroline's mom. "I can't think of any blue one besides the one Mrs. Hinkle lives in, and *she* certainly didn't move away. . . ."

"Um," said Aria, who didn't like lying and wasn't very good at it. "It's actually more of a green house. Blue green."

"Ah," said Caroline's mom. "Well, we'll have to have your family over for dinner sometime. Do you have any siblings?"

"No," said Aria. "Just me."

"I bet Caroline *wishes* she were an only child, don't you, sweetheart?"

Caroline made a sound that could either have been a *yes* or a *no*.

"So, Aria, how are you liking Westgate? It's an amazing school. Fabulous athletic program. Do you play sports? Caroline here was thinking about joining the swim team. She's an excellent swimmer . . ."

Caroline's mom went on like that for the rest of the ride to school, filling the car with chatter. Which was fine because Caroline remained silent. When the car stopped, she unfastened her seat belt and stormed out without saying good-bye to her mom.

Or waiting for Aria.

By the time Aria got out of the car, Caroline was halfway to the front doors.

"Hey," she called, jogging after her. "Hey, Caroline, wait up!"

chapter 13

CAROLINE

Caroline had seen *everything*.

She'd been getting ready for school, and for the first time she wasn't dreading it. Because she wasn't going alone. She'd be with Aria. The thought made her feel light. And then, as she was pulling on her shoes, she looked out her bedroom window at the front yard below, and she saw them.

Lily Pierce leaning across the fence talking to Aria. Lily was smiling, not her mean smile but her nice one, the one she only used around her friends. It was like a punch in the stomach. And then Aria leaned in as Lily whispered something in her ear. Lily looked up when she said it. At the bedroom window on the second floor.

At Caroline.

And Caroline had realized in that moment what was happening.

What *must* be happening.

It was all some kind of sick game.

Caroline reached her locker, grabbed her books, and slammed it shut. She hurried down the hall, past the other students, wiping away stray tears.

"Caroline?" came Aria's voice behind her, but she kept walking.

She should have known. The more she thought about it, the more it made sense. The reason Aria was being so nice. The reason she was so intent on spending time with her. The reason she wasn't afraid of making Lily mad.

It was a setup.

Lily was so determined to make her life a nightmare that she'd talked the new girl into pretending to be friends with Caroline. And then what? One day, Lily would snap her fingers, and it would all go away.

"Caroline!" called Aria, catching up.

"Just stay away from me." Caroline stormed into the stairwell.

"What did I do?" asked Aria, following.

Caroline reached the top of the stairs and started toward a door, but Aria blocked her way. "Talk to me," she said, breathless. "Please. I don't understand —"

"I saw you talking to Lily."

"So?" said Aria, looking confused. "She showed up while I was waiting for you."

Caroline shook her head. "I've been trying to figure it out."

"Figure what out?"

"You. Why you're so determined to hang out with me. And I get it now, so just admit it."

Aria stared at her, eyes wide. "Admit what?" she asked, tugging on her blue charm bracelet.

Caroline's chest tightened. "You don't even want to be my friend, do you?"

Aria's eyebrows went up. "Of course I do! Caroline, why would I hang out with you if I didn't want to?"

"Because Lily put you up to this," said Caroline, backing away. "To trick me. She —"

"Lily didn't put me up to anything," insisted Aria. "I promise. I'm —"

"I don't believe you," said Caroline, taking another step back. "This is what you and Erica were writing notes about in class. . . ."

"It's not like that. I'm here to help you."

"You probably were even at their pool party last night —"

"Caroline —"

"So you could all figure out the best moment when you'd switch from being my friend to my enemy and —"

"Caroline," said Aria, exasperated. "You're wrong. I'm not their friend, and I'm not your enemy. I'm your —"

Caroline took another step back. Only there wasn't any more landing, only concrete steps, and Caroline lost her balance, and slipped, and started to fall.

And then something happened.

Something *impossible*.

Aria, who was all the way at the other side of the landing, too far away to catch her, *disappeared*. The ground beneath her flashed a brilliant white, and swallowed her up, and an instant later it spit her out. Now she was right next to Caroline, and her hand closed around Caroline's wrist, catching her before she could fall.

Caroline's heart raced as she stared at Aria, wondering if she was going crazy.

"I've been trying to tell you," said Aria, pulling Caroline safely back onto the landing. "I'm not their friend. And I'm not your enemy. I'm your guardian angel."

chāptēr 14

ARIA

It wasn't exactly how Aria had planned on telling Caroline.

In fact, Aria hadn't *planned* on telling her at all. Or at least, she hadn't thought that far ahead.

But when Caroline had taken that step back, and Aria had used her shadow to catch her, well —

It was kind of hard *not* to tell Caroline after that.

The words had tumbled out, and now that they were there, Aria couldn't take them back.

Caroline's stare was perfectly blank.

Disbelief. Aria could handle that. She braced herself for the onslaught of questions, but the first thing Caroline said, very quietly, was, "So Lily *didn't* put you up to it?"

Aria broke into a smile. "No."

Caroline's brow furrowed as the rest of her questions caught up. "How can you be a guardian angel?" she asked.

"I just am," said Aria. "It's all I've ever been."

"But you don't *look* like a guardian angel. And what do you even *mean*, guardian angel? Like, *literal* guardian angel? Like wings and miracles and halos guardian angel?"

Aria scratched her head. "Um, well, I'm still earning my wings, and I can't really do miracles. . . ."

"What about the thing you just did with the light?" challenged Caroline. "What was that?"

Aria looked down at her shadow and shook her head. "I'm not really sure," she admitted. She'd never moved like that before. She guessed she hadn't *needed* to before. The shadow had appeared when she needed to reach Caroline. "I guess that was a kind of miracle! But I don't have a halo." She patted on top of her hair to be sure.

Caroline kept shaking her head. "You can't expect me to believe this."

"You don't have to," said Aria. "But it doesn't change the fact that it's true. I'm here to —"

The door at the top of the stairs burst open and a handful of sixth graders stormed past them. Caroline and Lily waited for the girls to disappear. And then Caroline's eyes grew larger and she let out a surprised sound.

"Wait. *You're* the one who put the ketchup on Jessabel's gym clothes," she said.

"Technically," said Aria, "Jessabel put the ketchup on *your* gym clothes. I just put your gym clothes in *Jessabel's* locker."

Caroline cracked a smile. "Magic," she whispered, still looking at Aria in wonder. "So have you been, like . . . watching me my whole life?"

Aria shook her head. "I only show up when someone needs my help."

Caroline nodded, her smile fading. "I guess I could use some," she said quietly. Aria could tell it was a hard thing to admit. "So if Lily really *didn't* put you up to this —"

"She *didn't*," insisted Aria.

"Then why were you talking to her?"

Aria sighed, and leaned back against the banister. "She was trying to get me to ditch you. So was Erica. They told me I should sit with them. Hang out with them." She straightened. "But *I stood up to her*. I told her *no*. That I'd rather hang out with you."

Caroline sighed. "Thanks, but you shouldn't have done that. Now Lily is going to make things awful for *you*."

Aria grabbed Caroline's hand and squeezed. "I'm not too worried."

Caroline looked at Aria, dazed. "Hang on. You didn't tell Lily you were a guardian angel, did you?"

Aria smiled. "No way. That should be our secret for now."

Unfortunately, it turned out that Caroline was right about Lily — she *was* going to make things awful. For both of them.

It was gym, and Aria and Caroline were still in the locker room, after everyone else had gone to their next class. They were searching for their uniforms, both of which had mysteriously gone missing from their lockers. There was no doubt it was Lily's handiwork.

"We're going to be late!" cried Caroline.

"Can't we just go to class in these?" asked Aria, gesturing down to her gym clothes. "We can explain what happened."

"No, we can't," said Caroline. "And I can't go back to Ms. Opeline." Aria didn't know who Ms. Opeline was, but Caroline seemed adamant. "Besides, the uniforms have to be here somewhere."

Aria had already offered to summon two new uniforms into existence, but Caroline had refused. "I'm sick of losing my own," she'd said. "I want it back." Caroline still didn't seem *entirely* convinced that Aria was an angel. She kept shooting glances at her as if she was trying to catch sight of Aria's non-existent halo.

"How did she even get into our lockers?" wondered Aria aloud as she stood on a bench.

Caroline sighed and shut the last of the unassigned lockers at the end of the aisle.

"Duct tape," she said. "She put duct tape on the inside of the locks so they wouldn't close all the way."

"Huh," said Aria, hopping down. "That's kind of clever."

"Come on, let's check outside." Caroline pushed the doors open. She scanned the field, the flagpole, the track, the pool . . . and then she looked up.

"Oh no," she said.

"Well at least we found them," said Aria, following Caroline's gaze.

Two plaid skirts rippled in the breeze. Four polo sleeves fluttered. Aria and Caroline's uniforms were hanging from the tallest diving board.

Caroline looked like she might cry. "I'm afraid of heights," she murmured. "Lily knows that. I told her when we first met," she added. "She tried to make me bounce too high on the trampoline, and I freaked out, and she teased me about it, about having a trampoline and not wanting to use it. And I told her that I liked to lie down on it, and watch the sky, and after that, Lily insisted we rename the trampoline an observatory, and said it couldn't be used for jumping, only cloud watching and stargazing." Caroline's hands curled into fists. "She knows I'm afraid of heights, Aria. She did this on purpose."

"It's okay," said Aria softly. "I'm not scared of heights. I'll go get them."

Caroline looked at her, eyes wide. "Are you sure?"

"I'm your guardian angel," said Aria, flashing her a smile. "It's the least I can do."

There was a metal fence around the pool with a gate, but thankfully it wasn't locked. Aria pushed it open, walked across the concrete rim of the pool to the ladder, and looked up at the uniforms draped across the highest diving board.

The highest diving board was, as the name suggested, very high off the ground.

Aria *wasn't* afraid of heights, but the thin ladder and the narrow board did make her a *little* nervous. It didn't help that the whole structure groaned as she started to climb. Nor did it help that Aria knew she couldn't fly (she had tried once, and it hadn't gone very well).

But Caroline was clearly upset, and Aria could help. And in truth, she kind of wanted to impress Caroline. So up she went.

When Aria finally reached the top and stepped out onto the board, she looked down. She could see the crisp blue water glittering in the sunlight, and Caroline standing there, looking much smaller than Aria expected. Caroline shielded her eyes against the sun and Aria waved. The board wobbled faintly under her feet.

"Be careful!" Caroline called up.

And Aria was. But as she started to gather up the uniforms, one of the sleeves got caught on the corner of the diving board. She tugged it free, and it came loose faster than she thought it would.

"Uh-oh," said Aria as she stumbled back . . .

And over the side of the board . . .

And down toward the pool.

She'd fallen once before, from a much higher place (the top of a seven-story apartment building), and her shadow had caught her. But this wasn't *that* high and the world beneath was water instead of sidewalk, so Aria wasn't terribly surprised when she just kept falling toward the water, and hit it with a giant splash that stung her skin and knocked the air out of her lungs.

Aria had never been underwater before.

Overhead, she could see the uniforms floating.

There was only one problem. A problem Aria hadn't thought of until she was there in the cool blue pool, looking up.

She didn't know how to swim.

chapter 15

CAROLINE

Caroline had been standing at the edge of the pool, looking up at Aria, trying to decide if she believed the girl was *actually* a guardian angel.

She had never really believed in things like magic or angels. She believed in science, in the stars in the sky, and the world she could see with her own eyes. But she could see Aria, too, so she knew she was real, and she'd seen her disappear and reappear with her own eyes, even if she didn't understand how.

And really, when she thought about it, the universe was so big that even scientists didn't understand *everything* about it. In fact, one of her favorite things about outer space was that, no matter how much they found, no matter how much they thought they knew, there were more still things to be discovered. More mysteries to be solved.

Maybe Aria was one of those mysteries.

Maybe . . .

Caroline's thoughts were interrupted by a sound — a voice saying "uh-oh" — and she looked up just in time to see a small redheaded shape plummeting down toward the pool.

Aria landed with a splash, followed a second later by the uniforms, which floated down and settled on top of the water. Caroline groaned and waited for Aria to bob back to the surface.

But Aria didn't come up.

Caroline could *see* her there, under the water, and it didn't occur to her at first that Aria might need help, because if she really was a guardian angel, surely she didn't need saving.

And then Caroline realized she didn't know anything about guardian angels, because she'd never met one before, let alone had her own, and it appeared that *this* guardian angel or girl or whatever she was couldn't swim.

And Caroline could.

She pulled off her shoes and socks, took a deep breath, and dove into the water, the way she had a hundred times at Lily's pool. She swam out to the deep end, and then down until she reached Aria.

Aria didn't seem very concerned — she was just kind of hovering there, dragging her arms and legs back and forth —

and when she saw Caroline, she actually *smiled*. And then she tried to say something, and a stream of bubbles came spilling out, followed by a lot of gasping and coughing. Caroline hooked her hands under Aria's arms and dragged her toward the surface, and a couple seconds later they both broke through the water.

Caroline hauled a spluttering Aria up beside her. She grabbed the uniforms floating on the surface and dragged two sets of clothes and one maybe-guardian-angel to the edge of the pool.

"Why didn't you come up for air?" Caroline snapped as they clung to the concrete rim. "You weren't even *trying* to swim."

"I don't know how," said Aria simply.

"Why would you offer to go up on the diving board if you don't know how to swim?"

"I didn't *know* I didn't know how to swim. I've never tried before. And I didn't expect to fall in."

"You could have drowned!"

"Oh," said Aria, thinking. "No, I don't think so."

Caroline let out an exasperated sound, and splashed water at her. And then despite herself, she laughed. Aria started laughing, too.

They were cut off sharply by a stern voice.

"What on *earth* are you girls doing?"

The laugh died in Caroline's throat as she looked up to see Mr. Cahill looming over them. She opened her mouth to explain, and so did Aria, but Mr. Cahill didn't give them a chance.

"Get out of the water," he snapped. "*Now.*"

Caroline and Aria sat in the headmistress's office, their hair still damp from the pool. Ms. Opeline had found them some dry clothes but the girls both looked pretty ragged. *Hardly the image of excellence and grace on the cover of the Westgate pamphlets*, thought Caroline.

Caroline sat perfectly still and stared straight ahead at the nametag on the headmistress's desk. When Aria noticed the sign, her eyes widened.

"Ms. Pierce?" she said aloud. "As in *Lily* Pierce?"

Caroline nodded. "The headmistress is her mom."

"Why didn't you tell me?" asked Aria.

"I didn't think it mattered."

Aria opened her mouth to say something more, but then the door opened, and Mr. Cahill walked in, followed by the headmistress.

Caroline had always been terrified of Ms. Pierce. She was dressed in a white blouse and black pants, and like Lily, she had perfect black hair and perfect teeth. But unlike Lily, Ms. Pierce never smiled. She took a seat, and rapped her manicured nails on the table as she considered them.

"I found the girls in the pool," said Mr. Cahill. "I don't know what possessed them to go in, but it wasn't even gym period, which means they were breaking half a dozen school rules, from swimming without supervision to skipping class to —"

"All right, Mr. Cahill," cut in Ms. Pierce. "I'll handle it from here. You can go back to the office."

The bespectacled man nodded and ducked out, mumbling ". . . kids these days . . ." as he went.

"So," said Ms. Pierce, "you two decided to go for a swim? During class?"

"I fell in," explained Aria. "Caroline dove in to save me."

"Is that true?" asked Ms. Pierce with a raised black brow. Caroline nodded. "But what were you doing out by the pool in the first place?" she pressed.

"Trying to get our uniforms back," said Aria. "Someone hung them from the diving board."

Ms. Pierce frowned and sat forward. "Do you know who?"

Aria started to speak, but Caroline cut her off. "No," she said. "It was just a stupid prank."

"Caroline Mason," said Ms. Pierce sternly. "If you know who did this, you need to *tell* me. Lying is a serious offense at Westgate." When Caroline said nothing, Ms. Pierce looked back at Aria. "Do *you* know who did it?"

Aria squirmed in her seat. She looked to Caroline, clearly confused, but finally shook her head.

"I can't hear you," pressed Ms. Pierce.

"No," said Aria, still looking at Caroline. "I don't know for sure who did it."

Someone knocked on the door, and a teacher stuck her head in. Ms. Pierce got up. "I'll be right back. Stay here."

The moment she was gone, Aria spun on Caroline.

"Why are you covering for her?" she hissed. "You *know* who put the clothes up there, Caroline."

"So?"

"So why won't you tell Ms. Pierce?" pressed Aria. "Lily's her daughter, so *tell her*. Tell her Lily is tormenting you. Tell her about the uniforms, and the locker, and . . ." Aria waved her hands emphatically. "Everything else," she said. "This is your chance."

Caroline looked down at her lap. It wasn't like she hadn't thought about it. It wasn't like she didn't want to. But she couldn't. If she did, it would all be over. There would be no going back. "No."

Aria looked at her, wide-eyed. "Why not?"

"If I tell on Lily, she'll never forgive me. She'll never . . ."

"Never what?"

Take me back, Caroline wanted to say.

"Caroline," said Aria. "Talk to me. I'm here to help, remember?"

Caroline looked up as it dawned on her. If Aria really was a guardian angel, then she *was* there to help. Aria could make things right. She straightened in her chair, and swallowed. "If you really are my guardian angel —"

"I am."

"— and you really do want to help me —"

"I do."

"Then help me get my old friends back."

chapter 16

ARIA

Aria stared at Caroline, dumbfounded.

After everything Lily had put her through, Caroline still wanted to be her friend?

Aria was at a loss. She *was* there to help, and Caroline had told her how she wanted her to help, but if this was how she was *supposed* to help, why did it feel so wrong?

"Well?" pressed Caroline.

Aria started to speak, but was saved by Ms. Pierce striding back in.

"Where were we?" she asked, taking her seat. "Ah, that's right. I'm giving you both Saturday school."

Aria's spirits rose at the prospect of something new but Caroline seemed upset.

"But it was an accident!" she cried.

"I'm sure it was, Miss Mason, but since you won't tell me who *is* responsible . . ." The headmistress paused again, waiting to see if Caroline had changed her mind, but she obviously hadn't. ". . . I have no choice. Rules were broken. There must be consequences. And if either of you decides to come back and tell me who *did* put those uniforms on the diving board, they'll be joining you on Saturday. In the meantime, I'll be notifying your parents."

Parents, thought Aria, biting her lip. She wasn't sure how *that* would go. She could magic up a clean school polo, or some pillows for the tree house. She didn't think she could magic up a mother and father.

"Miss Blue, there's no number listed on your information sheet," said Ms. Pierce, producing a crisp piece of paper. "In fact, there's nothing listed but a name. We must have had a technical malfunction. If you could fill out the rest . . ." She handed the paper to Aria, who stared down at the blank lines marked with things like *parents* and *address* and *home phone*. Her chest tightened a little, that strange dull sadness that floated up whenever she was reminded that she had nothing more than a name on a bracelet. And then she brushed it away, and filled in the blanks.

Her parents became *John* and *Kendall Blue* (she liked the names).

Her address — which in her head was *the blue-green tree house* — became *23 Tree House Lane*.

As for the phone number, Aria picked ten numbers — there were ten spots —at random, and then did her best to imagine a phone in her tree house to go with them.

The whole time she was writing, Caroline stared at the floor and listened to Ms. Pierce lecture her on the importance of honesty. "I have to say, I'm disappointed in you, Caroline. Integrity is an important part of Westgate's code. I depend on girls like you and Lily to be models of behavior."

A noise — somewhere between a sigh and a scoff — escaped through Aria's nose. Caroline shot her a look. Ms. Pierce didn't seem to notice.

"A Westgate girl," she continued, "does not lie, even to protect her friends."

"But why would Caroline's *friends* do something like this?" asked Aria pointedly. "Hanging our clothes up there was *mean*."

Ms. Pierce folded her hands, considering. "That's true. But why else would you protect them?"

"I'm not protecting anyone!" said Caroline. "I don't know who did it."

Ms. Pierce sighed, disappointed. "Very well. You two had best be getting to class, while there's still class left."

Caroline and Aria got to their feet and shuffled out. At the door, Aria paused and looked back. Ms. Pierce didn't seem like a very happy person. Aria thought maybe a bit of color would cheer her up. It certainly couldn't hurt, so she turned the little black bows on Ms. Pierce's black heels a sunny yellow.

"Is there something you want to say?" asked the headmistress, looking up. Aria only smiled, and shook her head, and followed Caroline out.

As soon as they were in the hallway, Caroline slumped against the wall. Aria touched her shoulder.

"So, will you help me?" asked Caroline.

Aria sighed. And whether she willed the bell overhead to ring, or it was simply time for lunch, the sound saved her from answering.

"Let's get some food," she said, hurrying away before Caroline could do anything but nod and follow.

But Caroline wouldn't let it go.

The first thing out of her mouth after they got their trays was, "Well? Are you going to help me?"

To which Aria said, "I'm starving." Even though she wasn't.

When they were standing in line, Caroline asked the question again. To which Aria said, "Should I get applesauce, or an orange?"

But once they sat down, there was no escape.

"Aria, are you going to help me get my friends back or not?"

Aria looked up, holding Caroline's gaze through the ring of blue smoke.

"No," she said.

Caroline frowned. "What do you mean, no?"

Aria hadn't used the word very often. She didn't even realize she was going to use it until it tumbled out. "No," she said again, "I can't do that. Or, I guess, I won't."

"I don't understand."

Aria thought about how to explain, that even though Caroline wanted to get her old friends back, it wasn't what she *needed*. There was a difference.

Yes, Aria could technically help Caroline get her friends back, but she knew in her bones and her shadow and the beginnings of her wings that it wouldn't help. It wouldn't make the blue smoke go away and it wouldn't make Caroline any happier. Going back wouldn't fix things. She had to go *forward*.

Aria was about to say this to Caroline, but Caroline didn't give her a chance.

"I thought you were supposed to be on my side," she said.

"I *am* on your side," insisted Aria.

"No, you're not." Caroline looked like she was about to cry. "You act like you're my friend, you say you're here to help me but you won't give me the only thing I want." She pushed up from the table. "What kind of a guardian angel are you?"

Aria felt like she'd been struck. "Caroline, listen . . ." she started, but the other girl was already storming away. Aria sighed. This could have been such a good day.

Now, sitting at the table by herself, the eyes of the other girls in the cafeteria turning toward her, Aria discovered how it felt to be abandoned. She could see her reflection in the waxy apple on her tray, distorted, but there. She poked her fingernail into the apple, drawing two small crescents just above the shoulders. Like wings.

What kind of guardian angel are you?

The single feather on her charm bracelet jingled faintly as she set the apple down, and stood up.

She was carrying the lunch trays to the return station when she heard Erica say, "Aw, did you two have a fight?"

Aria looked up to see Erica, Whitney, and Lily standing there.

"I told you not to waste your time on her," said Lily. "She's hopeless."

"She's a loser," added Whitney, a little halfheartedly.

Aria had had *enough*. "Why?" she asked Whitney. "Because she stood up for you?"

Whitney frowned. "What are you talking about?"

Aria felt her face get hot. "You were supposed to be Lily's victim this year. But Caroline stood up for you. That's why she is where she is, and you are where you are. Think about that the next time you decide to call her names."

Whitney looked at Lily and Erica, uncertainly. "Is . . . is that true?"

Erica rolled her eyes. "Whatever, it doesn't matter, Whit. Don't get worked up."

"You're one of us now," said Lily. "Isn't that what you want?"

Aria looked at Whitney. Whitney looked at the ground. Lily put her hand on Whitney's shoulder, and leaned in. "Do you want to go back to being a nobody?" she whispered in the girl's ear.

Whitney took a deep breath. Then she put on her best smile, looked at Aria, and said, "Caroline Mason is a nobody. I'm not."

Aria's heart sank. She remembered what Caroline had said that night on the trampoline. *Everyone just wants to belong.*

"You should have taken my advice," chided Lily.

Why? Aria wanted to ask. *Why are you doing this?*

"She didn't turn you in, you know," Aria told Lily. "After what you did with our uniforms. She wouldn't."

Lily shrugged, even though her blue smoke swirled violently around her shoulders.

"I feel sorry for her," said Aria.

"Because she's an outcast?" jabbed Erica.

"No." Aria shook her head. "Because even after all you've done to her, she'd come running back to you. I feel sorry for her," she said, "because she can't see that none of you are worth it."

And with that, Aria dumped the trays, and went to find Caroline.

chapter 17

CAROLINE

Caroline sat in the stairwell, her knees drawn up. She didn't know how long she'd been sitting there — it was still lunch — but she was about to drag herself to her feet when she felt her cell phone buzz in her backpack. She frowned and dug it out. Caroline's cell phone hadn't buzzed with a text — at least one that wasn't from her mom or sister — in weeks.

The message was from Lily.

I miss you, it said. *Come over after school. Pool party. Like old times.*

Her chest started to ache. Did Lily really want her back? Had she gotten bored of tormenting Caroline? Or was this just another prank?

I'm not falling for it, she texted back.

But a second later, the phone buzzed again. *Come on, Car.* Caroline could picture Lily draping her arm around her shoulders, resting her black curls against Caroline's straight blond hair. *Please come. We can talk.*

Caroline read the texts once, then twice, then a dozen more times before the stairwell door swung open. Without looking up, she knew it was Aria. Maybe it was the way the overhead light brightened slightly, or the faint jingle of the girl's charm bracelet.

"Look," said Aria, sitting down beside her. "I'm trying to understand where you're coming from."

Caroline shook her head. Aria *couldn't* understand. Had she ever been a person before she was an angel? Had she ever had best friends? The kind you love even when you don't like them? The kind you miss even when they make you miserable? "I only want things to go back to the way they were."

"Do you think they can?" asked Aria.

Caroline's stomach tightened.

"Do you think they *should*?" pressed Aria. "Look at science. Things move forward. Not back."

"I wish you would just help me," said Caroline.

"I'm *trying*," said Aria. "But it seems to me like Lily Pierce is a bully. The girls who hang out with her are bullies."

"I'd rather be a bully than a nobody," mumbled Caroline.

"You act like those are the only two options," said Aria, sounding exasperated. "Like there's nothing in between. But there are so many things between, Caroline. There's nice. And funny. Kind. Smart. Strange. Cool . . . And there are girls at this school who are those things. They may not be the most *popular*, but they're not nobodies."

Caroline swallowed hard. "It doesn't matter. Even if I wanted to make new friends, all the other girls ignore me."

Aria shook her head. "No," she said. "A few of them ignore you. *You're* ignoring everyone else. You act like Lily is the only person at Westgate worth being friends *with*. But this school is full of other people. I can help you find them."

Caroline's eyes burned. She didn't want to start over. She just wanted to go back. Back to the moment when she tried to stop Lily from pranking Whitney. She would do everything differently.

Suddenly, Aria's face brightened. "Ah!" she said, "Why didn't I think of this before?"

"Think of what?"

"We'll let my shadow decide!"

Caroline had no idea what Aria was talking about. "How is your shadow supposed to help?"

"Because it's not *just* a shadow," explained Aria. "It's also a door."

"A door . . ." echoed Caroline, confused.

Aria nodded. "One that takes me wherever I'm supposed to be. Which means it will take *you* wherever you're supposed to be. So if we go through, and it takes us to Lily, I'll help you get your old friends back." Caroline's spirits lifted. "But," added Aria, "you have to promise me that if it takes us somewhere else, you'll let me help you *my* way."

Caroline hesitated. She thought of Lily's texts and stared down at the shadow beneath Aria's feet. "Does it ever make the wrong choice?" she asked.

Aria shook her head. "No."

Caroline took a deep breath. "Okay," she said. "Deal."

Aria broke into a grin, and hopped up. "Let's go."

"We can't go *now*," said Caroline. "Lunch is almost over."

"We won't be gone long," Aria assured her. And then she looked down and tapped her foot a few times. Her shadow turned on like a light. The same light that had surrounded Aria when Caroline almost fell down the stairs.

Caroline gasped. If she didn't believe before, she was starting to now. . . .

Aria held out her hand. "Come on."

Caroline stood up and surveyed the pool of light on the ground. She took Aria's hand, squeezed her eyes shut, and stepped through.

A second later, Caroline opened her eyes. All she saw were trees, and fences, and sky. She wasn't at school. The ground wobbled under her feet, and when she looked down, she saw that they were standing on the trampoline in her backyard.

Caroline's heart sank. She realized how badly she'd wanted the shadow door to take them to Lily. But why had it taken them *here*?

"I don't understand," she said, turning on Aria. "What does this mean?"

Aria bounced a little on her toes, considering the trampoline. "I'm not sure."

Caroline sighed. "This doesn't tell me anything."

"Well," said Aria, "It didn't take you to Lily..." Caroline's throat tightened. She felt Aria's hand on her shoulder. "It's for the best."

Caroline nodded numbly. "We'd better get back to school."

Aria snapped her fingers, and the light blossomed at their feet. An instant later they were back in the stairwell, as if nothing had happened. The light went out, and Aria's shadow was nothing more than an ordinary stretch of darkness on the floor.

"Are you all right?" asked Aria.

"A deal's a deal," said Caroline, hollowly.

The bell rang overhead, and Aria turned toward the door. When Caroline didn't follow, she looked back. "Are you coming? It's time for science."

"You go ahead," said Caroline. "I'll catch up in a second."

She waited for Aria to leave, and then she dug her cell phone from her bag and read Lily's texts one last time.

Come on, Car.

Maybe Aria had lied about the shadow taking her where she *needed* to go. Maybe it only went where Aria *wanted*. After all, she didn't want Lily and Caroline to be friends again. She didn't understand.

Please come.

Caroline chewed her lip, and then typed one word — *OK* — and hit send.

Caroline's bikini was blue and green and white.

Lily had picked it out for her over the summer. She and Lily and Erica had spent a whole day at the mall, trying on bikinis and one-pieces.

"Car!" Lily had cried when Caroline tried on this bikini. "You're like summer on a stick! It has to be that one! Look," she said, holding up her own choice, blue and white, "we match!"

Erica had picked out an orange one-piece, but when she saw theirs, she shoved it back onto the rack and chose a green one instead. Lily had smiled and patted Erica's hair. "Perfect. Now we *all* match."

Caroline checked herself in the mirror now. For an instant, she wondered if she *shouldn't* head over to Lily's. But then she pulled on a pair of shorts, slung a towel over her shoulder, and went downstairs. Her mom, dad, and Megan were in the kitchen.

"Where do you think you're going?" asked her mom, who was *not* happy about the Saturday school news. "Haven't you had enough swimming for one day?"

"Oh, what did Car do now?" asked Megan.

"She got herself a weekend detention after skipping class to go for a swim."

"It wasn't like that," said Caroline.

"Nicely done, little sis!" said Megan in a rare display of affection.

"Megan, don't encourage her," said her dad. But then he

smiled. "Not that Westgate doesn't need to loosen up a little."

"Was it Aria's idea?" asked her mom.

"No," Caroline tried to explain for the zillionth time, "it wasn't *anybody's* idea. She fell in; I had to go get her because she can't swim."

Oh yeah, and she's also apparently my guardian angel.

Caroline thought it best not to mention that part.

"That's not nearly as cool," said Megan, pulling out her phone.

"Yeah, well, it's the only reason your sister isn't *grounded for life*," said Caroline's mom.

"So can I go or not?" asked Caroline.

"Where are you going?" asked her dad.

"Lily's."

Her mom's face broke into a smile. "I'm so glad you two are making up," she said. "Is Aria going with you?"

Caroline shook her head. Of course she hadn't told Aria what she was doing.

"Have fun," said her dad.

"Be home by eight," added her mom.

Caroline walked across the lawn, and up Lily's front steps. She could hear music and laughter and splashing in the backyard, sounds of summer, of good days. She closed her eyes, took a deep breath, and rang the bell.

No one answered.

She rang the bell again.

Again, nothing.

Caroline's heart started to race, but she told herself it was fine. They probably couldn't hear her, with the music turned up. She went around to the back fence door, the one that led straight to the backyard, and pulled on it.

It was locked.

Caroline hesitated. She could still hear the music, and the slosh of water, but the chatter had stopped.

She was about to knock.

And then she heard the giggle.

It wasn't loud, but soft and stifled, as if someone had put their hand over their mouth. It was coming from right on the other side of the door. Lily and Erica and Whitney were there. And they were hiding from her.

Caroline was standing in Lily's yard in a blue and green and white bikini.

And she felt like an idiot.

Because of course things weren't going back to the way they were before. They were never going back. Lily wasn't her best friend anymore.

She didn't miss her.

She just wanted another chance to humiliate her.

And Caroline had fallen for it, because she hadn't wanted to believe it was really over.

It took all of her strength not to start crying right there. She turned and padded back across the lawn toward her house, tears streaming silently down her face. But halfway there, she slowed, and stopped.

She couldn't go home. Not yet. Her family had just watched her leave, and if she came back now, she'd have to tell them *why*.

But she couldn't just stand there either, so she crossed the street to a giant tree in her neighbor's front yard. And when she was on the far side of the tree, hidden from view, she sank down among the roots and sobbed.

A few moments later, she felt arms fold around her, and with them a strange, familiar comfort.

Aria said nothing, not "I told you so" or "you should have known" or "how could you be so stupid?" Instead she just sat there with her arms wrapped around Caroline's shoulders, and let her cry.

chapter 18

ARIA

Aria had seen it all.

She'd had a bad feeling something was going to happen — Caroline had been quiet all afternoon, her smoke thickening around her. So after school, Aria had sat at the windowsill of the tree house, watching, willing Caroline not to do it, and knowing that she couldn't stop her. That was the problem with being a guardian angel. You were there to help someone, but they had to *want* that help. They had to be ready for it. And apparently Caroline Mason wasn't quite ready for it yet.

It was still hard to watch.

Now, Caroline buried her face in Aria's shoulder. "I'm so stupid," she whispered. Her voice hitched from crying.

"No, you're not," said Aria, hugging her tighter.

"All I wanted was to get my life back." *Hitch.* "All I had was that. I don't know how" — *hitch* — "to move on."

"It's going to be okay," Aria whispered into Caroline's hair. Not "it's okay," because it wasn't yet. But it would be.

"How do you know?" asked Caroline, pulling back.

"Because I'm here to make sure of it," said Aria honestly. "Caroline, I wouldn't be here if I *couldn't* help you. And I'm not going anywhere until I have, okay?"

Caroline pulled the towel around her, and used a corner to wipe her eyes. "Okay," she said quietly. She leaned back against the tree and sniffled, and the two sat there for a few minutes like that, wrapped in Caroline's smoke and Aria's comfort.

"Where did you come from?" asked Caroline, breaking the quiet.

Aria's brows went up. She wasn't sure how to answer that. "You mean like, in the beginning?"

Caroline let out a small, tired laugh. "No, I mean, just now."

"Oh." Aria looked up. "There."

"The sky?" asked Caroline.

Aria smiled. "No, silly. The tree house."

Caroline seemed to notice it for the first time. "Oh."

"Come on," said Aria, tugging the girl to her feet. "I'll show you."

Aria led Caroline past a small sign that read *23 Tree House Lane* — she was quite pleased with that addition — and to the rope ladder. Caroline hesitated, and Aria remembered her fear of heights.

"How can you love the sky and the stars and be afraid of heights?" Aria asked. "Isn't space the highest thing there is?"

"It's different," said Caroline, looking up through the tree limbs. "Space is so high up I don't really think of it as high. Just far away." She wrapped her fingers around the rope ladder. "In space, there's no gravity. That's what I'm afraid of. Falling."

"I won't let you fall," said Aria.

Caroline looked at her, for the first time without doubt, and said, "I know."

And then slowly she started to climb. Aria waited until she was at the top, and then followed her up. Inside the tree house, Caroline got to her feet (a little shakily), then broke into a smile.

"You okay?" Aria asked.

"Still in one piece," Caroline said. And then her eyes widened. "Whoa," she said, looking around. "This is where you live?"

Aria nodded. "For now."

"So this guardian angel thing," said Caroline, "it doesn't come with a house, or a family, or a fake identity, like if you were a spy?"

"No," said Aria, picking at the hem of her skirt. "Just me."

"That's got to be hard."

Aria shrugged.

Caroline noticed the picture of herself and Lily tacked to the wall. She traced her fingers along the blue lines that wrapped around them.

"What's that?" she asked.

"Smoke," said Aria. "You look at you and just see you," she explained. "When *I* look at you, I see blue smoke around you. It's how I found you. How I knew you were the one I was supposed to help."

Caroline's hand fell away as she turned back to Aria. "So what are we going to do about Lily?"

"Nothing," said Aria.

Caroline frowned. "What do you mean? There has to be a way to get revenge."

Aria understood the urge. She'd certainly been tempted to pull a few magical pranks, but bullying bullies didn't seem like the right answer.

"You told me I needed to stand up for myself," Caroline pointed out.

"There's a difference between standing up for yourself and getting even. Besides, this isn't about fighting back. It's about moving on. Are you really ready to move on?" pressed Aria. "To make new friends? Because I can help you," she said. "If you're willing to let me."

Caroline swallowed. And then she nodded. "Okay," she said. "I'm ready."

And as she said it, Caroline's smoke finally started to thin.

Aria and Caroline sat in the tree house until dark, stretched out on the floor, watching the sunset through the branches, and talking.

And the longer they talked, the more Aria became convinced that Caroline — not the version of her who had followed Lily's orders, or the version who'd been lost in space the last few weeks, but Caroline as she was under all of that — was great. She was funny and she was smart, and full of random facts like how far they were from the moon, and why it was so bright, and what the constellations were called. Aria loved learning all this. It made the world seem even more magical.

"Hey, Aria?" said Caroline when it was dark and they could see the stars.

"Yeah, Caroline?"

"I think I know why your shadow took me to the trampoline today."

"Why's that?"

"Well, I go out there to look at stars. It's always been the place I feel most like *me*," she said. "Lily and I were on the trampoline when she told me that it was more important to be popular than be myself. And I believed her."

"And now?" asked Aria in the dark.

"Now I want people to like me for *me*. Do you think that's possible?"

Aria smiled. "Absolutely."

When it was almost 8:00 p.m., Aria walked Caroline home.

"See you in the morning?" asked Aria when they reached her door.

"Yeah," said Caroline. "It'll be a fresh start. Caroline 2.0."

Aria cocked her head. "I don't know what that means."

Caroline smiled. "It's like, when you have a computer, and you update the software. Same person, new version."

Aria thought about it a long moment. "Yes!" she announced. "Like that."

She wondered, as she walked away, if she was Aria 2.0, too.

Aria found her feet carrying her across the lawn, and through the white picket fence to the Pierces's house. She took a deep breath, and made herself invisible before approaching the kitchen window.

Erica and Whitney and Lily were standing around the counter, their hair wet from the pool. But Lily didn't seem happy. Her hand went to her collar, as if reaching for a necklace. Weird. Aria had seen Caroline do the exact same thing.

"Come on," said Erica, "you have to admit it was funny."

"That's not the point," snapped Lily. "You shouldn't have used my phone."

"Well, I couldn't exactly use *my* phone. Caroline would never have come. She's not *that* stupid."

"I still can't believe she fell for it," chimed in Whitney. There was a new meanness in her voice. As if she was trying to prove that she fit in.

"Yeah, well, she did," said Lily, sounding put out.

"You're no fun today," said Erica, resting her head on Lily's shoulder. Lily shrugged her off.

"Hey," said Erica, scrambling. "What are we wearing to the dance next week?"

"I don't care," said Lily. "I have a headache. And homework. I'll see you tomorrow."

The two girls stared at her, clearly shocked by her cold tone.

"Are you mad?" asked Whitney with a pout.

Lily mustered up a smile that Aria could tell was fake. "No," she said. "Of course not."

But as soon as Erica and Whitney were gone, Lily slumped down at the kitchen table, her smoke swirling darkly around her shoulders. She looked miserable. And lonely.

Aria didn't get it.

Why was Lily tormenting Caroline? And if she didn't want to do it anymore, why didn't she simply tell the other girls to stop? What was she afraid of?

Aria remembered Caroline's words.

I'd rather be a bully than a nobody.

Was Lily scared of losing her place at the top?

Aria was about to leave when Lily dug her hand in her pocket and pulled out a necklace. She held it up to the light, and Aria saw a silver pendant on the end of a chain. It looked like half of a circle. Lily stared at it for several long moments, then put it back in her pocket.

chāpter 19

CAROLINE

Caroline was halfway to her bedroom when she heard her sister's voice.

"Hey, Car, get in here."

Considering Megan spent most of her life keeping Caroline *out* of her room, the order made her nervous. She hovered on the threshold, racking her brain. Had she borrowed anything? Broken anything?

"Sit," said Megan, pointing to her bed. "I'll braid your hair."

Growing up, Megan played with Caroline's hair all the time. But it had been years since she'd offered to do it. Still, as Caroline climbed onto her sister's bed and Megan drew the brush through her hair, Caroline began to feel sleepy and safe.

"Talk to me," said Megan.

"Why?" asked Caroline.

"Because I'm your big sister. Because you used to ramble in my ear about every little thing in your life. Because I know something's up with you and Lily, and I can tell you didn't go swimming." Caroline looked down at her lap. "What's going on with you?" asked Megan. There was no accusation, no jab in her tone. It was the closest thing she had come to sounding concerned.

"We're not friends anymore," said Caroline. It hurt her throat to say it. "We haven't been for a while."

Megan set aside the brush, and moved to face her sister. "I know it hurts. I know it feels awful and huge and like it will never really get better. But it will."

"How do you know?" asked Caroline quietly.

"Because it's the way life works. I wish I could tell you that every friendship lasts forever, but it doesn't. People change. Sometimes for the better, sometimes for the worse." Megan brought her hand to rest on Caroline's head. "The trick is remembering who *you* are. But I'm sorry things have been hard, Car."

Caroline nodded, and wrapped her arms around her sister. "Thanks, Megan."

"No problem," she said. "Now get out of my room."

· · ·

"I'm not ready," said Caroline the next morning.

She'd gone to bed feeling ready and woken up feeling sick. It was one thing to *say* you were ready in the safety of a tree house at night, and another to *be* ready surrounded by girls you were pretty sure wanted nothing to do with you.

"You are," insisted Aria. They were in gym class, passing a soccer ball back and forth on the field.

"I can't do this."

"Yes," said Aria. "You can. It's easy. We're passing a soccer ball, they're passing a soccer ball, everyone's passing soccer balls. You have something in common already! Let's go see if we can join another group."

Caroline groaned. Aria made it sound so easy. Like it was the first day of school. Like the whole grade didn't hate her, or at least fear Lily's wrath enough to pretend they did. Caroline never used to be shy, but now her nerves rattled in her chest.

"When people think about you," said Aria, "they think about you and Lily. You have to get them to see who *you* are outside of her."

"But how? No one will even talk to me."

"Have you talked to *them*?" asked Aria.

Caroline opened and closed her mouth, but said nothing.

Aria sighed and kicked the ball back to her. "What are you afraid of, Caroline? That they'll say no?"

"That's exactly what I'm afraid of." Caroline kicked the ball back hard. "And then I'll look even more pathetic."

"Did it ever occur to you," said Aria, stopping the ball, "that not everyone here cares about your fight with Lily? That even though it feels really big to you, maybe it's not the center of *their* universe?" Aria picked the ball up. "Maybe they're not all talking about you behind your back. Maybe some of them are even waiting for *you* to make an effort."

Caroline looked over at the other groups of girls laughing and chatting and passing the ball. She wanted to believe Aria, but . . .

"You don't believe me, do you?" asked Aria. She crinkled her brow, thinking. And then she broke into a smile, and looked around. "Come on," she said, dropping the ball back to the grass. "I have an idea."

Caroline followed Aria off the field, and over the track, and around the corner of the building. "I don't know if this will work," Aria said.

"If what will work?"

"Give me your hand."

"Why?" asked Caroline, suspicious.

"Trust me," said Aria, and Caroline did. She took Aria's hand. "Now, don't freak out."

"What would I freak out abou —" But the words fell away as Caroline saw their hands, followed by the rest of them, *disappear.*

"Hey, it worked," came Aria's voice, even though Caroline couldn't see Aria. Or herself.

"What did you do?" whispered Caroline, her pulse racing. Were they *invisible*?

"Come on," said Aria, and Caroline could feel herself being pulled back toward the soccer field. "I want you to hear what people are saying."

It was kind of cool to be invisible — to be *actually, magically* invisible, and not just *feel* invisible and ignored. But Caroline also had a bad feeling about this. As they wove through the groups of girls, she braced herself for gossip, expecting to hear her name on everyone's tongues.

But to Caroline's surprise, no one was talking about her. Most of the girls were talking about their weekend plans, or the upcoming dance with Eastgate, or how eager they were for gym to be over.

And then, finally, she heard her name mentioned. Not by Lily or her group (Lily seemed off today, quieter than usual) but by a girl named Ginny. She had sun-streaked hair and a band of freckles across her nose, and Caroline didn't know much about her except that she was on a local swim team.

"I'm just saying," Ginny was rambling to her friend, a dark-haired girl named Elle, "that I think Caroline Mason seems pretty cool."

"Drama," said Elle. Caroline cringed. "Way too much drama. And it's not worth wading into it, not with Lily Pierce in the mix."

Ginny scoffed. "Like I care what Lily thinks."

"Don't let *her* hear you say that. . . ."

Caroline was so shocked — by the fact that someone thought she was cool, and the fact that they weren't afraid of Lily — that she didn't even notice that the bell had rung until Aria was dragging her toward the lockers.

Caroline asked Aria if they could stay invisible for the rest of the day, but Aria said no. Aria also said Caroline had to try sitting at a new table at lunch. No more Table 12.

Now Caroline stood in the cafeteria, her heart hammering in her chest. "Couldn't you just summon up some friends for me?" she asked Aria, only half joking.

"No," said Aria, handing her a tray.

Some guardian angel, thought Caroline, staring out at the sea of tables that waited past the checkout. "This isn't going to work," she said again.

"Of course it is," said Aria, setting a vanilla pudding cup on her tray. "Eleven tables. Infinite opportunities for friendship."

"Infinite opportunities for embarrassment," mumbled Caroline. "You act like I can just *magically* make new friends."

"It's not magic," insisted Aria. "The problem is you've never looked beyond your group. Lucky for you, there are tons of girls at this school worth being friends with." Aria looked around the lunchroom. "You see the two girls at Table Eight?" she said. "Jasmine and Nora? They run a music blog. Renée and Amanda at Table Two want to be in the World Cup someday, whatever that is. The girls at Table Six are all in drama or dance, and half the girls at Table Four are in the science club, and the girls at Table Ten want to start a band, but they can never seem to settle on a name."

Caroline looked at her, wide-eyed. "How do you *know* all of that?"

"Because I *listened*," said Aria. "I paid attention."

"You were also probably invisible."

"The point is," said Aria, "maybe it's time for you to start listening. Get to know them," she pressed. "Let them get to know you."

Caroline took a deep breath and stepped forward without looking, accidentally bumping into a girl in front of her. "Sorry," she said quickly.

The girl glanced back. "No worries," she said. It wasn't just any girl. It was Ginny, from the soccer field.

Normally, the conversation would be over, but Caroline thought about what Aria had said, about listening, and paying attention, and how *she* had been the one doing most of the ignoring.

"Hey," continued Caroline. "You're a swimmer, aren't you?"

Ginny raised a brow. She shot a glance across the cafeteria toward Table 7 — toward Lily — but then nodded and said, "Yeah. Backstroke." Ginny paused and said, "You like to swim, too, don't you?"

Caroline brightened. "How did you know?"

Ginny gave her a crooked smile. "I heard you got a Saturday school for cutting class to take a swim. Is that true?"

Caroline groaned. "Yeah. Kind of. I mean, not really."

The line moved forward and so did they. "I did go in the pool, but I didn't really have a choice."

"I can't swim," said Aria behind her. "I fell in, and Caroline jumped in and pulled me out."

Ginny's eyes widened. "Whoa, is that true?"

They hit the checkout, paid, and made their way toward the tables.

"It's no big deal," said Caroline.

"She totally saved my life," said Aria. "You should have seen it!"

Ginny smiled. "That's pretty cool," she said as they reached her table. "Hey, Elle," she said to the dark-haired girl already sitting down. "Did you know Caroline here saved Aria's life?"

"No way," said Elle, looking up.

"Yes way," said Aria. "I almost drowned. Lucky for me Caroline's a good swimmer."

Caroline blushed. A few other girls turned toward her, and she realized they were hovering at the edge of Table 2.

"Well?" said Ginny. "You want to sit down?"

Caroline spent the rest of lunch telling the girls at Table 2 about the swimming pool incident. It didn't help that Aria kept making the story bigger, the diving board higher, the fall more dangerous, the fear of drowning ever-present (even though Caroline was pretty sure the guardian angel could have stayed underwater for days and been perfectly fine).

"Yeah," said Elle, "but what were you guys doing by the pool in the first place?"

Caroline glanced across the cafeteria at Table 7, and was surprised to find Lily staring at her.

"*Someone*," said Aria, "stole our uniforms, and hung them on top of the diving board."

Ginny rolled her eyes. "This school."

The bell rang, and for the first time in weeks, Caroline didn't want lunch to end. It had been so nice to have a table to sit at. To have people to talk to. And then, as they all got up to clear their trays, Caroline overheard Elle whisper in Ginny's ear. "Did you see the way Lily was looking at us?"

Caroline's chest twisted, but Ginny only shrugged.

"Let her look," said Ginny. "If she hangs *my* clothes from the diving board, I'll go and get them down."

"Try not to fall in," said Aria earnestly.

The girls broke into laughter, and Caroline let out a sigh of relief. Aria was right. Apparently not everyone at Westgate worshipped at the altar of Lily Pierce.

"Hey," said Ginny, turning to Caroline, "want to sit with us tomorrow?"

Aria beamed, and Caroline felt like she was glowing from the inside out. "I'd love to."

Her heart raced when she said it. Not with fear, but excitement. It felt like the first day of school. Like the first day of *life*.

It felt, she realized, like a fresh start.

chapter 20

ARIA

That night, Aria sat in her tree house, trying to decide what to do. She fiddled with her charm bracelet as her mind drifted, like smoke, through the problem. Caroline was on her way, but Lily —

A car door slammed across the street. Aria watched as Lily Pierce got out and went inside her house, tendrils of blue smoke trailing behind her like a cape.

While Caroline's smoke was thinning, Lily's was thicker than ever. It coiled around her, the way it had the night before, when she snapped at Erica and Whitney. The way it had at lunch that day, when Caroline smiled and laughed with Ginny and Elle.

Aria knew she was supposed to be helping Lily, too. But how? She'd tried to talk to her in the hallway at school that afternoon, but Lily made it clear that she wanted nothing to do with her. She walked right past Aria, as if she were invisible, even though she wasn't (Aria had checked to make sure).

Aria heard someone padding toward the tree. She got up, expecting Caroline, but as the rope ladder groaned under the person's weight, Aria could tell it wasn't her.

She had just enough time to make herself invisible before a small blond head popped up through the space in the floor. It was a boy. His eyes went wide. Aria may have made herself vanish, but she hadn't vanished anything else, not the pillows or the schoolbag or the phone or the pretty twinkling lights.

The boy looked around and took a deep breath. "*Mooooom!*" he called out at the top of his lungs, before disappearing back through the hole in the floor. "Mom!" Aria heard him shouting as he ran across the lawn. "Someone is living in my tree house! A *girl* is living in my tree house!"

As soon as he was gone, Aria snapped her fingers, and the pillows and the schoolbag and the phone and the pretty twinkling lights disappeared one by one, like candle flames. By the time the boy managed to drag his mother out of the house, across the lawn, and up the ladder, the tree house was as empty — only a beanbag and a shelf — as she'd found it. Aria perched on the windowsill and crossed her arms, invisible.

"Jamie," said his mom, exasperated, "what on earth has gotten into you?"

"There was someone's stuff here!" exclaimed the boy. "I swear —"

"You and your imagination."

"But I *swear* —"

"Enough. This is why you can't have candy before bed." And with that, she dragged him away.

Aria sighed and became visible again. One by one, her things flickered back into sight. The last twinkling light reappeared just as she heard Caroline call from the base of the ladder and start climbing up.

"You're getting better at that!" said Aria as Caroline hoisted herself up into the tree house.

"I am," said Caroline, only a little shaky. "As long as I don't look down . . ."

Aria smiled. And then she saw the plastic box under Caroline's arm. "What's that?"

Caroline held up the container. "Cookies," she said. "Mom made them. I hope you like chocolate chip."

Aria had yet to find a kind of cookie she *didn't* like. The two girls sat on the tree house floor and ate. But Aria could feel her attention tugging now and then toward Lily's house. She fiddled with her charm bracelet again.

"How come it only has one charm?" asked Caroline.

"I have to earn the rest," said Aria.

"What do you mean?"

"Do you see these three rings?" asked Aria, pointing to the small metal circles on her bracelet. "Every time I help someone, I get a feather on one of them."

"Ah, so you're, like, literally earning your wings."

Aria nodded. "I earned my first feather," she said, touching the small silver pendant, "for helping a girl named Gabby. And once I help you, I'll earn another feather. But see how this ring is different?" She held it up so Caroline could see the way the middle ring was actually two rings, intertwined. "That's because you're not the only one I'm supposed to be helping here."

"Who else . . ." started Caroline. And then her eyes went to the photo on the wall, the one with threads of blue smoke wrapping not just around Caroline, but around Lily, too. "No," Caroline said quietly. "No way."

"I don't pick who I'm here to help."

Caroline jumped to her feet, her face red. "But why would *Lily Pierce* need a guardian angel?"

"I don't know." Aria sighed. "And I don't know how to help her."

"You told me this was about me," said Caroline. "But it's about us, isn't it? Both of us. Maybe if you help one of us, the other will get better."

"That's what I thought," said Aria. "That's what I hoped. But your smoke is getting better, and Lily's smoke is getting worse. And she doesn't seem to *want* my help."

And then Aria froze, a cookie halfway to her mouth. She repeated the line in her head, only this time she changed the emphasis. *She doesn't seem to want* my *help.*

But what about Caroline's? Maybe Aria wasn't supposed to help Lily, not directly. Maybe she was supposed to help *Caroline* so *she* could help Lily.

"Lily's always been stubborn," Caroline was saying, shaking her head. "I still care about her, I guess. Even after all she's done. Even though we can't be friends. It's weird, isn't it? I like her, even though she obviously hates me."

"I don't think she hates you," said Aria. "I think she's lost."

"Part of me never wants to see her again," said Caroline, "but the rest of me wishes we could just *talk*. One on one. Without Erica and Whitney and everyone else watching."

A light went off inside Aria's head. She smiled and took another cookie. "Maybe you can."

chāpter 21

CAROLINE

Caroline half expected it all to be a dream. Or worse, another prank. She thought she'd get to lunch on Friday, and sit down at Table 2, and Ginny and Elle and Renée and Amanda would look at her like she was crazy. But they didn't. When she brought her tray over, Ginny looked up and grinned at her.

Relief poured over Caroline and she sat down.

"There you are," said Ginny. "We were just talking about you."

Caroline's smile faltered. "You were?"

"Yeah," chimed in Elle. "We're having a sleepover on Friday. Do you want to come?"

Caroline brightened. "Really?" she asked, a little too excited.

"Relax," said Elle. "It's just a sleepover."

"Yeah," said Renée. "It'll be fun. Movies. Popcorn. Pillow forts."

Caroline's spirits lifted. "Can I bring Aria?" she asked, pointing back toward the lunch line, where the guardian angel was holding Jell-O cups up to the light.

The girls at Table 2 looked Aria's way, and for a moment, it was like they'd forgotten who she was. Like she'd slipped out of their minds (which was weird, because Aria was the brightest, boldest thing in Caroline's life). It wasn't the first time it had happened. Caroline had asked Aria about it, and Aria had only shrugged and said, "People notice me when they need to."

But after a second of staring, Ginny shrugged and said, "Sure."

"Give me your phone," said Elle. "I'll put in the address."

Caroline pulled her phone out and passed it to Elle as Aria finally came over and sat down.

"You want to come to a sleepover tonight?" Caroline asked Aria, eyes pleading. Nothing would go wrong if Aria was with her.

"Sure," said Aria with a smile, and then a second later, "What's a sleepover?"

The girls at the table looked at her like she was an alien. Which wasn't too far off. "You know," said Caroline, nudging

Aria with her elbow. "Where everyone gets together at some-one's house and plays games and *sleeps over.*"

"Oh . . ." said Aria. "Oh, yeah, of course. Obviously."

"Great," said Ginny. "Oh, and bring a swimsuit," she added.

Caroline stiffened. "Why?"

"I have a pool and the weather is supposed to be warm," she said. She looked over at Aria. "You going to be okay? There's a shallow end. We can teach you how to swim."

Aria beamed. "That would be great," she said. "I know how to float, but only underwater."

The girls laughed, but Caroline felt a ripple of panic roll through her. She saw herself standing in front of Lily's house in her blue and green and white bikini. Heard herself knocking on the door, and the muffled giggle on the other side, and —

Then Aria squeezed her arm. Caroline blinked, and the memory dissolved.

"We'll be there," Aria was saying. "We can't wait."

"You've never been to a sleepover?" asked Caroline as they walked to class.

Aria shook her head. "There are a lot of things I haven't done."

"Like what?"

Aria shrugged. "How do I know if I haven't done them?"

"Well," said Caroline. "Have you been to the ocean?" Aria shook her head. "Eaten pizza? Been to a dance? Had a crush on a boy?"

Aria blushed. "No."

"We're going to have to work on that," said Caroline. They passed Ms. Opeline's office. She was standing in the doorway, and smiled at Caroline as they went past. Caroline smiled back, but kept walking.

"Are you excited about tonight?" asked Aria.

"I'm nervous," admitted Caroline. "It's just . . . what if . . ." *What if it's all a trap? What if they don't like me? What if . . .*

"You have to give people a chance," said Aria. "They're giving *you* a chance, aren't they?" It was true. Ginny and Elle didn't have to invite her along. "Besides," said Aria, "they might surprise you."

But that's what Caroline was afraid of. She felt like she was walking through a booby-trapped world, waiting for the mines to go off.

. . .

Friday after school, Aria sat cross-legged on Caroline's bed while Caroline packed an overnight bag, stressing over every single hair clip and sock.

"Sleepovers are supposed to be fun, right?" asked Aria, fiddling with her laces, which she'd turned bright blue.

"Yeah," murmured Caroline, dumping out her bag for the fifth time and starting over.

"So why do you look so miserable?"

Caroline sighed. "I'm not. I just . . . I want to get this right." After spending the whole week in a uniform, picking out regular clothes seemed impossible. What should she wear? What would *they* wear?

"Just be you," said Aria, hopping down off the bed. "Here, close your eyes."

Caroline sighed and did as Aria said.

"If no one was going to see you, what would you wear?"

Caroline started to say that it was a stupid question, since people *were* going to see her, but she stopped herself and tried to think of an answer. On weekends, around the house, she usually wore jeans and a T-shirt. Her favorite was this shirt with a galaxy on the front. It was soft from wear, but the colors were still bright. And she had these pink flats that

Lily had told her were out of style, so Caroline had stopped wearing them.

Caroline kept her eyes closed as she told Aria about the outfit. She felt a breeze around her, a flutter of fabric, and when she blinked and looked down, she was wearing the clothes, just as she'd described them, which was amazing because she'd lost that galaxy shirt three months ago.

"How . . ." started Caroline, but she realized it was a silly thing to ask a girl who could make things out of nothing. Instead she smiled and said, "Thanks, Aria. I feel . . ." She looked down at her shoes. "Like me."

Aria beamed, and the lights in the room brightened. Then Aria summoned up a new outfit for herself, too — pink jeans and a bright blue top.

Caroline checked her watch and groaned. "We're going to be late." Her parents were really happy that Caroline was going to a sleepover, but they weren't home yet to drive the girls over. And walking would take a while.

Aria's smile widened. "Don't worry," she said. "I know a shortcut."

She snapped her fingers, and her shadow turned on like a light.

·　·　·

347

Aria's shadow put them out in front of a pretty yellow house with a green door. Aria reattached her shadow while Caroline stared up at the house as if it might eat her.

Don't think of Lily's. Don't think of Lily's. Don't think of Lily's, she willed herself, even though she couldn't *not* think of Lily's place.

"After you," said Aria. Caroline took the lead, and Aria followed her up the front steps. When they reached the door, she took a deep breath, and willed herself to ring the bell.

At first, no one answered.

Oh no, thought Caroline. *No. No.* It was going to be like Lily's place all over again.

"This was a mistake," said Caroline, taking a step back. "Maybe we should —"

And then the door swung open, and Ginny stood there, breathless.

"Sorry," she said. "We were out back, didn't hear the bell."

"It's okay," said Aria, even though Caroline felt woozy.

"Come on in," said Ginny. When Caroline hesitated, she laughed. "We don't bite."

Aria put her hand on Caroline's shoulder and nudged the girl over the threshold.

"Oh hey," Ginny added. "Cool shirt."

chapter 22

ARIA

Aria quickly decided sleepovers were her new favorite thing. Better than cupcakes, or fresh apples, or fall leaves. Sleepovers were made of snacks and laughter, swimming pools and music. And everyone seemed so relaxed.

She was used to being around sad girls, girls twined in smoke and trouble, girls who needed her help. But it was nice, for once, to be surrounded by happy ones. And it helped that those girls seemed to make Caroline happy, too. The more Caroline was around them, the more her smoke seemed to thin.

Aria sat on the lip of the pool, her legs sloshing back and forth in the water. She was wearing a sunshine-yellow bathing suit, and these strange floaties on her arms like little plastic wings (Aria didn't think she needed them, but Ginny's mom had insisted, and they made Caroline smile, so Aria didn't mind, even if she looked a little silly).

Sitting there, Aria felt like a normal girl. Like she belonged. It wasn't something she'd ever wanted before, ever thought of, but she liked it. She made herself stop and remember that it wouldn't last, that she wasn't like the other girls. But that made her sad, and since she didn't want that sadness or worry to rub off on Caroline, she decided to just enjoy the feeling while she could.

Aria stared down at her reflection in the water, squinting at the empty space over the shoulders of her yellow bathing suit. If she made the world blur, she could almost see the start of wings.

And then she heard Caroline laugh — not a tight, nervous sound, but something genuine — and Aria looked up in time to see another tendril of blue smoke disappear.

When they'd first arrived, Caroline wouldn't leave Aria's side. But now she was doing flip turns in the pool with Ginny while Elle, Renée, and Amanda bounced a beach ball between them.

Something tugged in Aria's chest — the feeling that she was in the right and wrong place at the same time — and she knew it was because of Lily. But at least Aria had a plan in motion now. She only hoped it would work.

"Truth or dare!" said Ginny later.

They were all sitting in a pillow fort (Aria and Elle had made it from scratch, not in a magical way, just a "let's use everything we can find around the house" way).

Elle was playing with Aria's hair, and Caroline was sitting cross-legged between Amanda and Renée, and Ginny was perched on a massive cushion.

"Dare," challenged Amanda with a smirk.

"Hmmmm . . ." said Ginny.

"Oh, I know!" said Elle. She whispered in Ginny's ear, and Amanda was instructed to put six marshmallows in her mouth and then call and order a pizza. She couldn't get out the word *cheese*, so she had to hang up, which sent everyone into giggles.

Renée picked truth.

"Do you have a crush on anyone?" asked Elle.

Renée spent the next ten minutes talking about a boy named Jimmy, who was taking her to the dance, and who apparently had the bluest eyes in all of Eastgate. Everyone else seemed to know who he was. Aria simply nodded along.

Ginny boldly chose dare, and had to smear peanut butter on her face and go over to the neighbors' asking for jelly. A boy who couldn't have been more than five or six actually brought her a jar of strawberry jam.

Ginny beamed, victorious, and wiped her face on a towel while the other girls fell over laughing.

Before they were back to Ginny's house, Ginny turned to Aria and said, "Okay, truth or dare?"

Aria came to a stop on the sidewalk and chewed her lip. "Dare."

Ginny flashed a mischievous smile, and pointed to the nearest house.

"Go knock on the door," she said, "and if someone answers, you have to kiss them on the cheek."

The group let out a mixture of gasps and giggles. Aria's eyes widened.

"That's not nice," said Caroline. "You should let her pick again."

"She chose dare!" said Elle.

"Yeah, but —"

"I'll do it," said Aria decidedly.

"Really?" said the girls at once.

"Are you sure?" asked Caroline.

"You don't have to," said Ginny. "I can think up something else."

But Aria shook her head. "No," she said. "It'll be fun." Still, her heart fluttered as she made her way up the front steps. She glanced back and saw the girls looking on with awe. And then Aria turned, and knocked, and waited.

She wondered who would answer (if anyone did), whether it would be an old lady or a little kid or a mom or —

The door swung open. It was a boy. Not just a boy. But a boy with a summer tan and brown hair and green eyes. A boy Aria's age. Aria had met boys her age at Gabby's school, but she hadn't planned on kissing any of them.

"Can I help you?" he said, flashing a smile that made a dimple appear in his cheek. Aria felt her face redden.

"Um," she said.

"You okay?" asked the boy.

"Yeah, I . . ." Aria searched her brain for words. "Can I tell you a secret?" she blurted out.

"Uh, sure?" he said. He leaned in a little, and so did she. And then Aria kissed him on the cheek. The boy pulled back and looked at her with surprise, and Aria felt like her face was on fire. She started to back away. "Sorry," she said. "It was just this silly game and I —"

"Wait," said the boy. Aria stopped. "You forgot something."

"I did?" asked Aria. He motioned her closer, and then he leaned forward and kissed *her* on the cheek. Then he pulled away, smiled, and went back inside.

The door shut, but Aria stood on the front steps, her heart racing, her face hot. For a second, she forgot who she was. What she was. Not in a bad way, or a scary way, but in a strange, wonderful, totally new way. And then she turned back toward the girls, and smiled so wide that the whole evening — street lights and setting sun and all — seemed to glow brighter.

The girls cheered, and Aria gave a sweeping bow.

Several minutes later, when they were all collapsed back in Ginny's bedroom, Aria still hadn't stopped smiling. And then Ginny pulled a pillow into her lap, turned to Caroline, and said, "All right, truth or dare."

Caroline hesitated, smoke curling around her.

And then to Aria's surprise, she took a deep breath and said, "Truth."

Suddenly Ginny got very serious. "Okay," she said. "What happened between you and Lily Pierce?"

chapter 23

CAROLINE

Everyone went quiet.

Caroline felt like she'd been punched in the stomach. The light and happiness began to leak out of the room as Caroline looked from Ginny to Elle, Elle to Renée, Renée to Amanda, and then finally to Aria.

Caroline couldn't read Aria's mind, but her expression seemed to say one thing.

Tell the truth.

All Caroline wanted to do was forget. To put the past behind her and start fresh. But she couldn't. Going forward sometimes meant looking back, and if she really wanted to make new friends, they deserved to know what had happened with her old ones.

So she told them.

About Lily and Erica. About standing up for Whitney, and being kicked out of the group for it.

When she was done, the room stayed quiet. Ginny frowned, and for a second Caroline thought she was mad at her. Then Caroline realized Ginny was mad *for* her. "I can't believe they'd stoop that low," she growled.

"Can't you?" challenged Elle. "They're the meanest girls in school."

"I'm so sorry," said Renée.

"We just figured you two got in a fight," added Amanda.

"We didn't know," said Ginny, squeezing Caroline's shoulder.

"Does *Whitney* know?" asked Elle.

Caroline started to shake her head, when Aria cut in. "Yeah, she knows."

Caroline shot Aria a surprised look.

"And she still hangs out with them?" snapped Ginny. "Why would *anyone* put up with that?"

"Maybe she's scared," Caroline said quietly.

"Maybe she's *crazy*," countered Elle.

"Well," said Ginny decidedly, "if she isn't willing to stand up for herself, that's her problem. Can't help someone who doesn't want to be helped. You did the right thing, Caroline."

"Thanks," said Caroline, hugging a pillow to her chest. She let out a deep breath, and for the first time in weeks, she felt like she could breathe.

Ginny cleared her throat. "Now back to business," she said. "So, Elle, truth or dare?"

That night, when the girls were asleep, a tangle of pajama-ed limbs on the pillow fort floor, Caroline lay there, looking at the ceiling as if it were the night sky. And then, as she gazed up, tiny dots of light — like stars — began to pepper the darkened room.

"Hey, Aria," she whispered in the dark. "Are you doing that?"

"Yeah," Aria whispered back. There was a moment of silence, and then Aria said, "This was really fun." It was strange, the way she said it. Happy and sad at the same time.

"Thank you," said Caroline.

"For what?" asked Aria.

"For everything."

"We're not done yet," said Aria, and Caroline could hear the smile in Aria's voice as the stars began to soften and blink out. "But we're on our way."

Caroline's mom picked them up early the next morning for Saturday school. Caroline was still rubbing sleep from her eyes and pulling her hair back into a messy ponytail as she got in the car, Aria bobbing behind her. Aria didn't look tired at all. If anything, she seemed peppy.

"What's it like?" she asked as they rode to Westgate.

"What's what like?" asked Caroline with a yawn.

"Saturday school," said Aria.

Caroline shrugged. She had never gotten a Saturday school before, so she didn't know what to expect. Would they be sweeping the floors? Picking up trash? Dying of boredom at a desk? The possibilities were endless.

When they got to school, Mr. Cahill was waiting for them in the office. He led them to the gym, where rolls of colored paper and buckets of paint were waiting for them.

Mr. Cahill swept his hand over the crafts and said, "Dance prep."

"We're going to dance?" asked Aria, her face lighting up. "That doesn't seem like much of a punishment."

"No, you're going to *prep* for this week's dance."

Aria considered the gym. "But can we dance while we're prepping?"

Mr. Cahill sighed. "Sure," he said. "But don't have too much fun. This is Saturday school after all." He *almost* smiled when he said it. "The theme is 'In the Clouds,' so I need you girls to start painting clouds on the blue paper roll. Think you can handle that?" Aria and Caroline nodded. "Great. I'm going to find coffee."

Mr. Cahill left. Aria started to roll out some of the blue paper. "What a perfect theme," she said. "It was made for you."

"It's weird, isn't it?" said Caroline. The whole school had voted, and she'd been sure they were going to choose something flowery and pink. But Caroline had kept thinking how cool it would be to dance in the sky.

Aria shrugged. "Sometimes things just work out," she said with a mischievous smile.

There was a radio in the corner, and Aria turned it on. Music echoed through the gym while they worked. Soon they were singing along — Aria cheerfully off-key — and laughing, and Caroline was just starting to think Saturday school wasn't so bad at all.

Then the gym doors banged open, and in walked Lily Pierce.

chapter 24

ARIA

Caroline froze. "What is *she* doing here?" she hissed.

Aria shrugged. "Not sure," she said, even though she knew *exactly* what Lily was doing there.

She hadn't turned Lily in for the swimming pool incident (in part because she didn't have proof, and in part because she wasn't sure Ms. Pierce would make Lily come today). But Aria *had* read the entire pamphlet on Westgate's rules. So, all day on Friday, Aria had made sure that Lily broke just enough of the rules to land in Saturday school.

"My phone was turned off!" Lily had told the teacher after history class.

"Then how did it ring during my lecture?" he demanded.

"Mr. Cahill," Lily had said at lunch, aghast, *"I swear my shoelaces were black this morning."*

"Mhmmm," said Mr. Cahill, "so they just magically turned green."

"I don't know how the popcorn got in my locker," Lily had said later that day, exasperated.

"I could smell it all the way down the hall," said the eighth-grade monitor. "And where did you even find a microwave?"

(That one had *kind of been Lily's own fault.* She'd brought the bag of popcorn to school herself. Aria had simply made it pop.)

"Three strikes," her mother, the headmistress, had snapped. "What's gotten into you?"

Aria had almost felt guilty for setting Lily up (especially when she saw her face after leaving her mother's office), but Aria had to do *something* to get Caroline and Lily together alone, and in neutral territory.

Now Lily marched over, and, without saying a word or looking at either one of them, she picked up a paintbrush and started making clouds.

"I'm going to go wash my hands," said Aria, holding them up to show they were covered in white paint.

Caroline gave her a look that very clearly said, *Don't leave me here.*

And Aria gave her one back that said *You said this was what you wanted. A chance to talk? So go ahead. Talk.* (Though

Aria wasn't very good at giving people looks, so she wasn't sure that all came across.)

Caroline shook her head. *I changed my mind.*

Aria frowned. *Change it back.*

By this point, Caroline and Aria had been staring at each other for several long moments.

"So go already," said Lily, annoyed.

Aria slipped out into the hall and wiped her hands together, the white paint vanishing. Then she willed herself to disappear. Invisible, she stood on her tiptoes and looked back through the glass insert of the door.

Caroline and Lily were not talking.

They were not talking in that way that said they clearly wanted to — the whole room, not just the smoke, was filled with things they weren't saying. But neither one of them would go first.

A minute later Mr. Cahill came back with a mug of coffee and a newspaper under his arm. When he pushed the gym door open, Invisible Aria followed him inside.

"Miss Pierce," said Mr. Cahill, turning down the music. "I never thought I'd see you here."

"Yeah," grumbled Lily. "Me neither."

Caroline opened her mouth as if to speak, but didn't. She and Lily went back to silently painting puffy white clouds on the blue paper. Aria, still invisible, came up beside Caroline and wrote a word in the wet paint of the nearest cloud.

TALK.

Caroline's eyes widened a little. She glanced over at Lily, but Lily hadn't seen the trick.

"What are you staring at?" asked Lily without looking up.

Caroline blinked. "Can you pass the paint?"

Lily lifted the bucket and dropped it between them. It splashed, dotting both their clothes with white. Lily groaned. Caroline laughed.

"It's not funny," snapped Lily.

Caroline's giggles trailed off. "Do you remember that time," she said, "when your dad was painting the window, and left the bucket on the ladder, and Erica knocked into it?"

Lily rolled her eyes. "Oh god, she was *covered* in red paint."

"She was so worried about her hair. Not her clothes or her shoes or her skin. She was just terrified it would dye her hair."

Lily cracked a smile. "She didn't want to be a redhead."

Caroline started to laugh. This time, Lily did, too. The blue smoke that circled both of them thinned a fraction.

When their laughter trailed away, Lily said, "Hey, do you remember that one time when —"

But she was cut off by the sound of the gym doors banging open, Aria turned to see Erica and Whitney barging inside. Aria groaned inwardly. Caroline grimaced, and to Aria's surprise, *Lily's* smoke began to darken at the sight of the two girls.

"What up, losers?" said Erica loudly, her voice echoing through the gym.

"Language, Miss Kline," warned Mr. Cahill.

"What are you doing here?" asked Lily.

"We came to save you," said Whitney, "from being stuck with trash." The second part she said too low for Mr. Cahill to hear, but Caroline clearly heard.

Aria could see Lily's expression falter. Just for a second. Her mouth opened as if she was going to defend Caroline, but then she put on a stiff smile and said, "Ugh, thanks. Let's get some fresh air." She dropped her paintbrush back in the bucket, splashing flecks of white on Caroline. This time, neither one of them laughed. Anger rolled through Aria, and she had to resist the urge to stick out her foot and trip Lily.

"Can I take a break, Mr. Cahill?" Lily called out. "The smell of paint is making me sick."

Mr. Cahill sighed, and nodded. "Fine," he said. "Ten minutes."

He turned to Caroline. "You can take one, too, if you want."

Caroline's knuckles were white around her paintbrush. "That's okay," she said as Lily and Erica and Whitney vanished through the doors. "I'll stay here."

Mr. Cahill looked around. "Where's Aria?" he asked.

When his back was turned, she flickered into sight.

"I've been here the whole time," she said, cross-legged on the floor.

"Oh," said Mr. Cahill, blinking. "Well, carry on."

Caroline kept painting, even though tears were rolling silently down her cheeks. "I thought . . ." she whispered. "I thought . . . just for a moment . . . we could . . ."

"So did I," said Aria. She really thought, if she could get the two of them alone . . . and for a second, it had worked. Lily's smoke had thinned, and Aria had been able to see a side of Lily she hadn't before. But it wasn't enough.

And when Lily finally came back from her break, she didn't say another word to Caroline.

chapter 25

CAROLINE

All day a cloud hung over Caroline. Somehow getting a flash of old Lily made the new Lily even worse. And the *worst* part was that Caroline could see the old Lily in there somewhere, under all that mean, but she couldn't get her out.

Just when she felt like she'd never shake the dark cloud — did her smoke look the way this felt? — she and Aria got back to her house, paint-streaked and tired, and saw Ginny and Elle waiting for them on the steps.

"There they are, our little rule-breakers," said Ginny.

"Tell us, what's it like to be juvenile delinquents?" teased Elle.

"Messy," said Aria, holding up her paint-covered hands. "We painted clouds for the dance."

"What's the theme again?" asked Ginny.

"The sky," said Aria, and Elle tilted her head to one side.

"Hmm," she said. "That might be tricky to shop for. Ginny and I were going to the mall to look at dresses for the dance. Can you come?"

Standing there with Ginny and Elle, Caroline felt her spirits begin to lift. They didn't care who was most popular. They weren't bullies or nobodies. They were just themselves. Caroline nodded enthusiastically.

"You coming like that?" asked Ginny. "I mean, paint-splattered is a good look."

Caroline laughed. "No," she said. "Let me go inside and change. And actually I need to ask my mom if I can go."

As Caroline suspected, her mom was more than happy to let her go to the mall with new friends. It seemed Saturday school was now forgiven.

Shopping at the mall was a lot of fun, and Ginny and Elle didn't care if the dresses Caroline picked out matched their "color scheme" or not. There were no rules, and for the first time in a long time, Caroline just enjoyed herself without feeling self-conscious. Aria seemed to be enjoying herself, too — she'd never gone shopping before, she explained to Caroline in a whisper. Aria didn't buy a dress for herself — Caroline knew she could summon one up for the dance — but Caroline picked out a shimmery blue one with a poofy knee-length skirt.

By the time Monday rolled around, Caroline wasn't even dreading school.

Lily stayed out of her way, and didn't shoot her dirty glances. In fact, she didn't look at her at all. Erica still glared, of course, and Whitney whispered something harsh under her breath when she and Erica passed Caroline in the hall.

"Ignore them," said Aria, and to Caroline's surprise, she did.

For the first time all year, she had fun in gym. They were playing dodgeball and by some miracle, she got through most of the class without being hit a single time (she suspected she had Aria to thank for that).

"Hey, do you actually go to class when we're not together?" Caroline asked Aria as they walked down the hall together.

"Yeah," said Aria cheerfully. "Well, everything except math." The teacher had claimed that math was a kind of magic, explained Aria, but she remained unconvinced. To her, it just looked like numbers.

"What class do you have now?"

"Math."

"So what are you going to do instead?"

Aria shrugged. "Wander," she said. "Invisible, of course."

"Of course," said Caroline. "Well, have fun. I'll see you at lunch."

She watched Aria go, and then, just as she was rounding a corner, a girl slammed into Caroline *hard*. Hard enough to make her drop the books and papers she was carrying. It was Jessabel.

"You're still nothing," she muttered, then bounced cheerfully off to class. The blow knocked the wind out of Caroline, and the words made it worse, and she crouched in the hall, trying to gather up their things. And then she felt someone kneel down to help.

"Thanks," said Caroline. "You don't have to."

"I know," said the girl. Caroline looked up to see that it was a seventh grader named Jen.

"Hey," said Caroline, straightening. "You're in the science club, right?"

Caroline knew that because in sixth grade Lily had told her to fill Jen's locker with bugs — mostly crickets and a couple of worms, because she liked biology — and Caroline had done it. And she'd laughed along with everyone else when Jen opened the locker. Jen probably hated her. She had every right to.

They hadn't said a word to each other since then. Now Jen gave her a guarded look. "Yeah . . . why?"

Caroline offered a genuine smile. "I was thinking about joining the club."

Jen raised a brow. "*You?*"

"Yeah," said Caroline. "Why not me?"

"It's just, you never struck me as a science nerd."

"I love science," said Caroline. "Astronomy is my favorite, but really, I like all of it. I just never joined before because —"

"Because you were too cool then?" cut in Jen. "And now you're not cool enough for it to matter?"

Caroline cringed. Jen's tone made her want to hide. But she didn't. She had to face the fact that she'd done bad things. "You're right," she said. "I didn't join because I thought it was nerdy and uncool. I didn't know what cool *was*. I always thought being popular was what made you cool. But it's not. Liking something — really liking it — that *is* cool. So I think it's awesome that you like science. I think it's really cool."

Jen considered her a moment, clearly trying to decide if this was some kind of trick. Caroline recognized the distrust. But then Jen pulled a flier out of her bag and handed it over. "We meet after school on Wednesdays," she said.

Caroline brightened. "Do you get to do experiments?" she asked. "Like crystal-growing or how to get the colors in fireworks?"

Jen smiled, this time a real smile. "Yeah," she said. "Last week we got to make our own bouncy balls out of polymer."

"No way," said Caroline. "That's awesome. How did you do it?"

The second bell rang overhead.

"We have English together, right?" asked Jen. Caroline nodded. "Well, walk to class with me; I'll tell you about it. . . ."

chapter 26

ARIA

Instead of going invisible, Aria went looking for Lily.

She'd spent all weekend thinking about what to do, how to get through to her. Now she thought she finally understood what Lily needed to hear.

As Caroline's smoke had thinned, and Lily's hadn't, the pull toward the second girl had gotten stronger. Aria wove through the halls of Westgate to the headmistress's office, and paused outside. The office door was ajar, and she could see Lily standing in front of the headmistress's desk — her mother's desk. Her blue smoke was swirling around her.

"This is unacceptable," Ms. Pierce was saying, waving a test paper. A grade was written on the top in bright red pen: *B*. "I don't know where your head is, but it clearly isn't here. First the infractions —"

"I didn't do any of those —"

"And now this."

"It's just a B, Mom. It's not the end of the world."

"Just a B?" snapped Ms. Pierce. "This isn't *just* a B, because you aren't *just* a student, Lily. You're an example for every girl here at Westgate. I told you when you started here there would be expectations. How do you think it looks when the headmistress's daughter doesn't embody the excellence expected by the school? And for goodness' sake, stand up straight." Ms. Pierce sighed and rubbed her eyes. "Maybe you're spending too much time with your friends, and not enough on your work."

Lily let out an exasperated noise. "It's called a social life! Isn't having one part of being a well-rounded Westgate girl?"

"Don't you take that tone with me."

"What more do you want from me?" snapped Lily. "I run track in the fall. I play tennis in the spring. I'm class president. I'm the most popular girl in this school!"

"Exactly. All eyes are on you. Every girl here should look up to you, should want to *be* you. You owe it to them to be the best example."

"I just —"

"No," Ms. Pierce cut her off. "No excuses."

Lily's shoulders slumped. The bell rang. "Go to class," said her mom. "The last thing you need is an infraction for being late."

Aria felt bad for Lily. No wonder she trying so hard to be in charge. And no wonder she had become a bully. Her mom was one, too. Aria didn't think Lily's mom would change anytime soon. But Lily could. She had to.

Lily pushed the door open, and nearly ran straight into Aria. Her eyes narrowed.

"Why can't you just stay out of my way?" she barked.

"Lily Ann Pierce," warned her mother from the office doorway. "You're going to be late!"

Lily looked back in the office and forced a smile. "I was just talking to Westgate's newest student," she said tightly. "I wanted to make sure she felt welcome."

"I'm sure she does," said Mrs. Pierce. "And I'm sure you two can talk and walk at the same time."

Silently, Lily nodded, and started walking away. Aria followed.

"I'm sorry," Aria said.

"For what?" Lily grunted. "Getting in the way?"

"For your mom," said Aria. The answer seemed to catch Lily off-guard and she glanced at Aria, her face paling. "It's not fair to put that much pressure on you."

"That's not really any of your business," Lily snapped, recovering.

Aria shrugged. She wasn't going to back down. "I couldn't help but overhear, okay? It hurts, doesn't it. Being singled out by somebody. Being picked on." Lily's eyes narrowed as she saw where Aria was going with this. "If you ever want to talk —"

"Why would I ever want to talk to *you*?"

"Because you have to talk to someone," Aria said. Erica and Whitney didn't seem like good listeners. Mimickers, sure, but not listeners. Caroline had been Lily's listener, until Lily had pushed her away. "You can't just bottle everything up and then take it out on others," pressed Aria.

Lily threw her hands up. "I don't get it. What do you *want*?"

"To *help*," said Aria.

"I don't want your help," said Lily. "And I certainly don't need it."

"Do you miss her?" asked Aria.

Lily came to a stop. "Who?"

"Caroline. Do you miss her?"

The blue smoke coiled around Lily's shoulders.

"I know what happened between you two," continued Aria. "I haven't had very many friends, but I don't think friends are supposed to do what you did."

375

"You don't know anything —"

"I know she stood up to you," said Aria. "And instead of listening, or letting it go, or just saying you were sorry, you decided to ruin her life."

Lily stared at her, wide-eyed.

Guilt. Aria could practically see it woven through the smoke. Guilt, and sadness. But Aria knew now: Lily didn't need a hug. She didn't need support. She needed someone to stand up to her. And maybe that someone needed to be Caroline. But first, Aria could make a few cracks in the armor of *Mean* Lily so that when Caroline *did* stand up to her, the words would get through, and Lily would finally hear, finally listen.

"How dare you talk to me that way?" said Lily. "You are nothing. You are no one."

"The girls at this school aren't nice to you because they like you," said Aria. "They're afraid of you. But I'm not. Nothing you do can hurt me."

Lily clutched her books to her chest. "You think Caroline's your friend," she said, "but she will *always* come running back to me."

"Are you sure about that?" asked Aria. "What happens the day she doesn't? What happens when she realizes she's not afraid of losing you anymore?"

Lily stood there, speechless. Aria thought she might finally have gotten through. Then the bell rang again, and the sound jarred Lily free.

"You are nothing," she said again. "I'll prove it to you."

And with that, she stormed away.

"I think it's time we pick a new target."

Lily and Erica and Whitney were walking to lunch. Lily still walked in front, the other two trailing, but Erica and Whitney's arms were linked, and now and then they passed a secret look between them. A smile. An eye roll.

"Getting soft?" asked Erica.

"No," snapped Lily. "Getting bored. Caroline's no fun anymore. And frankly, this group is lame without her."

"Ouch," said Whitney.

"Harsh," said Erica.

"Honest," said Lily. "But the point is, we need a change."

"Because you're slipping," said Erica. She'd stopped echoing Lily, and started speaking up. She was getting bolder.

"Did you know someone *turned Jessabel in* for being mean?" said Whitney. "It's like they actually care what happens to Caroline."

"It's Aria," snapped Lily. "It's all *her* fault. And that's why we're going to make her the newest target."

"You sure that will work?" challenged Erica. "People seem to like her."

"You think they'll actually freeze her out?" asked Whitney.

"*They're* not going to," said Lily. "*Caroline* is."

Erica raised a brow, and a second later, so did Whitney.

"Ouch," said Whitney.

"Harsh," said Erica.

But they both smiled as they said it. The three girls pushed open the cafeteria doors and vanished within.

For a moment, the hall was empty.

Then the air shimmered and Aria became visible again. She'd heard everything. And she knew what she had to do.

Nothing.

It was up to Caroline now.

Aria took a deep breath, smoothed her skirt, and went to lunch.

chapter 27

CAROLINE

Caroline was halfway through the lunch line when she felt an arm loop through hers, and looked up to see Lily beside her. Caroline tried to pull free, but Lily tightened her grip.

"Hi," said Lily. *Hi*. Like they were still friends.

"What do you want?" asked Caroline.

"Look," said Lily. "We need to talk."

"We were talking, on Saturday. And then you decided to stop."

"I'm sorry."

Two words Lily almost never said, but Caroline didn't buy it.

"I'm sorry about Saturday school," Lily went on, "and I'm sorry about the diving board, and I'm sorry about the pool party last week. That was Erica, not me. She took my

379

phone. I didn't even know about it until I came out and saw them giggling."

"Whatever."

"You don't have to believe me," snapped Lily. "But it's the truth." She waved her free hand. "Anyway, that's not the point."

"What *is* the point?"

"I've been talking to the girls, and we all agree. It's time for you to come back to the group."

Caroline stared at Lily. She didn't know what to say. "Even Erica?" she asked.

"Even Erica," said Lily. Caroline didn't believe her.

"Come on, Car," cooed Lily. "I miss you."

"I miss you, too," said Caroline. The words came out before she even thought of stopping them. And they were true. She did miss Lily. In spite of everything.

"There's just one thing you have to do," said Lily. "To prove you want back in. To show you're one of us."

Caroline's heart sank. "What?"

"If you do it," Lily went on, "then things can go back to the way they were. The way they're supposed to be. Don't you want that?"

Caroline swallowed. Her eyes traveled over the lunchroom. She saw Aria sitting with Ginny and Elle. Aria's back was to her, so she didn't see Caroline standing there with Lily. Caroline remembered how she'd said there were more choices than being a bully or a nobody.

"Well?" pressed Lily.

Caroline frowned. "What do I have to do?"

Lily smiled, and leaned in, and whispered in her ear.

Caroline stood there, clutching her tray.

She could feel Lily and Erica and Whitney watching her, all waiting to see if she would do it. She made her way toward Aria.

The drink on her tray was filled to the brim with an icy red concoction. As she crossed the cafeteria, she had to focus on not spilling it.

Dump it on Aria, Lily had said when she set the drink on her tray. *Dump it on her, and everything will go back to the way it was before.*

When Caroline finally reached the table, she hovered at Aria's shoulder. Aria looked up.

"Hey," said Aria cheerfully. "You going to sit down?"

The other girls at the table looked up, too. Ginny, Elle, Renée, and Amanda. It felt like the whole cafeteria was watching her. Caroline tightened her grip on her lunch tray.

This was it.

The moment of choice.

She took a deep breath.

And then she sat down next to Aria.

As soon as she did, the fear and the stress went out of her. She knew she'd made the right decision. Aria reached over and squeezed her arm, as if she *knew*. Knew what Caroline had thought of doing. Knew what she'd decided *not* to do.

"Hey, Ginny," said Caroline, a little shaky, "can you pass me a —"

A hand came down on her shoulder, hard, and she jumped. When she did, the icy red drink spilled over the table, and the girls all jumped up out of its path. Caroline spun around to find Lily looking furious.

"What do you think you're doing?" she hissed. "This isn't how you get back in the group."

Everyone at the table — everyone in the *cafeteria* — was staring at them. Sixty-two pairs of eyes.

"I don't want to be back in the group," said Caroline. Her voice trembled but she kept going. "I don't want to be your friend anymore, Lily. I don't like the person you've become."

Lily turned red. It started in her cheeks, and spread

across her face and down her neck, and for a moment, Caroline thought she was going to cry.

Erica appeared at Lily's shoulder. "Lily, are you seriously going to let her talk to you like that?" she asked.

"You can't let her do that," Whitney chimed in, appearing on Lily's other side.

"You're supposed to be —"

"Back off," snapped Lily. "Both of you." She turned and stormed out of the cafeteria.

Erica and Whitney stood there, shocked, before slowly retreating back to their own table.

Caroline felt Aria squeeze her arm again. She took a deep breath and turned back to Ginny, and Elle, and the rest of Table 2 watching with a mixture of surprise and approval. She looked down at the icy red slush on everything, and sighed. "We're going to need more napkins."

By the end of the day, everyone in school seemed to know about the lunchroom scene. Caroline hadn't realized how many people *wanted* to stand up to Lily Pierce until girls started coming to thank her. Everyone treated it like a victory . . . so why did Caroline still feel strangely defeated?

"You did the right thing," insisted Aria.

"I know," said Caroline.

"Miss Mason," called Ms. Opeline as they passed her office. "Is everything all right?"

"Yes, ma'am," said Caroline.

"I haven't seen you in a while. No more accidents? No wardrobe malfunctions?"

"No," said Caroline with a smile. She and Aria started to walk away, but Ms. Opeline stepped forward.

"I know it hasn't been an easy year," she said. *You have no idea*, thought Caroline bitterly, before reminding herself that it wasn't Ms. Opeline's fault. Caroline hadn't *told* her. "But I'm glad that things seem to be getting better."

"They are," said Caroline.

"Middle school is . . ." started Ms. Opeline. "Well, actually, the world is full of bullies. But being mean never earns you friends, only enemies. I think that's a hard lesson, don't you?"

Caroline nodded.

"I'm still here," said Ms. Opeline. "If you ever want to talk."

Caroline paused and turned back. "I know," she said. "And thank you."

"Who's that?" asked Aria once they were outside.

"Ms. Opeline, the school counselor."

"Do you ever talk to her?" asked Aria.

"I don't need to talk to her. I have you."

Aria hesitated. "Caroline," she said slowly, "I won't be here forever. You know that, right?" Caroline's gaze dropped to the floor. She hadn't thought about it. Hadn't wanted to. "I told you in the tree house," pressed Aria. "I'll be here until your smoke clears and you don't need me anymore. But then I have to go."

"Why?" asked Caroline. "Why not stay?"

"I don't have a life here," said Aria. "I don't have a family. I have a mission. And once it's over, I have to move on. Just like you do, with your new life. We both have to keep moving forward. But promise me," added Aria, "that if things get hard after I'm gone, you'll talk to Ms. Opeline, or your mom, or your sister, or *someone*. Okay?"

Caroline nodded.

"And hey," said Aria, slinging her arm around Caroline's shoulders. "I'm not gone yet. I have to see what this dance thing is all about."

chapter 28

ARIA

"Keep your eyes closed."

Aria was sitting on Caroline's bed, and Caroline was putting her hair into a French braid for the dance. Aria was excited to see what it would look like.

"There," said Caroline when she was done. "What do you think?"

Aria blinked, looked at herself in the mirror, and beamed.

"It's like I'm someone else," she said.

Caroline smiled. "It's just hair."

"Where did you learn to do that?"

Caroline shrugged. "My sister taught me."

"Oh," said Aria.

"Here," said Caroline. "I'll show you how."

She started to take the braid apart, but Aria stopped her. "No," she said. "Leave it like this. It's perfect."

386

Caroline's own hair fell in loose blond waves down her back. Aria thought she looked beautiful in her blue dress.

"What are you going to wear?" Caroline asked.

Aria looked down at her school uniform. She snapped her fingers, and the plaid skirt and polo shimmered and shifted and transformed into a yellow skirt, a red shirt, and a pair of bright blue leggings. Her shoelaces turned violet, and Aria smiled proudly at her handiwork.

Caroline laughed. "You can't wear that."

"Why not?" asked Aria.

"You kind of look like a walking rainbow."

Aria shrugged. "I like rainbows," she said.

Caroline giggled. "Never mind," she said. "You look like you."

"Caroline," her mom called up, sounding happy. "Your friends are here."

Ginny and Elle were waiting on the porch. They met up with Renée and Amanda, and then they all went out for pizza, which Aria quickly decided was her new favorite food.

When they got to the gym, Aria was amazed by how the massive room had changed, transformed from wood and bleachers into a giant stretch of sky. Bundles of white balloons were everywhere, and painted clouds hung from every rafter. Streamers in sunset colors ran back and forth over-head. Aria loved it.

The gym was full of Westgate girls and Eastgate boys. Elle, Ginny, Renée, and Amanda immediately started danc-ing. Aria wanted to join in but she noticed Caroline looking around, her expression a little tense, her thin blue smoke swirling. Aria knew she was looking for Lily.

Then Erica and Whitney strolled in, arm in arm, fol-lowed by Jessabel. The three of them were wearing matching pink dresses.

And Lily wasn't with them.

"Where's Lily?" asked a girl with shiny black hair as the trio passed her by.

Whitney giggled. "Probably still waiting for us."

Erica shrugged and said, "She couldn't keep up, so she got left behind."

"About time," said Jessabel. Together, the three girls strode onto the dance floor.

Aria sighed. She needed to leave, and she was about to make an excuse, when Caroline beat her to it.

"Come on," she said. "Let's go find Lily."

• • •

Aria's shadow put them out across the street from Lily's house, under the branches of the tree house tree. Lily was sitting on the front porch, her knees pulled up to her chest. She was wearing a purple dress, and picking at the hem while tears streamed down her face.

Aria stayed behind — far enough to give them space, close enough to hear — as Caroline crossed the yard, made her way up the front steps, and sat down beside her ex-best friend.

When Lily saw Caroline, her thick smoke began to ripple.

"Are you happy now?" muttered Lily.

"No," said Caroline.

"Did you come here to gloat? To rub it in my face? Congratulations, Caroline Mason, you're popular and I'm not."

"That's not why I came. I wanted to see if you were okay."

"Why do you still care?"

Caroline sighed and pulled her knees up. "I never stopped caring, Lily. Even when you were horrible."

Lily wiped her face with the back of her hand. "You said you didn't want to be friends with me."

"I don't," said Caroline. "I don't know if we *can* be friends again. But you still matter to me. You always will."

Caroline dug her hand into her skirt and pulled out the silver half circle necklace. Lily's eyes widened, and then she pulled her own pendant from beneath the collar of her dress.

"I'm sorry, Car," Lily whispered. "It wasn't supposed to be this way. None of it was."

"But it is," said Caroline. "So what are you going to do now?"

Lily shook her head. "I don't know."

Caroline stood up, and put the necklace back in her pocket. "Come to the dance," she said.

"I can't," said Lily.

Caroline crouched down to look Lily in the eyes. "Why not? Because they hurt your feelings?" She shook her head. "If you don't go, you're letting them win," she said. "Besides, we spent all that time painting clouds. Don't you want to see them? They look amazing."

Caroline straightened and held out her hand. "Come on, Lily."

Lily looked up. Then she reached out, and took Caroline's hand.

As she did, her smoke *finally* began to thin.

Aria smiled. She knew it. Lily didn't need her help. She needed Caroline's.

"But how are we going to get to the dance?" asked Lily, looking around. Her parents didn't seem to be home, and Caroline's already thought she was at the dance.

Aria stepped forward. "I have a way," she said. "But there's something I should probably tell you first."

Aria wasn't sure Lily believed her, even after the trip through her shadow door to the school.

"*How* — how — how did you do that?" stammered Lily, as the three girls stepped out of the light-filled shape and onto the path in front of the gym.

"I told you," said Aria for the fifteenth time. "Guardian angel."

"No way," said Lily for the fifteenth time.

"Way," said Aria.

"Way," said Caroline.

Lily looked up at the gym. Fear flickered across her face, and what was left of her smoke coiled nervously around her shoulders. But Caroline took her hand and gave it a small squeeze.

"Come on," she said. "There are some pretty cool girls at this school. I'll help you meet a few."

Aria followed Caroline and Lily up the stairs, watching as the blue smoke around them got thinner, and thinner, and thinner. By the time the two girls stepped into the gym, it was totally gone.

Aria felt something cool on her wrist, and looked down to see a new feather charm twinkling on her bracelet. It was actually two feathers, linked together on the interlocking rings. When Aria shook her wrist, the charms jingled faintly, like far-off bells.

There was only one ring left to fill, and she could feel it tugging at her. This was her least favorite part. Even though she knew she'd done her job and made Caroline and Lily better, and all of that made her happy, that also meant it was over.

It was an ending, and endings were always sad.

But they were just as important as beginnings. And somewhere else, another girl was waiting for Aria's help.

So Aria watched Caroline and Lily slip into the crowd of the dance.

And then her shadow flared, and she stepped backward, into the light.

chapter 29

CAROLINE

Although Caroline had a nice time at the dance, she kept looking for Aria, afraid that she had left without saying good-bye. As soon as the dance was over, Caroline hurried home, and sighed with relief when she found Aria sitting in the tree house, legs dangling over the open window edge.

"There you are," said Caroline, breathless from climbing up the ladder. "Why did you leave the dance?"

Aria swung her legs back inside. "Because it was time," she said.

"It wasn't even eight. There was still an hour left."

Aria shook her head. "That's not what I meant," she said. "How was the dance?"

Caroline smiled. "It was good. Ginny and Elle weren't too thrilled to see Lily, but they were polite to her. And I wish you'd stayed to see Erica's face . . ."

She trailed off, and a silence fell between them.

"Caroline," said Aria, "it's time for me to go."

"Go where?"

Aria held up the bracelet so she could see the newest feather charm. Caroline paled. "Stay," she pleaded. "Everything is so much better with you here."

"You don't need me anymore," said Aria. "And we all have to move forward."

Caroline felt her chest tighten. "Promise me you'll come back."

Aria smiled. "I promise I'll try. But only if you promise me something."

"What's that?"

"That you'll never go back. Not to the way things were. Mean is easier than nice, and I know it's hard, and it'll only get harder, but promise me if you're ever faced with being a bully or a nobody again, you won't choose bully."

Caroline smiled. "You act like those are the only two options," she said, echoing Aria's own words.

Aria beamed, and threw her arms around Caroline.

"So, where are you going?" asked Caroline when she pulled away.

Aria shook her head. "I won't know until I get there."

"Caroline?" called a voice from the street. It was Lily.

"You'd better go," said Aria. "So should I."

Aria smiled and snapped her fingers, and the cushions, the star lights, and all the little decorations she'd summoned to make the small space cozy disappeared. She and Caroline stood there a moment, two girls in an empty wooden box up in the branches of an old oak tree.

Caroline saw Aria's shadow fidget beneath her feet.

"All right," said Aria. "All right."

She tapped her shoe, and the shadow turned on like a light.

"Good-bye, Caroline," she said.

"Good-bye-for-now," corrected Caroline.

Aria smiled, and nodded, and disappeared.

Caroline snuck back to the tree house later that night, after everyone was in bed.

She climbed the ladder, half expecting, fully hoping to find Aria there again, sitting in a sea of pillows.

But Aria was gone. She'd watched her go.

Caroline sat cross-legged on the floor. Even though Aria and her decorations were gone, Caroline still felt as if she was there, somehow. She couldn't explain it. She looked up through the branches at the twinkling stars.

"Things are going to get better," she said aloud, as if Aria could hear her. Maybe she could. Caroline still didn't know exactly how guardian angels worked.

"After you left," she went on, "Lily and I went out to the trampoline, and we just talked. Finally. About everything. About the last month and the last year and how it all got out of hand. And she said she was going to talk to her mom, about all the pressure she was putting on her. I hope Mrs. Pierce listens. I told Lily she could always talk to Ms. Opeline, too." Caroline sighed. "I don't think she and I can ever be best friends again, not the way we were before. I know we can't go back. But I hope we can go forward. All things go forward, right?" she said, remembering Aria's words. "It's science."

Caroline got to her feet and was about to go, when she noticed the photo of her and Lily. It had slipped to the floor, but when she picked it up, she saw that the blue lines Aria had drawn around them were gone. Instead, a small blue stick figure of a curly-haired girl was drawn between them, with her arms wrapped around both.

Caroline broke into a smile, pocketed the picture, and went home.

chapter 30

ARIA

Aria came back one day at lunch.

Caroline didn't know it. She was sitting at Table 2, with Elle on one side and Ginny on the other. Jen, who was in the science club with Caroline, was sitting across from them, and they were all talking about a movie they had seen.

Caroline wasn't at the center of the universe, but she had an orbit. And she seemed genuinely happy.

Aria watched as she twisted in her seat and started talking to a girl at the table behind her. A girl with black curls and pale skin and a pretty smile. Aria noticed that for once, Lily's smile wasn't fake or forced. She and Caroline leaned their heads together and shared a secret, a comment, a joke, and then they turned back to their separate tables, separate lives.

Over at Table 7, Erica threw her head back and gave a

sharp laugh, and shot a dirty look at another girl across the room. Whitney and Jessabel mimicked her.

Some things didn't change.

There would always be an Erica or a Jessabel or a Whitney, girls who wanted to be on top, and would do anything to get there. But for every one of them there was a Ginny, or an Elle, or a Caroline.

Girls who found a way to be themselves.

Aria stood there watching until the bell rang and the girls put away their trays and filed off to class. She followed behind Caroline, a small pang of sadness in her chest. If she were still here, they'd be going to science class together. Instead, Caroline had her arm looped through Jen's. But once, Caroline glanced back, and Aria wondered if she could feel her there, trailing like a shadow, or if she was just remembering.

Caroline disappeared into the classroom. As the door swung shut, Aria reached out and brought her fingers thoughtfully to the wood. Her hand fell away, and she smiled at her handiwork.

The classroom door was now *covered* in stars. Just a little something for Caroline to see when class was over.

Aria's shadow fidgeted at her feet. *All right*, Aria thought. She didn't belong here anymore.

She still had work to do.

Last Wishes

chapter 1

MIKAYLA

Mikayla Stevens was made of gold.

That's what Miss Annette was always saying, but tonight it was true. She was wearing a gold leotard, and her dark skin was dusted with glittering powder — every time she rubbed her face, some came off on her hand. She considered her reflection in the mirrored wall, and realized she looked like one of those figurines they put on the tops of trophies.

Only gold girls go to Drexton, she recited to herself. But as her gaze drifted down from her face to her body, she cringed, taking in the catalog of imperfections: She wasn't tall enough. Her legs were too short. Her waist wasn't that narrow. *Stand up straight*, Miss Annette would say. *Legs together.*

She forced herself to stand tall and smile. A practiced smile. A *winning* smile.

Halfway down the same wall Mikayla's classmate, Sara, was warming up on a barre. Sara was a foot taller than Mikayla, long-limbed, and rail thin. She wore a shimmering green leotard, her blond hair pulled back in a perfect bun. The younger members of the Filigree Dance Company were across the room, a huddle of eight- and nine- and ten-year-olds, rehearsing their group number.

Only Sara and Mikayla were competing in solos.

The practice room was loud and full of dancers from across the region — ranging from little kids all the way up to teens, some in simple leotards, others in more ornate costumes (Mikayla envied those, even though Miss Annette said they were a distraction from talent), all waiting their turn to take the stage. A banner above the door read NORTHEAST DIVISION REGIONAL CHAMPIONSHIP.

"Five minutes, girls!" Miss Annette called, crossing her arms over a glitzy Filigree Dance Company sweater. Sara would be performing first, followed immediately by Mikayla.

Panic fluttered through her, the way it always did before she went on stage. Her stomach coiled nervously. She knew her dance routine backward and forward and upside down. She knew it inch by inch, and second by second, so it should be perfect.

It *had* to be perfect.

"Filigree dancers," trilled a voice through the intercom. *"Sara Olbright, Mikayla Stevens."*

The room snapped back into focus as Miss Annette gave a definitive clap and ushered Mikayla and Sara out of the room and down a hall toward the stage.

"Good luck, Sara," said Mikayla.

The other girl gave a thin smile. "I don't need luck," she said, heading toward the darkened backstage area. Mikayla reached for the door, but Miss Annette put a hand on her shoulder and crouched to look her in the eye.

"I don't want silver," Miss Annette said sternly. "And I don't want bronze. So what do I want?"

"Gold," replied Mikayla.

Miss Annette smiled, her teeth unnaturally white. "Exactly." She straightened and gave Mikayla a push. "I know you won't disappoint me."

Mikayla swallowed and nodded while Miss Annette scurried off into the audience to grab a seat.

When Mikayla snuck a peek through the velvet curtains, she could see the judges at their long table, the trophies beside them, the cash prizes in elegant envelopes beneath. She *needed* to win. Her parents needed her to win.

Behind the judges sat the audience, a mass of families and friends and coaches and dancers who'd already gone and were waiting for the awards at the end. Mikayla's mom was out there somewhere, filming on her iPad. Sometimes, Miss Annette told them, there were scouts in the audience, too. Mikayla had seen a poster one time that said DANCE LIKE NOBODY'S WATCHING, but Miss Annette said that was ridiculous; someone important was *always* watching.

Mikayla's pulse thudded in her ears. She closed her eyes, and tried to clear her head, but all she could hear was Miss Annette saying *gold gold gold gold*.

A routine ended, the music giving way to applause, and three cheerful girls bounded offstage, arm in arm, in matching blue outfits.

Sara stepped through the curtain, let out a breath, and disappeared onto the stage. The audience went silent, and the music began, and Mikayla put away the voices and pulled herself together.

She was up next.

chapter 2

ARIA

The shadow took shape on the curb outside.

It appeared out of nowhere, tucked in the dark between two streetlights. Everyone was inside watching the dancers, so no one saw the shadow grow or fill with light. No one saw the trace of wings above the shadow's shoulders. No one saw a twelve-year-old girl with curly red hair and a blue charm bracelet rise out of the brightened shape. And no one saw the girl tell her shadow, "Good job," and tap her foot until the light went out.

No one *saw* Aria step out into the world, but there she was. In a new place for the third time.

The last time.

Aria felt a rush of excitement. One more girl, one more mission, and she would finally have her wings. And then . . . Well, Aria didn't know what would happen after that.

First things first.

She exhaled, marveling as her breath made a cloud in front of her. She brought her hand to the fog, which fell apart before she could touch it. How strange.

It was much colder here than the last place she'd been, and she shivered and pulled her coat close around her before she even realized she was *wearing* a coat. She also had on jeans, a sweater, and brown boots. After a moment, she turned the boots a pretty shade of purple, and smiled.

In the distance there was a beautiful skyline: a cluster of tall, skinny buildings stretching toward the sky. A *city*. Aria had never been to a city before, and she was excited to explore.

And then Aria heard music. It was coming from the building to her right. She turned to look. A sign outside the building announced that the Northeast Division Regional Championship — whatever that was — was going on inside. Aria headed for the door; she could tell in her bones that this was where she was supposed to be.

Inside, the lobby was filled with boys and girls hurrying around in strange outfits, but none of them were marked by the blue smoke Aria knew to look for. Glitter and makeup and gossamer, yes, but no smoke.

The music was coming from an auditorium, and Aria nudged the door open and slipped in. It was crowded, so crowded that Aria worried she wouldn't find whomever she was looking for. A few hundred people sat in the audience, some in costumes and others in normal clothes, while on stage a blond girl in a green leotard was dancing. The girl was tall and thin, and her motions were elegant in a practiced way. Aria watched her leap and turn and tumble across the stage, landing on one knee just as the music ended. The audience applauded, and so did Aria, scanning the room for a wisp of blue smoke. Nothing. The girl on stage curtsied, looking pleased with herself, and then scampered off into the wings. A panel of judges sat at a table in the front row, scribbling on their papers.

And then the crowd grew quiet again. Aria's gaze drifted back to the stage, and she saw her.

The girl was pretty, her dark skin dusted with glittery makeup, and her black hair pulled back into a bun and tied with a gold ribbon. She was dressed in a shimmering gold leotard with a simple gold frill of skirt, and she sparkled from head to toe beneath the auditorium lights.

The only thing that didn't match her outfit was the ribbon of blue smoke coiling around her shoulders.

Aria straightened up at the sight. This was her. The girl Aria had to help. The last girl.

No one else in the audience could see the blue smoke surrounding the girl. But Aria could, bright and clear. It was the same color as Aria's charm bracelet, and her hand went to the third and final loop that hung on it. Waiting. The only loop without a feather on it.

Aria smiled, and the spotlight above the dancer brightened.

The girl struck a pose, draped backward like a flower, so far that Aria was sure she'd lose her balance. But the girl didn't. Even the smoke twisted around the girl with an elegant grace.

Then the music started, and the girl began to dance.

She was small, but when she danced, she seemed to fill the stage. Aria watched her carefully, in awe of her talent. There was something mesmerizing about the girl, the way she moved, like an extension of the music. Aria had to remind herself that the rippling smoke wasn't part of the routine, that it was being caused by something in the girl's life.

But what?

The girl's face was a mask of calm, but there was a moment — a fraction of time — when she closed her eyes and a small, private smile found its way onto her face. In that instant, the blue smoke thinned. But it was only an instant, buried in the middle of the routine. When she came to a stop, draped in the exact same position she had started in, the smoke was thicker than ever.

The crowd applauded, the judges scribbled, and when the girl smiled again, it was a different smile. A stiff, practiced smile. She vanished backstage and Aria got up to follow. She couldn't exactly go up on stage, so she ducked and circled around, drawn to the girl by a simple tug, as if a rope were running between them.

She rounded a corner and found the girl leaning back against a wall, head down. She didn't look like the girl on stage anymore. The girl on stage had been proud, confident, in control. This girl looked miserable.

Aria was about to step toward her when a woman appeared.

"Mikayla," said the woman, who had the girl's same dark skin (minus the glitter) and the same bright brown eyes. Aria guessed it was her mother. "You were wonderful."

Mikayla, thought Aria. What a pretty name.

The girl looked up but didn't smile. "I missed the turn," she said softly.

"Which turn?"

"At the end. I was supposed to spin four times, and I only did three."

"Well, no one noticed."

"*I* noticed." Mikayla's eyes shone with tears, and her mom tsked and ushered her back toward the audience.

"Hey," said Aria to her as she passed. "You were really amazing out there."

Mikayla flashed her that same hollow smile. "Thanks," she said. But Aria could tell she wasn't really listening. Mikayla's mind seemed miles away as Aria trailed her into the auditorium.

The rest of the dancers were good — some *very* good — but none of them were as good as the girl in gold. So Aria wasn't surprised when she won first place for her category. The blond girl in green took second.

When Mikayla Stevens (they called her full name) got up to take the trophy, and the cash prize, her smoke got even denser. Aria frowned, confused. The girl had won. What was making her so upset? Aria squinted at the smoke, as if she could see the problems in it, but all she saw was Mikayla's gold form beneath a blur of blue.

chapter 3

MIKAYLA

"There's my golden girl," said Miss Annette outside the auditorium, squeezing Mikayla's shoulder. "We'll work on that turn tomorrow."

Mikayla held the trophy to her chest, along with the check, and nodded.

The second-place trophy hung from Sara's hand. She held it with only the tips of her fingers, like she didn't want to touch it.

"What do you expect?" Miss Annette said to Sara. "It was a silver performance."

Sara's parents were standing nearby. They either didn't hear, or they pretended not to. Sara looked like she was about to cry. The rest of the Filigree girls were gathered around. The group routine had gotten bronze, but Miss Annette didn't seem to mind.

"Come on," said Mikayla's mom. "Let's get you home."

Mikayla pulled her Filigree Dance Company jacket on over her gold costume.

"Your dad wanted to be here tonight," said her mom, zipping up her own coat.

"I know." Mikayla's dad used to come to every event, back before he lost his job at the firm. Now it seemed like he spent every waking moment looking for work. She could picture him hunched over his laptop at their kitchen table, nursing a mug of coffee in one hand and furiously typing with the other, sending out résumé after résumé. He only left the house for interviews, and so far none of them had worked out. Her mom still had a job — she worked as a graphic designer for a small company. But she didn't make very much money, and it felt like their lives were tipping out of balance, about to fall.

"I filmed it for him, though!" Her mom waved her iPad. "We can all watch it when we get home."

On the way out, they passed that girl again, the redhead who'd told her she'd been amazing. The redhead smiled. Mikayla smiled back. There was something about her. Mikayla couldn't put her finger on it.

"I'm so proud of you," her mom was saying. "We should get a hot chocolate or something, to celebrate." Mikayla shook her head. She was already the shortest dancer in her bracket. She couldn't afford to put on weight. Not with the Drexton audition coming up. "What's wrong, M?" pressed her mom. "You just won, and you don't even seem happy about it."

Mikayla's smile must have faltered. She forced it back in place. "I *am* happy," she insisted. "Just tired."

The competition was outside the city, in New Jersey, so they'd had to drive instead of taking the subway. Now they climbed into the car and pulled away, the venue disappearing in the rearview mirror. They drove past a movie theater and a mall. Mikayla slumped back against her seat. She couldn't remember the last time she'd *seen* a movie, or gone shopping for something that wasn't for dance. A strange feeling twisted in her chest.

Her mom's cell phone rang. It was Dad.

"We're on our way home now," said Mikayla's mom, answering at a stoplight. "Yes, she was perfect." Mikayla cringed at the word. "Another gold. Yeah, I filmed it all. Okay. We'll see you soon."

The Stevenses lived in a townhouse in Brooklyn. It stood shoulder to shoulder with its neighbors, tall and thin, like a dancer, and made of pretty, dark bricks. Mikayla loved the house.

Which was why she hated the boxes. They hovered by the front door, and in the corners of the rooms, looming like shadows. A threat, a constant reminder that if her father didn't find another job, and soon, they'd be out of their lovely brownstone, crammed into a smaller apartment in a faraway neighborhood.

The boxes had shown up one at a time, throughout the house. At first her mom said she just wanted to clean up, clear out the things they weren't using anymore. Simplify their lives. But after she was done simplifying, the boxes kept coming.

"We have too much stuff," her dad said. "We don't need it." What he meant was, wherever they were going, there wouldn't be enough room.

"There's my girl," he said now, pushing up from the kitchen table. He looked tired but still threw out his arms, and she launched herself into the bear hug, the way she had when she was a kid. His arms still swallowed her up, made her feel small.

"Hi, Dad."

He pulled back and admired the newest trophy. "We're running out of space," he said, setting it on the table. Mikayla wondered if the trophies would be boxed up soon, too.

Chow, Mikayla's overly excitable spaniel mix, bounded up from under the kitchen table and leapt on Mikayla, licking her face. She giggled, feeling her spirits lift. By the time he was done, the dog's black fur was dusted with gold. Her mom let him out into the narrow back garden and began collecting her dad's coffee cups, which had multiplied.

Mikayla pretended not to see the bills stacked next to the coffee pot as she set the prize money silently beside it.

The first time she'd won after Dad had lost his job, she'd brought the check straight to him.

"Will this help?" she'd asked.

She hoped the sight of the money would make him happy, but, if anything, he looked more miserable than ever.

They'd always put Mikayla's competition winnings into a special college fund for her. But now she knew her *parents* actually needed the money. They didn't want to say it, as if by not saying the words out loud, they could somehow protect her from the fact that they were broke. But the truth was all around them. Just like the boxes.

"We can put it toward my Filigree classes," Mikayla had added, seeing her dad's hesitation as she held the check out to him. "That makes sense, right? Dance paying for dance."

"Okay," her dad had replied, reluctantly. "We'll put it toward Filigree. But only until the audition."

The audition. The only one that mattered. The one for the Drexton Academy of Dance. The most prestigious dance school in the city. Places rarely opened, auditions were once a year, by invite only, and every Drexton dancer was given a full scholarship. Enough to pay for the academy, for school, for competitions.

For *everything*.

Which meant she *had* to get in.

"So let's see this first place performance," her dad was saying now, nodding toward the iPad her mom was pulling from her purse.

Her mom propped the iPad up on the kitchen table and they all gathered around the screen as the video started.

Her parents beamed. Mikayla watched the gold-dusted girl take the stage. She looked like someone else.

Mikayla knew it was a good performance, but all she could see were the flaws. The mistakes that had cost her points. Yes, she'd won, but not by much. She could have lost. Could have taken second, which was the same as losing.

The judges had gone easy on her.

The Drexton committee wouldn't.

"I'm *so* proud of you, M," said her dad when it was over.

"So proud," echoed her mom. "Why don't you go change, honey, and then add this to the collection?" She gestured to the trophy.

Mikayla knew that was code for her parents needing to talk in private. Ever since her dad lost his job, they'd conversed in low, worried voices, and Mikayla could sometimes make out words like *costs* and *rent* and *benefits*.

Mikayla took her trophy and went to her room, changing out of her leotard and into stretchy pants and an old T-shirt. She scrubbed the rest of the gold dust from her face and undid her bun, finger-combing her thick dark hair. She could hear her parents' muffled voices in the kitchen.

Out in the garden, Chow was barking at something. Probably a squirrel. Chow was obsessed with squirrels.

With her trophy in hand, Mikayla slipped out of her room and padded downstairs to the basement.

For as long as she could remember, the basement had been her space. She'd played dress-up down here, watched movies with friends, made forts, and pinned up art. That was back when dance was just one of a dozen hobbies. Before it became the center of her life.

Three years ago, for her ninth birthday, the basement had been converted into a private dance studio, complete with a mirrored wall and a barre and shelf after shelf of trophies.

There were a few silver and bronze, but the vast majority were gold.

She set the newest trophy in one of the last open spots on the wall.

There were no boxes here. Not yet.

Next to the trophy shelves hung a wall calendar. On a date that looked dauntingly close, she'd written the word *Drexton* in red capital letters, a red circle drawn around it.

Mikayla rubbed her eyes, exhausted. But she turned toward the mirror and stretched. She raised her arms and started to spin, just as she'd done in the middle of the routine. Only this time she managed one, two, three, four turns before coming back to a stop.

She did it again.

One, two, three, four.

The shelves of golden trophies blurred as she kept her eyes on the mirror and spun, and spun, and spun, and stopped one turn shy, not because she'd messed up, but because something in the mirror had caught her eye. Well, not in the mirror, but in the window behind her. It wasn't a true window, not the kind you open or climb through, just a strip of glass near the top of the wall that looked out onto the grass in front of the townhouse. But she *thought*, for a moment, that she'd seen someone's face. Which was silly, because the face would have to be lying on the ground just to see her. Mikayla shook it off and lifted her arms again.

"Mikayla!" called her mom from upstairs.

She let her arms fall back to her sides. "Coming!" she called.

She cast a last glance back at the window, but of course, there was no one there.

chapter 4

ARIA

"That was close," whispered Aria to her shadow.

She had, in fact, been crouching on the ground in front of Mikayla's house, peering in through the tiny window into the basement below.

Aria had made it to the Stevenses' house before Mikayla (traveling by shadow was faster than traveling by car). She'd gone through the low gate and into the little back garden, but she'd been met with unexpected resistance in the form of a dog. The little barking creature had been able to sense her, even when she was invisible, so she'd come back out front. She'd let herself become visible again, and was about to wander away when she saw the light turn on in the basement window.

She'd crouched down, and watched Mikayla spin and spin and spin — she felt dizzy just watching her — and hadn't thought about the mirror or the fact that she was visible, not until it was too late.

She pressed herself back against the bricks, invisible again, and waited for the basement light to turn off. Then she looked up at the townhouse and wondered which room was Mikayla's, even though it didn't matter; she couldn't get inside, not without permission.

Just then, the front door opened, but it wasn't Mikayla; it was her father. He was carrying out the trash, but she could see past him into the townhouse and was surprised to see boxes stacked inside, as if they were getting ready to move. And then the dog — Chow, they'd called him — bounded out in the man's wake, and headed straight for Aria. He barked and wagged his tail and prodded her invisible knees with his wet nose.

"Good dog," whispered Aria.

"Chow!" snapped Mr. Stevens, dropping the trash in the can. He came over and picked up Chow, hauling the barking dog back inside and closing the door.

Aria let out a breath of relief and became visible again, an instant before a boy on a bike pulled up to the townhouse next door. He hopped down, took off his backpack, and tugged off his helmet. He had shaggy brown hair and blue eyes, and was roughly the same age as Mikayla.

He saw Aria standing there in front of Mikayla's house, and paused.

"Hey," he said.

"Hi," said Aria.

"You a friend of Mikayla's?"

Aria nodded. It was a small lie. And it wasn't so much a lie as an out-of-order truth, since she intended to *become* friends with Mikayla.

"I didn't think she had *time* for friends anymore." There was something in the way he said it. An edge, like hurt. "What with all the dancing." Aria didn't know what to say to that. "Sorry," the boy added, shaking his head. "That was harsh. I just miss her."

Aria smiled kindly. "What's your name?"

"Alex," he replied, locking his bike to the railing of the steps. "Well, tell her I said hi." And with that, he went inside.

Aria turned her attention back to Mikayla's house. She couldn't just stand around all night, waiting for morning or Mikayla. (Well, she could, but that didn't seem like a good use of time.)

So Aria started walking.

It was a cold night, but Aria wanted to see as much as she could. The single featherless loop on her bracelet whispered against her skin, a reminder that this was her last task, that everything that starts must end. It wasn't that she was afraid, exactly; she just didn't want to waste any time sitting still.

As she walked, she wondered about Mikayla Stevens — who she was, and why Aria had been sent to help her. She thought of the pieces of Mikayla she'd seen so far: the competition, the gold trophy — the *wall* of gold trophies — and her practiced smile. The moving boxes, and her father's troubled eyes, and Alex's comment on how she was never around. Aria wondered which thing was causing Mikayla's blue smoke, or if somehow they all were.

Whatever it was, Aria would find a way to help. She always did.

Meanwhile, the streets had quieted around her, but they still felt *alive*. There was a pulse to this place, an energy the other places she'd visited hadn't had. Aria liked it.

She walked on, her legs burning pleasantly, following the clusters of light that marked large buildings. She crossed a big circle, edged around a park that was sprawling and dark, and passed a massive stone building.

Then Aria looked up, and found herself standing in front of a large, curving gate. The gate was lovely, and covered in carved silver leaves, and bore the words BROOKLYN BOTANIC GARDEN.

Aria didn't know what *botanic* meant, but she knew what a garden was, and this one seemed impressive.

When she looked through the gate, she could see paths and trees, flowers and grass that seemed to go on forever.

The gate was locked, but not in the way that meant she had to be invited in. This place didn't belong to just *one* person or family. When Aria brought her hand to the gate, something clicked inside, and it fell open beneath her touch, just far enough for her to slip through.

Aria reached the edge of the entrance path, and her eyes widened.

Fairy lights hovered on the path, illuminating the gardens wherever she went. Many of the flowers had retreated against the chill, but as Aria walked past them, they blossomed again, pink and red and white and yellow.

"Isn't it wonderful?" she said to her shadow, and though her shadow never spoke, its head seemed to bob in the flickering light.

Everywhere she wandered, there was something new to see.

A field with trees lined up in perfect rows.

A lake with moonlight and lily pads floating on top.

A building made entirely of glass.

When she stepped inside the building, it was like walking into another world, the groomed gardens and cool fall air traded for a leafy green indoor jungle.

She couldn't think of a better place to spend the night.

The city, thought Aria, as she slipped back through the gate again around dawn, *is a magical place*.

Almost as magical as her.

chapter 5

MIKAYLA

WINNERS NEVER QUIT. QUITTERS NEVER WIN.

It was the first thing Mikayla saw when she opened her eyes each morning. The poster was taped to the back of her bedroom door, a pair of ballet shoes suspended beneath the words. It was one of Miss Annette's favorite phrases. She was full of sayings.

If it doesn't hurt, you're not trying hard enough.

You're only as good as your next dance.

Only gold girls go to Drexton.

Mikayla sat up, tired and sore. Her eyes traveled to the boxes in the corner of her room, then to the homework spread at the foot of her bed. She'd stayed up until midnight working on math problems but hadn't finished. She knew she had to keep her grades up if she wanted to stay at Coleridge.

Coleridge was the prestigious private school Mikayla had been going to since kindergarten. The prestigious private school her family couldn't afford anymore.

Mikayla had overheard her parents talking about it.

(Mikayla overheard her parents talking about a lot of things.)

Apparently Coleridge had agreed to give her a scholarship, so long as she kept her grades up. But it wouldn't take effect until after Christmas. By then, it might be too late. The Drexton audition loomed in her mind, more important than ever.

She got out of bed and went through her morning stretches, limbering her arms and legs, ankles and feet, working the stiffness out of her limbs. There was a floor-length mirror in her room, and she stood in front of it, assessing. Scrutinizing.

"Mikayla!" her mom called up the stairs. "Bye, honey. I'm leaving for work now. Don't be late to school!"

"I won't!" Mikayla called back. "Have a good day!" Her mom always left the house earlier than she did. There was a time when her parents would go to work together. Now, Mikayla knew, her dad was downstairs alone. At least he had an interview today.

Quickly, she showered, dressed, and packed up her school stuff, along with her Filigree dance bag. She swung the bag over her shoulder and grabbed a granola bar on her way out. Coleridge was located in Manhattan, just off the 3 line. Mikayla took the subway to school — she'd just been allowed to start taking it by herself.

"Good luck on the interview," she told her dad as she tugged on her coat.

"Thanks, hon," he said, looking as tired as she felt. *Please let him get this job*, she thought as she walked outside.

Next door, Alex was just swinging a leg over his bike.

"Hey," he said.

"Hey, she said.

Then there was an awkward pause, where they both opened and then closed their mouths. And then it was over. He waved and she nodded and he went off on his bike and she went off on foot.

Mikayla and Alex used to be inseparable, back when they were kids. She'd invite him over to build forts in the basement and he'd invite her over to play video games or go bike-riding in Prospect Park. And then at some point, Mikayla started saying no — for the same reason she said no to everything, because she had dance. And then, eventually, Alex stopped offering. They were still nice to each other, and she missed him, of course — sometimes on her way home from dance, she'd hear him laughing with friends in his backyard, or playing video games when the windows were open, and she wanted to join him — but dance came first. It had to. And besides, she told herself, they probably didn't have anything in common anymore.

She hurried down the steps into the subway station. The train was just pulling in, and she ran to catch it. It was already half-full, and she sank into a seat and pulled out the last of her math homework while the stops ticked past.

About halfway to Coleridge, she finished her homework and glanced up. A girl her age was sitting beside her. She looked familiar.

"Hi again," said the girl with a smile.

Mikayla frowned. At first, she couldn't figure out where she'd seen her before. And then it clicked. It was the redhead from the competition the night before.

"Hi," said Mikayla. "You were at Regionals last night."

The girl nodded.

"So you're a dancer, too?"

"I'm an Aria," she said.

"Like the music?"

The girl smiled. "No. Like the person."

"Oh," said Mikayla. "Well, hi again."

Aria swung her legs back and forth. She had on cute purple boots, Mikayla noticed. "Small world, huh?" she said.

Mikayla nodded, even though it wasn't really a small world. It was a big city, with millions of people. What were the odds that they'd bump into each other? "Where are you headed?" she asked.

Aria's gaze drifted down and landed on Mikayla's bag. There was a Coleridge School button on it. Aria brightened and pointed at it. "There!"

"No way," said Mikayla.

"It's my first day," said Aria, "so it's nice to know I'll know *someone*."

"Yeah," said Mikayla. What was it about this girl? She was open and chatty in a way that was out of place in the city. Mikayla had been taught not to talk to strangers. Aria looked like she would probably talk to anyone. It wasn't a bad thing. Just one more thing that made her stand out.

"What is it?" asked Aria, feeling the weight of Mikayla's gaze.

"It's just weird, crossing paths," said Mikayla. "You're not following me, are you?"

It was a joke, but the girl's eyes went wide and she looked nervous. "No . . . I mean, not really," she said. "Must be a coincidence. The world is full of those, you know. Unless you believe that everything happens for a reason, and then I guess maybe we were *supposed* to cross paths. What do you think?"

Mikayla shook her head, dazed. "I don't believe in fate," she said stiffly. "It just seems like an excuse for people who don't want to take responsibility for things." Her words came out harsher than she'd meant them, but it bothered Mikayla when people chalked things up to the universe. In dance, you were responsible for yourself. When you messed up, it wasn't because it was *supposed* to happen, it was because you failed to get it right.

"Well," said Aria cheerfully. "One way or another, I'm glad our paths crossed." She sounded like she meant it. Aria smiled, and it was crazy, but the train's fluorescent lights seemed to get brighter at that moment. Then Aria leaned forward, as if she had a secret. "You know, you really *are* an amazing dancer."

Mikayla felt embarrassed. "I could be better."

"Well, I hope so," said Aria, sitting back. "Wouldn't it be boring if you were already the best you could be? There'd be nowhere for you to go!"

Mikayla frowned. She'd never thought of it that way. But there *was* such a thing as *best*, especially when it came to competition. Mikayla turned to explain this to Aria, when she saw the girl gazing in awe at the subway map on the opposite wall. The train jerked forward and Aria swayed in her seat, crashing into Mikayla's shoulder. She apologized with a laugh.

"You're not from New York, are you?" ventured Mikayla.

Aria shook her head. "I just moved here."

"From where?"

Aria thought for a moment and then said, "California."

"Wow, that's a big change."

Aria beamed. "You have no idea."

Mikayla found herself returning the smile as she looked back at the subway map. She was so used to all the colorful lines and dots that she'd come to take it for granted. The train slowed, and she pushed to her feet, ready to elbow her way through the crowds. She glanced down at Aria.

"Come on! This is our stop."

chāpter 6

ARIA

As they climbed the subway steps and emerged onto the street, Aria's mouth fell open.

The subway itself had been a new adventure — the not-terribly-pleasant smells on the platform, the passengers shoving and maneuvering around one another, the way the train snaked through the tunnels like a giant beast. But what waited for her on the other side was even more amazing. Brooklyn had been green and leafy and relatively quiet. This part of the city was stuffed full of dizzying skyscrapers, honking yellow cars, carts selling food, giant stores, and more people than Aria had *ever* seen. She looked around, mesmerized.

"What is it?" asked Mikayla.

Aria couldn't stop gazing at the city.

"It's *incredible*," she whispered.

Mikayla looked around, as if trying to see the streets and the people the way Aria did, but Aria knew she couldn't. To Aria, things were still strange and exciting. So many experiences were still foreign and new, which made the world a place of wonder and discovery. She wished more people could see life the way she did, could notice the things they'd gotten used to. She thought that if they could, it might make their lives a little more magical.

"Are you coming?" asked Mikayla.

Aria dragged her attention back to the girl and her blue smoke, and she nodded, determinedly.

"Have you always lived in the city?" Aria asked as they hurried down a busy street. She noticed how briskly Mikayla — and everyone else here — walked.

"Yeah," said Mikayla. "What about you? Had you always lived in California?"

Aria shook her head, thinking of the first place she'd visited, where she'd met Gabby. "No. I move around a lot."

"That's got to be hard," said Mikayla.

Aria shrugged. "I figure, I go where I'm supposed to be."

Mikayla chuckled. "You really do believe in fate and destiny and all that."

Aria chewed her lip. "I think there's a path. If that makes sense."

"Like the steps in a dance routine?" offered Mikayla.

Aria nodded. "Yeah. Sometimes you have to improvise, but I guess I believe there's a routine. A course things are supposed to take. So when it leads me to places, or to people, I assume I'm there for a reason."

Mikayla's brow crinkled, but she didn't say anything more.

At the end of the block, they rounded the corner, and there it was.

Coleridge School was a large brick building that looked like it had been there for a hundred years. The last school Aria had "attended," Caroline's school, had been very strict, with the girls in uniforms. Here, there was a mix of boys and girls, and no uniforms.

But everyone here, Aria noticed as she and Mikayla climbed the front steps, wore very *nice* clothes. The girls had on soft-looking creamy sweaters and jeans that fit perfectly. Velvety short skirts over patterned tights and shiny, brand-new boots. Luxurious-looking puffy coats. Mikayla, too, wore a pretty sweater dress with boots, but Aria noticed that her boots were a little scuffed, as if they weren't brand-new. Somehow, Aria could sense that this bothered Mikayla, even though Aria didn't understand why. She saw Mikayla glance down worriedly at her boots, then straighten up and adjust her smile until it was the perfect, practiced one.

"Mikayla!" someone called.

Mikayla waved and headed toward the voice, Aria trailing like a shadow.

Two girls were standing on the front steps, one with a tennis bag slung over her shoulder, the other holding a drawing pad to her chest.

"Hey," Mikayla said to the girls. She turned to Aria. "This is Beth," she said, gesturing to the girl with the tennis bag. "And this is Katie." She nodded toward the girl with the drawing pad. "This is Aria," she explained to her friends.

The girls, neither of whom had seemed to notice her yet — people rarely did, unless they needed her — smiled cheerfully. "Hey," they said in unison. And then they started chatting with Mikayla about homework and boys and a dozen other topics, all started and dispatched with lightning speed. Mikayla listened and nodded, and Aria wondered why she was wearing the practiced smile, instead of a real one.

And then the bell rang. Mikayla pointed Aria toward the main office. "If we're not in the same classes, then come find me at lunch," she said, before vanishing down the hall with Beth and Katie.

Aria hoped getting into Coleridge wouldn't be too hard. And it wasn't. Not with a little bit of magic. The man at the front office found Aria's name in the computer, with all the proper boxes already checked. Aria gave her best smile and was given a schedule in return.

She hadn't thought to arrange her schedule so that she shared classes with Mikayla. Still, she figured she might learn about the school and Mikayla's world by just attending the classes with the other students.

To her relief, Coleridge was pretty much like the two other schools Aria had been to. There was English, and history, and math. (Aria didn't like math, and she supposed she could just skip it, but that felt somehow like cheating.)

By lunchtime, Aria *had* learned a little bit about algebra, and about something called the Revolutionary War, and that a poem called "The Road Not Taken" was very beautiful. She'd also learned that all the Coleridge students seemed wealthy, but not all of them seemed snobby. But she wasn't much closer to learning what was behind Mikayla's smoke.

The cafeteria was huge and noisy, and she saw Beth and Katie sitting at a table with a few other girls, but no Mikayla. She scanned the room and saw Mikayla standing at the end of the lunch line, tray in hand, her blue smoke twisting thickly around her. She looked distracted. Aria wondered what kind of help the girl needed, and she knew she wouldn't find out by watching. So she grabbed a tray and headed over.

"Cookie for your thoughts?" she said cheerfully.

Mikayla blinked and looked up. For a moment Aria expected her to paste on that smile and say, "Nothing," but instead she said, "I can't remember the last time I went to a movie."

It wasn't what Aria had expected her to say. And she didn't know how to answer. She couldn't remember the last time she'd been to a movie either, because she'd *never* been to a movie.

"Beth and Katie were talking about this movie they saw over the weekend," explained Mikayla. "They're always going to movies. Plays. Concerts."

"So why can't you go with them?" asked Aria, setting an apple on her tray.

Mikayla sighed. "Dance," she said automatically, as if that was the answer to every question. "And money," she added, and as soon as she said it, she looked down at her tray and blushed furiously. Aria didn't see why Mikayla should be embarrassed (Aria knew that most people couldn't just magic money out of their pockets whenever they needed to). But Mikayla seemed upset. Aria thought of the boxes she'd glimpsed stacked inside Mikayla's front door and wondered

440

if that had anything to do with the smoke. Or was it the fact that she was so hard on herself? That even first place didn't seem good enough?

In Mikayla's smoke, Aria could make out the edges of worry, and doubt, and stress, but it was all tangled, like a knot.

Aria opened her mouth to change the subject, but Mikayla was already heading for the checkout. By the time she led Aria toward a table where Beth and Katie were already sitting, she had that practiced smile back on her face.

As they were sitting down, Aria caught a glimpse of a familiar blond bun. Across the cafeteria was the tall, thin girl who'd won second place the night before.

"That's Sara," offered Mikayla.

"You two dance together, right?" asked Aria.

"We both go to Filigree," said Mikayla, as if the two statements were very different. "We usually walk there together after school."

"Speaking of," said Beth, taking a bite of her lasagna, "how were Regionals last night?"

"I did all right," said Mikayla, but Aria spoke up.

"I was there," she said, "and Mikayla was amazing. She won first place!"

Katie, who'd been doodling on her drawing pad, smiled.

"She always does." She sounded sincere, Aria realized, but there was something else in her words. A kind of sadness. Like she was proud of her friend, but also missed her, even though Mikayla was right there.

"Not true," said Mikayla. "Sara's getting better. If I'm not careful, she'll beat me."

Beth gave a dramatic gasp. "Because coming in second would be the end of the world!"

Mikayla managed a thin smile, but Aria could tell it was hollow, could tell that underneath the mask, beneath the perfect posture, the thought of coming in second was a horrible thing.

"Silver would clash with everything," said Katie thoughtfully. "We all know Mikayla only wears gold."

chapter 7

MIKAYLA

Mikayla had just left Coleridge with Sara, feeling the usual dread in her stomach whenever she had to spend time with the girl. They were halfway down the busy street, Sara listening to music through her earbuds, when Mikayla heard the sound of rushing steps behind her. She turned to find a breathless Aria catching up.

"Hey," she said. "Can I walk with you guys to Filigree?"

Mikayla's eyes widened. First the competition and then the subway and then Coleridge and now this? How could this Aria girl be everywhere?

Maybe we were supposed to cross paths. Aria's voice echoed in her head. Mikayla didn't believe in magic or things like fate, but even she had to admit this was getting weird.

Sara scrunched up her nose and tugged one earbud out. "Since when are *you* part of Filigree?"

"It's my first day," said Aria, apparently immune to Sara's attitude. She fell into step beside them. "Actually, that's why I was at Regionals last night."

"To scope out your competition?" asked Sara.

Aria frowned. "No," she said, earnestly. "Just to see you guys dance."

"Are you any good?" asked Sara.

Aria looked at her like she didn't understand the question.

"Of course she's good," said Mikayla, coming to her defense. "She wouldn't be coming to Filigree if she weren't."

Aria swallowed.

Sara shrugged, put her earbud back in, and cranked her music up. They were walking along Columbus Avenue. People were rushing past them, chattering into cell phones and holding coffees. They passed a hairdresser, a dry cleaners, restaurants with tables outside. Mikayla caught Aria looking around, so entranced by the city that Mikayla had to pull her out of the way of grumbling pedestrians. Twice.

"So," said Aria as they walked. "How long have you been dancing?"

Mikayla squinted, thinking back to herself as a chubby

little girl, in tights and a tutu for the first time. "Since I was five," she said. So it had been seven years. But sometimes it felt like forever.

"Wow," said Aria. "That's a long time. How often do you do it?"

"Six times a week." Back when she first started, she used to dance only twice a week, with foundations in ballet, jazz, and modern. But now her focus was contemporary, and somewhere along the way two times a week became four and then four became six. The only reason it wasn't seven was because Miss Annette took Sundays off. Now Mikayla felt like she was measuring dance not in times per week but in times per *day*.

It made her tired just thinking about it.

"You must really love it," said Aria as they stopped at a crosswalk. Sara stood beside them, lost in her music and cracking her gum.

"It's my life," replied Mikayla, feeling a strange heaviness when she said it. She forced herself to smile.

"So," said Aria. "What do you do when you're *not* dancing?"

Mikayla opened her mouth to answer, but nothing came out. She thought of Alex, and of Katie and Beth, and felt a pang of sadness. But she was spared from having to answer when they crossed the street and came to a stop in front of a small brick building. The sign on the front read FILIGREE DANCE COMPANY in bold, curving letters. "We're here," she said, dodging the question.

Aria looked suddenly very nervous. Mikayla brought a hand to rest on her shoulder. "You'll do fine," she said, trying to assure her. Sara had already vanished inside, and she started up the steps. When Aria didn't follow, Mikayla looked back. "You coming?"

Aria straightened, and nodded. "You go ahead," she said. "I'll be right behind you."

Mikayla went inside, surrounded by the familiar sight of mirrored walls and wooden floors, the familiar sound of music and Miss Annette's voice critiquing someone in a studio. But when she heard the sound of Aria at the front desk, she hesitated in the hall and listened.

"Can I help you?" Pam, the woman at the desk, asked.

"Hi, I'm Aria Blue. I'm here to join Filigree." Mikayla frowned. So Aria hadn't actually been accepted yet.

"I'm afraid we have a waiting list," said Pam. "You can't simply walk in."

"Oh," said Aria. "Sorry; I should be in the computer."

The click of keys on the keyboard, and then, "Sorry, you're not in here."

"Oh," said Aria again, sounding confused. "Can you check again? Aria Blue?"

"Sorry," said the woman after more typing. "No luck."

"Apparently not," said Aria. Mikayla chewed her lip.

"Filigree is a very competitive dance school," Pam said. "We can't exactly take on *everyone*. Admission is at Miss Annette's sole discretion. If you want to join, you'll need to audition."

"Great," said Aria, her voice brightening, "when can I do that?"

Pam started typing away again. "Hmm," she said. "Looks like the next opening is in just over three weeks."

"But I need to start now," insisted Aria. Mikayla didn't understand the urgency. Mikayla didn't understand what Aria was doing here at all, for that matter. It was starting to seem less like Aria had wandered into her life, and more like she'd marched.

"I'm sorry," said the woman, "Miss Annette is a very busy woman."

"Well," said Aria after a minute, "since I came all this way, could I at least join in today? I won't cause any trouble."

There was a long pause. "How much experience do you have?"

"I'm a very fast learner," she said.

The woman sighed. "Well, go get changed. You can stand in the back of the group lesson, and if Miss Annette has a few minutes, maybe she can fit you in. . . ."

Just then, Mikayla heard Miss Annette's voice boom out from one of the studios.

"What was that, Eliza?" she was shouting. "Was that supposed to be a ballonné? I can't even tell."

Mikayla heard Eliza's quiet apology, and she knew she better move quickly. Her own class was about to start. She hurried to get changed, nearly bumping into a beaming Aria outside the dressing room.

What are you doing here? Mikayla wanted to say. *Why are you here* now?

Instead she just said, "Do you have your dance clothes?"

"Of course," Aria replied, even though she only had a bookbag, not an extra dance tote like Mikayla did. But in the minute it took Mikayla to turn around and quickly change into her leotard, she looked back and saw that Aria was in a leotard herself. Mikayla didn't even know where Aria's school outfit had gone. It was as if the leotard had magically appeared. Weird.

Aria smiled, blue eyes bright. "I'm ready," she said. She turned to go, her red hair waving behind her.

"Wait," called Mikayla, pulling a hair tie from her wrist. She wrangled Aria's hair up into a ponytail, and then a bun, so it wouldn't get in the way.

"There," Mikayla said. "*Now* you're ready."

chapter 8

ARIA

Aria didn't know what had happened with the Filigree computer — she'd always been able to magic herself onto school rosters. She'd done it just that morning!

The only time her magic *didn't* work was when it wasn't *supposed* to (though she never knew what was allowed and what wasn't until she tried). So if she couldn't magic herself into Filigree, there must be a reason.

Or maybe her powers were just being ornery.

It didn't matter, she decided as she entered the classroom Mikayla had pointed her toward. Because she was here now. Standing in the back of a group lesson that was filled with eight- and nine-year-old girls.

Aria was a head taller than all of them, so she stood out like a tree in the middle of a garden.

Mikayla had gone into another studio, where Miss Annette taught the more advanced class.

In this one, a man named Clyde instructed the girls in Aria's group to do things like *chassé* and *pirouette.*

Aria had no idea what those words meant, but she'd told the truth to the woman at the front desk — she *was* a fast learner — and soon enough she was doing a half-decent job of keeping up.

"Jeté," instructed Clyde, and again, everyone but Aria seemed to know what that was. They lined up against the wall, and a small girl with a tight braid went first. She took a few fluid steps and then leaped high into the air. Aria watched in awe as the girl landed soundlessly on the wooden floor. She did three more flawless jumps, making her way to the opposite wall.

Aria felt suddenly very out of her element.

For a second she wondered if she should make herself invisible and duck into Mikayla's studio. But a good guardian angel didn't just watch. They became involved. They *intervened.* At least, that's what Aria told herself as the number of girls on her side of the room dwindled. She was secretly relieved that the other girls' jumps weren't all as impressive as the first girl's, but they were still *good.*

Soon it was just Aria against the wall, waiting.

Aria took a breath, and forced herself to go.

She took a step and then sped up. The wind whistled past her ears as she leaped into a jump. She stumbled as she landed, feeling clumsy.

"Try again," Clyde said, not unkindly.

Aria did. *Step, step, step, leap, split, land.*

She'd done it! It had actually felt nice, the sensation of being airborne for a moment. Aria couldn't fly, but this came close.

Aria smiled at the small victory. The fluorescent lights of the studio brightened.

When Clyde told them they could take a break, Aria turned to leave her studio to visit Mikayla's. But then the studio door opened and in marched an imperious-looking woman. Aria guessed she was Miss Annette.

"Clyde, I had a —" Miss Annette began, then paused when she saw Aria.

"What's this?" Miss Annette asked, scowling down at her.

Aria bristled — she was a *who*, not a *what* — but she managed to say, "I'm Aria."

"Where did you come from?"

"California," said Aria.

"And what are you doing here in my school?"

"I'm new. The woman at the desk said I could stay and that you might have time . . ." she trailed off under the woman's scrutiny.

Miss Annette gave her a long, head-to-toe look. "What kind of dancer are you?"

Aria wasn't sure how to answer that question. A new one, obviously. But she had heard Mikayla use the word *contemporary*, so that's what she said.

"Well," Miss Annette said. "Show me." The eyes in the room began to turn back toward Aria. "Let me see you do a pas de chat."

Aria stared. She had no idea what that was. "Um."

Miss Annette put her hands on her hips. "Fine. A plié."

Mikayla had slipped into the room. Aria could see her standing behind the instructor. At the word *plié*, Mikayla brought her hands up in front of her, like she was holding a basket, and dipped down, her legs bowing. Aria did her best to mimic this. Miss Annette made an exasperated sound.

"A grand jeté."

At that, Aria smiled. She knew how to do that one: the jump! She took a few steps back, then managed her best running leap. She was quite proud of herself, but Miss Annette only clicked her tongue.

"Do you at least have a routine you can show me?"

"Right here?" asked Aria. "Right now?"

"You are standing in a dance studio, and yes, now."

Aria swallowed. She wasn't self-conscious — she was a terrible singer and had still belted out tunes to help Gabby Torres — but this was different. Aria didn't usually care about looking silly or stupid, but here, she knew that if she wasn't good enough, they'd kick her out, and if that happened, it would be a lot harder to help Mikayla. She looked down at her shadow, but she knew it couldn't help her, not with this.

"Well?" pressed Miss Annette.

Aria nodded. "All right."

"Do you have music?" Miss Annette asked, pointing to the iPod speakers at the front of the room.

"Oh," said Aria. "No. Any song will do."

Miss Annette looked skeptical, but crossed to the iPod. A dozen dancers had now appeared in the studio to watch her, but it was Mikayla's gaze Aria could feel as she closed her eyes and took a breath. The music started. It was a pop song, one of the ones she'd sung with Gabby back in her room. Weeks ago. Lifetimes ago. Aria listened to it for a few moments, bouncing on her toes, finding the beat.

And then, as smoothly as she could, she started moving her arms and legs. There was something about the music, something cheerful, and as she danced, she thought of the gardens in Brooklyn. She thought of trampolines, of sleepovers and swimming pools. She thought of cupcakes and fall leaves and singing with Gabby. She thought of things that made her happy. Things that made her feel alive. Real. Human. She let that feeling move her, literally.

And then, all of a sudden, the music stopped. Aria blinked, and looked up to see Miss Annette watching her, eyes narrowed in thought.

Aria didn't know what to do. She wasn't sure what came next.

The room was painfully quiet, and Aria glanced at Mikayla, hoping to find an encouraging smile. But to her surprise, the other girl didn't look happy at all. If anything, she looked sad and lost. Aria didn't understand.

What had she done to make her upset?

chāpter 9

MIKAYLA

Mikayla stood against the wall with the other girls and watched Aria dance.

It had taken Aria a few moments to find the beat, to sink into the music. But then she was gliding across the floor. It wasn't perfect, far from it, but there was something to the movement, a kind of reckless abandon Mikayla envied. And *missed*.

Because back when Mikayla first started dancing, back before she cared about nailing every step, before she'd been afraid of making a mistake (before she'd even known what the mistakes *were*), she had moved like that, like Aria. The music would start, and she would just fall into it. Disappear.

She'd stop being Mikayla Stevens and become a melody, a rhythm, a beat. She'd stop thinking about the steps. She'd lose herself, and when that happened, she could be anyone, anything, for the length of the dance. It was the best feeling in the whole wide world.

Or at least, it used to be.

These days, the doubt and the fear and the pressure followed Mikayla wherever she went, and whenever she danced. Once in a while, when the music was perfect and nothing ached, the voices in her would quiet, and she'd start to lose herself again, just for a second. She'd forget how much it mattered, to her and to Miss Annette and to her parents. But those moments never lasted.

Now, Aria . . . Aria had danced like it didn't matter.

Like she didn't care if someone was watching.

Didn't care if she was messing up, or if she was good enough.

She just . . . danced.

"You're a beginner," Miss Annette said at last. It wasn't a question.

"I am." Aria nodded. "But," she added, "everyone has to start somewhere."

"Your form is a mess," added Miss Annette. "Your lines are far from straight and your hands need work, and it was, on the whole, a fairly rudimentary routine."

Aria kept her head up, but her smile flickered, and her gaze drifted not to the floor, but to the wall where Mikayla was standing.

"*But*," continued Miss Annette. "You have some natural talent. You dance with your heart. It's not enough, of course, but it's a start. I can teach you to dance with the rest."

"So I can stay?" asked Aria softly.

Miss Annette crossed her arms. "For now."

At that, Aria smiled like she'd just won Nationals.

As Mikayla returned to her Advanced studio and went through her arabesques and pirouettes, her tumbles and turns, she couldn't stop thinking of Aria's smile. Or the look on her face when she was dancing, lost in the music.

The girls at Filigree always looked focused, or tired, stressed or aching or worried or determined.

But Aria just looked *happy*.

The sun was going down by the time dance class ended. Mikayla and Sara and Aria all pulled on their jackets and descended the steps to the street. Sara peeled away — she lived on the Upper West Side and could walk home — and Mikayla and Aria made their way to the subway together.

"You're awfully quiet," said Aria as they walked.

"Just thinking," said Mikayla. "And tired."

Aria yawned. "I know," she said. "I can't believe you do this six days a week."

Mikayla shrugged. She tried not to focus on that, because it was a slippery slope from tired to whiny, and Miss Annette had a zero-tolerance policy when it came to complaints. Of course Mikayla was tired — exhausted in a bone-deep way — but she'd gotten over it, or at least gotten used to it. It was just another sacrifice.

Success requires sacrifice. One of Miss Annette's many sayings.

When the train came and they got on, Mikayla snagged two seats. Aria slumped down beside her. "How do you do it all?" she asked, sounding genuinely amazed.

Mikayla shrugged again. She didn't just do it for herself. She did it for her parents, who had sacrificed so much for so long to make it possible. The Drexton audition loomed in the back of her mind. She was so close. If she could just get in, she'd finally be able to make it up to them.

Aria stretched, obviously sore after the long lesson. The subway train sped through several stops. It was an express.

Mikayla hesitated, then said, "Why did you decide to come to Filigree today?"

Aria's forehead crinkled. "What do you mean?"

"I mean, I know you hadn't been accepted yet. Which means you just . . . decided to come."

Aria tugged her red hair out of its bun and shrugged. "Maybe I was inspired by you. Maybe I just felt drawn to it. Like fate."

Mikayla sighed. "It's not fate if you *make* paths cross, Aria."

Aria gave a half-smile. "Even though I nudged our paths a little," she said, "I still think we were supposed to meet."

And it was weird; Mikayla couldn't explain why, but she felt the same way. "I'm glad we did," she said. "It was pretty bold of you to just dance like that, in front of everyone."

"Oh man," said Aria with a chuckle. "It was pretty bad, wasn't it?"

"No," said Mikayla. "I mean, okay, technically there were issues, but that's just because you're new."

Aria sighed. "There's *so* much I don't know."

"I could help you learn." It wasn't an *entirely* selfless offer. Some small part of Mikayla hoped that maybe by being near Aria, she could rediscover the way dance used to feel, even though all afternoon it had been a reminder of something she'd lost.

Aria laughed and sat forward. "I'm supposed to be the one helping you."

Mikayla frowned. "What do you mean?"

Aria's eyes widened, as if she'd surprised herself. "Nothing," she said, blushing. "Sorry, my brain must be tired. And thanks. That would be great."

The subway train shuddered to a stop, and the doors dinged open. People pushed on and off, and then the doors closed. Mikayla was glad they'd gotten seats.

"I'll do what I can to help," she told Aria. "My form's not perfect."

"You're *way* too hard on yourself," said Aria. "You're an incredible dancer. And *perfect* is kind of a silly word."

"How so?" Mikayla bristled a little.

"Well," said Aria. "There's no such thing as perfect. It doesn't exist."

"Of course it does."

"Where?" challenged Aria. "If perfect means without flaws, then there's no such thing as a perfect tree, or a perfect apple, or a perfect sky."

"What about a perfect score?" asked Mikayla. "That exists."

"Even if *you* got a perfect score," said Aria with a devious smile, "I bet you'd find mistakes."

Mikayla found herself blushing. She didn't know how Aria knew that, but she was right.

"Perfect is this thing in your head," continued Aria. "If you think, *I'll be happy when I'm perfect*, then you'll never be happy! I just don't think perfect is a good thing to shoot for."

"Well," said Mikayla. "You still have to try."

"Why?" asked Aria, sounding genuinely curious.

"Because," said Mikayla with exasperation, "even if there's no such thing as *perfect*, there *is* such a thing as *best*. And in the world of dance, being the best is what matters. It's *all* that matters."

The smile slid from Aria's face, and Mikayla felt bad for saying those words so harshly. But it was true. Aria could let go, dance like she didn't care, but for Mikayla, it wasn't about having fun, not anymore.

It was about *winning*.

A silence fell between them as the train rattled toward Brooklyn.

"This is my stop," Mikayla said when the train screeched to a halt in her station. "I'll see you tomorrow, okay?" She wondered where Aria lived, but she wouldn't have time to stop and ask if she wanted to make it off the train.

"Sure thing," said Aria, summoning a smile. Mikayla got off, but when she looked back, just before the train pulled away, she was surprised to see the smile slide from Aria's face, replaced by worry.

Mikayla pulled her jacket tight around her and hurried home. When she reached the front steps, she hesitated, dragged down by the thought of her father hunched at the kitchen table, the boxes looming in the corners, the gold trophies lining the basement walls. A lump filled her throat.

She brought her forehead to the front door.

Here's what will happen, she told herself. *Next week, I'm going to nail my audition at Drexton. I'm going to get the scholarship, and Mom and Dad won't have to pay for dance or Coleridge anymore, and Dad will get a new job, and we won't lose our house, and everything will be perfect. Because I will be perfect.*

And then she took a deep breath, readjusted her smile, and went in.

chapter 10

ARIA

Aria didn't get off the train.

She'd thought about following Mikayla, but instead she hung back and watched the girl go, tendrils of blue trailing in her wake.

Aria needed to think, and something about the motion of the train, as it made its winding path, was soothing. A map on the wall showed the whole city — it looked so small and so large at the same time — and all the train lines criss-crossing over the top of it, labeled things like A and B and 1 and 2 and 3. They were all different colors, too.

Aria ran a thumb absently over the bare ring on her charm bracelet, trying to sort through the mystery of Mikayla Stevens. Back in California, Caroline's problem had been fairly obvious, and, at least in retrospect, Gabby's had been clear, too. But Aria was having trouble understanding Mikayla.

As the train clattered along, Aria thought about all the things Mikayla had said — about money, the need to be the best, the way her life revolved around dance — and all the things she hadn't. She thought of the boxes at Mikayla's house, but also the weary sadness that wove through her voice when she spoke of dancing.

Aria thought about Mikayla as a dancer. After Aria had performed for Miss Annette, she'd made herself invisible and watched through a crack in the door as Mikayla danced in the Advanced studio. Mikayla had seemed fidgety. She was constantly adjusting her posture, holding in her stomach, forcing a smile she obviously didn't feel. Like she wasn't comfortable in her own skin. Aria had seen the self-criticism swirling in her smoke.

But then . . . there were those moments, embedded in the middle of a routine, when it was like all that fell away, and she seemed genuinely happy to be dancing. And in those moments, the smoke around her changed, too. Didn't lessen or thin, exactly, but shifted. *Reacted.*

So did that make dance the *problem*, or the *solution*?

Or could it somehow be both at once?

Aria looked down at her shadow, as if it had something to say. But it didn't, so Aria leaned back. She stayed on the subway, riding it from end to end, changing from the blue line to the red to the green, trading As and Cs for 1s and 2s and Gs.

As it got later, she started to stand out more and more (apparently twelve-year-old girls didn't ride the subway alone after a certain time), and finally, between stops, when no one was there to see, Aria took a breath and willed herself to disappear.

She didn't like being invisible, but it definitely made things easier sometimes.

As evening turned to night, the crowd on the subway thinned. There was a man with a bike. A tired-looking woman with grocery bags. A figure stretched out sleeping across three seats. And that's how Aria realized, with some surprise, that she wasn't the only one without a place to call home.

At different stations, Aria began to see these people: slumped or dozing on the benches, looking lost and tired and ragged. None of them were surrounded by blue smoke. None of them were marked for Aria's help. But that didn't mean she couldn't try and make their lives a little better. She put coins in cups, mended coats and blankets and shoes with an invisible touch. Even if the acts of kindness were small, and wouldn't bring her any closer to helping Mikayla and earning her wings, they still made her feel useful.

After she'd ridden a few more trains, Aria decided to get some fresh air.

When she got up to the street, she was amazed to find that the sparkling city was still very much awake. It felt even bigger at night, and Aria felt even smaller. But it wasn't a bad kind of small. It made her feel like a piece of something. Connected. She wandered down the sidewalk, past dimly lit restaurants and brightly lit markets, and businesses closed for the night.

She passed a handful of chalk murals on the sidewalk, stepping gingerly around them so she wouldn't mess them up. They were so beautiful and colorful and intricate that it took her several moments to realize they were words. Sayings like *This Too Shall Pass* and *Take a Deep Breath, It Will All Be Okay* and *Find Your Joy*.

Clever sidewalk, she thought.

A streetlamp behind her cast her shadow forward so that it almost looked like it was part of the picture, the words of encouragement bubbling around its head.

A bucket of chalk sat nearby, with a small sign that said, ADD YOUR VOICE.

Aria wondered what she should write, and was still wondering when she heard the sound of laughter. She followed it, and found a group of teenage boys passing a basketball back and forth, taking leisurely shots at a net. Farther down the block, a movie theater was spilling out a group of girls, arms linked. Across the street, a cupcake shop was jam-packed with laughing customers.

All these people had something in common.

They all looked like they were having *fun*.

Maybe *that* was what Mikayla was missing. Aria thought back, and realized that even though they'd spent most of the day together, she'd never once heard Mikayla laugh. Not even with her friends at lunch. She had that smile, but it faltered when no one was looking. And even though she had perfect posture, she seemed to be bending under the weight of her life. The pressure. The expectation. The responsibility.

Maybe that was it. Maybe Mikayla was taking on too much.

After all, she was only twelve.

When was the last time she'd acted like it? Maybe Mikayla Stevens needed to shrug off that weight, and have a little fun. It couldn't hurt.

Aria retraced her steps toward the mural.

She smiled, and took up a piece of blue chalk and added her own message to the edge of the swirling letters. Two small words.

Have Fun.

chapter 11

MIKAYLA

"Stop, stop, stop," snapped Miss Annette in dance class the next afternoon.

In the midst of spinning, Mikayla lost her balance and staggered.

"Where's your head?" challenged her coach. "Because it's not here."

Miss Annette was right.

Mikayla hadn't slept. She couldn't stop thinking about what Aria had said on the subway, about there being no such thing as perfect. In fact, ever since the strange redheaded girl had showed up in Mikayla's life, her words had been burrowing into Mikayla's thoughts, snagging there like thorns.

You're way *too hard on yourself.*
You're an incredible dancer.

There's no such thing as perfect.

Mikayla had lain there in her bed, looking at the poster across the room.

WINNERS NEVER QUIT. QUITTERS NEVER WIN.

Downstairs, she'd heard her parents talking. About her. About money. About dance.

We'll find a way . . .

She's worked so hard . . . we have to . . .

"I'm sorry," said Mikayla to Miss Annette now, trying to shake the questions and the voices of out of her limbs.

"I don't want sorry," snapped Miss Annette. Mikayla cringed. Miss Annette often seesawed between treating her like a star and being harder on her than she was on anyone else. Mikayla guessed the two were connected — Miss Annette insisted she was tough on Mikayla because she believed in her, believed she was made of gold, but it didn't feel that way. "Just do it again," Miss Annette added sharply. "And do it right."

Mikayla took a deep breath and started the turn again. She focused, agonized over every motion, so intent that she didn't even feel the dancing, didn't hear the music, only the marks she was supposed to hit. By the time Mikayla came to a stop, she felt strangely hollow and sad, but she'd made it through without another mistake.

471

"That's more like it," said Miss Annette. "Ten minute break!" she called out to the rest of the room, clapping her hands.

Mikayla escaped before Miss Annette could decide to make her stay and go again.

Aria's class was also on their break and Mikayla saw Aria in the common hallway, putting on her sneakers. She and Aria hadn't interacted much at school that day, but Mikayla had been pleasantly surprised when Aria had again walked along with her and Sara over to Filigree. Something about Aria's presence made Mikayla feel lighter. Even scowling Sara didn't seem quite so bad when Aria was around.

"Come on," Aria said now, hopping to her feet.

"Where are we going?" asked Mikayla, wiping the sweat off her brow.

Aria nodded at the window, toward the small park behind Filigree's building. "Outside."

Mikayla shook her head. "We only have ten minutes." During the class breaks, the girls would stretch in the common hallway, or use the restroom, or work on nailing their turns. True, there was no explicit rule that they couldn't step into the park. . . .

Aria smiled. "You can do a lot in ten minutes," she said. "And it's gorgeous out, not cold at all. Didn't you notice on the way here?" Mikayla hadn't. "Besides," added Aria, "you look like you could use some fresh air."

Mikayla suddenly realized that fresh air was *exactly* what she needed. A few moments of freedom from Filigree. So she ducked into the changing room and slipped on her own shoes, adding her jacket as well. When the other girls stretching in the hall noticed that Aria and Mikayla were heading out, they glanced over with something like envy.

"Everyone here looks like they could use a little air," Aria observed, glancing around. "And maybe a little *fun*. When's the last time you had some?"

Mikayla rolled her eyes, even though the truth was, she couldn't remember.

Clearly intrigued, a few of the other girls took Aria up on her offer. Donning shoes and jackets, they trailed outside. Even Sara, who looked skeptical, came along. Aria led the way, and Mikayla walked beside her, feeling at once guilty and excited to be stepping out of the building for a bit.

The park was a small stretch of green fenced off and dotted with trees. Mikayla looked up at the streaks of cloud and the bright blue sky. It really *was* a pretty afternoon. She wondered how Beth and Katie were spending it, if Alex was out on his bike. She wondered how *she'd* spend the afternoon, if she weren't here. Which was a stupid thing to wonder, so she forced herself to stop.

The girls gathered in a loose circle, eyeing Aria uncertainly.

"Well?" asked one of the dancers from Mikayla's class, Elin.

"What are we doing out here?" asked another advanced dancer named Nissa.

Aria tapped her shoe and chewed her lip. "Why don't we play a game?" she offered.

Sara groaned. "Games are for little kids," she complained, just as Nissa asked, "What kind of game?"

At that, Aria smiled, reached out, and touched Sara's shoulder.

"Tag," she said. "You're it."

At first, nobody moved. Mikalya wanted to say that they needed to conserve their energy for class, that she was still sweaty from her turns. The other girls seemed to feel the same way, standing and waiting for someone to do something.

And then, it just kind of *happened*.

Sara took a single step forward, and on instinct, everyone else jumped back.

She took another step, and everyone took off running, including Mikayla.

It felt nice to run, to move her body without worrying about tempo and getting the steps right. The girls ran in every direction, and in seconds the park was filled with the sounds of laughter. Sara went after Nissa. Mikayla's heart raced as she ducked behind a tree. Aria lunged behind the one beside her.

Sara skimmed Nissa's arm, and they reversed direction, Sara fleeing as Nissa took off after Elin, who then took off after Aria and Mikayla. Aria ran ahead, her red curls flying, but she was tagged next. Aria and Mikayla exchanged a look — Mikayla could feel herself smiling — and then Aria took off after her, and Mikayla ran, the two sprinting across the grass.

For a few, glorious strides, Mikayla felt *happy*. Like the weight of the world — her parents, the boxes, school, Miss Annette, the Drexton audition — just fell away and she could breathe.

She didn't notice the root sticking out of the grass, not until it caught her shoe and sent her sprawling forward hard. A sharp pain shot up her ankle. She gasped, more from the shock of the fall than the pain. Then she tried to stand, and this time the gasp was a mix of pain and panic, because something was very, very wrong with her foot.

The girls immediately rushed around her.

"Mikayla?"

"Can you stand?"

"What happened?"

"Stay still."

And then Aria was there, crouching next to her. Her blue eyes were full of regret. "I'm so sorry," she said. "It wasn't supposed to go this way. I just wanted to —"

But she didn't get a chance to finish. Miss Annette had burst through the back doors and was hurrying across the park. She shoved the girls out of the way.

"Everyone get back! What are you doing outside during break? What on earth has happened here?"

"We were just —" started Aria again, but then Miss Annette saw Mikayla on the ground, holding her ankle, and she let out a sound of dismay.

Miss Annette crouched beside her and prodded Mikayla's sore ankle. Mikayla bit her lip to keep from crying out.

Mikayla saw that Aria was still watching her worriedly. It was the strangest thing, but the shadow at Aria's feet seemed to waver. Mikayla decided she had imagined it, that she was delirious from the pain.

"Is she okay? Can you help her stand up?" Elin asked worriedly.

Miss Annette's face became a rigid mask of concern and anger, but for once she was silent as she scooped Mikayla into her arms, and stormed away.

chapter 12

ARIA

Aria saw it all happen a second too late.

If she had seen it just in time, her shadow might have come to life and carried her over to catch Mikayla before she fell. But it had all happened too fast, and now Aria sat cross-legged on a very uncomfortable bench in a hospital hall, feeling horrible and helpless and totally responsible. She was just trying to help — she was always trying to help — but she'd somehow made things worse.

She looked down at her bracelet and wondered if an angel could *lose* feathers for messing up.

Mikayla was in with the doctors and Miss Annette, getting her ankle examined. Her mom was on her way. Aria hadn't been in a hospital since her time with Gabby. Those had been different circumstances, of course, and a different hospital altogether. But the pale halls still felt sadly familiar.

Aria fiddled with the empty loop on her charm bracelet, feeling like she had her own cloud of smoke hanging around her shoulders. It wasn't that Aria thought a game of tag would suddenly solve all of Mikayla's problems. But she hoped it would get Mikayla out of her head and show her that not everything was win or lose. Some things were just for fun. It certainly couldn't hurt.

Only, it had.

Miss Annette stomped out of Mikayla's exam room, flustered, and turned her attention on Aria. She didn't ask what Aria was doing there, or even how she'd gotten there. (Miss Annette had driven Mikayla to the hospital herself.) Instead, she knelt down and glowered in Aria's face.

"What were you thinking?" she growled.

"We were just playing a game," said Aria. "I didn't think —"

"No, you didn't think. You just gambled with my best dancer. She could have broken her ankle! And with Drexton coming up." Miss Annette shook her head, as if she couldn't bear to think about it. "As it is, she'll be off for days. DAYS."

Aria was glad to hear that Mikayla's ankle wasn't broken, and thought *days* didn't seem like long at all, especially if it meant she'd be okay. But Miss Annette acted like it was the end of the world. "I've changed my mind about you," the teacher went on ferociously. "You're no longer welcome at Filigree."

Aria's heart sank. "But I —"

Before Aria could say anything else, Miss Annette straightened up and stormed off down the hall, muttering to herself, "I don't have time for this. . . ."

Aria watched, glad when she was gone.

Then she stood and glared down at her shadow. "You could have helped me," she said, even though she knew it wasn't the shadow's fault. Or maybe it was. But for all her talk about fate, she had a hard time believing this was how things were supposed to happen.

Aria sighed and knocked on Mikayla's door. A moment later she heard a quiet voice say, "Come in."

Mikayla looked up from where she lay on the exam table. She'd obviously been expecting a doctor and was surprised to see an Aria instead. Surprised, but not angry.

"Aria," she said. "What are you doing here?"

"I was worried," answered Aria. "The game was my idea, and I had no idea this would happen. I'm so sorry. . . ."

"Don't be," said Mikayla, shaking her head. "It's not your fault. You couldn't have done anything to stop it."

Could I? Aria wondered, sinking into a nearby chair. *I'm your guardian angel.* Somehow the fact that Mikayla didn't seem mad at her made Aria feel even worse.

Mikayla's ankle was wrapped and propped up on several pillows.

"How bad is it?" Aria asked, wishing not for the first time that she was a different kind of angel, one who could actually *fix* broken things.

"It's just twisted," said Mikayla.

"That must be a relief," said Aria.

"Yeah," mumbled Mikayla. But Aria was surprised to see a shadow cross the girl's face, and her blue smoke darken and coil around her.

"I'm sorry," said Aria, feeling like if she said it any more times, it would start to lose its meaning.

Mikayla sank back against the exam table. "The doctor said I'm supposed to stay off of it," she said. "Just for a few days. So no dancing." She tipped her head back. Her smoke swirled. "Do you really believe that everything happens for a reason?"

Aria hesitated, then found herself nodding. "Why?"

"It's just . . . I don't know . . . lately I've been wondering what my life would be like if I weren't spending every single moment dancing. And then . . ." she gestured to her ankle. "This happened."

Aria looked down at her shadow, thinking. She *did* believe things happened for a reason. Or at least, that everything had the potential to matter. Now she wondered if somehow this, the fall, the twisted ankle, was supposed to happen because Mikayla needed a break. A chance to step away from dance. To see that a person was made up of more than one thing. This was her chance. Maybe it would help.

Or maybe Aria was just trying to make herself feel better.

"It *was* fun," Mikayla spoke up, and Aria looked at her, surprised but glad. "At least for a little while." Mikayla almost smiled. Aria started to smile, too. Silence fell over them like a blanket. Then Mikayla said, "Can I tell you something?"

"Of course," said Aria.

"You promise not to judge me?"

"I don't judge anyone," said Aria. "I'm just here to help."

Mikayla considered her ankle, while Aria considered the girl's blue smoke. "When I fell," she said at last, "the first thing I felt, after pain, wasn't fear or sadness. It was *relief*. I was *relieved* at the thought of not having to go back into Filigree. Of having an excuse to not dance."

And there it was. The heart of Mikayla's problem, the reason Aria was there.

Mikayla looked up, her eyes wide. "Isn't that awful?"

"No," answered Aria. "It's just honest."

Mikayla sighed.

Aria took a deep breath. "I think that sometimes people have a really hard time being honest with themselves."

Mikayla's stress and conflicting thoughts were all tangled up in her smoke. She had probably been feeling these things for a long time, and simply hadn't stopped to look at them. Hadn't wanted to.

"Sometimes," Aria went on, "something has to happen to make someone face what's wrong in their life."

"But dance *is* my life."

"Do you love it?" asked Aria.

Mikayla opened her mouth. Closed it. Opened it again. "I . . . I did." She put her head in her hands. "I mean I do. I don't know, Aria."

"It's okay."

"No it's not. This is my life. It's who I am."

Aria wanted to say that people were more than what they

did, but then the door burst open and Mikayla's mom was there, a whirlwind of worry and nervous energy, of *oh no* and *how are you feeling* and *I came as soon as I heard* . . .

And Aria knew that this wasn't the time or the place, so she stepped back, and slipped out the door.

chapter 13

MIKAYLA

Mikayla's mom let her stay home from school the next day.

It was a Friday, and Mikayla's first thought was that she couldn't miss dance, before she remembered that she couldn't *go*. It took her by surprise again, the wave of relief that came before the dread.

The Drexton audition was only a week away, and she knew she needed the practice. But for the next few days, dance was off-limits.

But without dance, and without school to distract her from its absence, she felt lost.

What did people actually *do* with their free time?

It was a drizzling gray day; her mom had stayed home from work and was bustling around the house — as far as Mikayla could tell, she was putting things in boxes — and her dad was at another interview. Chow was asleep at her feet. Mikayla was propped up on the couch with her ankle wrapped in ice.

Both Beth and Katie had texted to check on her, and Katie even asked if she should come over after school. But Mikayla had looked around at the moving boxes and said no, she was fine.

And now, for the first time in forever, she almost felt *bored*.

It was such a strange thing, sitting still. She tried to do homework, but her thoughts kept wandering. She flipped through the channels, but nothing held her interest. Finally she put her earbuds in and cranked the music up, even though it made her want to get up and move, and she couldn't.

And then — she wasn't sure how much time had passed, how many songs had gone by — someone tapped her shoulder, and she jumped, sending a tiny wave of pain through her foot. She tugged the earbuds out and twisted to find Aria standing in her living room.

Chow hadn't heard her come in either, and now he sprang to his feet, barking. But when Aria reached out and started petting him, he promptly flopped over at her feet.

Which was surprising. Chow wasn't usually that friendly to strangers.

"Sorry," said Aria. "Didn't mean to frighten you. Your mom let me in."

"What are you doing here?" asked Mikayla. She checked the clock on the wall. It wasn't even noon. "Shouldn't you be at school?"

Aria smiled, and readjusted the backpack on her shoulder. "I thought you could use some company," she said, adding, "I don't think they'll miss me."

"Are you going to Filigree later?" asked Mikayla. "Miss Annette has a really strict no-skipping policy."

"Yeah, about that . . ." said Aria slowly, "I kind of had my acceptance revoked." Mikayla felt her eyes widen. "But it's okay!" added Aria quickly. "Filigree and I weren't a good fit."

Mikayla stared at the other girl. She couldn't make sense of Aria Blue. This girl who had just walked into her life and turned it upside down. But she was glad Aria was there.

"So do you have any siblings?" asked Aria, looking around. "Are they dancers, too?"

"No," said Mikayla. "I'm an only child. You?"

"Same," said Aria. "It's just me."

Mikayla fell silent a moment, and then she said, "I sometimes wish I had siblings."

"For the company?" asked Aria.

"No," said Mikayla. "Not really."

"Then what?" Aria put a hand on Mikayla's shoulder, and Mikayla could feel the words about to spill out.

She looked down. "For the pressure," she said. "When you're an only child, all eyes are on you. You're always the one responsible . . . Sometimes I think it would be nice if my parents had someone else to focus on. Then I wouldn't feel like everything was riding on me." Aria's hand slipped away, and Mikayla blinked. She hadn't meant to open up like that, and she shook her head. "I shouldn't complain," she scolded herself. "Honestly."

"I think it makes sense," said Aria. And then, to Mikayla's relief, she changed the subject. "So," she said cheerfully. "No dance. No school. What will you do with all your time?"

"I have no idea," said Mikayla.

"Sure you do."

Mikayla shook her head. "You asked me the other day, what I do when I'm not dancing, and I didn't answer because I couldn't think of anything. Because I'm never not dancing."

"You're not dancing right now," observed Aria casually.

"Right, and I'm *bored stiff*," Mikayla shot back. "I don't even know what to do."

"Cut yourself some slack," said Aria with a laugh. "I bet it's hard to think of things to do when you're confined to a couch."

Aria started digging through her backpack. And then she pulled out a notepad and a pen, and perched on the arm of the couch.

Mikayla shook her head. "It's more than that," she said, lowering her voice. "Dance is not just what I *do*. It's who I *am*. So I don't know how to be me without it." It scared her to admit that.

Aria rapped the pen against the pad a few times, thinking. "Okay, so dance is your life," she said. "It defines you." Mikayla nodded. "But it's a thing," Aria went on. "You're not a thing, you're a *who*. A person. And people are more than one thing. They're messy, in the best way. They're made up of everything they've done, everyone they've been, and everyone they'll be. Even though you're an amazing dancer, it's not *all* you are."

Mikayla's heart sank. She wanted to believe that, but she didn't see how it was true. She nodded at the pen and paper. "What's that for?"

Aria brightened. "We're going to make a list," she said. "Together. And then, when you're feeling better, you can do the things on it. So," she held the pen out between them, as if it were a microphone, "if you had all the time in the world, what would you do?"

Mikayla opened her mouth to protest, because she'd never have all the time in the world, and even if she did, she probably couldn't afford to do half the things she wanted. But then she stopped. There was something about Aria's expression, the simple, unguarded hope, that made her play along.

"I'd go to the movies," Mikayla answered. "I'd see everything that's playing in the theater."

Aria scribbled this down.

"And I'd ride my bike through Prospect Park with Alex."

"He says hi, by the way," cut in Aria. "I met him the other day." Mikayla's chest tightened. "Okay, what else?"

"I'd . . ." Mikayla bit her lip. "I'd bake cookies. I'd reread all the Harry Potter books. I'd get frozen hot chocolate at Serendipity with Beth and Katie. I'd play tennis with Beth and draw with Katie, and I'd walk along the High Line, and go the Met museum, and sleep in and . . ." she trailed off, breathless, her head rushing from all these possible activities, and feeling guilty that none of them were dance.

Aria finished writing and turned the list toward Mikayla with a smile. "I think that's a good start. So . . ." She tore the page free of the notepad and held it out to Mikayla. "What should we do first?"

chapter 14

ARIA

"Wait!" said Mikayla. "I think you're supposed to *measure* the ingredients before you put them in."

"It's more fun when you guess," said Aria, scooping sugar into the mixing bowl.

They were standing in the kitchen — well, Aria was standing, Mikayla was sitting on a stool — making cookies, because that was one of the only things on the list that didn't require the ability to walk. Chow circled their legs, lapping up anything that fell.

"Girls," called Mikayla's mom from the living room. "Try not to make a mess."

Aria looked at Mikayla, who was covered in flour, and Mikayla looked at Aria, who was covered in sugar, and the two burst into laughter.

Aria didn't realize how old Mikayla had looked before, until she started laughing and looked much younger. Her smoke thinned a little. Aria knew it wasn't enough, that it was a shallow kind of happy, but it was still nice to see her laugh.

"So . . ." said Aria as they put the first batch of sugar cookies in the oven. "Are you guys moving?"

"What?" asked Mikayla, brushing flour from her T-shirt.

"The boxes," said Aria, looking around at the containers gathered in the corners of the room, the yet-to-be-assembled ones slouched in the hall.

"Oh," said Mikayla slowly. "I don't know. I guess it just depends." She looked down at her hands, and Aria could see the fears swirling in her smoke.

Aria reached out and touched the girl's arm, even though it left a sugary handprint there. "On what?"

Mikayla swallowed. "On whether my dad finds a new job soon. He's an engineer," she went on. "He used to work for this big product design firm. But it went under a few months ago, and he's been looking for a new position ever since. I wish I could do something. . . ."

"It's not your fault," said Aria softly. "And it's not your job —"

"I haven't told anyone about Dad," Mikayla went on, her cheeks flushing. "Not even Beth or Katie."

"Why not?" asked Aria.

"It's not like they can say or do anything to help, and . . ." she trailed off, obviously embarrassed, though Aria didn't see why she should be. "Beth and Katie are great," she added. "We've been friends forever, but they've never had to worry about money. I'm pretty sure they were given credit cards when they started kindergarten. I don't want them to get weird, to treat me like I don't belong."

"Do you honestly think they would?" asked Aria.

Mikayla dusted off her hands. "I don't know."

"Well, I'm glad you told *me*," said Aria, even though she didn't know how to help. She couldn't get Mikayla's dad a new job, couldn't save their house, any more than she could have cured Gabby's brother. She could only help Mikayla make the right choices when it came to her own path.

"I don't want to move," said Mikayla, so low Aria almost didn't hear. "I hate these boxes. I hate everything they mean."

"You know," said Aria after a moment, looking at the boxes again, "a house isn't really walls and a roof. It's the people inside, and you get to keep those no matter what. As far as these boxes, I think sometimes it's good to sort through our things, pack some away, pull others out. It reminds us who we've been, and who we are, and sometimes it helps us figure out who we want to be."

Just then, the timer dinged, and Aria hopped up to pull the cookies out of the oven. "These smell great!" she said, shuffling them onto a plate. "One item on Mikayla Stevens's Dance-Free To-Do List, done!"

Mikayla smiled, and found the flour-dusted list on the counter, and was just crossing off *bake cookies* when she heard the front door open, and close *hard*. She dropped the pen as her dad stormed in. He didn't even seem to see them as he slammed the briefcase down onto the table hard enough to make Chow jump. Then he sank into a chair.

"Dad?" whispered Mikayla as he put his head in his hands. He didn't seem to hear her, either.

Mikayla's mom appeared, took in the scene, and gave the girls a look that said it was time for Aria to go. Mikayla mouthed *I'm sorry* and Aria smiled and mouthed *don't be*, and then they managed a kind of *see you later* in a mix of nods and waves.

Aria slipped into the hall toward the front door. But she didn't leave. She opened the door, then closed it again, still standing in the foyer. She brought her hand to the wood, watching as a moment later her hand disappeared, along with the rest of her.

Invisible Aria crept back to the kitchen doorway and saw Mikayla still sitting on the stool, her smoke swirling darker as she watched her mom try to comfort her dad. He loosened the tie at his throat and looked like he might cry. Aria watched Mikayla get down from the stool and use her crutches to hobble off toward her room. Aria didn't follow, not at first. She hung back, listening to the girl's parents.

"They've decided not to hire right now," said her dad, pulling the tie over his head.

"Don't give up," said her mom. "The Stevens aren't quitters."

"I don't know what to do. I'm running out of options."

"It'll be all right. We'll make it work. . . ."

He just kept shaking his head, and Aria wished that *he* was wreathed in smoke, marked for someone's help. Then she turned and followed Mikayla, slipping into her bedroom just before she closed the door.

Mikayla's room was so organized. No clothes on the floor. The bed was made and the desk was clear. The walls were covered in posters, and every single poster was about dance. Some showed girls leaping, or sitting elegantly on the floor; others were midturn, arms aloft. Aria turned and saw a poster on the back of Mikayla's door. A pair of dance shoes and a saying that made her frown.

WINNERS NEVER QUIT. QUITTERS NEVER WIN.

It seemed so . . . harsh. As Aria looked around, she realized that most of the posters had similar messages, about discipline, sacrifice, strength.

VICTORY IS WORTH THE PRICE.

NO PAIN, NO GAIN.

These were the words Mikayla read every morning and night? Aria shook her head. None of these sayings were about letting go, having fun, being happy. And dance was about that, too.

Aria watched, invisible, as Mikayla hit PLAY on her computer. Music filled the room, drowning out her parents' voices down the hall.

Aria sank onto the edge of the bed and watched as Mikayla tacked their to-do list up above her desk. Mikayla stared for a long time at the paper, and the question in her head and in her smoke was so loud, Aria could almost hear it.

Who would I be without dance?

Aria wanted to tell Mikayla there was only one way to find out, and that was to go looking for herself, for the person she'd been before, the one she wanted to be now. And then, as if Mikayla could hear her, her gaze drifted to the empty boxes. She hobbled to the edge of the bed and sat down facing her closet. Then she reached for the nearest box.

chapter 15

MIKAYLA

She knew she had to start, sooner or later. She might as well start now. Mikayla didn't have anything else to do — well, she could start rereading Harry Potter — but her mom had been nagging her for weeks to go through her closet.

You don't have to pack everything up, her mom had said. *Just go through, and see what you want to keep, and what you want to get rid of.*

Mikayla had been avoiding the chore as long as possible — she didn't have time, she was tired, she hoped that if she just ignored the boxes, they'd disappear . . . but they hadn't. And now, as she sat in front of the closet doors, she thought about what Aria had said. Not just about moving, but about finding who you are, who you want to be, and about the fact that people were made of more than one thing.

Mikayla couldn't remember a life outside of dance, but it had to be there, somewhere, buried.

She took a breath, leaned forward, and slid the closet doors open.

She pushed aside her school clothes and dance leotards and found a box of medals — silver and bronze, mostly. But behind that box, she found old dance costumes, as well as an album of pictures from her early days in dance. In these photos, Mikayla was nine, eight, seven, six, and beaming, even though she hadn't placed in half the competitions. Her costumes were strange and fanciful, the kind of thing Miss Annette would scoff at now. There were frills and gossamer, bright colors and ribbons and wings. Mikayla couldn't help but grin. They were fun. Whimsical.

Now Mikayla was taught, and reminded, to be her best self, her gold self. But looking at these things, she remembered a time when dancing had meant *transforming*, getting to be someone else. It had been an escape.

Dragging the costumes aside, Mikayla felt her way deeper into the closet, and came out with something else entirely.

A box of notebooks. The box itself was doodled and drawn on, with a ribbon tied around to hold it closed, as if it were precious.

Property of Mikayla Stevens, it said in a nine-year-old's handwriting.

She'd forgotten all about this. Inside she found a stack of notebooks, covered with drawings. Mikayla used to love drawing as much as dance. They both told stories. That was how she and Katie had first become friends, by bonding over drawing.

How had she forgotten about that?

As she flipped through the notebooks, she saw scribbles of story, along with doodles of dragons and fairies, ghosts and angels.

And the thing was, nine-year-old Mikayla had actually believed in them. Or at least, she'd wanted to. She'd been the kind of kid who wondered if her stuffed animals came to life when she was out of the room. The kind who left windows cracked for sprites and believed that old places were haunted. When her third-grade teacher had taken them to the American Museum of Natural History, and she'd seen the massive skeletons of dinosaurs, they'd made her believe in dragons. Because a world that could make such massive, incredible creatures could surely have made other monsters, too.

Mikayla had wanted to believe the world was full of things she couldn't see. Of higher powers, or at least *other* powers.

It seemed silly now. Childish. Mikayla Stevens had long since learned that the world wasn't full of magic and mystery, that there was no such thing as angels or ghosts or fate. *You* had to take responsibility for your own life, for your successes and your failures. That's what dance had taught her. What Miss Annette had taught her.

But sitting on the floor, surrounded by her childhood, Mikayla missed the girl who'd made these drawings, who'd worn these costumes and believed in magic. And she wondered, as she set the box of notebooks aside, if there was a way to get that Mikayla back, or if it was too late.

"It looks like a storm blew through here," said Aria the next day.

She was perched on Mikayla's bed, and the room was still covered in the contents of her closet. Mikayla had fallen asleep last night reading through one of her old notebooks, her costumes beneath her like a pillow.

When she'd woken up that Saturday morning, she'd avoided her parents, and it had been a welcome relief when Aria rang the doorbell, bright-eyed and holding fresh muffins from the local bakery.

"Sorry," Mikayla said now, massaging her still-sore ankle. "I decided to sort through some things last night."

"And what did you find?" asked Aria, biting into her muffin. "Mmm," she added, momentarily distracted. "This is kind of like a cupcake."

"Hang on," said Mikayla. She swiveled so that she and Aria were sitting side by side on the bed. Together, they flipped through the notebooks, and Mikayla tried to show Aria the person she'd been before dance, or at least before dance became so important, so big that it swallowed everything else.

Aria picked up a photo album and turned through it, pointing out photos of a goofy kid that Mikayla didn't even remember being. A kid who was eating a giant ice cream cone, making a mess and laughing. A kid who wore her dark curls in pigtails, big brown eyes shining as she stood outside the Central Park Zoo. If anything, the girl in the photos reminded Mikayla of *Aria*.

"When did things change?" asked Aria.

"I don't remember," said Mikayla, which was the truth. She felt like she should be able to pinpoint a day, a dance, a win — some moment when the gravity shifted and being the best became more important than having fun. But it must have happened over time, so slowly she didn't notice.

"I want to meet this girl," said Aria, tapping the album.

"I'm not her," said Mikayla. "Not anymore."

"Why not?"

"Because I was a kid. Monsters and magic, those are kids' ideas. I know better now."

"I still believe in magic," said Aria simply.

Mikayla rolled her eyes, even though Aria sounded completely serious. "Do you believe in monsters, too? Ghosts? Unicorns?" she asked teasingly.

Aria chewed her lip, as if thinking. "I believe the world is big and strange and full of wonder," she replied.

Mikayla was quiet. When Aria put it like that, it didn't sound quite as silly. Something in Mikayla's chest fluttered.

"What is Drexton?" asked Aria lightly, and the question jarred her. It sent a cold spike through her chest. Aria was pointing at the calendar on the wall, where the word was written in bold red letters. "I also heard Miss Annette mention it."

"Drexton Academy," said Mikayla. Aria looked at her blankly, so she explained. "It's the most prestigious dance school in the city. Probably in the *country*. They only take in a few new dancers each year — the auditions are invite-only — but if you get accepted, they pay for *everything*. Lessons.

Travel. Costumes. Competitions. Even a stipend for schooling."

"Wow."

"An audition window is coming up," continued Mikayla. "And I got an invitation to try out."

"That's amazing," said Aria.

"Yeah," said Mikayla, feeling nauseous.

"No matter what happens, you should be proud."

A heavy silence fell between them. Aria held out a muffin to Mikayla, and after a beat of hesitation, Mikayla accepted it and took a big bite. It had been ages since she'd let herself have something so sweet.

As she was eating the muffin, Aria glanced behind her, toward the shimmering pile of costumes on the bed. "Ohhh!" she said. "What are these?"

Mikayla let out a massive breath, relieved by the change of subject. "Old costumes," she said, swallowing, as Aria grabbed up a short iridescent dress. It seemed to change colors in her hands.

"I like this one," she said.

"Oh, that goes with these." Mikayla wiped her hands and reached past her into the closet. She pulled out a pair of iridescent wings. Aria's mouth fell open. "Here," said Mikayla. "Try them on."

Mikayla helped Aria drag the dress on over her clothes, and then she showed her how to slip her arms into the wings. When she was done, Aria turned to look at herself in the mirror on the wall. Her face broke into a huge grin, and Mikayla couldn't help but think that the wings suited her somehow.

Aria must have agreed, because she wore them the rest of the day.

Saturday went by in a blur of costume wings, old photo albums, and bad TV, books and drawings and laughter. Mikayla invited Aria to spend the night, and she happily stayed, sleeping on an air mattress on Mikayla's floor. Sunday was rainy, and the girls hid in Mikayla's room, reading random passages of Harry Potter inside a makeshift pillow fort (Aria was *really* good at making forts). Mikayla couldn't remember the last time she'd had so much fun. She almost forgot about her ankle, and Filigree, and the studio downstairs filled with trophies.

She might have succeeded, if Miss Annette hadn't called three times in those two days to check on her, and to remind her of the upcoming audition for Drexton.

Aria left Sunday night. By the time Mikayla got up for school on Monday, her ankle was stiff, the pain a dull ache. But she could walk more easily now, so there was no question it was getting better. Some small, guilty part of her wished that it wasn't healing so fast, even though the rest of her knew that it had to be better in time for the audition on Saturday. Her parents were still counting on her, and she couldn't let them down.

Her mom offered to drive her to the subway, but it was a gorgeous day, and she decided to walk and think through what to do with Aria after school. She was tying her laces gingerly on her front step when she heard a door open. She looked up to see Alex heading out.

He paused to adjust the chain on his bike. He'd gotten taller and his brown hair was longer and shaggier. How long had it been since she'd stopped and *really* looked at him? She felt her face grow warm.

"Hey, Alex," she said as she made her way down the steps, then leaned her elbows on the low chain fence between their houses.

He looked over and smiled. "Hey, stranger. How's dance?"

Mikayla glanced down. "It's fine," she lied, adding softly, "That's not *all* I do, you know."

"Could have fooled me," he said, teasingly.

"We should go ride our bikes in the park sometime," Mikayla said, looking back up at him and thinking of her list.

Alex smiled. "I'd like that," he said. "If you can find the time."

She blushed, but said, "I'll make time."

Alex swung his leg over his bike. "You want a lift to the subway?"

"Is that thing safe for two?"

Alex held out his hand. "Come on, M. Have a little faith."

chapter 16

ARIA

Aria sat on the school steps, working on her own list. She didn't want to tell Mikayla that she was making one, because it would be too complicated to explain.

But, sitting on the train the previous night, she'd conjured a piece of paper and pen and started writing. It wasn't much, just a list of places in the city she wanted to see, and things she wanted to do, before her time here was up.

Sometimes she cheated and added a place she'd already been — like the Botanic Garden — but she figured that was okay, since the list was just for her.

Go to a movie, she wrote.

Find the tallest building.

Visit Times Square.

"What's that?"

She glanced up to see Mikayla, looking well rested and happy, her dark hair loose instead of pulled back in its bun. Her smoke swirled around her, a little thinner, but still there.

"Just some notes," said Aria, getting to her feet. She was about to ask Mikayla how she was feeling, when Katie and Beth appeared, lavishing worry.

"M! How are you feeling?"

"Are you going to be okay?"

"Are you going crazy without dance?"

"I'm fine," said Mikayla, her smile shifting into the practiced one.

"How long are you off?" asked Sara snidely, who'd just appeared on the steps.

"Just a few days," said Mikayla, looking stiffer than ever.

"So you're still planning to audition at Drexton?" Sara pressed, narrowing her eyes.

Mikayla's smile flattened. "Of course," she said. Sara shrugged and went inside. The bell rang, and Mikayla and the others followed. Aria trailed after, watching the way Mikayla's smoke got darker every time she talked about dance.

Aria knew she needed to stop trying to *distract* Mikayla from her problems, and help her face them.

But she didn't know *how*. And she feared it wouldn't be easy.

"Park or museum?" asked Mikayla after school.

Without Filigree filling up her schedule, she'd taken it upon herself to show Aria around the city.

"Park," said Aria, looking at the sky. It was a beautiful day, a little cool, but sunny.

"We could do Prospect if we wanted to go back to Brooklyn now," Mikayla mused out loud. "But Central Park is much closer. Come on!"

They took the subway to Columbus Circle. Aria had ridden to that station before, invisibly at night, but she hadn't gotten off, had no idea what waited above. And nothing could prepare her, as they emerged, for the low stone gate that surrounded a massive, gorgeous sprawl of green.

"It's huge," she whispered to herself. Mikayla giggled. As they followed a path in, Aria stared around in awe at the trees and the rocks and the way the whole city just seemed to disappear, replaced by a forest, a lake, a hiking trail.

"Magical," Aria sighed, taking in a sloping green lawn that ended at a glittering pond.

Mikayla smiled. "Lots of people say that." She looked

around. "I guess I'd stopped seeing it. But you're right, it is." She smiled, a genuine, private smile. "I used to think Central Park was full of fairies, that they hid in the cracks of the big rocks, or in the lake. . . ."

Aria liked that idea. As Mikayla led her through the paths, Aria kept her eyes peeled for fairies. All around them, people were walking, jogging, laughing. Pushing strollers and walking dogs, eating ice cream and holding hands. Then, when Aria thought it couldn't get any better, she and Mikayla arrived at a zoo.

Aria had seen animals, of course. But she'd only been a person for a couple of months, so her experience had been limited to cats and dogs and birds and, since she'd arrived in New York, a few subway rats. Now, walking through the Central Park Zoo, Aria was *captivated.* She'd always thought that being an angel — or at least an angel-in-progress — was pretty cool, but the snow leopards, the penguins, and the monkeys seemed even cooler.

"You act like you've never seen a sea lion before," said Mikayla as Aria gaped at the incredible creature.

And the way she said it, like everyone — or at least everyone who had been someone for long enough — *had* seen them, made Aria say, "Not . . . like this. It's just so different when you're up close."

Aria held up her hand, and to her surprise — and everyone else's — one of the sea lions waddled toward her, as if eager to converse. *This*, thought Aria, for the fifteenth time that day, *is magical*. And then suddenly, as the sea lion wandered away, she felt a strange pang of sadness at the thought that the world was so big, so big that even if she had a thousand missions instead of three, she'd never get to see it all.

"What's wrong?" asked Mikayla.

Aria shook her head. "Nothing," she said, taking the girl's arm. "Where should we go next?"

"What do you want to see?" asked Mikayla.

Aria broke into a smile. "Everything."

Over the next few days, they went to the Museum of Natural History (where Aria could have stood staring at the dinosaur bones for hours), the Statue of Liberty (Aria loved the cool spray on her face from the ferry ride, and the grandeur of the statue on that tiny island), and Times Square (which was the strangest and brightest place Aria had *ever* seen; she was pretty sure there was more color and sound there than in the whole rest of the city, and Mikayla ended up having to lead her away).

Aria happily crossed items off her secret list just as Mikayla crossed items off hers. But as the week went on, and Mikayla's ankle got better, her smoke got worse, and she seemed more and more distracted. They'd avoided talking about dance, but Aria knew that avoiding a problem wasn't the same thing as overcoming it.

And it was time to talk.

It was Wednesday night, and they were sitting on her bed, reading from the Harry Potter books out loud and tossing out questions like, "Which house would you be sorted into?" (Aria felt she was strongly Hufflepuff, while Mikayla was certain they'd both be in Gryffindor) and "What would your Patronus look like?" But Mikayla kept glancing at the calendar on her bedroom wall.

"What's going on?" asked Aria at last.

Mikayla took one look at Aria, sighed, and said, "I'm going back to Filigree."

"When?"

"Tomorrow," she said. "My Drexton audition is on Saturday. I need to practice my routine."

"Are you ready?" asked Aria, and they both knew she wasn't asking about the strength of Mikayla's ankle.

Mikayla didn't answer that. Instead, she said, "I have to go back."

Aria chewed her lip. "Do you remember what you told me in the hospital? About being relieved?"

"Of course I do."

"Well," said Aria, slowly. "Don't you think there's a reason you felt that way? Something you should consider?"

"I was just tired," said Mikayla, sounding like she was trying to convince herself more than Aria. "I needed a break, but it's time to get back to work."

Aria reached out and touched her shoulder. "But if you don't love it anymore, then why —"

"Because I have to," she said.

"But do you *want* to?" asked Aria. Mikayla had been dancing for so long that people had stopped asking her if it was what she *wanted*. She had stopped asking herself. Nobody gave her the choice, because everyone assumed they knew the answer. But maybe someone needed to ask the question. The simple, important question.

"Mikayla," Aria said. "Do you want to quit dancing?"

chapter 17

MIKAYLA

At first, all Mikayla heard was *quit*. She recoiled at the word.

"No," she said automatically. And then, "Of course not." And then, after a longer pause, "I *can't*."

"Of course you can," said Aria simply. It actually started to annoy Mikayla, the way Aria acted like it was such a small thing, to up and quit the biggest part of her life.

Mikayla shook her head, thinking of Miss Annette and Filigree and her parents and the wall of gold downstairs.

"You deserve to be happy," said Aria.

"Happy has nothing to do with it," snapped Mikayla.

"Shouldn't it?" countered Aria with a frown.

Mikayla shook her head. *Happy*. She struggled with that word. It was true, she'd felt happier these past few days than she had in ages. She certainly hadn't felt happy at the competition. Or in dance class.

It's just nerves, Miss Annette would say.

It's natural, her parents would insist.

This is the way it is, she'd tell herself.

After all, this was how it had been for as long as she could remember. No, that wasn't totally true. Mikayla thought of the girl in the photo album. Hadn't there been a time, in the beginning, when she danced because it made her happy? A time when she didn't dread getting on stage, didn't fear the failure of second place? What happened to that version of herself?

Mikayla shook her head again, as if she could clear the thoughts. Happy was simple, and this was complicated.

"I *miss* dancing," she insisted. And it wasn't a lie. She did. She didn't miss what it had *become*, but she missed what it used to be, when she first started, back before it all mattered *so* much. She hadn't missed Filigree, hadn't missed competing, hadn't missed feeling like no matter how hard she worked, it wasn't enough.

But she *wasn't* a quitter.

"The Drexton audition —" she started.

"Are you sure you want to do it?" challenged Aria.

"I have to," said Mikayla. "I don't expect you to understand."

"Then help me understand," pressed Aria.

Mikayla looked at her, long and hard. And then she stood up. "Okay," she said. "Follow me."

Mikayla flicked the switch in the basement, and the light glinted off the trophies. Mikayla hadn't been down here since her accident. She'd been avoiding the room, as if she could somehow avoid everything it represented. Out of sight, out of mind.

"Wow," said Aria quietly, taking in the wall of gold.

"The thing people don't understand," said Mikayla, running her fingers over a shelf of medals, "is that it's not enough to become the best. You have to *stay* the best. It's exhausting. People are always waiting for you to slip up, to go from gold to silver, to fail."

"Silver doesn't seem like failing."

Mikayla's fingers slid off the shelf. "It is when you're gold."

"All the gold's not worth it if you're miserable, Mikayla."

Mikayla's shoulders slumped. "You saw the boxes, Aria.

We don't have enough money. If dad doesn't get a new job soon, we're going to lose the house."

Aria eyed her thoughtfully. "But what does that have to do with Drexton?"

"Drexton would pay for dance, and school. It would help."

"So would quitting Filigree," observed Aria. She glanced up at the ceiling. "It's not your job to save this house, Mikayla. You can't take that on."

Mikayla's throat tightened. "My parents have given up so much, for so long. They've poured money into my classes. It's my job to make it worth it. It matters too much now. They need me to succeed. If I give up — if I *quit* — then it was all a waste. Every one of these gold trophies was for nothing. If I can just get through the audition . . ."

"Then what?" pressed Aria. "What happens when you get accepted?"

"If," corrected Mikayla.

"*If* you get in, Mikayla, then everything goes back to how it was, right? Only worse. You said Drexton was the most prestigious dance school in the city, right? So it's even *more* intense than Filigree. Are you sure you *want* to get in?"

Mikayla felt frustration bubbling inside her. "I've been working toward this for *years*, Aria. It's everything I've been training for. I can't just walk away."

Aria ran a hand through her curly red hair. "Why do you have to?" she asked. "Why does it have to be all or nothing? If what you miss is dancing, why can't you just . . . *dance*?"

Mikayla's chest tightened. "It's not that simple," she said.

"Why can't it be?"

"Because it's *not*," shouted Mikayla.

The words echoed through the small room.

"I'm sorry," said Mikayla, feeling bad for snapping at her friend.

"It's okay," said Aria. "I shouldn't have pushed you."

A moment later, Mikayla's mom appeared.

"Is everything okay?" she asked, looking worried.

Mikayla pulled her face into a forced smile. "We're fine," she said. "I was just telling Aria how excited I am to get back to dance tomorrow."

Her mom looked relieved. She crossed the room and kissed the top of Mikayla's head. "I'm proud of you," she said. "And I know you'll do wonderfully."

Mikayla found Aria's eyes in the mirrored wall, a crease of concern between them, but she turned away. "Thanks, Mom."

The next day, Mikayla went back to dance.

She said good-bye to Aria after school, part of her wishing they could go on another adventure. Like seeing paintings in a museum, or shopping in Union Square. But instead she followed Sara to Filigree, telling herself she just had to get through the Drexton audition.

Aria's question — *Then what?* — echoed in her head, but she pushed it away.

"What, no shadow?" asked Sara, obviously referring to Aria.

"She decided she didn't like Filigree," said Mikayla, not wanting to tell Sara that Miss Annette had kicked her out.

"Well," said Sara, smugly. "Quitters never win." The words Mikayla was so familiar with sounded meaner than usual, coming out of Sara's mouth. Or maybe they'd always been harsh.

As they climbed the stairs to the dance studio, Mikayla asked, "Did I miss anything?"

Sara shrugged, smirking. "I guess we'll find out."

Inside, Miss Annette wrapped Mikayla in a sequined embrace. "You gave us a scare," she said, pulling back. "Are you still my golden girl?"

Mikayla's chest tightened, and she felt herself slip back into her performance smile. "Absolutely."

Class started. Mikayla had only been gone for a few days, but she already felt like she'd fallen behind. Why hadn't she stretched more on her time off? She could have stayed limber, could have practiced her stance and her arms. Now her leaps weren't as high as they'd been, her lines weren't as perfect. She tried to stop the negative thoughts, tried not to beat herself up for the tiny flaws.

To her surprise, Miss Annette didn't beat her up, either.

"You'll find your stride again," her teacher said. It was probably the nicest Miss Annette had ever been to her. And then she added, "Just find it *quickly*."

Mikayla went through her audition routine for Drexton under her coach's scrutiny, Miss Annette punctuating the music with corrections like, "Leg up, elbow higher, posture, that's too rough, that's too soft. . . ."

And then, after she'd gone through the routine half a dozen times, she looked up, and Miss Annette wasn't there. Mikayla looked around, wondering for a second if she might have finally willed the coach away. And then she heard the woman's abrasive voice in the next room over.

Mikayla frowned, following it, and found Sara practicing a solo, Miss Annette scrutinizing her limbs and motions the way she'd done earlier with Mikayla.

Mikayla watched as Sara moved with elegance across the floor. She didn't make a single mistake. Sara had always been good, but recently, she'd gotten even *better*. But their next competition wasn't for weeks. Why did she have a new solo routine? What was it for? Sara finished at the same time as the music, coming to a stop in a graceful pose. In the mirror, Sara saw Mikayla watching, and smiled.

"How did it go?" asked Aria that night.

They were sitting on Mikayla's front stoop. Mikayla was icing her ankle while Aria cuddled Chow.

"Surprisingly okay. Miss Annette actually went easy on me."

"I didn't know Miss Annette *had* an easy setting."

"Me neither," said Mikayla, laughing. "So what did *you* do today?" she asked, feeling vaguely jealous of Aria's adventures, even before she heard about them.

Aria scratched Chow's head. "Just wandered, mostly. I love how big this city is. I love how, if you just start walking in any direction, you find something fascinating. Like this one place . . ."

Mikayla tried to listen, but her thoughts were already drifting back to Filigree. She couldn't stop thinking about Sara's routine, how *good* she'd been, and the smug way she'd looked at Mikayla.

Like she had a secret.

It wasn't until Friday that she found out what Sara's secret was.

After practice, Miss Annette dismissed the other dancers, but told Mikayla and Sara to stay behind.

"Girls," she said, clasping her hands. "My golden girls."

Mikayla frowned. That had always been Miss Annette's name for *her*.

"Tomorrow," she went on, "is an important day for both of you."

Mikayla felt herself freeze. *Both* of them?

"What do you mean?" asked Mikayla.

"Oh, you must have missed it while you were home sick," said Sara. "I got an invitation to audition at Drexton."

Mikayla's stomach turned. She looked to Miss Annette for an explanation. The invitations had all gone out weeks ago. Their teacher must have pulled strings to get Sara a last-minute chance.

"I couldn't exactly put all my eggs in one basket," explained Miss Annette, gesturing to Mikayla's ankle, "especially an injured one. My school has a reputation to maintain."

Mikayla swallowed hard. For the last *six years* a Filigree dancer had taken the coveted opening spot at Drexton, and Miss Annette obviously wasn't taking any chances. Which meant she no longer thought Mikayla was gold.

Sara's smile spread, and Mikayla felt tears burning her eyes. She didn't let them show, not even as she walked out of the studio, changed, and left with Sara.

"I guess we'll finally see what all those medals have bought you," said Sara when they were alone on the sidewalk. "Or if they were all a waste."

Mikayla fumed all the way to the subway.

She had always assumed *she* was Miss Annette's only candidate. It never occurred to her that Miss Annette would make sure Sara got an invitation.

Mikayla was the best dancer at Filigree. She'd sacrificed everything to *stay* the best.

But Sara had been working just as hard to close the gap. It wouldn't take much for them to switch places, for Mikayla to be the one walking away with silver. But for the Drexton audition, there was no silver, no second best. It was all or nothing.

She *couldn't* lose, not now.

She had to be best.

She had to be gold.

chapter 18

ARIA

Aria found Mikayla in her basement that night, soaked in sweat and grimacing every time she spun on her bad ankle.

"She's been down there all evening," Mikayla's mom had said as she opened the front door for Aria. "She won't come up. I know she's nervous about tomorrow, but still. You'd think it was a matter of life and death."

"I think to Mikayla it sometimes feels that way."

Now, Aria stood at the bottom of the stairs and watched Mikayla finish her routine.

Aria felt like the last week had never happened. The girl Mikayla had been, the one she was becoming again — fun-loving, whimsical — was gone, all Aria's progress washed away. What had happened?

The song ended, and Mikayla stood for a moment, breathless, before walking over to the music player and starting the song over. She took a pose and was about to go again when she saw Aria. She straightened, and the music played without her.

"Hey," said Aria.

"Hey," said Mikayla, clearly distracted.

"Why don't you take a break?" said Aria.

"I can't," said Mikayla.

"It's a nice night," pressed Aria, "and I bet you'll feel better if we —"

"I said I *can't*," protested Mikayla, her face hardening. "I need to practice. It's still not —"

"Perfect?" said Aria with a sad smile. "I thought we talked about that word."

"Not now, Aria," said Mikayla darkly.

Aria braved a step forward into the room. "Why are you so upset?"

When Mikayla didn't answer, Aria crossed the small room and put her hands on Mikayla's shoulders. "Look at me," she said, even though she wished she could say, "Look at you." She wished there was some kind of magic to show a person multiple versions of themselves, so Mikayla could see what all this pressure was doing to erase the beautiful, happy girl she'd become. "This is why you didn't want to go back, remember?"

But Mikayla shrugged her off. "I'm just nervous," she said.

"Well, all you can do is your best."

"But what if it's not good enough?" asked Mikayla, her voice on the edge of tears.

Aria held out her hands. "Then it wasn't meant to be."

Mikayla rubbed at her face, clearly frustrated. "Sara's auditioning."

Aria didn't understand. "So?"

"So she's *good*, Aria. She's amazing. And she hasn't spent the last week injured! She could take the spot at Drexton instead."

Aria sighed. "Maybe she *should*."

Mikayla gasped and put a hand to her cheek, as though Aria had hit her. "How can you *say* that?"

"I just mean" — Aria took a deep breath — "maybe it would be *better*. You don't *want* this, Mikayla. Not really." Once she started, she couldn't seem to stop. "I know you want to make your parents proud, but you don't want to go to Drexton, and you're going to be miserable if you get in, and you might be disappointed if you don't, but maybe then you'll accept that this isn't healthy, and finally give yourself a break. Not from dance, necessarily, but from *this*. The pressure and the feeling like nothing is good enough. Like *you're* not good enough. So, yeah," she said, looking Mikayla in the eye. "You're the best dancer I've ever seen, and there's no question you deserve to get into Drexton. But I think you deserve to be happy, too. So for that reason, I hope Sara gets the spot."

Mikayla stared at Aria long and hard. And then her face changed, morphed from sadness and frustration to *anger*. Her blue smoke was so thick it looked like it could choke someone.

"Get out," she snapped.

"Mikayla," started Aria, but the other girl threw up her hand and pointed at the door.

"You obviously don't get it. You're not helping anything, not helping *me*, so just *go away.*"

Aria recoiled. She could *feel* Mikayla's order, the same way a person might feel a bucket of cold water. It was tangible, real, and Aria felt her shadow shift beneath her feet.

She retreated through the door and up the stairs, and the last thing she saw was Mikayla turning away before Aria's shadow came to life and swallowed her whole.

· · ·

Aria didn't know that someone could banish a guardian angel.

It wasn't the only time she'd been told to go away, but the first time it happened, with Gabby, she thought she'd disappeared out of sheer embarrassment. Now, as she sat on a bench in a subway station, she wondered if human girls had some magic of their own.

When the train came, Aria got on. She didn't know where she was going. She just wanted to be going somewhere. She'd spent quite a lot of time on the trains the last few nights, and something about the motion helped her think. Aria leaned her head back against the seat.

She wished there was something she could do to keep Mikayla from going to the audition, but she couldn't think of anything, besides pushing the girl down some stairs, and that didn't seem very angelic.

The problem, Aria was beginning to realize, was that even though Mikayla's accident had given her something that she needed — a break, a chance to step back — it had only been because of an *accident*. And if Aria had learned anything from helping Gabby and Caroline, and from *trying* to help Mikayla, it was that people had to *choose* change. Aria couldn't choose for them. When it came to whether or not to stop dancing, Mikayla needed to make the decision for herself.

531

Aria felt a pang in her chest. She'd felt it before, the sinking weight that came when someone she was trying to help was about to do something wrong, and she had to let them do it.

Because sometimes people had to make the wrong decision first, so they could make the right one later.

That was life, thought Aria. Choice after choice after choice, some of them wrong, and some of them right, and all of them important.

Aria told herself it would all work out. But the truth was, she didn't know what would happen. Didn't know how she could help change Mikayla's path.

And then she looked up and noticed another girl on the train. She looked to be a couple years older than Aria, maybe about fourteen or fifteen. She was pretty, with curly brown hair and a band of freckles across her nose.

The girl had big headphones on, music whispering out into the subway car. But that wasn't what caught Aria's attention.

No, it was the girl's charm bracelet, a red one, laced with a handful of tiny gold feathers.

Aria straightened in her seat when she saw it.

Because the girl wasn't just a girl.

She was an *angel*.

Aria thought of the teenage boy back in Gabby's hospital, the one with the green bracelet and the black feathers. She wondered how many kinds of angel there were. As many as there were colors in a box of crayons? Or more?

Aria wondered if this teenage angel was riding the subway just to think, like Aria, or if she was on her way to help someone.

And then, as the train slowed, the girl looked up, straight at Aria, and she winked.

Which wouldn't be that strange, except that Aria was invisible.

Aria sat there, stunned, as the girl stepped off the train. Then she found herself scrambling to her feet and following the girl out, ducking through the doors just before they slid shut. She trailed the girl through the subway station, up to the street and down the block, drawn along by some invisible rope, the same way she was pulled toward those she was supposed to help.

"Hey, wait!" Aria called, running to catch up.

But the girl rounded a corner, and by the time Aria rounded it, too, the other angel was gone, and she was alone on the street. Aria turned in a circle, looking for her, but the angel had simply vanished.

Aria stood there on the sidewalk, trying to get her

bearings. Where was she? What was she doing here? And then she heard the music overhead.

She looked up to see light two stories up, a row of floor-to-ceiling windows revealing an adult dance class.

Great, thought Aria. Just what she and Mikayla needed. More dance.

But something about this place was different. It wasn't like Filigree. The adults were dancing in pairs, spinning across the floor with their hands on waists and shoulders, smiling and laughing. Having fun.

The sign in front said PARK SLOPE COMMUNITY DANCE CENTER.

Aria climbed a short set of steps to the front door, where a poster announced:

ALL AGES WELCOME.

ALL LEVELS WELCOME.

UNDER 13 DANCE FREE UP TO 4X/WEEK.

A folder taped to the wall by the door held pamphlets, and Aria took one, opening it to find a calendar listing different classes on different days. Everything from jazz to modern to hip-hop and freestyle. On the back of the brochure was a quote from the owner, a woman named Philippa Rask.

Dance is expression, it read. *Dance is motion and emotion. There are no mistakes, so long as you dance what you feel.*

Aria smiled.

Maybe she'd been wrong. Maybe this was *exactly* what Mikayla needed.

Aria pocketed a brochure. Then she looked over her shoulder, half expecting the girl with the freckles and the red bracelet to be standing there.

Aria didn't know if guardian angels had guardian angels of their own. But if they did, she had a feeling she'd met hers tonight.

chapter 19

MIKAYLA

The day of the Drexton audition, Mikayla woke up feeling horrible. Her body ached from practicing too long — her shoulders were stiff, her legs sore, her ankle tender. But she felt even worse about yelling at Aria. Mikayla was still annoyed at her friend for not understanding, but her head was also full of thoughts and questions and fears.

She couldn't afford to think about failing, or her dad's unemployment, or the boxes, which just kept multiplying. Nor could she think about the fact that maybe she was mad at Aria because Aria was *right*.

She couldn't afford to think about anything but Drexton.

Her mom tried to get her to eat breakfast, but she wasn't hungry. She took a few bites of French toast and fed the rest to Chow, who seemed perfectly happy to take it off her hands. Her dad, normally hunched over his laptop, was dressed and ready to go. He and her mom would be accompanying Mikayla to the audition.

They took the subway into Manhattan, Mikayla's stomach in a knot the whole time. Before she knew it, they were walking down Broadway toward Drexton Academy.

"You're quiet, hon," said her mom, rubbing her shoulder.

Mikayla managed a smile. "Just nervous."

"You've got this," said her mom.

"You're going to do great," said her dad.

Finally Mikayla said, "It's not the end of the world, if I don't get in." Her voice was quiet and shaky.

"You will," said her dad.

"But if I don't —"

"It's okay to be nervous," said her mom. "But think positive."

Mikayla opened and closed her mouth to say something, but it was clear they wouldn't hear her.

"Just stay focused."

"Listen to the music."

"Make us proud."

"We're already proud."

"We're *always* proud."

Mikayla swallowed as they reached the steps of Drexton.

It loomed overhead, a large white stone building with its emblem — a cursive *D* and *A* intertwined to look like dancers locked in an embrace — on a marble pillar out front.

Beneath the dancing letters ran the Drexton Academy motto:

EAT SLEEP BREATHE DANCE.

The first three words were set in smaller type above the fourth, to emphasize the last word's importance.

And leaning up against that pillar, beneath the motto, was a girl whose hair shone copper in the sunlight. Aria! She was dressed in her usual colorful style — green pants and a purple-and-blue striped shirt.

Mikayla expected to feel anger rising up in her chest, but she was surprised to feel a sudden wave of relief instead.

"What are you doing here?" she cried.

Aria smiled. "I wanted to come and wish you good luck."

Mikayla crossed her arms. "Do you still want Sara to win?"

Aria's smile softened, but didn't disappear. "I want *you* to be happy," she said. "So if this is what you want, if winning the spot here will make that happen, then I hope you get it." She sounded like she really meant it. "I believe in you."

Mikayla looked down at their feet. The laces on her sneakers were white. Aria's were purple. "I'm sorry I got so mad at you," Mikayla whispered.

"It's all right," said Aria, and something about those three simple words helped Mikayla breathe again. Then Aria surprised her by throwing her arms around Mikayla's shoulders. Mikayla felt something well up in her, her fear and her doubts and everything she couldn't afford to face. She swallowed hard.

"Mikayla," said her mom. "We better get inside."

Mikayla pulled away. "I have to go."

"Can I come over after?" asked Aria.

"Yeah," said Mikayla.

Aria smiled. "Good luck," she said, stepping out of the way. "I'll see you on the other side."

The holding room was *packed*.

Mikayla hadn't expected there to be *so many* other kids, girls and boys, all warming up, all waiting, and wanting. Their nervous energy and their stretching made a kind of rhythm in the room. *Tap tap woosh.* They were all contemporary dancers, like Mikayla, and they were all *good*.

How many spots had Drexton opened up? One? Two? Three?

Suddenly Mikayla realized that Sara wasn't the only one she had to beat.

As if on cue, she spotted the other Filigree girl across the room, her blond hair pinned back, wearing her signature green leotard. She watched as Sara did a quadruple pirouette, nailing the turn Mikayla had struggled over. Their eyes met, and Sara smiled tightly.

Mikayla's stomach jumped just as a man in a suit and a thin woman with a bun appeared before a set of wooden doors.

The man had a walking stick and he rapped it against the marble floor, the sharp sound echoing even in the crowded space.

"Parents, friends, and anyone who's not auditioning today, please wait in the foyer. Dancers, stay here."

Mikayla's parents gave her a last hug and a kiss and retreated into the outer room. Mikayla was secretly glad when they were gone. Her face was starting to hurt from holding up the smile, and the moment they were out the door she let it fall away,

"Gather round," said the twiglike woman. "You've all been invited to audition today for a spot here at Drexton. When your name is called, you will come through this door behind us, introduce yourself, turn on your music, and perform your piece."

"But before we begin calling names," said the man, "we want all of you to understand what it means to be a Drexton dancer. As our motto suggests, we expect our performers to *eat*, *sleep*, and *breathe* dance. Every moment of the day. Every day of the week. That is the kind of dedication it takes to make it in this industry. And there's always someone ready to take your place."

Mikayla's chest tightened. Aria's voice echoed in her head. *What happens once you get in?*

"If you do not have what it takes," cut in the woman, "leave." No one moved. The man and woman smiled, even though they didn't seem happy. "Very well, let's begin."

Mikayla stood against the far wall, watching as dancer after dancer vanished into the audition room, the crowd thinning. When Sara was called, Mikayla forced herself to go over and wish her good luck. She'd expected a snarky reply, but Sara must have been just as scared as Mikayla was, because she only said, "You too."

Then it happened. "Mikayla Stevens!" the woman with the clipboard shouted. Her name had been called.

This was it.

Mikayla was terrified, and she realized in that moment, just before she pushed open the doors, that she didn't know what she was more afraid of: messing up or getting in.

Gold, she told herself, glancing down at her shimmery leotard. This was everything she'd worked for. Everything that mattered.

As Mikayla pushed the doors open, she noticed the Drexton Academy motto carved into the wood.

EAT SLEEP BREATHE DANCE.

In her head she heard, *Every moment of the day. Every day of the week.*

Only gold girls go to Drexton.

Make us proud.

You don't want this.

I don't have a choice.

You always have a choice.

She carried the voices — Drexton's and Miss Annette's and her parents' and Aria's and her own — with her, all their hope and expectation. Mikayla felt it all wrap around her, weigh her down.

Beyond the doors was a dance studio, wood-paneled floors and a mirrored wall. The admissions committee — the thin woman and the man with the cane, as well as a young man with a mustache and an older woman — sat behind a large table, waiting.

Mikayla padded into the center of the room and introduced herself, and the committee stared at her over their papers.

She could hear her pulse pounding in her ears as she went to the speakers, plugged in her iPod, and hit PLAY, then retreated back to her place and took her pose.

After a few seconds that felt like *forever*, the music finally started.

But Mikayla didn't.

In that moment, her whole mind went blank. Her body froze.

She knew the routine backward and forward and upside down, but standing there, in front of the admissions committee, her limbs went numb. The hesitation only lasted a moment, but it was a moment too long.

By the time Mikayla started dancing, she was off-tempo, a step behind the music.

She couldn't catch up.

She faltered on a kick.

She fell out of a turn.

She felt every inch of her body, and knew it wasn't working.

When the song finally ended and Mikayla toddled to a stop, she felt sick.

She had performed hundreds of times — *hundreds* — in front of thousands of people, and she'd never, ever choked. Why did she have to choke *today*?

She'd messed up, beyond repair. She could see it in the admissions committee's crossed arms. Their tight mouths. Their hovering pens.

Mikayla stood before them breathless, hopeless, heartbroken.

"You can go now," said the woman with the bun.

"Have a nice day," said the man with the mustache.

"We'll be in touch," added the man with the cane.

"Next!" called the older woman.

Mikayla gave a single, tight bow, and backed out of the room.

It was over.

She'd failed.

"Well?" asked her mom excitedly when she came outside.

"How'd it go?" asked her dad, opening his arms for a hug.

But Mikayla said nothing, only shrugged.

"Mikayla?" pressed her mom, looking worried. "What happened?"

"I don't know," she whispered.

"I'm sure you were fine," said her dad.

Mikayla shook her head. She felt her eyes burning.

"It's okay, honey," said her mom.

"It's okay," echoed her dad.

But it wasn't okay. How could they think it was okay?

She'd failed. Failed them, failed Miss Annette, failed herself.

On the subway ride home, she kept her lips pressed together. She could hear her parents whispering, but she pretended not to hear.

"I just need some time alone," she said as soon as they got home, and they let her go.

She went straight to the basement studio and shut the door.

It was over.

It was all over.

She'd had her chance, and she'd ruined it.

She looked at herself in the mirrored surface, eyes puffy from held-back tears, a wall of gold at her back.

And then she turned, picked up one of those trophies,

and threw it against the ground as hard as she could. It broke into several pieces, skidding across the floor. She took up a medal and chucked it at the mirror, splintering the glass. And then she picked up and threw down another trophy, and another, and another, until everything else was ruined, too.

chapter 20

ARIA

Aria found Mikayla sitting on the floor, surrounded by her broken trophies.

She'd cleared the shelves in the room of every single prize.

Aria had seen everything, of course (being invisible had its perks). She'd watched the audition, which was pretty disastrous, and Mikayla's sullen reaction to her parents. She could feel the breakdown coming like a wave, and she'd let it break.

Now she stood in the studio, visible again, while Mikayla sat on the floor, staring at her splintered reflection in the broken mirror. Her smoke swirled heavy and blue around her shoulders.

"What do you want, Aria?"

"To help," she replied, stepping carefully around the mess of broken trophies and cast-away medals.

Mikayla looked up, her eyes red. "I choked," she said. "After everything, all that work, all that worrying . . . it was all for nothing."

"I doubt that," said Aria, sitting down beside Mikayla with her back against the wall, so their shoulders and knees bumped together. "Nothing is for nothing."

Mikayla shook her head and looked down at the years of trophies littering the floor. "I just thought . . . if I could get through the audition . . . but I saw the motto and I panicked."

"Eat, Sleep, Breathe Dance," recited Aria.

Mikayla tipped her head back and wiped her nose on her sleeve. "You were right. Going to Drexton was a bad idea. But I couldn't not go, either. There was no way to win."

Aria leaned her shoulder against Mikayla's. "Not everything in life can be divided into win and lose. Which is probably a good thing. But it means having to make choices. Some of them hard."

Mikayla looked around. "When did everything get so messy?" she asked, and Aria knew she wasn't talking about the trashed studio.

"It's going to be okay," said Aria. "We can fix this."

"How?" whispered Mikayla, and Aria knew she was finally ready to listen.

Aria got up and picked up two pieces of a broken trophy. Then she knelt in front of Mikayla. "Anything can be fixed," she said. "If you know how to put it back together."

As she said it, she fitted the halves of the trophy together, one into the other. There was a small flash of light, and an instant later, the trophy was whole again. She held it up for Mikayla to see.

Mikayla's eyes grew wide with disbelief.

"How — how — did you . . ." she stammered.

"I told you," said Aria with a bright smile. "I'm here to help. But I guess I should explain. . . ."

Mikayla's face was frozen in shock. "A guardian angel . . ."

Aria nodded. "*Your* guardian angel, specifically."

Mikayla shook her head so hard her bun loosened. "Come on. You actually expect me to believe that?"

"You told me that you used to believe in lots of things," Aria pointed out.

"When I was a *kid*. And then I grew up and realized they weren't real."

Aria gestured to the repaired trophy. "I'm real."

"But that doesn't mean you're an angel." Mikayla blinked, and hugged herself. "Maybe I'm going crazy."

"You're not," Aria assured. She was making her way around the studio. She held up another broken statue, and fixed it with another flash of light. "You saw me do that, right?"

"I guess. I have no idea. How did you do it?"

"Magic."

"Magic doesn't exist," said Mikayla flatly.

"Of course it does," said Aria, setting the mended trophy on the shelf. "I told you, the world is big and strange and full of wonder. Is it really so hard to believe in me?"

"Actually, yeah, it kind of is."

Aria brought her hand to the broken mirror, and the cracks across the front traced backward. It was pretty cool — Aria hadn't been totally sure she *could* mend things until she'd magicked the trophy back into one piece (it would have been awkward if that hadn't worked).

Mikayla watched silently, her head tipped to the side. "How am I *supposed* to believe you're my guardian angel?" she challenged.

Aria wasn't surprised that Mikayla was resisting her. She thought of the best way to explain.

"Think about it, Mikayla. I just . . ." She made a *poof* motion with her hands. ". . . appeared in your life, right when you needed me. At the competition, at the school, at Filigree. I wasn't here, and then I was. Do you honestly think it's a coincidence?"

Mikayla made a noncommittal *hmm* sound. And then she squinted at her.

"I guess it kind of makes sense," she said at last.

"Really?" said Aria, brightening.

Mikayla gave a wan smile. "No, I mean, it's still totally crazy, but I guess it makes sense in a crazy kind of way. It makes *you* make sense. The way you just showed up in my life. The way you always know what to say. And the way you dance. I guess we really were supposed to cross paths."

Aria nodded. "I thought you'd be excited," she said. "I mean, I'm basically proof that magic is real! Score one for Young Mikayla."

"Does that mean monsters are real, too?" Aria could see the flicker of light in Mikayla's eyes, some old part of her shining through the skepticism. "Dragons and fairies and stuff like that?"

Aria chewed her lip. "I have no idea. I've never met one. But who knows? Maybe one day I will. Or you will."

Mikayla frowned. "Why didn't you just tell me what you were?"

Aria set another trophy back on the shelf. "Would that have made you listen?" Mikayla bit her lip. Aria smiled. "You couldn't see past Drexton until you *got past Drexton*."

At the mention of the academy, Mikayla groaned. "Ugh, I can't believe I bombed the audition." She looked up sharply. "Wait, if you're really my guardian angel . . ."

"I am," said Aria, suddenly nervous. She'd seen that kind of excitement before, and it was usually followed by a bad idea.

"Then can't you use magic to go back and change it? Make it so I didn't mess up?"

There it was. Aria laughed. "I'm an angel, not a time-traveler," she said. "And even if I could change the past," she went on, "I wouldn't."

"What about my dad?" asked Mikayla, urgently.

"What about him?"

"Can you help him? Can you use your magic to get him his job back?"

Aria's heart sank. "I'm sorry, but I can't."

"Why not?"

"He's not the one who needs my help," she said. "You are. And I can't fix people's problems." Mikayla looked devastated.

"Not even for you. Only *you* can fix your problems. But I can help you."

Mikayla drew her knees up to her chest and wrapped her arms around them, but she nodded. "Okay."

"Okay." Aria was quiet, watching Mikayla. She could see that some part of the other girl was starting to believe in her. "So, the question," said Aria, "the smallest, biggest, simplest, hardest question is this: What are we going to do about dance?"

Mikayla put her head on her knees. "I honestly don't know."

Aria put her hand on the girl's shoulder. "I think you do."

Mikayla sighed and wiped her eyes. "I guess I'll have to quit. I don't *want* to," she said. "But without the Drexton scholarship, my parents can't afford to keep paying for my classes. So it doesn't make sense."

"What if money weren't a factor?"

"Money is always a factor."

"But what if it weren't? What if dance were free, and it was just about whether or not you *wanted* to do it? Then what would you do?"

Mikayla's eyes went to a set of photos on the wall by the door. In among the more recent pictures were a few older ones from the album she'd found, in which a young Mikayla posed with a group of girls, all in matching blue outfits. The young Mikayla beamed, not a fake smile, but a real, delighted one.

"I meant it when I said that I missed dancing," she said, "the way it used to be. Back when it wasn't about hitting every mark, or being the best, or winning gold. It was just . . . fun. Freeing."

"Okay," said Aria, standing up. "So we need to make it about the dance again."

"You make it sound so easy."

"Maybe it is," said Aria. "Maybe it *can* be. If you're willing to give it a try."

Mikayla's smoke tangled around her, but Aria could see, woven through it, a tired but persistent hope. Her eyes had lit up when she'd talked about dance the way it used to be.

For once, Aria had to help someone back instead of forward.

"I have an idea," Aria said. "You only have to do one thing."

"What's that?" asked Mikayla.

"Will you trust me?" Aria asked.

Mikayla hesitated, gazing around the studio, now put back together as if nothing had happened. And then she nodded. "I trust you."

"Okay," Aria said. "I'll come back here tomorrow to pick you up. And you'll see."

chapter 21

MIKAYLA

"I don't know about this, Aria."

"Come on, Mikayla. You said you'd trust me."

They were standing on a sidewalk in front of a building marked PARK SLOPE COMMUNITY DANCE CENTER.

"I did say that," said Mikayla. "But I didn't say I'd join another dance academy."

"This isn't a dance academy," Aria said. "It's a *community dance center*." She accentuated every word. "And my advice is to try it. One class. If you don't like it, you don't have to go back."

It wasn't just the thought of dancing in the wake of yesterday's failure that made Mikayla's stomach twist. It was Filigree. If Miss Annette found out that she was taking lessons somewhere else —

As if she could read her mind — was that a thing guardian angels could do? — Aria said, "It's Sunday. You wouldn't be at Filigree anyway, so it's not like you're cheating."

Aria started up the steps, but Mikayla still hesitated. Aria looked back.

"You told me you miss the way dance used to be. No pressure. No expectation. That's what this is. So give it a shot. You might enjoy it. Besides, it's free!"

Mikayla took a deep breath. She did want to get back to that kind of dancing that made the world fall away. She wasn't sure if she *could* find her way back, but she knew she could try. She owed Aria that much.

"Trust me," said Aria with a mischievous grin. "I'm your guardian angel, after all."

Mikayla laughed — she'd been up most of the night, seesawing between belief and disbelief about Aria — but she climbed the steps. Aria held the door open for her, and the two went in.

Inside, the dance center was alive with noise and motion.

A man at the front desk smiled warmly. "Morning, girls. Here for the one o'clock class?"

Aria nodded. "We're new here. I'm afraid we don't know where to start."

The man produced two small slips of paper. "Start with these. Your passes," he said. "You're both under thirteen, right? So you get four free classes a week." He punched a hole out of each card. "Just keep these with you. The studio is through these doors."

"Anything else we should know?" asked Aria.

The man smiled. "Just have fun."

Mikayla quickly discovered that the Community Dance Center was *very* different from Filigree. Different from any dance class she'd ever taken. First of all, the dancers ranged in age from nine and ten to late teens, and in experience from beginners to, well, Mikayla. She didn't recognize any of the dancers from competitions, but she supposed that made sense. A handful of adults lounged in a low set of wooden bleachers at the side of the studio, but everyone else was on the floor, casually warming up.

The instructor, Miss Rask ("Just call me Phillipa," she said), was middle-aged, with long hair coiled in a loose braid around her head. She was tall and lithe, built like a prima ballerina, but there was a relaxation to the way she held herself.

"Hello, everyone," she said when it was time to start. Mikayla's heart fluttered nervously. "I see we've got a couple new faces." She nodded at Aria and Mikayla. "Welcome." She held a remote in one hand, and when she pressed a button, the room filled with soft music. "Let's get started. . . ."

The warm-ups were easy: basic stretches, calisthenics. Mikayla did each movement quickly, almost automatically. She noticed Aria stretching and looking content. *My guardian angel*, Mikayla thought, observing her. No wonder Aria seemed to give off light wherever she went. It all added up now.

Next, Phillipa began teaching everyone a routine. She demonstrated a handful of steps, linking one into the next, and then everyone would repeat them back a few times until they got the hang of them. Meanwhile, Phillipa would walk around and help.

Mikayla picked the steps up within her first two tries, so she was surprised when Phillipa stopped beside her.

"Did I do it wrong?" asked Mikayla, nervously.

Phillipa smiled. "No," she said. "But you dance like you're afraid of messing up." She took her by one arm, and shook the limb slightly. "Relax," she said kindly. "Don't worry about it. Just let go."

Phillipa held on to Mikayla until she physically felt her shoulders loosening, her breath moving more smoothly. When the instructor let go, and Mikayla did the move again, it came easily. It wasn't perfect, but it felt right. Good.

Mikayla's heart raced, but this time with excitement. How long had it been since dancing *felt good*?

Phillipa had everyone dance the segment, then moved on to a second, and a third, stringing them together each time, slowly building something bigger.

More than anything, stressed Phillipa in between segments, you had to listen to the music. "Every single time you dance, it's going to be different, but as long as you move with the music, instead of against it, you'll be fine."

Mikayla had never thought of it that way, but it made sense. How long had she been moving against the music? Fighting it, and her body, like they were a current?

As the class neared its end — how had the two hours gone so quickly? — Phillipa had them string all the segments of dance together and run the entire routine from start to finish. And to Mikayla's surprise — and delight — something clicked. The music filled her head and the room fell away.

She felt the way she had back when she first started dancing. Happy. Free.

When the music stopped, Mikayla realized she was smiling. A real, genuine smile. She stole a look at Aria, who was beaming triumphantly, as if she could see the change in her.

The class did the whole routine three more times, more and more students finding their stride, and by the end of the third, Mikayla was breathless, but giddy. How could Filigree and this feel so different? How could they both be called *dance*?

"Good job, everyone!" called Phillipa. To Mikayla's surprise, the instructor applauded, and the other students applauded back, the room momentarily swallowed by the sound.

The class broke apart, and Mikayla followed Aria outside.

"Well?" said Aria. "That wasn't so bad, was it? I thought —"

Mikayla surprised both of them by throwing her arms around her guardian angel.

"Thank you," she said into the angel's shoulder.

"You're welcome," said Aria. "Just doing my job."

Mikayla's excitement about the new dance class followed her home, but it died the moment she and Aria stepped inside.

Her father was hunched at the kitchen table, her mother whispering to him, and Mikayla could tell that yet another job had fallen through.

Doubled over like that, he looked broken, and Aria tugged her away by the arm, the two retreating to Mikayla's room.

"I wish there was something I could do for my dad," Mikayla said, shutting the door.

"There is," said Aria, and Mikayla brightened before the angel added, "Be there for him."

"That's not what I meant."

"But it is what you can do," said Aria.

"But maybe if I had gotten into Drexton . . ." said Mikayla, but she trailed off, knowing that it wouldn't have fixed everything. As much as she wanted there to be a simple solution, there wasn't one. "He just used to be such a happy person," said Mikayla. "Now he's always on edge."

"That sounds familiar," said Aria with a smile.

"What do you mean?"

"Well, *you* used to be happy, too. Until you became so afraid of letting everyone down. That's probably how he feels. The same way you're scared of disappointing your parents, he's probably scared of disappointing you."

Mikayla had never thought of it like that.

She slumped back against the bed, but Aria got up to go.

"Hey. Where do you go at night?" Mikayla asked. "Do you just disappear until I need you again?"

Aria shook her head. "Sometimes I'm *invisible*, but I'm still real. Mostly I explore the city. I want to see everything."

"People live here for years and still don't see it all," said Mikayla.

"That's okay," said Aria. "I want to see as much as I can before . . ." she trailed off, frowned, and picked back up. "Before I'm done."

"How will you know when you're done?" asked Mikayla when Aria was at the door. Mikayla felt a stab of worry. She didn't want Aria to not be a part of her life anymore.

Aria looked down at her bracelet. "I'll know," she said. "But we're not done yet."

Mikayla watched the door close behind the girl, and swore she saw Aria *disappear* as she stepped through. She sat there a moment, staring at the poster on the back of the door.

WINNERS NEVER QUIT. QUITTERS NEVER WIN.

Mikayla got up and took the poster down. She rolled it up and tucked it in one of the moving boxes. It was a small step in the right direction.

Then she went to find her father.

He was still sitting at the kitchen table, typing away, and Mikayla wrapped her arms lightly around his shoulders.

"Hey, honey," he said, distracted.

At first Mikayla didn't know what to say. But if Aria was right, her dad really felt the same way she did, so she told him what she'd want to hear.

"I'm proud of you," she said. "No matter what happens."

At that, he stopped typing and looked up, his eyes shining with tears. "Even if we have to move?"

Mikayla could almost feel Aria there with her, a touch on her arm, as she said, "A house is just a house. Home is the people in it."

Mikayla went back to her room feeling lighter than she had in ages. For the first time, the boxes didn't scare her.

chapter 22

ARIA

Aria had made quite a dent in her to-do list, and yet it wasn't getting any shorter.

Every time she crossed an item off, two more seemed to pop up. Mikayla was right, there was just too much to see, even if someone had a whole life in which to see it.

But Aria didn't. Mikayla's smoke was thinning, which meant Aria was running out of time.

"Where did you come from?" Mikayla asked Aria as they rode the subway to school that Monday.

"I told you, California," said Aria.

"Why California?"

"I was helping a girl named Caroline."

Mikayla swung her legs back and forth on the subway seat. "What was her problem?"

"Bullies."

"And who did you help before that?"

"Gabby. Her brother was sick."

"And before that?"

Aria shrugged. "Gabby was the first girl I helped." She held out her bracelet for Mikayla to see. "See these rings?" she said. "I get a feather for each girl I help." She touched the silver feather that belonged to Gabby, then the linked silver feathers from Caroline and Lily. And then the empty ring. "This one is you."

Mikayla frowned. "What happens after me? Where will you go when you're done?"

It was a question that Gabby had asked, as well as Caroline. But with those girls, Aria had known what to say — *to the next girl who needs my help* — and now she didn't.

"I don't know," she admitted. "Wherever I'm supposed to be."

Mikayla nodded thoughtfully, and Aria was grateful when she changed the subject. "So," Mikayla said cheerfully, "were you able to get through any of your math problems?"

Aria was pleased that Mikayla seemed to be in bright spirits all day. Up until lunch, that is, when they took their seats and Beth said, "OMG, I texted you but didn't hear back — how was the Drexton audition?"

The natural smile slid from Mikayla's mouth, her smoke twitching and twisting. "I don't know," she said. "I don't think it went well."

"No way. I'm sure you did great," said Katie.

"You're just being hard on yourself," Beth chimed in.

Mikayla looked down at her food and managed a nod. Then she felt Aria squeeze her arm. "To be honest," she said, "I'm kind of relieved. I'm not sure it's what I wanted. Anyway, it's not the end of the world. One way or another."

Beth gaped at Aria. "What have you done with Mikayla Stevens?" she teased. Aria smiled, picking up an apple from her lunch tray.

"Speaking of body snatchers," said Katie. "There's a Broadway show opening on Friday, all about aliens. We should get tickets."

Mikayla went quiet. "I can't," she said at last.

"Filigree?" asked Katie, in a voice that made it clear they were used to this excuse.

"No," said Mikayla. And then, after another deep breath, she said, "Money's really tight right now. I can't afford it."

Aria held her hand under the table, knowing how hard it was for Mikayla to finally be honest about her circumstances.

She was tense, obviously worried about how the girls would react.

But Kate simply said, "Okay, no worries." And Beth added, "Let's do something free, then. There's a concert in Central Park. . . ."

And just like that, the conversation — and the world — went on.

Mikayla squeezed Aria's hand back, and let go. "Sounds great," she said.

The last bell rang, and Mikayla and Aria grabbed their things and made their way outside.

Sara was a few strides ahead, already heading for Filigree. But she looked back, saw Mikayla, and stopped, obviously waiting. Aria skipped down the stairs and took a few steps in the other direction. Toward the subway that would take them to the Community Dance Center.

This was the moment of truth.

Mikayla stood there between them, at the literal intersection of two paths.

Aria hadn't said anything, hadn't tried to tell her what she thought was right. It had to be *her* choice. Go back to Filigree, and everything that came with it — the hours of training, the harsh criticism, the kind of dance that won medals and left her feeling hollowed out. Or go to the Community Dance Center and . . . dance. No gold trophies, no prestige, but no pressure, either.

Mikayla didn't have to decide for forever, but for now.

"Aren't you coming?" asked Sara, impatiently.

Mikayla hesitated, and looked from one girl to the other. Then she shook her head.

"Not today," she told Sara. "You go on ahead."

And then she took another step in the right direction.

chapter 23

MIKAYLA

"Welcome back," said Phillipa, holding the door open.

Mikayla and Aria stood there, breathless from running, ready to dance.

And for two hours, everything was perfect. Not perfect in the technical, no-points-lost kind of way, but perfect in the simple, wonderful way that comes with doing something that you love. And Mikayla did love it. She was remembering *how* to love it.

There was one thing, though, that caught Mikayla by surprise. She'd gotten there, ready to revisit the dance from the day before, but Phillipa never brought it back. Instead she taught the class something new. And it was great, half-full of moves Mikayla had never tried before, but it left her with a question.

When the class broke apart, she approached Phillipa at the front of the room, Aria trailing behind.

"Ah," said the woman, "my little Filigree."

Mikayla was startled. "How did you know?"

Phillipa smiled. "The way you danced yesterday," she said. "And the fact it's on your jacket."

Mikayla realized she was wearing her competition jacket, and felt silly.

"What's your name?" asked Phillipa.

"Mikayla," she said. "And this is Aria. And I was just wondering, when do we perform?"

Phillipa gave her a quizzical smile. "We don't, dear."

Mikayla's brow crinkled. "Then what's the point of learning a routine?"

"The point?" Phillipa tapped a finger on her chin. "Well, my dear, I imagine it's to grow, to stretch, and to have fun."

Mikayla saw Aria break into a smile that seemed to brighten all the lights overhead.

"Oh," said Mikayla.

"Each class, you learn a routine," explained Phillipa. "You spend the whole class with it. Embrace it. Enjoy it. And then you let it go."

"But . . . why?"

"We let it go because it served its purpose, Mikayla. This isn't a class for the audience. This is a class for the dancer. Does that make sense?"

Mikayla nodded. After years of competition, that idea would take time to sink in. But she was willing to try.

When Mikayla got home, her mom was making dinner.

"How was dance?" she asked, and Mikayla felt a pang of guilt as she said, "It was fine." She knew she'd have to tell her, but couldn't bring herself to do it. What if she got mad? What if she made Mikayla go back to Filigree?

"Sit down," said her mom, and for an instant, Mikayla thought she knew, that she could see it in her eyes. But when Mikayla slid into the nearest chair, her mom said, "Are you ready to talk about Drexton?"

Mikayla looked down. She hadn't been able to bring herself to say it, but now she took a breath and said, "I choked."

"Was it your ankle?" asked her mom. "If it was bothering you, maybe we could ask for a redo or —"

Mikayla shook her head. "It wasn't my ankle. I just panicked and I . . . I blew it. I'm sorry."

Her mom wrapped her arms around her. "Don't be. We all stumble. The important thing is getting back up. If you keep working hard, I bet Miss Annette can get you another chance and then —"

"Mom, I . . ." she cut in, and then trailed off. Silence hung in place of the truth. *There's something I need to tell you*, she wanted to say. *I don't want to compete anymore.* But all that came out was, "I'm tired. I better go finish my homework before dinner."

Then she escaped to her room.

"When are you going to tell them?" asked a voice as she shut the door. Mikayla jumped and saw Aria standing there. Being a guardian angel apparently came with the ability to sneak up on people.

"Soon," said Mikayla. Saying it out loud — *I'm quitting* — would make it so real, so final.

As if Aria could read her mind, she said, "Try not to think of it as quitting. It's just changing course."

Mikayla swallowed, and nodded. "I'll tell them tomorrow."

But Mikayla didn't tell them tomorrow. Or the next day.

Every day, after school, she and Aria hit the front steps of Coleridge, and Sara went toward Filigree and Mikayla didn't. Every day she and Aria went to the Community Dance Center and had a great time, so great that all the way home Mikayla would say that was it, she'd decided, and tonight she was going to tell her parents. And every night she'd get home and her dad would be worried or her mom would be tense and she'd chicken out. She was stuck in a cycle of doubt.

Then, on Thursday, everything changed.

She got home and found her father at the kitchen table, hugging her mother.

He was crying, and a horrible pit formed in Mikayla's stomach until she realized that he wasn't sad. He was *happy*.

"What's going on?" she asked, and he pulled her into the family hug.

"I got a job," he said, his voice shaky. "It won't pay nearly as well as the old job, but it's something."

Mikayla felt her whole chest lighten, even under his embrace, and as she pulled away, she thought, *This is it*. This was the right time to tell them, when they were relaxed and relieved.

As the celebration died down, she said, "Mom, Dad, there's something I need to tell you. . . ."

"What is it?" asked her mom.

Mikayla hesitated. "It's about dance. . . ." she started.

But she didn't get a chance to explain, because just then the phone rang.

It was Miss Annette.

And she was *furious*.

chāpter 24

ARIA

In the end, it was Aria's fault.

By Thursday, the secret was still tangled in Mikayla's smoke, and Aria was starting to think she would never tell her parents.

She couldn't push Mikayla over the threshold, couldn't use plain words or magic to force her to change. But sometimes, Aria realized, when someone won't seek out change, you have to bring the change to them.

It had started with Sara after school.

Aria beat Mikayla to the front steps, where Sara was waiting, as she had been every day. "Is she coming?" asked Sara impatiently.

When Aria shook her head, Sara frowned. "Well, quitters never win."

"She's not a quitter," said Aria.

"Could have fooled me," snapped Sara.

"She hasn't stopped *dancing*," said Aria. "Just because she's taking a break from Filigree."

Sara's eyes narrowed, and she opened her mouth to say something, when Mikayla showed up, eyes bright with excitement, obviously eager to get going.

"Ready?" Mikayla asked.

"Ready," said Aria.

As they made their way to the Community Dance Center, Aria could feel Sara following, but she didn't look back.

Now she sat perched on the Stevenses' couch, invisible legs crossed, waiting for the call or the knock or whatever it would be.

She'd been shocked when Mikayla actually started to tell her parents herself. And then the phone had rung. Because of course Sara had told Miss Annette.

Mrs. Stevens answered the phone and Aria listened intently. "Why hello, Miss Annette. How can I . . ." she trailed off, then frowned. "No, I *didn't* know that Mikayla hadn't been at Filigree all week." She shot a look at Mikayla, who shrank away. "Well, I'm sure there's an expla-nation . . . Excuse me? No, I've no idea why she would go there . . . No one is going behind anyone's back . . . Well, obviously there's a reason . . . Yes, I'll be sure to find out."

And with that, Mrs. Stevens hung up the phone. Aria saw Mikayla watching her mother with trepidation.

"What was that about?" asked Mikayla's father.

"That," her mom said slowly, "was Miss Annette. Apparently Mikayla hasn't been to class all week." She turned to her daughter. "What's going on?"

Mikayla stood there, rocking back and forth on her heels.

"Mikayla," said her father sternly, and Aria got up, walked over, and put her invisible hand gently on the girl's shoulder, for strength.

At her touch, Mikayla exhaled and then said, "I've been going to classes somewhere else. A community dance center. It's open to everyone, and it's free."

"You're not quitting dance," her father said sternly. "I didn't raise a quitter."

Mikayla cringed at the word. "It's not quitting," she said. "It's just changing direction."

"But why?" asked her mom. "You've worked so hard —"

"Because . . . I stopped loving it."

"You're upset about Drexton," said her dad. "That's natural. But —"

"It's not just the audition," said Mikayla.

"Where is this coming from?" pressed her mom.

"Filigree is expensive," Mikayla said, "and I'm not having fun."

But her father only seemed to hear the first part. "We'll find the money. We'll make it work. Especially now —"

"But I don't want to make it work," Mikayla pressed on, sounding stronger than Aria had ever heard her. "I don't want to compete anymore. I don't want to focus on every flaw. I don't want to spend every minute of every day worried about being the best, stressed out by the idea of getting silver instead of gold." Her voice cracked, and tears slid down her face. "Winning isn't worth it if you're miserable. And I've been miserable for a long time. I'm sorry if I'm letting you down. I'm sorry if this makes me a failure."

As the words poured out into the air, so did the smoke, uncoiling from Mikayla's shoulders and dissolving into fog and air and nothing. Aria watched it happen.

Only the barest tendril remained as Mikayla stood facing her parents. Finally, they both folded her into a hug.

"You're our daughter," said her mom. "Of course we don't think that."

"Why didn't you say anything before?" asked her dad.

Mikayla wiped her eyes. "I'm sorry. I didn't want to disappoint you."

"We're only disappointed that you didn't tell us you were so miserable," her dad said softly.

"You've given up so much . . ." Mikayla started.

"We didn't give it up for you to be a star," said her dad. "We gave it up for you to be *happy*."

"So this community dance center," said her mom. "You're happy there?"

Mikayla broke into a grin, wiping away tears. "Yeah," she said. "It's great. Every time, we learn a new routine. . . ." She told them about the punch card, and Phillipa's philosophy, and the way she felt when she was dancing there.

"It sounds great," said her dad, wiping away another one of her tears.

Her mom smiled. "Can we come and watch you dance sometime?"

"It's nothing fancy or formal," said Mikayla. "But sure, you can come if you want. They have some seats in the back."

"We'd watch you dance anywhere," said her mom.

"We're proud of you," said her dad.

"Even now?" Mikayla asked.

"Yes," said her mom. "Especially now."

Aria looked down at her bracelet, expecting to feel the cool grace of the third charm on her wrist, but it wasn't there. She was surprised to feel a flicker of relief that it wasn't quite time to go yet. But she wondered what could possibly be left to do.

Mikayla got up and made her way down to the basement, and Aria trailed after. When the girls were alone, Aria flickered into sight, and began turning the gold trophies on Mikayla's wall pink and blue and green and purple.

Mikayla laughed and turned to see Aria there.

"I thought it might help," said Aria. "You know, take your mind off the gold and silver. . . ."

"It was you, wasn't it?" said Mikayla. "Somehow, you told Miss Annette, or . . ."

"I maybe tipped off Sara," said Aria, apologetically. "But I didn't know you'd actually tell your parents!"

"Have a little faith," teased Mikayla, shaking her head. "But maybe I needed the push. So, did you hear *everything*?" she asked. "Or do I need to catch you up to speed?"

Aria smiled bashfully. "I heard."

The two sat down on the floor, underneath what had been rows of gold trophies and were now rows of rainbows.

"So I guess that's that," said Mikayla. "No more Filigree. No more competitions, for now. Just dance."

"Are you happy?" asked Aria.

"I'm . . . relieved. Like a weight's been lifted, and I can breathe."

Aria nodded, knowingly. "Secrets are heavy," she said.

They both looked at the mirror. Aria studied the last clinging tendril of blue smoke around Mikayla's shoulders.

"You won't need me much longer," she said at last.

"You sound sad," said Mikayla.

Aria tried to smile. "Not at all!" she said, too cheerfully.

But staring at Mikayla's remaining blue smoke, Aria couldn't help but wonder what she was missing, and why she was so afraid of finding it.

The letter from Drexton came on Saturday.

It was sitting on the stoop, a shoe print on the envelope from where someone had stepped on it as they passed, obviously mistaking it for trash. But it wasn't trash. Aria could tell by the way the envelope made her feel just looking at it. It was important.

Aria hesitated. She understood, as soon as she saw it, what it was. What it *meant*.

This was the last step, the reason Mikayla's smoke hadn't disappeared.

The reason Aria was still there.

And then, out of nowhere, a thought occurred to Aria Blue.

Staring down at the letter, she realized that this was her chance. Her chance to avoid the unknown of what came next. To stay. To have a *life*. Mikayla didn't *know* the letter was coming. She wasn't expecting it. Only Aria knew that something was missing. If she didn't give the letter to Mikayla, then Aria wouldn't have to move on. She wouldn't be able to. And neither would Mikayla.

But . . . Mikayla *had* moved on. In almost every way. She'd found balance. She was happy.

Why shouldn't Aria be happy, too?

Her heart fluttered defiantly.

She knew it was wrong, to be afraid of the unknown. She knew it was breaking a rule — the most important one of all — to put herself before the girl she was supposed to help. But part of her still wanted to stay.

She could remain here, in this incredible city. She could see everything there was to see. . . .

But there were holes in her imagination, things she couldn't dream up, because she knew she couldn't magic them into being. Things like a family. A future. A normal life. Aria would never be a normal girl.

And deep down, she knew she wasn't meant to be one.

So she knelt down, picked up the letter, and slid it under the door.

chapter 25

MIKAYLA

The letter from Drexton came on Saturday.

It was sitting on the kitchen table, waiting in the spot where her dad's laptop usually was. Aria and Mikayla had just gotten back from a movie with Beth and Katie. It turned out Aria had never *been* to a movie theater before (something she confessed to Mikayla in a whisper as the previews started). It was crazy, the simple things she'd never done, and the joy she got out of doing them.

All the way back to Mikayla's house they'd chatted, Mikayla about the movie itself and Aria about how big the screen had been, and the peculiar buoyancy of popcorn. When they got to Mikayla's house, Aria seemed to see the envelope first. Mikayla followed her gaze and recognized the emblem: the two dancers woven together to form the *D* and *A* of Drexton Academy. Mikayla came to an abrupt stop.

Mikayla's mom was standing beside the table, waiting.

"It came today," she said. "I hope you'll forgive me, I snuck a peek."

Mikayla looked from her mom to Aria to the letter on the table, and then she picked it up with nervous fingers, and began to read aloud.

"Dear Mikayla Stevens," she read, voice trembling, "Congratulations. The Admissions Committee at Drexton Academy would like to offer you a place . . ."

Mikayla stopped reading and looked up.

"I don't understand," she said. "It must be a mistake."

"It's not," said her mom. "I called Drexton, and apparently one of their talent scouts has a daughter who takes classes at the Community Dance Center. She saw you dance."

Mikayla smiled sadly, and laughed.

"What is it?" asked her mom.

"Miss Annette used to say that someone important was *always* watching. I guess she was right." She looked at her mom. "What am I supposed to do?"

"It's your choice," said her mom. "It has to be your choice."

Mikayla looked down at the paper in her hand. For a second, she felt once again like the girl who only wanted to be gold. It was hard enough to move past something when you'd lost. But it was even harder to walk away from something when you'd *won*.

Even if it wasn't what you wanted anymore.

The silence in the room grew heavy.

And then Mikayla closed her eyes and set the letter back on the table. She put her hand over it, ran her fingers over the emblem embossed on the paper.

And then she pushed it away.

"I love to dance," she said. "But I don't want to eat and sleep and breathe dance." She smiled. "I want to eat and sleep and breathe *and* dance. It's an honor to be offered a place, but it's not for me. Not right now."

Mikayla's mom brought a hand to her shoulder and squeezed. "Okay, then."

"Okay," Mikayla echoed. And for the first time in ages, the word was true.

Then, out of the corner of her eye, she saw Aria slip through the front door and onto the porch.

Mikayla hurried after, afraid the girl would just disappear from her life as easily as she had first appeared. But she found her standing on the front step looking down at her charm bracelet, where a third feather charm now glinted in the afternoon light.

"Hey," said Mikayla.

"Hey," said Aria.

For an instant, she seemed . . . insubstantial, like Mikayla could put her hand right through her. But when she reached out and touched the angel's arm, it was solid, still there.

"I thought of another place to take you," said Mikayla. "We can go tomorrow after dance. There's a great cafe with these amazing cookies, and —"

"I'm sorry," said Aria gently. "I don't think I'll be able to come with you."

"Oh," said Mikayla. There was a moment of sad silence — they both knew what the feather charm meant — but then Mikayla said, "Can you stay for dinner?"

And to her relief, Aria burst into a smile. She pulled a piece of folded paper from her pocket, and held it up for Mikayla to see. It was titled *Aria Blue's Things to Do*, and there in the middle of the page, amid a sea of checked-off tasks, many of them big and exciting, was a simple desire that made Mikayla's heart twist.

Eat dinner with a family, it said.

"I'd love to," said Aria.

And Mikayla was glad that, for once, she could be the one helping.

chapter 26

ARIA

"Come on, give it back," said Mikayla, wresting a tennis ball from Chow's mouth. "Let go."

They were sitting on her back steps after dinner — after the best and only home-cooked meal that Aria had ever had — tossing the ball into the garden for the excitable dog. It was cool, but not too cold, and the sunset was leaving bright streaks of color across the sky. Aria gazed up at it, trying to convince herself that it was a gift, this last sunset. Trying not to think that word: *last*.

Then Aria's gaze drifted down to her charm bracelet. Along with the third and final feather, she'd felt something else settle over her, a simple, solid certainty that she was done here. That it was time to go.

Go where? she wondered to herself, a thread of panic weaving through the calm. She was always telling the girls she helped to look forward, to not be afraid of change. Now she had to take her own advice.

Mikayla wrapped her arm around Aria's shoulders, and the two sat there for a moment in silence.

Aria's shadow fidgeted beneath her. "I better get going," she said at last.

Mikayla started to nod and then bounced to her feet, eyes bright with an idea.

"Wait!" she said, turning to go inside. "Stay here. I have something for you!"

Before Aria could say anything, the girl was gone. She got slowly to her feet, and stretched, and waited.

Suddenly, though, Aria's shadow began to glow. And as it filled with impossible light, she could see the hint of wings.

A strange panic filled her chest.

Mikayla wasn't back yet, but there was something about the pulse of light, something unspoken, that told her it would be okay. This wasn't an end. Just another step. Her shadow knew best. It always did. So she took a breath, and looked up at the sky one last time, just in case, and stepped into the light.

·　　·　　·

One moment Aria was surrounded by white, and the next moment she found herself standing in a girl's bedroom. She recognized it at once. The walls had been painted purple since her last visit, and were now covered in art and photos. Gabby was sitting cross-legged on the bed, hunched over homework, a thin stream of music pouring from the headphones around her neck. She was singing along softly. Her voice was lovely as always.

Aria smiled. "Hi," she said.

But Gabby didn't look up.

Aria frowned, realizing that Gabby couldn't see her. Which was weird, because she could still see herself. She was all there, from her green sweater to her blue tights down to her pink-laced shoes. But when she brought her hand to the corner of the bed, it went right through.

It didn't make sense. Her shadow had sent her, so she knew she was supposed to be here. But if not for Gabby, then for whom?

And then Aria understood.

This trip was for *her*.

One last look.

Someone knocked on the doorframe. A lanky teenage boy. Gabby's older brother, Marco.

He had a cane in one hand and was clearly tired, but he looked much better. Stronger. The color was in his cheeks and his eyes were bright. He looked right through Aria at his sister.

"Hey, Gabs," he said. "Dinner."

Gabby nodded. She tossed the headphones onto the pile of homework and got up, walking within inches of Aria.

Aria noticed that her laces were purple.

"Bye, Gabby," she said, right before the girl vanished through the door. To her surprise, Gabby stopped, and turned back. She couldn't have heard her, but her eyes still hovered on the air near Aria's head.

"What is it?" asked Marco.

"Nothing," said Gabby after a moment. "I just thought I heard something."

"Must be ghosts," said Marco, with a teasing stomp of his foot.

Gabby grinned, and gave him a playful shove toward the kitchen. She cast one last glance back. "Must be," she whispered. And then she was gone.

Aria smiled after her.

The shadow at her feet began to glow again.

"Okay," said Aria, looking down. As she stepped into the light, she had a feeling she knew where it would take her next.

There was a campfire in the backyard.

A handful of girls huddled around it, elbow to elbow as they toasted marshmallows on metal skewers and traded stories. It was dark, but Aria could see the outline of the trampoline behind them. She recognized Ginny and Elle, and Lily.

And there, blond hair pulled into a ponytail, was Caroline.

Caroline tilted her head back, and so did Aria. It was a clear night, and unlike in the city, here the sky was full of stars. Aria smiled, and one shot across the sky.

Caroline broke into a grin. "Did you see that?" she asked, but the girls had been staring down at the fire, and looked up too late. She was met by a chorus of *no* and *see what*.

"A shooting star." Caroline pulled her marshmallow from its stick and sandwiched it between two crackers along with some chocolate. It looked strange and wonderful and delicious, and Aria was secretly sad that she'd never gotten to try one. "Did you know that when you look up at the sky, you can see for almost twenty quadrillion miles?"

"Cool," said Ginny.

"Weird," said Elle.

"Random," said Lily, adding, "but still cool. Only you would know that."

"I didn't even know quadrillion was a word," said Ginny.

Elle squinted up. "That's a really long way."

"Yeah," said Caroline. "And all that empty space up there? It's not actually empty. It's full of stuff we just can't see. Some of it we can't even explain . . ."

Aria smiled, and beneath her, the shadow began to glow again with light.

Aria expected to find herself back in front of Mikayla's house. Instead, she wasn't really anywhere. She was standing in an empty place, everything blank like the screen before a movie started. Then, instead of going backward, or staying put, time began to roll *forward*.

Of course. Because she wouldn't be there to see it.

Aria stood still as Mikayla's future unfolded around her, not solid but ghostly as smoke, the images twisting into one another, tangling.

Aria saw Mikayla at the Community Dance Center, but she wasn't alone. Beth and Katie were with her, all of them breathless from dance and laughter.

She saw Mikayla going to movies, and school parties, riding her bike with Alex, and drawing with Katie, and playing tennis with Beth. She saw her tossing the ball for Chow and reading on the front stoop.

She saw her packing up the trophies and the rest of the house, saw her in a new apartment — smaller, but still home. She saw her tacking the now battered list of goals up on the new wall, old lines crossed out, new ones added.

She saw her, taller now, stretched out in Central Park, listening to music, with Alex by her side.

And Aria saw Mikayla *dancing*. Threaded through every memory of a life not yet lived, she watched the girl made of gold fall back in love with dance.

The last thing Aria saw wasn't from months or years in the future. It was probably only a few minutes ahead of now. She saw Mikayla standing in her backyard alone, staring at the place where Aria once stood. She saw her turn and go inside, through the house and out the front door. She saw her take a deep breath and then turn to Alex next door, working on his bike. Saw her smile, and lean across the fence, and say, "Hey, stranger. Still up for that ride?"

· · ·

The light flared again, and Aria found herself back in Mikayla's yard as if nothing had changed.

And seconds later, Mikayla came through the door. "Good," she said. "You're still here."

Aria nodded. "I'm still here."

Mikayla hopped down the steps with something hidden behind her back. "You should have these," she said, revealing the gift: a pair of iridescent wings, the very same ones from Mikayla's dance costume.

The air caught in Aria's chest, and she smiled so wide that the setting sun grew brighter.

Aria took the wings, and slipped the straps on.

They were nearly weightless, but as they settled on her shoulders and against her back, they *changed*. The wings became heavier, more substantial. And when she looked down at her shadow, there they were, but they were different. The flimsy translucent material was gone, replaced by something that glowed with bluish light. The wings now arched gracefully over her shoulders and ended near her palms in feathered tips.

They weren't the stuff of costumes anymore.

They were real.

And they were *Aria's*.

It was better than anything she could have hoped for. It was the best gift. The best good-bye.

"Thank you," she said, still beaming.

"You've earned them," said Mikayla.

A breeze blew through, and the silver charms on her bracelet jingled faintly, like wind chimes.

"I wish you didn't have to go," said Mikayla.

Moments earlier, she would have said, "Me too," but now, after everything she'd seen, she said, "Don't worry. You're going to be amazing. Trust me."

"So will you," Mikayla said.

Aria took a deep breath and looked down at her shadow. The wings shimmered and then extended, stretched like welcoming arms toward her.

"Okay," she said to the angel's shadow. "I'm ready."

She tapped her shoe, and the shadow flared white.

Aria closed her eyes.

Endings are beginnings, she told herself.

And then she heard a flutter of wings, and stepped forward into the light.

DON'T MISS

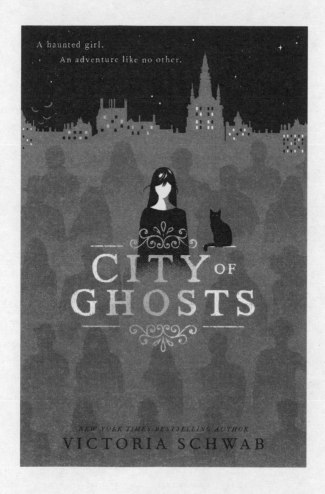

When Cass's family head off to Edinburgh, Cass meets a girl who shares her "gift" of entering the world of the spirits. Cass still has a lot to learn about the Veil - and herself. And fast...

A thrillingly spooky and action-packed tale of hauntings, history, mystery, and the bond between friends (even if that friend is a ghost...)

THE THRILLING SEQUEL TO VICTORIA SCHWAB'S
BESTSELLING *CITY OF GHOSTS*.

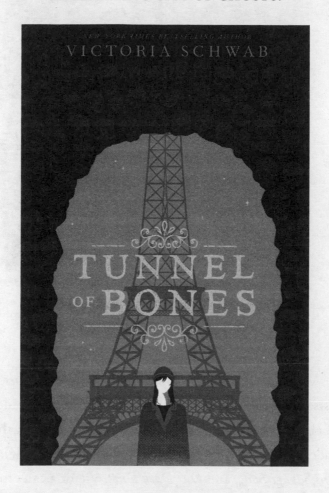

Cass is in Paris, where her parents are filming their TV
show about the world's most haunted cities. When Cass
accidentally awakens a frighteningly strong spirit in the
creepy underground Catacombs, she must rely on her still-
growing skills as a ghosthunter – and turn to friends both old
and new to help her unravel a mystery.

ABOUT THE AUTHOR

Victoria (V. E.) Schwab is the #1 *New York Times* bestselling author of more than a dozen novels for readers of all ages, including *City of Ghosts*, *Tunnel of Bones*, the Shades of Magic series, the Villains series, *The Near Witch*, *This Savage Song*, and *Our Dark Duet*. Victoria can often be found haunting Paris streets and trudging up Scottish hillsides. Usually, she's tucked in the corner of a coffee shop, dreaming up stories. Visit her online at veschwab.com.